THE CHAMPION OF THE SIDHE

The Fomor captain whirled about. Just inside the gateway, an imposing figure stood.

In dress, he seemed a warrior. He wore a simple tunic of white with a cloak of brilliant green. At his hip was sheathed a sword whose hilt was richly worked in gold and set with glittering stones. Still, his body, while tall and well muscled, had the slenderness and suppleness of youth.

"Just who are you?" the captain demanded harshly.

"My name is Lugh Lamfada."

"The one they call the Champion of the Sidhe? But you are just a boy!"

"That may be," said Lugh. "Still I am here to help these people." He drew his sword in a swift, single move. The blade glowed brightly and an aura of power from it seemed to envelop the young warrior. The boyish manner fell away and his voice turned deadly cold.

"This weapon is called Answerer. Leave here at once, or it will do my speaking for me. . . ."

CHAMPIONS OF THE SIDHE
by Kenneth C. Flint
A new tale of high adventure by the author of
RIDERS OF THE SIDHE

CHAMPIONS OF THE SIDHE

Kenneth C. Flint

BANTAM BOOKS

TORONTO • NEW YORK • LONDON • SYDNEY • AUCKLAND

CHAMPIONS OF THE SIDHE
A Bantam Book / December 1984

ISBN 0-553-24543-0

Published simultaneously in the United States and Canada

Bantam Books are published by Bantam Books, Inc. Its trade-
mark, consisting of the words "Bantam Books" and the por-
trayal of a rooster, is Registered in U.S. Patent and Trademark
Office and in other countries. Marca Registrada. Bantam
Books, Inc., 666 Fifth Avenue, New York, New York 10103.

BOOK I

BRES RETURNS

I

REBELLION

THE TOWER OF Glass thrust up from the sea like a blade of ice, chill and deadly.

The planes of its four sides were formed of glass panels, level upon level, joined by a web of lines so fine that at a distance each wall became a single sheet of shining material. Like enormous mirrors they reflected the ocean and the sky about with a cold, detached precision. In the slanting rays of the dawn sun, the eastern face was a painful glare of blue-white diamond light. It made the Tower seem all the more starkly alien, alone in that soft, sunflecked expanse of level sea.

The soaring structure was set firmly in a base of smooth grey stone. And this foundation was itself imbedded deeply in an island of jagged rock barely larger than the Tower itself.

The base, like the glass walls above, was devoid of openings, save at one point. On the southern side, a knobby elbow of the island thrust into the sea, forming a sizeable cove. Here, massive quays of the same smooth stone stretched far out into the waters of the cove. And here, in a line along the foundation wall, a dozen immense, square openings with heavy doors of a dull grey metal gave access to the Tower's interior.

At the quays, a score of slender ships of a curiously smooth black metal were tied. Men in close-fitting uniforms of silver-grey worked busily upon one of them, preparing it for sea and for the arrival of a special passenger.

A flat, hollow tone, like the repeated note on some great horn, began to sound echoingly across the quays. It brought the attention of the working men to the base of the Tower. There, with a piercing, metallic squeal, one of the metal doors began to lift.

It rose slowly, as if with an effort, accompanied by a tremendous clattering. Beyond the growing opening only the blackness of the Tower's interior was revealed.

3

When the door had risen halfway, it clanged abruptly to a stop. From the darkness appeared a double column of men, clad in similar grey uniforms, but wearing helmets—smooth, rounded skullcaps of bright silver—and carrying strange devices, like thick spears of metal tipped with balls of silver instead of points.

Twenty soldiers emerged from the Tower, moving in a brisk, high-stepping march. As the last moved onto the quay, they halted and the two lines executed sharp turns to face one another. They stood straight and exactly dressed and motionless, like chiseled granite figures lining some temple corridor.

The men on the ship had now ceased their work to watch with open curiosity the figure who walked from the shadowed depths of the Tower and down the aisle of soldiers.

He was, indeed, a figure worthy of note. His appearance was in sharp contrast with the men he strode arrogantly between. His dress was colorful, barbaric in this stark setting. A blood-red cloak was slung across his shoulders, fastened at his throat with an elaborate brooch of gold. Beneath it was visible a tunic of bright green richly embroidered in gold thread. A heavy belt at his waist supported a silver-fitted scabbard and a long-sword whose wide hilt was set with glinting jewels.

The garb was a complement to the striking nature of the man himself. Tall and wide of body, he was well muscled with no signs of extra weight. He carried himself with the unconscious easy grace of a warrior in full fighting trim. His hair was dark and very coarse, rolling back from his forehead in thick waves. His features were handsome but broad and crudely chiseled. The dark eyes were set deeply behind heavy brows and took in the preparations at the ship with sharp interest.

He strode down purposefully to the ship and stopped by its gangway. A uniformed man directing the work there moved to greet him. Several black bands encircling his lower sleeve were all that announced he ranked far above the rest.

"We sail in a few moments, High-King Bres," he announced to the brightly dressed arrival. "The tide is nearly at its peak."

"Very well, Captain," said the other in a voice edged with irritation. "I'll go aboard."

He went up the gangway but paused to look up toward the top of the Tower that loomed so far above him. There, a wider band of glass marked the structure's highest level. As distant as it was, he was certain that he could detect the dark shape of the one who watched. He was even certain that he could feel the heat of that damned eye.

He was right. From far above, an eye was trained upon him. The crimson blaze of the single, fiery pupil was shuttered by its metal lid to a mere thread of ruby light as it stared down at the ship below, and at the tiny figure climbing into it.

The face in which the eye was set was really no face at all. It was a rounded surface of burnished black, featureless except for the heavy lid that hung before the eye like a visor on a helmet. The head itself was no more than a barrel of metal, fixed to a short, thick neck that rose from massive, squared shoulders.

The whole being was enormous, three times the height and girth of a normal man, all armored in the same smooth metal, fully jointed in the arms and legs, with hands like metal gauntlets. Standing there at the window, motionless, it might have been a lifeless object, like the ships below, save for the power of that eye.

And then a voice addressed it.

"Do you believe Bres can succeed in Eire alone, Commander Balor?" it asked, its tone hesitant.

There was no immediate response. Then, with an agonizing slowness and a faint, grating sound of metal on metal, the vast head began to move. It pivoted around on the neck, bringing the crimson eye from the window to those in the room.

The room was vast, befitting its main occupant. Three stories high, its outer wall was all glass, giving a view of the sea around the Tower to the distant horizon. Against the bright background of the dawn sky, the giant figure seemed all the more dark, all the more ominous to the three men who stood before it.

The narrow beam of light from the single eye played over them. All wore the grey uniform. The many bands on the sleeves of each spoke of their exalted rank. The eye shifted from one to another, finally fixing on the center one. From the figure a voice sounded, a deep and hollow and clanging sound, like a great gong echoing from the depths of some cavern of iron.

"It is necessary for him to succeed, Sital Salmhor. If he is unable to organize our occupying forces in Eire and crush this foolish uprising soon, it may spread to all the de Danann settlements."

Sital Salmhor stared up at the figure. As often before, he wondered if there was a living being there, behind that armored front. He steeled himself for another question.

"But shouldn't we send some support to him? Send some forces from the Tower? That would insure a victory."

"No!" the being thundered. "No forces from this Tower will be involved. Bres has the power to crush them if he acts quickly. And, remember, it is his own kingship over Eire that he must regain."

The offending officer held himself rigidly under the heat of the flaming eye. But the torture was short. The giant head turned slowly back toward the windows, the gaze of the eye shifting down toward the ship again.

It had put to sea by now and was gliding out past the sheltering peninsula. It moved along quite steadily, although no sail was up. But as it left the cove and the winds caught it, a field of brilliant white blossomed around its mast and it picked up speed quickly, soaring away with the grace of a great bird.

Until the ship faded into the haze of the southern horizon, the crimson eye stayed fixed upon its course.

The woman was thrown from the doorway of the house and staggered, falling heavily onto her knees in the muddy courtyard of the ringfort. A roar of coarse laughter went up from the circle of monstrous beings who watched.

They were vaguely like men, with men's shape and stature, but they were disfigured in ways so horrible that they seemed more like insane parodies of men.

No two of them were deformed alike. In many the limbs were twisted, distorted to resemble the claws of birds, the paws of beasts, even the fins of fish. In some the limbs were missing altogether, replaced by crude appendages of metal and wood.

More grotesque were the faces that were, indeed, a mockery of anything human. And here, again, many of the deformities looked like the product of some obscene coupling of men and animals.

All were dressed as warriors, in ragged tunics and cloaks, and heavily armed with spears, swords, and leather shields.

The frightened woman looked up at them in horror as she pulled herself from the mud and stumbled away to join a huddled group of others penned against the earthen wall of the ringfort by the menacing band.

From within the round, wattle-sided house, a figure emerged. His head appeared to have been split from the top of the skull to the bridge of the nose by some massive wound that had healed to leave a deep trench ridged by thick scar tissue on either side. On both sides of the gap, the bald skull bulged up as if two heads had tried to form. Goggling eyes were set far out atop each bulging cheek like those of a frog. The mouth was tiny, shaped in a high bow, with a deep cleft that ran up into the wide, single nostril of the flat nose.

With obvious enjoyment he watched the frightened woman stumble away. He strode out into the center of the compound and looked around him at the ringfort's interior.

It was a small enclosure. The wrapping earthen bank with its crowning ring of upright stakes embraced only four of the round, thatched homes. It was clearly a very poor settlement, and its two-score inhabitants were near starvation.

The warrior looked them over appraisingly. There were a few scrawny men, some worn and haggard women, and a few wretched brats with swollen bellies who peeped out fearfully from the shelter of their mothers' bodies.

"Phaw!" he exclaimed disgustedly. "What a sorry catch we've got here. No food among 'em. No shiny little bits for us. And none of these women are worth our time. Seems a waste of effort even to kill them."

"There's no need to kill us," one of the captive men said pleadingly, moving forward from the group. He was a tall man with a lean face that had once been handsome. But years of hardship had ravaged him, and years of oppression had left him without pride. He begged for the salvation of his people. "Please, My Chieftain! We've never caused the Fomor any trouble. We've always paid our tribute to you."

"And I suppose you're not fallin' in with those rebels at Tara?" the Fomor leader said, smiling skeptically.

"Rebels?" the man repeated blankly. "No. We know nothing about a rebellion. Please, believe me!"

"Captain!" called a dog-faced warrior, coming out of one of the huts. He held up a battered sword in a thick paw. "Look here! We found these in a souterrain under this house!"

"A hidden escape tunnel?" the captain said, and turned a baleful look upon the hapless man. "And weapons?"

"They're for our defense from animals," the man tried desperately to explain. "We have to have something. The bears—"

"Bears!" the captain spat out contemptuously. He took a

swift step forward and swung out with a sudden blow of his fist that caught the man on the side of his head, dropping him heavily to the muddy earth.

"The bears will be eatin' of all your bony carcasses this day," the captain promised. He drew a heavy longsword from its sheath and lifted it to strike.

From the huddled group a wail of terror went up. A young boy pushed forward. A woman tried to stop him but he tore away and flew upon the warrior, grabbing his sword arm to drag it down.

Angrily the captain shook the attacker off and the boy was flung down into the mud beside the man.

"Filthy whelp!" the captain grated and lifted the sword again. "Now you'll be first!"

"I'd greatly appreciate it if you'd not do that," said a voice behind him.

II

THE CHAMPIONS

SURPRISED BY IT, the captain whirled about. Just inside the gateway through the outer wall a new figure now stood.

In dress, he seemed a warrior. He wore a simple tunic of white with a cloak of brilliant green. At his hip was sheathed a sword whose hilts were richly worked in gold and set with glinting stones. Still, in looks he seemed more of a boy. His body, while tall and well muscled, had the slenderness and suppleness of youth. The face was boyish, too, lean and boldly featured in chin and nose, with clear blue eyes sparkling behind high arching brows of pale gold. His fair hair swept back in thick casual waves.

He was altogether a fine and pleasant-looking young man, and he smiled on the monstrous clan before him in a most innocent and engaging way.

"Just who are you?" the captain demanded harshly, eyeing the newcomer suspiciously.

"My name is Lugh Lamfada," he stated in a matter-of-fact voice.

"Lugh Lamfada?" the Fomor officer repeated with some surprise. "The one that they call Champion of the Sidhe? But, you are just a boy!"

"That may be," the other said lightly. "Still I am here to give help to these people."

"You're going to help them?" the captain asked, smiling. He seemed vastly amused at the idea.

"I want you to take your warriors away from here and leave these people alone," the young warrior went on. "I'm asking you in a friendly way now, for I've no wish to see you come to harm, unless you allow me no other choice."

Now the captain laughed outright, joined by the others in a harsh chorus of derisive laughter.

"And are you challenging us, boy?" he asked, stepping toward Lugh. "You, alone?"

"I didn't say that I was alone."

"No, he surely didn't say that!" another voice sang out brightly.

The Fomor turned again to face this new voice. It came from a very strange individual now perched precariously atop the logs of the ringfort's palisade.

He was a loose-jointed and gangly sort of fellow dressed in the baggy, striped clothes of a clown. A tattered and filthy brown cloak was draped in heavy folds about him and battered leather shoes flapped on his enormous feet. He had a tangled mass of straggling yellow hair and beard that couldn't mask a sharp jut of nose and a wide, idiotic grin. He was casually juggling three small apples and swinging back and forth on the posts. His movements were so awkward that it seemed certain he would topple from his seat at any moment.

"Gilla Decaire is my name," he said in a breezy way. "And I'm pleased to meet you all, so I am. Even for so short a time of livin' as you're likely to have." He nodded toward the opposite side of the fort. "Now, would you be wantin' to meet another friend?"

From across the courtyard there came a splintering crash. Once more the Fomor were forced to wheel about. Directly opposite the clown, three of the logs that formed the palisade had suddenly shivered and then toppled back, sheared off at their base. Through the created opening stepped another man, the wide space barely adequate to allow passage of his body.

For he was a gigantic being, tall as well as broad. With a great barrel chest and thick, sinewy arms and legs, he was like an ancient tree that has survived centuries of storm to become the stronger, if more battered and gnarled. His round, weathered face was cheery, red-cheeked, his eyes aglow with pleasure, his wide mouth smiling. In broad hands he hefted the immense, gleaming battle-ax with which he had severed the three logs in a single blow.

"It is the Dagda!" cried one of the Fomor warriors. "My Captain, he is one of the de Danann's greatest champions!"

The others of the band seemed equally impressed, but their officer examined the newest arrival skeptically.

"So, this is the famous Dagda!" he said. "He's much older, and much fatter, than I expected." He looked from the champion to the other challengers, now forming a triangle about his men. "And is that all of you? Just you three?"

A Fomor warrior in the group behind the captain raised his spear suddenly to make a cast at Lugh. But from the sky swooped a large black form.

It drove straight into the face of the man with a harsh cry and a flutter of broad wings. The amazed Fomor saw it was a raven, larger than a hawk. It tore savagely at the warrior, great talons gripping his hands while a gleaming, sharp beak jabbed at his face. Helpless to fight it off, he flailed wildly, then dropped his spear and staggered back. The bird pulled away and left him to retreat, hands pressed to a face streaming with blood. It glided to the back of the courtyard, opposite Lugh, and settled lightly to the ground.

As the raven touched the earth, a strange glow arose from it, as if the sleek blue-black feathers had turned suddenly to silver flame. The glow grew quickly, swallowing up the form, then rose in a column taller than a man. It flared, then faded away, shrinking back to reveal a new form now, a tall and slender form wrapped in a clinging cloak of deepest black.

The face of a woman showed above the cloak, high-browed, hollow-cheeked, and pointed-chinned. Black hair was pulled back and tightly braided at the nape of the neck, giving the head an even harsher look, like the raven's skull. Dark eyes glinted like polished black stones from deep behind the brows, fixing on the Fomor with the hungry look a raptor has for its helpless prey. The thin mouth smiled, and the fine, sharp teeth parted as if ready for the taste of a victim's flesh. The arms unfolded, lifting from a gaunt, almost skeletal frame. The limbs revealed by the warrior's tunic that she wore were lank and wiry, like knotted cord. At each bony hip hung a sheathed longsword.

"Our number is four," the one called Lugh quietly announced.

"It is the Morrigan!" another of the Fomor gasped, voice touched with awe. The name and carnivorous reputation of this de Dannan warrior was well known to them. She was one of the few for whom the cruel beings had any fear.

The Fomor officer was still quite unimpressed.

"The Morrigan too," he said carelessly. He looked back toward Lugh. "So, is that it, then? Or are some more of your little band going to be leaping at us from somewhere?"

The young warrior shook his head. "No more."

"Too bad," the captain said with mock regret. Then the tiny mouth turned upward in a cruel smile. "But it's enough. We'll earn a fine reward for killing such a group of rebel champions."

"Leave this place now," Lugh told him. He drew his sword in a swift, single move. The blade glowed brightly and an aura of power from it seemed to envelop the young warrior. The boyish manner fell away and his voice turned deadly cold. "This weapon is called the Answerer. Leave here or, from now on, it will do my speaking for me."

The captain looked from the bright weapon to the suddenly determined face. He hesitated, feeling a faint, chill ripple of fear wash through him.

But he shook it off. Years of casual brutality had taught him that these weak and cowardly de Dananns had no chance of standing up against the Fomor power. He laughed again.

"Boy," he said in a blustering voice, "in a moment your sword will be hanging at my side!" He turned and shouted the order to his men. "All right, attack them now!"

Lugh and his companions made no move to meet the attack. This forced the Fomor to divide and charge four different ways.

The captain, easily the most skilled fighter of the group, drove forward to engage Lugh himself. He struck with his full power, expecting to finish the overconfident youth quickly. He was astonished to find his opponent swinging his own weapon in a lightning move that parried the sword thrust easily. He redoubled his effort, realizing he faced a trained adversary.

Gilla the Clown downed one of his own charging Fomor with

the throw of an apple, driving the hard sphere into his victim's eye. He then dropped from the wall to the yard with an agility surprising to the Fomor, landing in a fighting position, sword in hand, to face three more attackers.

The giant Dagda waded into the five men who swarmed upon him. The great ax flew about him like a scythe cutting through a field of grain, slashing through the Fomor with a force they could do nothing to defend themselves against. Not far away the raven-woman shrieked her harsh battle cry and flew against three more with both swords. Her flashing weapons were like tearing claws, and it seemed to them that a flock of blood-hungry crows were upon them.

The battle was brief and bloody. The inhabitants of the ring-fort watched the fighting with growing amazement and jubilation as the four wreaked devastation on the Fomor band.

Finally, Lugh pressed the captain back across the compound, teasing him now, nicking him here and there to drive him like a stubborn bull. The maddened officer made a desperate thrust. He found his weapon knocked from his hand and a bright, sharp blade pressed to his throat.

Lugh smiled and poked out with his sword. The captain tumbled backward into some of the deepest mud in the yard. Now the Fomor's recent captives laughed.

"Now, Captain," Lugh said, "look around at your warriors."

He did. There were only three left alive, and two of them were wounded. The rest were sprawled lifeless in the mud.

"Tell them to surrender. Quickly!" the young warrior demanded. There was no compromise in his voice now. Only deadly earnestness. The captain obeyed.

The Fomor warriors were quickly disarmed and directed out of the gateway. Then Lugh turned back to the fallen officer.

"Now you, Captain. Crawl out of here like the vermin that you are. Go and tell your fellows that if any of you come near this fort or any of the Tuatha de Dananns again, you will surely die!"

The captain began to crawl. Lugh gave him a slap across the rump with the flat of his sword to urge him along. The terrified Fomor slithered through the muddy yard with astonishing speed and disappeared out the gateway.

Lugh walked to the de Danann man and boy who had watched the battle from their own seats in the mud, afraid to move. He sheathed his sword and held out a hand to each.

"And you, get up from that mud," he told them forcefully.

"Stand up like men." Each took a hand and he pulled them erect. "It's time the de Danann people did that again."

The man stared at the young warrior before him, and then around at the rest of their saviors, still somewhat dumbfounded at the suddenness of their rescue.

"By all the Powers, you have saved us," he said weakly, as if he had just accepted the truth of it. "But how did you come here?"

"We've been traveling the countryside, trying to tell every settlement of the rising against the Fomor," Lugh said.

"Then there has been a rising?" the man asked. "That captain spoke of it."

"There has, that's certain," the Dagda assured him, moving up beside Lugh. "We seized Tara only days ago, drove out the Fomor garrison and deposed Bres."

"The High-King?" The man gasped in shock.

"Yes, but let's not speak of it right now," said Lugh. He had been examining the ringfort's inhabitants. "Your people look badly used and nearly starved. See to them and get them some food. Then we can talk."

"We've no food left," the man told him sorrowfully. "We were poor enough to start, and these Fomor raiding parties have taken what we had these past few days. That's why this last band was so cruel."

Gilla Decaire crossed the yard to them.

"I think we can take care of that ourselves, so I do!" he said cheerfully. He reached into the voluminous cloak and yanked out a tremendous leg of mutton. This he tossed lightly to the man who gaped in wonder. "Here. This'll start things nicely. And, here!" He reached in again, this time hauling forth a skin bulging with liquid and a fat, round loaf of bread. "Some nice ale here," he announced, passing it over to the man and tossing the bread to the boy.

The youngster stared wide-eyed at the loaf that filled his arms, then in awe at the marvelous cloak.

"Lost a whole lamb inside there once," the clown told him with a broad wink.

"I believe you," the boy said with great seriousness.

Five, six, seven, eight apples spun in a circle, flying at a dizzying speed high above Gilla's head as he juggled for an enthralled audience of children.

The clown was willingly entertaining them, bringing smiles

to faces so long marked by fear and pinched by hunger. So eager for his diverting tricks were they that, even though they were nearly starved, the food lay forgotten on their plates as they watched and laughed.

Gilla ended his performance at last by throwing the apples, one by one, to each child.

"Enough for now," he said. He held up his hands at their disappointed cries, promising, "I'll do more later, but only if you eat up all of that food!"

They fell to the task with a will, and he moved away from them, toward the rest of the company.

The children were grouped at one side of the circular room. The adults sat at low tables set around a central hearth. This was the largest of the ringfort's houses, the one used as a meeting hall for the inhabitants. It was a barren place, stripped of all the fine de Danann ornamentation. A tiny fire was the only spot of cheer.

As Gilla joined them, the Dagda was just concluding his account of the recent uprising at Tara. His booming voice and colorful speech made it a most gripping tale.

"And the people of Tara joined together to defeat the Fomor garrison," he was saying. "Under Nuada they are now organizing an army at Tara to challenge the rest of the Fomor in Eire and drive them all out."

"So Nuada has become our High-King once again," said the leader. "I cannot believe that Bres has finally been deposed."

"It was Lugh here who discovered that Bres was in league with the Fomor to destroy us, that he was half-Fomor himself!" the Dagda said proudly, clapping a massive hand to Lugh's shoulder. "Why, it was even his work that saw Nuada restored." He leaned across the table toward the other man to add emphatically: "I tell you, Febal, he is truly the one that the Prophecy said would come one day to lead us to freedom from the Fomor."

"I believe what you say," said Febal, eyeing Lugh with great interest. "I felt the power of a great champion in him when he appeared in our fort."

The modest young warrior tried not to look as abashed as he felt in this praising.

"Then you'll join us?" urged the Dagda. "We must gather every de Danann who can fight."

The man shook his head doubtfully. "My friend, I don't know. We are not warriors. We never have been. We came to

Eire to live in peace, to farm and herd and feel a oneness with a land of our own. We cannot fight."

"It's because you will not fight that this land is not your own," Lugh put in. The young man's voice was quiet, but urgent and truthful and carrying a force within it that claimed the attention of all present. "You will never have anything that is truly yours until you choose to earn it."

"Perhaps," Febal agreed. "But perhaps Bobd Derg is right."

"My son?" bellowed the Dagda angrily. "You'd listen to the whining of that coward and leave Eire?"

The leader looked over to the children. "At least our families were safe in Tir-na-nog. It was a place of peace and happiness."

"Listen to me, Febal," said Lugh. "If you return to the Four Cities, you will become as you were, children of Queen Danu's people, never a people of your own."

"Once, long ago, we called ourselves the sons of Nemed," the Dagda put in strongly. "Too many of us have forgotten that. But we were a proud race who gave in to no one, who battled any power for our place. That was what we were, Febal. Don't you remember?"

He did remember. All those years before when the young, hopeful band of adventurers had come to Eire, seeking their own land. Then they had met the Fomor, a race of raiders who meant to make these newcomers their slaves. They had fought, but the Fomor had nearly destroyed them. The battered remnants of their once-strong clans had sailed into the unknown Western Sea. There, lost and nearly dead, the survivors had been found by the people of Queen Danu.

The Sons of Nemed had been taken to Tir-na-nog, a peaceful and mystical land where four shining cities held marvels the outsiders couldn't comprehend. Danu had befriended them, given them homes, put her own teachers and druids and artisans to helping them learn and regain their strength.

In gratitude, the clans of Nemed had taken on a new name, Tuatha de Danann, the Children of Danu. But the time had come when their leaders decided that they must return to Eire. Danu's land and people were not their own. They were of another, harsher world, and they must return to it and prove themselves.

But, instead of doing that, their traitorous High-King Bres had used his power and their old fears to lead them into the Fomor control.

"Maybe it's not a warrior you are," the Dagda went on, "but

you've always believed in our coming to Eire to win our own life here. And you've always been willing to fight for that when it was needed."

"Yes, I've fought," the other agreed wearily. "I've seen our people nearly destroyed by the forces of the Tower of Glass. I've seen them die battling the Firbolgs, hurt and degraded by the Fomor animals. I've lost my children and friends and homes and all hope. Is this rocky, savage isle worth all of that? Isn't reason saying to us that we should give it up?"

"It's not reason we're speaking of," the Dagda said. "It's something in the heart, in the life force, that makes us what we are. You may as well ask a baby to stay protected in its womb instead of coming into the world to live, with all its dangers, with death surely waiting. That force drove our people to come to Eire. It's a fiercely protected part of us. The fear of losing it made us leave Tir-na-nog and come back here."

He moved closer to his old comrade, his voice filled with intensity, his rugged face alight with battle-fire. "You have to see our people at Tara, Febal. The rising has brought them alive again. They've a will they've not had in many years. Join them. Don't let it be lost again."

"Even if it means death?" Febal asked.

"Only our spirit made something of us," the Dagda said. "The Fomor took our spirit, took what we are. We have to get it back or we have nothing at all.

He stood up, a massive figure, to address them all.

"I say that we must never again allow the Fomor to rule us through fear. I say that Eire is ours and we cannot let them drive us from it! What do you say?"

Febal looked around at his gathered people. In their drawn and weary faces he saw a new determination, the rebirth of a glow of pride that had been extinguished for so long. They looked at one another and all understood. A silent agreement was passed.

"All right," Febal said to the champions with greater heart. "We will go to Tara, all that can. We'll join your rising."

"But what about the Fomor?" asked one of the others. "Won't they act to stop this rebellion?"

"We don't know," Lugh admitted. "To be truthful, we've no idea what the Fomor are planning to do. We've met no kind of organized resistance. We haven't even seen any Fomor parties in our traveling, except those who came here."

"We've seen more than our share," Febal's wife put in.

"Herds of the filthy beasts have been passing through for days now."

"Oh? And were all of them going the same way?"

This came from the Morrigan. She had just entered the room. She wiped a crimson smear from her mouth with the edge of her cloak. Lugh, realizing what she had been about outside, repressed a shudder. He couldn't get used to the raven-woman's grotesque habit of slaking her insatiable thirst with the warm blood of her victims, even if they were the beastly Fomor.

"They did all go the same way, I think," said Febal. "Didn't they?" He looked to his people for confirmation.

"Aye, they did," said another. "And all in a great hurry."

Morrigan stepped toward him, her dark eyes glittering, her dry, crackling voice sharp with interest.

"And just which way was it?"

"North and east," he told her. "Toward the sea."

III

THE DISCOVERY

"JUST A BIT higher now," the Dagda promised with a grunt of effort as he hauled his bulk up the rocky slope.

Behind him Gilla and Lugh scrambled along, their more agile forms still no match for the amazing litheness of the huge man. Panting and hanging on a rock for a brief rest, Gilla looked up enviously at the black bird that soared high above.

"I'd give a pretty to be havin' her powers, so I would," he said sincerely.

"Never mind," said the young warrior, grinning. "The sea lies just beyond this hill, I think. It must be where Morrigan's been leading us."

"I wish she'd remember that 'as the raven flies' is only the easiest route for a raven," the Dagda growled. "I feel as if we've climbed every hill in Eire. She likely did it on purpose, knowing her twisted mind."

But the crown of the ragged hill was just ahead, and beyond

it the sea did come into view, a fine, wide cove with a beach of yellow sand stretching around its curve.

The three climbed higher and were able to look down the steep slope to the section of beach just below. What they saw made them jump hurriedly back into some sheltering rocks.

The flat ground along the water's edge was swarming with Fomor!

They had encampments scattered far along the shore with crude shelters built and scores of fires burning. The smell of cooking food drifted up to the watchers.

"There must be nearly a thousand men there!" said the Dagda. "It looks like half the garrison forces in Eire are gathered."

"They must be planning to attack us," Lugh said. "But why are they gathering here? And what are they waiting for? There are more than enough here to challenge our forces at Tara."

"What's Morrigan about?" Gilla wondered, pointing.

The figure of the raven had soared out far beyond the Fomor, high above the sea and away until she had shrunk to a black fleck against the grey of an overcast sky. But, as they watched, she began to grow again as she returned, sweeping in from the sea with speed, soaring up over them and then fluttering down to alight on a boulder nearby.

She folded her great wings and then began to caw and rattle noisily. The Dagda listened carefully, then nodded.

"We may soon find out what this lot is waiting for," he told his companions. "She says there's a ship coming in now."

Gilla looked at the huge warrior skeptically. "You understood her?"

"Certainly I did," the Dagda answered indignantly. "We were married once, you'll recall. She taught me the speech. Made things much easier too."

"I can imagine that it would," said Gilla thoughtfully. "Or, maybe I can't." He flashed a broad grin. "You'll have to tell me more about your marriage sometime. It must have been quite an interesting match, so it must."

"Never mind that," the Dagda said tersely, clearly not amused. "Look. There's the ship."

They could just see the flashing speck that had appeared on the edge of the grey, rough sea. They watched it draw near, slowly revealing itself as a large, lean vessel of smooth black. Lugh and Gilla exchanged a meaningful glance. Both had seen such a ship before.

"It's come from the Tower of Glass," said Lugh.

"I've seen their like, long ago," the Dagda said, his voice darkened by a grim memory. "I told you of it, lad. When we went against the Tower those many years ago and were destroyed by the powers there. It was a fleet of such ships that came against us then."

The Morrigan crackled stridently.

"Aye," he said. "I know you were there too. And I'm certain you recall as well as I."

"But why is it here?" asked Lugh. He looked at Gilla. "Do you think it means that the forces of the Tower will join the Fomor?"

Gilla shook his head. "No. We heard that bloody iron monster himself declare that the island Fomor would have to hold Eire alone. I can't imagine Balor changin' his mind and riskin' the lives of any of his pure Tower people just to aid these poor, blighted brothers they've so kindly exiled to this place."

"Balor," Lugh said coldly, recalling the terrible one-eyed being. "If he comes, we are doomed. I watched the power of that red eye blast apart the fortress where I grew up. We could never face that."

The ship came smoothly in, its sail down, but still cutting swiftly through the waves, driving unwaveringly toward the shore, defying wind and sea with its unknown power. A large party of Fomor officers gathered from the massed forces and moved toward the water to meet it.

The ship eased up through the shallows and grounded. A gangway was run out from the side to rest on the shore. A man appeared at its head and strode haughtily down to be greeted by the officers. On the hillside above, the little band of watchers looked on with growing understanding.

"Not Balor," Gilla remarked, "but a monster nearly as bad."

"I'd hoped that he was dead!" the Dagda growled.

But he was not. Bres, once High-King to the Tuatha de Danann, had returned to Eire.

The hilltop fortress called Tara of the Kings was alive with activity.

After years of decay and apathy, it and the town below it had reawakened, preparing desperately for the coming struggle to hold on to the new freedom.

Within the enormous circling palisade of logs that crowned the rounded hill, many scores of warriors trained for battle.

The very few who had been able to keep up their warrior's skills through the long period of Fomor oppression were laboring to restore the ability and strength and confidence of the rest.

It was difficult work. Most had been so long undernourished and brutalized that the will to fight was very weak. But the inspiration and courage of one man who moved through them, constantly encouraging, was helping to bring new spirit to them.

His name was Nuada, the High-King. He was an aging man, his long mane of hair frosted heavily with grey, his face seamed by years of wear. But his powerful figure showed few signs of age, and his proud bearing gave him an aura of energetic youth. Beside him strode Angus Og, another son of the Dagda, a cheerful and vigorous young man who was helping to supervise the training.

One side of the great inner courtyard was given over to a line of men who practiced casting spears at man-sized targets carved of wood. Nuada stopped to watch and shook his head with doubt. After days of work, the targets were still distressingly free of spears that had hit their mark.

Across the court, other men were training with swords and shields. Most were clumsy and unsure, and doing themselves almost as much harm with the heavy weapons as they were their practice opponents.

Nuada watched this for a while, too, and then Angus heard him sigh heavily. But the High-King did not express his misgivings aloud. He only offered some ringing words of encouragement before passing on.

By the stables at the back of the courtyard, a large smithy had been set up beneath open sheds. Here a group of figures, black and streaming with sweat, labored over forges and anvils to shape weapons for the resurrected army of their comrades. At one of the forges, Goibnu, the master smith of the de Dananns, turned out the bright, slender, and lethal spearheads for which he was renowned with a speed and workmanship that seemed miraculous. Beside him worked a woman whose efforts matched his own. Her looks were as remarkable as her skill, for her face was divided, one side that of a beautiful woman, the other that of a withered hag.

When he saw Nuada and Angus approaching, Goibnu stopped to point proudly at the great pile of glinting spearheads beside them.

"We'll have all the weapons any army could need," he announced. "Bridget has learned the craft well."

"All we've need of now is hands that can use them with the same amount of skill that created them," said Nuada. Again Angus was aware of that doubting quality, not fully disguised by the High-King's attempt at heartiness.

"My King!" a voice called from above them.

Nuada and the others looked up toward the sentrywalk of the outer wall. A guard was hailing the High-King.

"Warriors are coming up from the town!" he proclaimed. "It's the party of Lugh Lamfada!"

"Are you certain?" Nuada called back.

"I couldn't be mistaking the figure of the Dagda," the guard replied with an irreverent smile.

"I wonder why they've come back so soon," Nuada said, that troubled note in his voice now clearly audible. He looked to Angus. "Come along. We'd better go meet them."

Angus nodded assent and the two started off for the main gates of the fortress. Those gates were open, as was usual during daylight, and the two men reached them just as Lugh, Gilla, and the Dagda rode through into the courtyard.

When Nuada saw them, his worry increased. They were worn by much hard travel, sagging on the horses' backs. The animals themselves were thickly caked with mud from fast travel on Eire's roads and plodded wearily, heads lowered. Even the great, stocky mount of the Dagda was near exhaustion.

As the three pulled up, the familiar black form sailed lightly down to land beside them and shimmer its way into Morrigan's shape. She was the only one of the party who looked fresh.

As Lugh and his friends eased their aching bodies from their horses, Nuada advanced toward them.

"What's happened?" he demanded. "Why have you come back so soon?"

"We've made a discovery," said Lugh. He and his comrades gave the horses over to a steward's keeping and Lugh moved closer to the High-King. "Let's move away a bit," he said in a confidential tone. "I don't think the others should hear this quite yet."

They moved away from the training area, into an open spot beside a small mound at one side of the yard.

"Tell me! What has happened?" Nuada asked urgently.

"We've discovered an army of Fomor gathering secretly," the

Dagda told his old friend bluntly. "Over a thousand warriors have joined it and more companies are arriving every day."

"There's something else," said Lugh. "Bres is with them. He's clearly been sent by those at the Tower of Glass to lead them in crushing us."

"He has enough men to do that now," said Nuada, clearly alarmed by this news. "Why is he waiting?"

"He seems to be gathering all the Fomor in Eire," said Lugh. "We think he plans to destroy the de Dananns totally."

"Then how much time have we before he is ready?" Nuada asked.

"There must be several thousand Fomor in Eire," the Dagda answered. "We can only be guessing, but I'd say it will be at least ten days before he is ready to march against us."

"Ten days!" repeated Nuada in a despairing way. "So little time!"

"We wouldn't have had that long if we hadn't discovered Bres's secret," Lugh reminded him. "Now we have a chance to organize a defense."

"Is that the truth?" Nuada replied, his voice sharply edged with irritation. "And just what is it you're planning to make this defense with?"

Lugh was taken aback by this sudden hostility from the king. But Nuada saw the surprise in his face and was at once regretful.

"I'm sorry, young Champion. I know the kind of hopeful fire that courses in your veins. For you, anything is possible. But age is turning my blood cold. It's harder to keep hope."

Lugh didn't understand. "But the de Dananns are gathering. You're forming an army here—"

"No, Lugh," Nuada interrupted. "Our own forces are only trickling in to join us from those few settlements close by. We haven't had time to reach the others. Most of the de Dananns in Eire can't even know there's been a rising here."

"He's right, Lugh," said Angus. "And to give them time to come, to arm and train them and make an army, they would have to host in a very few days. We can't reach them so quickly."

"But some will come, and you have some companies here," Lugh said, stoutly battling to counter their air of defeat.

"Look at them more closely," said Nuada, taking in the warriors in the yard with a sweep of the arm. "We have perhaps five hundred who could fight. But look at their condition. Even with weapons and training, they are far too weak. They've been starved and beaten for too long. The rest of our people are surely the same." He shook his head. His voice sounded weary. "Even if every de Danann were at Tara now, armed and ready to fight, they wouldn't have the strength to withstand the Fomor hordes."

Lugh realized how deeply this vision of defeat had plunged Nuada into despair. He recalled the condition the High-King had been in not many days before. Then Bres had ruled and Nuada had watched helplessly as the tyrant drained his people. His sense of failure had driven him into a drunken apathy. The fear and uncertainty that had come upon the once assured leader still threatened to grip him at times. They had to be controlled.

"Nuada, remember, when I first came to Tara, you were certain you could never act again. But you have, and so have your people. You cannot show any weakness or any doubt. You must keep the spirit and the others will too. We'll find a way to defeat the Fomor. You must believe that."

Nuada looked closely at the intense young warrior, then he smiled.

"I do believe you. The force in you always brings new vitality to me. We will find a way."

Lugh felt relief at having bolstered Nuada. He only wished he really knew what way they would find.

"We will have to discuss plans for action with all the advisors," he suggested. "Gather them, but do it without letting anyone know what's happening. There's little point in bringing worry to the rest until we've some idea what to do."

"True enough," agreed Nuada. "I'll have them gather in my quarters tonight, after the others are asleep."

"That's settled then," Gilla announced with relief. "Now maybe we'll have a bit of time for some rest and food."

"There's food and drink laid out in the main hall," Angus said. "The Druids are working there."

"Working?" asked Lugh.

"Old Findgoll's got them practicing their arts," Angus explained, laughing. "He says they've gotten tarnished, like an unused blade."

"Do you know where Aine might be?" Lugh asked, trying to sound quite casual.

Angus grinned more widely. "Ah, I wondered when you'd ask. She's in the sunroom with Taillta, working on some fool project. They're not in a good humor over it."

"My idea, I'm afraid," Gilla admitted lightly. "I put them to it before we left."

"Then you're the one they've been talking of torturing in so many interesting ways," Angus said. "Best be armed when you see them."

"No one can be angry with playful old Gilla the Clown for long," he replied in a breezy tone. "Come, friends. Let's find the victuals. My cloak's purely deflated."

With that he set off jauntily, humming a light air.

"There goes a lunatic for certain," said Angus, staring after him.

"There's no man, lunatic or not, I'd more want at my back," Lugh told him, and started off with the Dagda and Morrigan after him.

They crossed the yard to the main hall of the fortress. This immense, circular structure of wattled timber squatted in the center of the enclosure, the physical and spiritual heart of Tara's life.

As they passed from the sunlight of the yard, the hall's interior was like a dim cavern. But before their eyes could adjust to the darkness, a sudden flare of yellow light threw the vast room into sharp clarity and revealed to them a nightmare scene.

In the center of the hall, a monstrous form rose from the stone circle of the fire pit.

The body was like that of an enormous maggot that had crawled up from the earth's blackest bowels, flattened and marked with rings that divided the soft flesh into segments. It shone with a thick layer of mucous that oozed from it as it pushed upward past the stones circling the pit. At its upper end was a boneless head with staring, bulbous eyes fixed to slender stalks that seemed to grow from the pliant body. Below the eyes was a round, protruding mouth, like that of a leech, constantly pulsing, sucking, ready to fix upon some victim, drooling a venomous liquid that sizzled and steamed as it splattered to the floor.

It reared upward, drawing its huge form high and lifting the head toward the point of the peaked roof nearly thirty feet above. The eyestalks stretched out, bringing the eyes forward, and arched downward, directing the lidless stare at a group of bright-cloaked men huddled right below. The obscene, sucking mouth began to drop threateningly toward them.

The men stood, seemingly transfixed by fear, staring helplessly upward at the thing as it prepared to strike.

IV
—
THE SEA GOD'S PLAN

"NO. NO. NO! This will never do!" a fussy voice said with sharp disapproval.

A small figure dressed, like the others, in a multihued robe, appeared from behind the grotesque creature and stood, hands on hips, looking up at it and shaking his head.

"It is certainly disgusting. That I will admit. But what good would it be against the Fomor? Why, if they saw it, they would probably try to carve the poor thing up for their supper. And some of them are more ugly than it is." He waved a dismissing hand at the thing. "Now, get away with you," he ordered curtly.

And with miraculous obedience, the creature instantly began to disappear. It dissolved, like a cloud dissipated by a sudden wind, blown into tatters that floated up through the smoke hole in the ceiling's peak. Soon nothing remained but the embers of a small fire in the pit from which rose a thin thread of grey smoke.

Lugh and his companions all relaxed and released their grips on their weapons. All four had been ready to charge in. Now, seeing the little man, they understood. For he was Findgoll, High-Druid of the Tuatha de Dananns.

"Findgoll, I object to your criticism," said an imposing greyhaired Druid who pulled himself stiffly up to his considerable height to glare down at his small colleague. "I used some of my best skills to conjure that."

Findgoll stepped toward the group of other Druids. They were an imposing lot, mostly tall, lean, aristocratic men with strong features and an air of great dignity. Indeed, the Druids

were the most influential group in the de Danann society,
rivaling even the High-King in power. But Findgoll, a head
shorter than any of the rest, was not intimidated. His manner
toward them was that of a scolding teacher to unruly small
boys.

"If that is your best, then it only proves how decayed your
skills have become from long neglect," he replied uncom-
promisingly.

"What? Why, how do you dare to—" the other began in an
outraged splutter.

Findgoll cut him off. "Listen, you, and all the rest of you,"
he said fiercely, his high voice cracking like a whip, "while
most of you spent these past years cowering in your hiding
places and praying to Danu that the Fomor wouldn't find you,
I was at work. I was using my talent in sorcery to protect the
other teachers and artists Bres had condemned. My skills are
sharper than ever in my life, more than a match for any Fomor
and, I'm betting, more than a match for any of you. Or would
one of you be wishing to give them a test?"

He glared around at them, his eyes fixing most challengingly
on the tall Druid. None replied. They knew the truth of his
words.

"Fine, then," he said. "Now, you're all as out of practice as
our warrior friends outside. So we will practice, practice, and
practice. Every skill that we learned from our teachers in the
Four Cities may be needed."

"And sooner than we thought, I'm afraid," Lugh called
across the room to him, striding forward with his companions.

Findgoll looked around toward them. He had a small-
featured, cunning face set below a broad forehead. It lit now
with pleasure as he saw his friends.

"Well, you've come back!" he said. Then the ominous words
of Lugh registered and his expression clouded. "But what do
you mean? What's wrong?"

"It's the Fomor," Lugh explained. "They're gathering a huge
army, and Bres himself is leading them."

"Bres!" exclaimed the Druid, and murmurs of concern ran
through the group of his colleagues.

"We haven't many days in which to prepare," Lugh went on.
"We're meeting tonight in Nuada's quarters to discuss our
plans. But, until then, don't speak of this to anyone else."

"I understand," Findgoll said. "We'll surely all be there."
He looked at the other Druids. "In the meantime, we'd best

be going on with our work, hadn't we? From the look of our warriors, our magic may be the best defense we'll have."

The four warriors left the Druids and moved back through the hall to the raised platform at the back where the High-King and his champions sat at the feasts. On the long table there were set out plates of cheeses and bread, dried meat and fruit, and large pitchers of ale. The Dagda helped himself to a plate of food, took up a whole pitcher, and sat down heavily on one of the large benches.

"I'm going to watch this," he said. "It should be a good bit of entertainment."

Morrigan sat down, too, refusing the ale the Dagda held out, folding her cloak tightly about her and staring ahead, silent and expressionless.

"I'll be back to join you," Lugh promised. "I just want to tell Aine and Taillta that we're back."

He turned away toward the wooden stairway beside the platform and found Gilla falling in beside him. He gave him a curious look.

"I thought you were going to eat first."

The clown shrugged. "It'll wait a bit. I want to see them too."

Across the room, the Druids were back at their practice. Findgoll gestured one of the group forward. He was a young man, and looked very uncertain.

"Ce, you are the newest of our group," said Findgoll. "See what you can conjure that might frighten the Fomor."

As Lugh and Gilla started up the stairs, they heard the young Druid's incantation begin. They were nearing the top when there came a muffled boom and a bright flash of light from below. Then came Findgoll's voice, raised in sharp annoyance:

"I ask for frightening and what is it I get? A sheep! And a dead one at that!"

"I think it's only asleep, Findgoll," came the weak, defensive voice of hapless Ce.

"Is it? With all four feet straight up that way?" was the little Druid's biting retort.

Gilla flashed a broad grin at Lugh.

"Poor Findgoll. He's got his hands full with that lot of pompous tricksters. Only a handful of real sorcerers in the whole bunch of them."

The two reached the top of the stairs. There a long room ran along the back curve of the hall above the High-King's dais. It was open on the inside to the hall, edged by a low gallery rail. On the outside was a row of windows, now all open, allowing sunlight to flood the room.

The few tables and stools that furnished the room were moved to the sides, leaving the center clear. There two women sat upon the floor amidst piles of wooden plaques, sections of cloth and hide, metal sheets and thin slabs of slate, all marked with crude maps.

Both women were of striking appearance, but in quite different ways. One looked to be in her thirties, but still maintaining the freshness and physical vitality of a much younger woman. She was solidly built, not heavy-limbed but certainly not frail. She was quite handsome, broad featured, her face dark complected and crowned by a wealth of black hair lightly salted with grey. Her expression was at this moment set in concentration, her dark eyes flashing with energy. She was sorting the piles with sharp, impatient gestures and grumbling the while.

The other woman was much younger. From her face she seemed hardly more than a girl. Her features were open, smooth, and pleasant rather than beautiful, but somehow more natural and satisfying for that. Her cheeks were high and round and her small nose was dusted lightly with freckles. Fair hair with the cast of burnished copper was loosely plaited at her neck.

Her figure, however, belied her youthful look. She was in shape indisputably a woman. And as she sat there, unaware of the arrival of the men, Lugh let his gaze dwell on her admiringly. It took in the supple curves, the slender waist, the soft swell of hip revealed by the short, belted warrior's tunic that she wore. He lingered especially over the length of slim, white legs, the ankles accentuated by the leather thongs of her shoes winding about the calves. His eyes followed their line on up, past her knees, toward—

"Lugh!" said a surprised and happy voice.

He jerked and looked up, to meet the frank gaze of bright green eyes. He flushed guiltily, but she only smiled at him with warm welcome.

The woman beside her wasn't smiling, however. When she saw who had come, she bent a sharp glare upon Gilla that would have skewered him like a pig carcass if it had been of iron.

"So, you've come back from your bit of adventurin', have you?" she said with heat.

"It makes me feel good to know you're so glad to see us safe," Gilla replied with his usual foolish smile.

But she wasn't to be soothed. "Don't try your charming manner on me again, you standin' there so full of yourself, and with your face still rosy from the fresh wind and the sun on it." She jumped up from the piles and advanced on him. "Look at us, penned up here in this dark and smoky hall for these three days past, filthy from all these bits of trash, our backs breaking from going through them. We should have been with you."

"It was important work you were doing," Gilla told her in a defensive tone. "We'll need the map you can make from all these bits."

"It's done," she said, "but for our last checking. All the pieces of Eire in one great chart. And if it was so important, why weren't you here doing it yourself? Just because you're Manannan, the great Sea-God—"

"Taillta, please!" he protested quickly. He looked around toward the stair head to be sure no one else had intruded upon them and overheard this astonishing revelation.

For it was true that this peculiar, gawky being was actually Manannan MacLir, known to those of Eire as a god of the sea who inhabited a mystical isle protected by sorcery and savage monsters of the ocean depths. In reality, he was a subject of Queen Danu of Tir-na-nog, sent out by her to act secretly as a guardian for the proud de Dananns.

Not long after the de Dananns had come to Eire from the distant Blessed Isles, Danu had established an outpost for him on a small island near to Eire. She had granted him vast powers over the sea and its creatures, but these were only to be used to protect his outpost and mask the true nature of his presence there. For Danu had promised that she would not interfere with the de Dananns acting of their own free will. No magic of Tir-na-nog would be used in Eire unless that independent-minded race wished for it.

As a result, Manannan had nothing to sustain him while in Eire except his own cunning, his fighting skills, and a few conjuring tricks like his bottomless cloak. But to the lighthearted adventurer, this only made his task a more exciting challenge. In the disguise of an awkward, harmless clown, he was able to move about Eire unnoticed, helping the de Dananns in their struggle for freedom.

Now, having carefully made certain that he and his companions were alone in the hall's upper room, he abruptly dropped the higher voice and foolish manner of the clown, taking on the more assured and refined manner of Manannan.

"You must remember," he cautioned urgently, "only the four of us can know who I am!"

"And why is that?" she asked sarcastically. "It's so you can be free to play the fool—not that it doesn't suit you—and go off on more little adventures."

"Be careful, Taillta," Manannan cautioned, his voice tinged with irritation. "Even from you I'll take only so much."

"Besides, Taillta," Aine said reasonably, "my brother didn't force us to do this. We did volunteer."

"Thank you, sister, for that stout defense," the tall man said graciously. "And I assure you both that you'll not be made to do such a thing again."

"Well, all right then," Taillta agreed grudgingly. She walked to Lugh and threw her arms about him, giving him a great, crushing hug. "I am glad to see you back safely," she told him, smiling at last. As an afterthought, she threw to Manannan, "And you too."

"Show us what you've done," Manannan urged.

"It's over here," Taillta said, directing him to a large table against the outer wall. She unrolled a great dressed deer hide on which a large and detailed chart had been painstakingly drawn. Mountains, rivers, inlets, and other geographic features were included.

"See here," she said, pointing out small circles scattered across the island, "we've tried to mark where every settlement is and show the roads that link them."

"Marvelous work!" the tall man said, bending over it to examine its details more closely. "Really marvelous work. Don't you think so, Lugh?"

But Lugh was paying no attention. It was all on Aine. He stepped forward and held out a hand to help her up from her seat amidst the piles. As she rose, she brushed back some stray hairs from her face and then smiled to see how black her hand was.

"It really is filthy work," she said. "I must be covered with it."

"You look fine to me," Lugh assured her, continuing to hold her other hand.

Manannan looked back and noticed a familiar, foolish expression on Lugh's face. His eyes narrowed and he called sharply to the young warrior.

"Lugh!"

The young man tore his gaze from Aine and turned it to his tall comrade. "Yes?"

"We've got to talk now," the other said seriously, turning from the map and propping his lanky form against the table. "That's why I wanted to come up here. The others can't hear this."

Curious, Lugh and the two women took seats on the benches.

Her brother's tone of voice aroused Aine's concern.

"Manannan, what's wrong? And why are you back in Tara so soon?"

"Bres is not dead," the man answered tersely. "He's come back to Eire and is gathering an army of Fomor. We didn't guess those monsters could react that fast to the rising. Now all the de Dananns are in great danger. Lugh, what do you think are the possibilities of our friends gathering their forces or restoring strength to their warriors in time?"

"I would say it will be difficult," Lugh replied.

"Charitable. I'd say it will be impossible. To survive, they are going to need our help."

"But we are helping them," Lugh said, not understanding.

"It'll take a little more than that," Manannan said. "It will take the powers Danu has intrusted to us. Think, Lugh, of the Gifts of the Four Cities."

Lugh recalled his first visit to the isle that Manannan called his home. There, in the strange underground dwelling known as the Sidhe, this remarkable being had shown him the four objects that Queen Danu had sent to aid the de Danann cause. Two of those objects had already been put to use. One was the Lia Fail, the Stone of Truth, which had established Nuada's right to hold the throne as High-King. The second was the sword that Lugh carried, an unbreakable blade whose aura of strength endowed Lugh with the spirit of a champion. But there were two others still awaiting their time—a spear containing a terrible energy and a massive cauldron with its own unique powers. He understood what Manannan was speaking of.

"Of course! The cauldron! Its magic can restore the strength of anyone who eats from it."

Manannan nodded. "Danu foresaw that it would be needed, as she did the Lia Fail and your own Answerer."

"You're right," Lugh agreed. "We should start for it at once."

"No," said Manannan, lifting a restraining hand. "I'll see to that. You have another task. The cauldron will be little good if the warriors are not hosted. That's what you have to do. The Riders of the Sidhe can help you do it in time."

"But why do I have to do that?" the young warrior wondered. "Anyone could travel with them. I'd rather go with you."

"You must do this. You are Champion of the Sidhe. The Riders are charged by Danu to protect and obey you."

"Champion," Lugh said and laughed ruefully. "It's certain I don't feel like one."

"It doesn't matter what you feel. You are Champion. The son of Cian," Manannan reminded him. "You are the one the Prophecy has said will lead the de Dananns. They believe it. They can feel the power in you. You heard what Febal said. Only you can convince them that they can rise against the Fomor."

Lugh shook his head. "Manannan, I feel as if I'm being used by you as I was before. You're in control and I have no will."

"This is your own destiny using you, not me," the tall man protested. "And you freely accepted it. From the moment you chose to become the Champion of the Sidhe and fulfill the Prophecy, you had no self."

This idea had not been put so bluntly to Lugh by his mentor before. It seemed to Lugh that Manannan's nature had become more openly domineering and the idea disturbed him. He felt confused.

"I'm going outside for a time," he announced abruptly. "I need to think a bit."

He got up and crossed the room to a door in the outer wall. He pushed it open and stepped through onto a wooden bridge. It linked this upper level of the hall to the walkway around the top of the palisade.

He crossed to the walkway and stood staring out across the row of timbers to the countryside and the town below. He tried to make some order of the many feelings mixed within him.

He was mostly bothered by the sense that his life was still not his own. He realized that Manannan had controlled it since his childhood, manipulating him so that he would play out his intended role.

He felt a presence beside him. A hand moved out to rest lightly on his arm. He turned and looked into the eyes, so brilliantly green, so knowing that they could plumb every depth of him.

"You know, not so many days ago I was just a boy living on a tiny isle," he told her. "I thought then that my only destiny would be to stay there, fishing and playing my games. I wonder sometimes if I wouldn't have been happier knowing nothing else."

Her expression grew worried. "Lugh, what's wrong?"

"It's just your brother. I don't know. He's taken so much control."

"He's doing what he thinks is right to help the de Dananns win freedom," she reasoned. "If the time is short, it seems the only way."

"I suppose that's true enough," he admitted. "I only wish that it was my idea, or my choice, or anything to do with my own will."

"It will be over soon," she promised soothingly. "Then you can be your own. Both of us can."

Her smile raised a responding smile from him. He lifted a hand to lay against the softness of her cheek.

"I missed you," he told her.

"And I missed you. But that won't be happening again. This time we won't be separated. I'll ride with you."

"You will not," said Manannan's voice behind them.

They turned to see him crossing the bridge toward them.

"What do you mean?" Aine asked him, clearly puzzled.

"You're not going with him," he said flatly. "Lugh will ride alone. You and Taillta will stay here at Tara."

Her puzzlement turned to astonishment and anger. "What?" she cried. "But you just promised—"

"I promised that I wouldn't have you doing any more tasks like this map," he said, lifting the rolled-up chart he was carrying. "But you can join in the training of the warriors here. Or you can organize the de Danann women. Your help is needed at Tara. Lugh doesn't need it."

"Helping Lugh fulfill his mission in Eire is as much my work as yours, Brother," she said hotly. "You can't let him go alone."

"He's a warrior. A champion."

"He's a boy. He can't handle this by himself."

"Thank you!" Lugh put in, hurt by her evaluation of his skills. "You're not much more than a girl yourself!"

"I'm sorry, Lugh," she told him. "But you admitted to me that you still had doubts. And you know I've had more experience than you. I've been in more difficult places and fought more battles."

"Lugh doesn't need you now," Manannan said stolidly. "He needs to act alone and his last doubts will disappear. There's no reason for you to risk yourself unnecessarily."

"He does need me. And you can't speak to me of risks. Until now I've taken as many as you, and you've never been concerned. What is it? What's changed your mind? There's more to it than that."

Manannan hesitated. Then the words came reluctantly.

"All right. I've noticed the growing closeness between you. It might be . . . in the way."

"If you think that, then you don't think much of me," she said harshly. "When have I ever been other than your right arm? When have I ever failed you?"

"Never," he admitted.

"Then you've no right to think that I would now. I have feelings for Lugh. I won't deny them. But I have my own sense. This is as much my mission as it is yours. You sent me to Eire to help Lugh and that comes first. I'd never let anything interfere with that."

"You might think so," Manannan reasoned, "but you can't be certain. This is too important to take any risks. Lugh will act alone this time."

She appealed to Lugh, her eyes pleading, her voice urgent.

"Please, help me. Tell him you want me to go with you."

Lugh looked at her and wavered. When he spoke, it was with great reluctance.

"I don't know, Aine. I want you, but I'd be a fool not to want to keep you safe."

She stared at him, stricken by his words. Then she spoke in growing heat.

"You don't give much value to what I want, do you?" she said. She wheeled on her brother. "And you! I used to believe that you were always right. Now I agree with Taillta. You are a fool!"

Manannan drew himself up. His manner assumed a towering haughtiness.

"I am the guardian of these people. Danu herself has made me so. I'll do what I think I must to help them succeed. If you can't obey, you'll leave Eire."

"You really have taken too much control in this," she

stormed. "The chance to play the hero has made you drunk with power."

She spun on her heel and stalked away, too choked by her emotions to say more. Manannan and the stunned Lugh watched her go.

"It's for the best," the tall man said with great assurance. Then he slapped the chart he carried into his young friend's arms. "Here. We've got to go speak with the Dagda and Morrigan before tonight's meeting. There's much to plan."

V

SPY

THE MAP WAS unrolled on the plank table. Under the light of the many flaring torches, the Druids and chieftains of Nuada gathered close about to examine it.

"This will help us determine the best routes," Lugh explained.

They were crowded into the quarters of the High-King, a wedge-shaped section of an outer circle of rooms that surrounded the main hall. It was shut off from the larger room by a thick wall of wickerwork.

"This is most intriguing," Nuada said, leaning down to peer closely at the fine drawings of woods and hills and rivers. "How did you ever come up with such a thing?"

"It was the idea of Gilla," Lugh said.

"The clown?" Nuada asked in surprise. He looked up toward the lanky figure who smiled affably.

"It's something I learned of in my travelin'," he explained in the clown's high, foolish tones. "Far to the east it was. The people there use these all the time. Keeps them from being lost, it does that. Seemed useful to me. I'm lost all the time."

"It can help us to choose the safest, fastest routes we'll need to take," said Lugh. He placed a finger on the spot that represented Tara and drew it toward the west. "I will take the Riders of the Sidhe and sweep through Eire, calling every settlement to host. With their magic I can move at great speed. It'll take no more than three days to reach them all."

Nuada looked from the map to the young champion's face. "But hosting them isn't enough. You know how weak they are."

"I know," said Lugh, his voice sure, "but there is a way we can deal with that." He moved his finger across to the eastern sea, to the small island that showed not far from Eire. "Here, in Manannan's Isle is a cauldron. It has powers like none ever seen. It can never be emptied. And, more important," he looked around him at the listening men, "the food in it has the power to restore the strength of those who eat! It can restore the whole de Danann force!"

Impressed, the circle of advisors murmured amongst themselves.

"But why should this Sea-God give it to us?" asked Meglin, the haughty High-Druid. "He has always been aloof before, a distant and dangerous being, a mystery who surrounds his island with a deadly fog where monstrous beings lurk. Some say that he is a monster himself."

Lugh glanced at Gilla from the corner of his eye and saw the disguised "Sea-God" stifle a laugh.

"Let's say that I know he wishes to give us aid," Lugh said cryptically. "But his powers do not extend beyond the sea. It's up to us to bring the cauldron here."

"If this cauldron can be brought to Eire in time to nourish a hosting of our warriors," said Nuada, "we may have the strength to withstand the Fomor."

"If! If!" Another spoke up. He was a thin, sad-faced, sallow man dressed in the dark cloak and golden torc of a bard of the highest rank. His voice had the tense, shrill quality of a tightly strung harp. He seemed to vibrate with a nervous energy his frail body couldn't control. "It all sounds a very great risk to me. A great risk to be taken by this boy who is a stranger to us, who has appeared so suddenly from nowhere to help us, who claims to be Cian's son, with no proof of it at all."

"Be careful of your words, Bobd Derg." The Dagda rumbled like a threatening storm. "He has done nothing to earn our distrust. It was his courage that made this rising."

"A rising that could see us destroyed, Father," the other countered. He swept his brooding gaze around the room. "If Lugh fails, there will be no army for this magic cauldron to restore. If the cauldron is not brought, all our warriors will be gathered to make easy Bres's slaughter. If there is failure in both things . . ."

"We here will surely be destroyed," Nuada finished. "And Bres will do what he likes with the rest of our people. But if we do nothing at all, the end will be the same for us. There is no other choice."

"There is another choice," Bobd Derg replied.

"Yes, yes. We all know about your other choice," Findgoll said wearily. "We've all heard it scores of times." He mocked the bard's dismal tones as he recited: "We must leave Eire and return to Tir-na-nog!"

"We'd be accepted there," Bobd Derg said earnestly. "Queen Danu promised that we could return if we chose."

"To become the children of Danu again, not a people of our own," the Dagda put in heavily. He leaned across the table toward Bobd Derg. His body towered above that of his son. His words held the finality of death. "Listen to me for the last time. We will not abandon Eire. We will never return to a life of pampered ease in the Magic Isles. That is no life for us. It is no life at all. Eire is our land and I'll have it even if it only means I'll be buried in it. I stay, whatever the risk. Now, how about you all?"

He threw a challenging gaze around the room, searching each face in the flickering lights. Some hesitated, but many nodded their quick assent, faces determined. Finally all joined in agreement, leaving only Bobd Derg silent.

"There is your answer," the giant man said, smiling in triumph at his son.

"You and these others loyal to Nuada do not speak for the entire de Danann race," the poet said, still hostile, unwilling to accept defeat. "The rest might think otherwise if they thought no help would come."

"There is no reason for them to think that," Nuada said sharply. "And you will not suggest it or frighten our people with your talk of doom unless it becomes certain that these missions have failed."

"And when would we know that?" Bobd Derg asked.

Nuada looked to Lugh for the answer.

"Bres should take ten days to gather his forces and march," the young champion said. "If all goes well, our missions should take six, eight at the most. If Bres marches on Tara and we still haven't returned, then will be the time to ask the de Dananns if they wish to flee."

"How is this cauldron to be brought to Eire?" asked Niet, a captain of the household companies.

"I'll be fetching it," the Dagda said. "I'll go to Manannan's Isle with Angus, Morrigan, and Gilla Decaire."

"I want to go with you as well," said Findgoll. "I've a great curiosity about this Manannan MacLir, and you may be needing help of my sort."

"We need none of you wizard's tricks," the Dagda protested. "Only strong arms and true blades."

But Lugh saw the disguised Sea-God nod sharply at the Druid and wink. The young man moved quickly to support Findgoll's request.

"No, I think it might be a help. Manannan is a very . . . ah . . . peculiar man. I think he might enjoy meeting Findgoll."

"All right then," the Dagda agreed grudgingly. "But he'll be only an extra weight to us."

"It's settled then," Nuada confirmed. "We will use this map to decide and mark the best routes for both missions. Those of you most familiar with the countryside come here, closest to me."

They began to pore over the map, discussing the virtues of this route over that. A heated discussion began. Unnoticed at the back of the group, one youthful warrior listened with a special interest.

He was a fresh-faced youth, his boyish, guileless face topped by a tousled mass of bright red hair. Normally his manner was bright, his expression smiling But this night, as he listened, a strange coldness showed in his blue eyes.

Late into the night, the discussion ended. The planners departed to their beds. Nuada left to check the fortress guards. Then the youth returned, slipping past the wicker screen into the High-King's quarters.

He studied the chart still laid out on the table, now marked with the routes that had been decided. He slipped a piece of broken pottery from beneath his cloak and scratched a hurried copy of the map upon it with his dagger point. Then he left, slipping out into the darkness of the hall, creeping across the great, silent room to the main doors and out into the night.

No one saw him steal out through the small guard's door at the fortress's back. And no one saw him ride swiftly away from the town below on a sleek horse, galloping out to be swallowed by the night.

Through that night and the next morning the lone rider pushed his mount toward the northwest at full speed. He rode deeply into the territory of the Fomor, but without slackening pace. Boldly he passed by their patrols, flashing a strange metal device. Finally he made his way through a heavy picket line and entered the camp of the gathering army.

Not long after this, a sleek black ship slipped away from the sheltered bay into the sea and headed north.

It cut through the waves swiftly, holding a steady heading. Soon a tall, sharply glinting object seemed to rise up from the sea ahead. It was the Tower of Glass.

It was not long after the sleek ship had reached the Tower's quays that a soldier entered the stark, sunfilled room atop the Tower and approached the dark figure seated motionless upon the massive throne.

"My Commander," he said, "Bres has returned. He wishes to see you. He has a young de Danann here with him."

"Let them enter," the metallic voice commanded.

The soldier backed away toward the massive doors and pulled them open. Two figures moved into the room.

The former High-King strode forward fearlessly. The other came reluctantly, glancing up with obvious nervousness at the towering figure brooding there against the backdrop of bright sky. In the smooth black expanse that should have been a face, the crimson slit of eye showed like a sun just breasting the world's rim.

"Why have you come back here, Bres?" demanded the being. "And who have you brought with you?"

Bres smiled and extended a hand toward the red-haired youth.

"Balor, I would like to introduce my son, Ruadan."

"So, this is your son. The product of your secret and brief pairing with—who was it?"

"Bridget," Bres supplied. "Yes, only she and I know of his true parentage. The secret has marked her, but she has kept it."

"And you're certain your mother would not expose you, if she knew of your betrayal?" the one-eyed giant asked the boy.

"Never," came the arrogant reply. The innocent face beamed with a sly smile. "You see, she loves me far too much."

"The son is as treacherous as his father," Balor said. "Interesting. No matter how diluted is the Fomor blood, it still seems to taint the whole. But, what is it that this young spy has discovered that brings you to abandon your army?"

"The de Dananns have discovered that we are gathering our forces secretly," said Bres. "They are making plans to host their own warriors and restore them to full strength in only a few days."

The eye flicked a fraction wider at this news. The father and son felt the heat of it increase.

"How could that be?" The voice clanged out like a hammer on cold iron. "You told me such a thing would be impossible."

"It might be, but for the one called Lugh," Ruadan said, with more boldness. "He has shown them how they can do it."

"Lugh!" Balor boomed.

"He is planning to thwart us once again," Bres said in anger. "If he succeeds, my army will face an enemy equal in strength. We might be defeated in open battle. Then Eire would be lost to me—and you as well."

The black figure was silent for a long moment. Then, finally: "Come with me!" it ordered them.

And, with those words, the giant throne shuddered, squealed in agony, and began to move.

It traveled slowly and unevenly at first, but then with increasing smoothness and speed. It seemed to follow a thin line, a barely discernible crack in the hard, polished grey surface of the floor.

Bres and his son exchanged a look of wonder at the sight. Even the former High-King had never seen the giant move this way. They followed.

The massive throne and its terrible occupant rolled across the large room, into a wide hallway that led along one outer wall. At the far end, huge panels of a softly gleaming silver blocked the way. The Commander's transport came to a halt there, but only for a moment. The panels slid silently aside to reveal a square empty room, its blank walls sheathed in the same silver metal. It was high and wide enough to easily accommodate Balor. The throne slid forward into it, then stopped again and slowly pivoted to face the giant toward the doors.

"Come in," he told his visitors.

They obeyed, the young man peering about him apprehensively. He had been in such a room on his strange trip up the Tower to Balor's lofty quarters. He hadn't enjoyed the experience.

This one was no better. But this time the room was dropping, and the sensation of pressure was like someone lifting up his insides instead of trying to push them into his heels.

The sensation grew, along with a rising metallic whine. Just as both became almost intolerable, they faded. The room thumped softly and was motionless. The doors, without any visible hand on them, slid open.

They were looking into a strange twilight darkness alive with what seemed a constantly shifting galaxy of colored stars.

The throne moved again, carrying Balor forward. The two followed, peering about them with expressions both curious and uncertain at once.

They were in a wide hallway that ran ahead of them to disappear into a deeper night. The walls on either side were set with metal panels intricately decorated with designs alien to the visitors. Within these designs, countless points of colored light pulsed or glowed or ran in constant patterns. A faint but steady hum hung in the air.

The throne went on without pausing and the two men stayed very close to it. Neither wished to be left behind in such a place.

The corridor was lined with doors, and many of them stood open. As they passed, Bres and his son peeked into the rooms beyond them. Some of the spaces were vast, filled with boxlike metal shapes in row upon row. Like the panels on the corridor walls, they were alive with shifting lights. Enormous power pulsed in them, crackled in them like distant lightning or a blazing fire. The air was charged with their energy. They chattered and growled and chirped at one another constantly, as if they were some company of odd metal beasts arguing hotly amongst themselves.

In other rooms the men saw things that might have been human beds. But these were always surrounded by fantastic contrivances of metal fitted with grotesque and cruel-seeming appendages. To the ruthless Bres, the purpose of the things seemed obvious.

"They must be torture rooms," he murmured knowingly to his son.

Ahead, the corridor ended in another set of silver doors. As they moved toward it, the faint background hum increased. Father and son exchanged a questioning glance. Neither could guess—or really wished to guess—the giant's purpose here.

Balor's strange transport reached the doors and pushed right into them. The heavy throne base forced the metal panels aside and the three passed through into an enormous room.

It was square, and each flat wall was filled with the complex panels of light. More sinister devices loomed around them in the semidarkness. The shifting lights glinting in multiplied reflections from their array of gleaming parts lent them a chill beauty, like that of a fine jeweled ornament.

But the most striking feature of the room was a wide, circular column that rose from the floor in the center of the space to touch the flat ceiling. The visitors estimated that it was five or six times a man's height in thickness. Its curved surface seemed to them composed of some smooth substance, shiny and black as the surface of a still, moonlit pond.

Balor trundled forward, aiming for a square box that protruded from one point in the cylinder's side. There the throne jerked to a stop, its base touching the curved black wall.

As Bres and Ruadan approached the wall, they realized that it was not solid. Instead they looked through a glass surface into a darkened space. Within that space, more tiny lights were visible. And a large shadow, undefinable but somehow sinister, seemed to float there. Had Balor imprisoned some monster within this glass column, Bres wondered?

Slowly, slowly, one of the giant's massive hands lifted toward the protruding box. On its top, rows of small lights in red, green, and yellow burned steadily. The hand rose over them and then descended. The jointed fingers uncurled and rested carefully upon the lights.

At once the space beyond the glass leaped to brilliant white light. Its brightness made them start and they blinked, peering through narrowed eyes momentarily blinded.

And then they saw.

VI

THE DRUID

THEY WERE LOOKING into a circular room, walled off by the cylinder of clear glass. The ceiling was a circle of white light that flooded the space with an icy glow.

From various devices fixed in this bright ceiling were suspended a bewildering array of instruments and cables, branching limbs of metal, flexible tubes of some clear material through which liquids of various hues flowed. Together they formed a complex interlace as they ran together at a central point.

And there, enmeshed in the tangled net, like an immense spider in its web, was hung suspended the figure of a man.

It was difficult at first for Bres and Ruadan to even recognize that the thing before them was a man. It hung in a prone position, arms and legs spreadeagled. It was very like a spider. The body was encased in an armorlike shell, shaped like the insect's bloated body. The protruding limbs were spindly, knobbily jointed bones covered with a mottled, grey-white skin. The many devices suspended about the form all seemed attached to it by cables and the clear tubes. Some even penetrated the flesh of the wasted limbs, like the suckers of some mechanical parasite. Only the movement of the liquid within the tubes showed that it was entering his body, not being drained out.

The head of the being was suspended in a soft mesh cradle. It appeared to be little more than a skull, long, narrow, and high-domed. The flesh beneath the surface of stretched, dry skin was melted away, leaving the slender nose, long chin, and high cheekbones to jut up sharply, painfully, as if they would tear through.

Where the eyes should have been there were sunken pits, black depressions surrounded by crinkled folds of scar tissue. From these caverns into the depths of the skull, objects like some kind of tuberous plant seemed to grow. They filled the

43

deep sockets, bulging outward beyond the bony ridges of the
hairless brow, then tapered down to thin, stalklike cables that
coiled upward to holes in the white ceiling.

To Bres and Ruadan, it seemed impossible that this was a
living thing. But once again Balor's hand moved upon the
panel. This time a light appeared in a device beside the awful
head, and a low chime sounded from inside the cylinder.

The head shifted. With an enormous effort it rolled toward
them. As it did, a device suspended beside it rotated, too, and
a small circle of light set in one end, glowing greenly like a cat's
eye in the dark, fixed on them.

Immediately, a square panel filling half the outer wall
beyond the glass cylinder came to life. What had been
darkness now filled with a hazy light, like mist before the sun.
It brightened, and then it began to fill with shadows. They
took on color and firmer shape, grew clearer, but still uneven,
like the images reflected in a wind-rippled pool. At times a
greater disturbance washed through it, but still the figures that
finally appeared in the lighted square were recognizable.

They were a black giant with a slit of blazing eye and two
men, pale faced, expressions frozen with amazement.

"Why, that's us!" Bres gasped.

"That is what he sees," Balor explained, "with the help of
our old devices and his powers. It is reflected there, along with
the images created within his own mind."

"You can see his thoughts?" Bres asked in wonder.

"Only if he wishes it."

The image steadied further now, as if the being were coming to a fuller consciousness. Then the lipless slit of mouth
parted, moved back from the blackened stumps of teeth, and
there came to them, hollowly, as if amplified within the cylinder, a horrible whisper.

"So, Balor, you have finally brought Bres to me," it said.

Bres looked at the black giant. "Who is this being? How
does he know me?"

"I am Mathgen!" came the rasping, horrible reply.

Bres's head jerked back to that wasted face. "Mathgen!" he
cried in astonishment. "But you are dead! You must be
dead!"

"I am alive. Alive if you call this living nightmare that en-
traps me life."

"I have heard of you," Ruadan said in awe. "You were one of

the High-Druids in the old time. But . . . something happened to you. No one speaks of it."

"I tried to help the de Danann race. That was my crime," the voice wheezed out, the tones shifting from a soft hiss to a harsh rattle. "For that I was nearly destroyed and my memory erased by my own people."

"What did you do?" the boy asked, his curiosity overcoming his aversion to the grotesque being.

The image of Balor, Ruadan, and Bres faded, replaced by others in a swiftly moving series, rushing by so quickly that the watchers could scarcely identify them. There were some tantalizingly brief views of an extraordinary, glittering land and vast, glowing cities as the dry husk of a voice spoke in wistful tones of distant memory:

"For many years my people lived in the Four Cities of Tir-na-nog, helped and strengthened by the people of Queen Danu. The others were happy with the kindness we were shown, like puppies fawning at a master's heel. But I"—the faint voice took on a stronger note, as if some ancient will was reinforced by the memory—"I wanted much more! I saw the power that could be gained by using the magic of Tir-na-nog. I knew that it could be wrested from those weak and passive beings. I plotted for years to take control, learning all the skills I could, stealing the deepest secrets of magic from Danu's highest Druids."

At this, the images on the wall steadied to reveal a brief but starkly etched image of a sharp-featured man at work in a vast cavern of a room. Around him fires flickered beneath vats and beakers of bubbling liquids, sending colored, coiling streams of smoke into the air. Strange objects, bits of beasts and birds and even men were piled upon the table where he worked, feverishly mixing ingredients in a copper cauldron.

"Soon," Mathgen went on, "I became strong enough to rival them all in power! But when I finally struck, when I finally moved to seize those isles, it was by my own people that I was stopped."

There came another jumbled montage of images, this time of shifting forms and flashing weapons. This changed quickly to a view of two men bursting through a doorway.

Though they appeared much younger than he knew them, Bres still recognized the massive warrior and the tiny, bright-robed druid.

"That is the Dagda and Findgoll!" he said in astonishment.

"Yes. They were the ones who thwarted me. I escaped them and managed to leave the Magic Isles. But Danu sent her powers after me."

Another scene flickered across the wall at this. It was a confused blur of crashing seas, wind-blasted clouds, and lightning, ending abruptly in an explosion of light that wiped the picture away. The lighted wall faded into a blackness and then, slowly, the image of the three watchers in the room came back into view.

Mathgen's voice went on again, but very weakly now, as if the effort to recall this harsh memory had sapped its energy.

"They thought then that they had finished me," it said, "that I was dead."

"One of our ships found him floating in the sea," Balor said, picking up the tale. "He was burned and broken, barely alive. He would have died soon if my people had not returned him here."

"What is this place?" Bres asked, looking around him.

"It was meant for the use of our physicians," Balor supplied, "to treat and heal our people. Once, long ago, these devices would have regenerated him. But now, with the aid of his own powers, they only manage to sustain his life."

"Yes . . . my life," the Druid said with a renewed strength gained from a pride in this single victory. "I am still alive, and my mind is still my own. Through it, my powers are still intact. The knowledge of magic I took from Tir-na-nog can still be used. And I will use it to help the Fomor achieve the one end that we both seek—the complete destruction of the de Danann race!"

With his intention thus stridently proclaimed, Mathgen's voice again lost much of its energy. Reduced to little more than a soft rustling, its next words were, once more, addressed to the visitors.

"Now, what is it that you seek of me? I feel a certain urgency in you."

"Mathgen, we have need of your powers," Balor said. "You told me of the Prophecy. You helped me discover Lugh's hiding place. Now you must help me deal with him. He intends to save the de Danann cause."

"So, he plagues you again. And how will he do these things?"

"He knows of a magical cauldron that can restore full

strength to the de Dananns," Ruadan supplied. "And he will use the Riders of the Sidhe to warn every settlement that they must host."

"What are these Riders of the Sidhe?" the spiderlike being hissed.

"They are a company of mystical warriors," the boy said. "But not men . . . at least not living men. They move with the speed and fury of a fierce wind from the sea. He says that they will sweep him around Eire in only a few days."

"I've seen these warriors myself," Bres put in. "Lugh brought them when he appeared at Tara to help drive me out. They are a strange and terrible force, deadly fighters that seem unkillable."

As Bres spoke, the image of himself, his son, and Balor on the wall began to fade. Replacing it was a blurred image of a troop of men, not solid beings, but like the substance of the sunlit, silver clouds pushed by a powerful wind, sweeping over green meadows.

"I see them," Mathgen said. "They have a powerful aura of energy. But I sense that they are not totally invulnerable. There are forces that even they cannot withstand."

Then, as quickly as it had come, this image faded, too, and that of the three grouped by the cylinder returned.

"Tell me more, boy," the soft, sibilant voice urged. "What else have you discovered about this Lugh? Tell me everything you know about him, about who he is, where he comes from, what he is."

"There's little enough to tell," Ruadan said regretfully. "He appeared from nowhere to help the de Dananns. He's revealed nothing about himself except that he is the son of Cian, the one the Prophecy said would lead the de Dananns to freedom . . ."

"And destroy the Fomor power," the grating voice of Balor finished. "Yes, we know well enough about that Prophecy."

"The son of Cian," the voice of the wasted Druid mused, and another scene imposed itself upon the lighted panel. It was only a brief flicker—a scene of a warrior being cast onto the rocks of a sea-swept beach by the massive hand of Balor— and then the image of Mathgen's vision was gone again.

"But Cian had no powers like this boy Lugh," he said. "Where have they come from? You must have some idea of their source."

"Some say he has the help of Danu herself," the son of Bres offered hopefully. "The Lia Fail that he brought to Tara to proclaim the true High-King was from the city of Falias, in Tir-na-nog."

"Danu swore that she would never interfere in Eire," the hoarse whisper replied. "He has some other help. Now think, boy, think! There must be something else, some bit of information you have learned."

"I don't know," Ruadan said with some desperation. He searched his mind again, and this time came upon a notion. "It might be he is somehow linked to Manannan MacLir," he suggested timidly.

"Manannan!" The Druid's faint voice grew stronger, fueled by new interest. "Why do you say that?"

"Because this magic cauldron that Lugh intends to use is in Manannan's Isle," Ruadan explained. "He is sending a party to fetch it back to Eire."

"Who is in this party?" Balor asked.

"The Dagda, Morrigan, Angus Og, and a strange character called Gilla Decaire, along with the High-Druid Findgoll."

"So many of my old friends!" the being in the web hissed thoughtfully.

"And Manannan MacLir," Balor's iron voice rattled. "Is that sorcerer somehow involved in this? That nuisance who plagues my ships with his monsters and fogs and calls himself a sea-god? Tell me, Mathgen. What do you see?"

Once more the image of the room faded and new scenes formed. But they were shifting, foggy, and unclear. There were glimpses of an isle, of rolling hills, of a great mound, of silver warriors contending on a plain, all flowing together like water in a stream.

"It is his isle you see," the Druid said, "but it is hard. My powers are being blocked. He shrouds himself from my vision as he shrouds his isle, and I sense an even greater force behind his."

The images became a flood of colors that swirled and drained away. They left behind the picture of the room and its occupants.

"Still, I was able to sense that this place of his has some value to Lugh, and that these Riders of the Sidhe come from that isle," Mathgen told them. "Yes, Balor, I think that it is time we learned a great deal more about this Manannan."

"But what about me?" asked Bres. "It will take days for those mindless Fomor beasts you've exiled to Eire to be organized into a useful army. If Lugh and the others complete their missions, forces from the Tower may have to join us to insure a victory."

"No!" Balor rumbled. "You know my decision."

"Balor is right," the being in the web rasped. "To send the Tower forces is unnecessary. There are other ways to make it certain that you will win. There are ways to end this foolish uprising and leave the de Dananns nearly leaderless. Easy prey for your army."

"What are these ways?" Bres asked, clearly skeptical.

"It is quite simple." The image on the wall narrowed suddenly, seeming to shoot forward so that Ruadan's startled face filled the picture. "The boy, I sense, has a map."

"I have," Bres's son admitted, pulling the etched fragment from his tunic.

The image on the wall shifted to it, showing the fine lines scratched upon the pottery.

"You see, Balor," the Druid said, "with that and with the charts in this tower, you can trace the exact routes their warriors will take. They will be alone and far from help. They can be destroyed. Without them and their success, the de Dananns are finished. The Prophecy is finally ended, and I have my revenge."

"Even alone, the Dagda and Morrigan will not be so easy to kill," Bres said. "And my forces can't move quickly enough to catch them."

"Balor must help you if he wishes to keep from committing more of the Tower's forces," Mathgen replied. "He must provide you with the means to reach them and see them destroyed."

"What about Lugh?" asked Ruadan. "With these Riders of the Sidhe, he'll surely be even harder to stop."

"They may be supernatural beings, but I believe a way can be found to deal with them," the Druid said. "Lugh's mission can be stopped. Destroying the boy himself may be more difficult."

"You have doubts that it can be done, with all your powers?" Balor asked, the voice touched with an odd note of interest.

"The Prophecy, Balor," Mathgen said bluntly. "If he is fated to fulfill it, you are powerless."

"Your Prophecy does not make the future," Balor replied. "It only warns us of possibilities. They can be changed."

"Still, if the boy survives and is captured, have him brought here," Mathgen suggested. "There may be other ways to deal with him, and more we could learn."

"I'll do as you wish," said Balor. "But I'll take no chances on his escape again."

"And this Manannan," added the figure in the web. "He, too, cannot be treated too lightly. He may be dangerous. His powers over the sea may be real ones."

"Manannan MacLir I will see to myself," Balor promised.

The skeletal Druid's scarred mouth pulled into a ghastly smile. The hoarse whisper came softly, chilly, like a winter wind blowing fine, hard snow across the ice.

"I am content. Now, please, leave me to rest."

Obediently, Balor moved his massive hand across the lighted panel once again. The light faded and the being slipped back into an unnatural twilight where the stars were tiny, winking, colored lights.

A rising scream of metal upon metal echoed in the caverns of cut stone below the Tower. From the depths of a square pit, a platform lifted upward, carrying the huge objects slowly toward the light. As the floor of the moving platform reached a level with that of the storage area, the shrill whine died away. The platform jerked to a stop, and dozens of grey-uniformed men moved briskly forward to surround the two massive things.

Shrouded in blankets of heavy cloth, the masses—several times a man's size in height and length—were without identifiable form. The only visible portions were enormous, dull-black wheels that thrust beyond the covers. There were two wheels on either side of each of the hulking things, and they allowed the men to easily roll the objects from the platform and across the floor of the storage area, toward the huge, open doors that led onto the quays.

Sital Salmhor—Balor's chief aide—stood with Bres and Ruadan and watched the activity. His voice was heavy with a clear distaste.

"These machines were not intended for such uses as this," he said. "They are meant to help us restore our civilization on the day we leave this Tower. There are few of them, and they have been carefully stored away for a very long time. It was not meant that they should be used to save the likes of the Fomor of Eire."

Bres bridled at the man's superior air. The Tower Fomor were always very arrogant and uncaring in their attitude toward their deformed and exiled bretheren. Bres had no more love for the disgusting beasts himself, but he did see their value.

"You may never have a chance to leave your precious Tower if the de Dananns are not stopped," he said. "You should be grateful you've escaped giving me more help than this!" He put on a haughty manner of his own. "If these marvelous things of yours can really move quickly enough to head off the Dagda's party!"

Salmhor reacted to this as if it were a personal insult. He was an orderly, highly disciplined, and fastidious soldier of the Tower Fomor's elite officers' corps. He believed this untainted portion of his race to be far superior in every way to other beings, especially the upstart de Dananns. He saw Bres as inferior, too, despite the Fomor blood in him. He was a mongrel, an insult to the pure Fomor. A barbarian.

With an irritated tug on the tunic of his impeccable uniform, he replied icily to the former High-King.

"Of course they can move quickly enough. If things go well, they should allow us to destroy this de Danann band without even engaging the machines themselves. Their power is far beyond your ability to imagine, I am sure."

Bres was unimpressed. "Just so they succeed. And what about Lugh?"

"Mathgen has told us what to do," Salmhor said curtly. "Those drums are being loaded for that purpose."

He nodded to a far corner of the immense storage area, where more Fomor were loading large metal barrels from a towering stack onto small carts and wheeling them toward the quay.

"We're planning to use a company of Eireland Fomor for the actual operation," he went on. "They know the area, and even they should be able to handle such a simple task."

"And you avoid risking any more of your own grand lads as well." Bres added.

"That's nothing to do with you," Salmhor replied.

"It is if there are any mistakes and Lugh or the others escape."

"They will not escape. Our arrangements will guarantee that."

Bres shook his head, "I'm not so certain. Most of the de

Dananns are no threat. They are frightened and weak. But Morrigan, the Dagda, and this new champion are dangerous. It's a foolish mistake to underestimate them. I want there to be no chance that you will."

"Put your fears to rest," the officer told him with proud assurance. "No primitive warriors can withstand the forces we will use against them."

They looked out across the quay to where the huge and sinister machines were now being loaded onto one of the black ships. Bres watched the work with a vague uneasiness. He hoped that Sital Salmhor spoke the truth.

BOOK II

DESPERATE MISSIONS

VII

THE MISSIONS BEGIN

THE STARS FADED as the dark sky lightened. The rising sun revealed Lugh and his companions gathered on a hillside not far from the rounded dun of Tara. They were ready to make their departures.

The two separate missions were getting ready to head in opposite ways across the mist-softened, green countryside of the early dawn. The Dagda and his comrades—Gilla, Morrigan, Angus, Findgoll—stood at one side. Behind them waited the score of carefully picked warriors who would accompany them. Facing this group, stood Lugh, alone.

"Remember now, when your own mission is done, you must bring the Riders to the coast and await our return from Manannan's Isle," Gilla was telling Lugh.

"I will," Lugh promised. "With their help we can easily bring the cauldron back to Tara in time."

"Good enough," the Dagda said with satisfaction. "With luck, we'll see you in four or five days, then."

"You will," said Lugh. He took the hand of each in a last gesture of farewell. Gilla gave him the usual wide, foolish smile.

"I'll say hello to this Manannan for you," he said cheerily.

"Just don't you be joking with him, Clown," Lugh advised with pretended gravity. "He might get angry. He's quite mad, you know, and he's ugly as well."

The disguised Sea-God narrowed one eye at his young friend, but the idiotic grin never slipped. "He likely thinks the same of you," came the innocent reply.

Lugh finished the leavetaking and moved along the hillside away from them. There was a soft, chill wind blowing across the meadows and it ruffled the tall grasses around his knees and tugged his cloak and hair as he stood there, a solitary figure now, looking out across the countryside and up to the grey surf of rolling clouds scudding ahead of the wind.

He lifted his arms as Manannan had taught him and murmured the invocation that would bring the Riders from whatever nameless void they inhabited.

At once the light breeze freshened. It swept the clouds ahead and blasted across the hillside, carrying a booming sound of its rushing. And then, in the distance, a mounted troop came into view, rushing toward them with a speed no mortal horses could match.

At first view they were a blur, no single rider distinguishable, more a stream of light with gleaming points, like some sunlit brook cascading across the rocks. But as they neared, separate beings became discernible, the heads of sleek horses raised as they strode, the heads of riders glinting in helmets, the confused tangle of many speeding hooves. But no sound came from them save that of the rushing wind and a bright, melodic jingle.

In moments they were on the hill, drawing to a stop beside the young champion. They sat in two columns, the horses tall and slender, fine heads proudly raised. The warriors sat stiffly upright upon them, clad in glowing cloaks that fluttered about them as if the wind still rushed past. Silver helmets masked their faces so nothing could be seen of them but the grim set mouths and the chill lights of their gleaming eyes. Each carried a lance at his side, its hilt encircled by fine silver rings that jingled together as the company rode, to create the fine, high music that surrounded them.

At their head was a riderless horse, a grey-white mount with a sleek, muscled body. It stood waiting, the energy within it making the body luminous, like a white cloud before the sun.

Lugh approached the horse and prepared to mount. But he paused and turned as someone called his name. Aine and Taillta were moving up the slope toward him.

Taillta held back and let Aine walk up close to Lugh alone. The young woman laid a hand upon his on the reins and met his smile with an emotionless face.

"Angry as I am, I had to come to give you a farewell," she said in a tightly controlled voice. "All fortune ride with you, for the good of the de Dananns. They are all that matters now."

"Aine—" he began, moving a hand to her shoulder. But she pulled back.

"No," she said curtly. "There's no time for that anymore. You have to go. You are the Champion of the Sidhe now."

Before he could reply, she turned and walked away, her head high and her stride proud, the burnished hair shimmering like red fire about her shoulders in the early sun. His eyes followed her and a knot tightened in the center of his chest. He wanted to call out to her, to tell her to come with him. But he held back stubbornly. She and Taillta would be safer here, he told himself. And Manannan was right about him. It was time that he was truly on his own.

Taillta moved up beside him and he looked at her, seeing that familiar, knowing expression in her eyes.

"You're being as great a fool as that gawky clown, you know," she said bluntly. "I'm angry, too, at being left behind." Then a faint smile touched her lips. "But you're still as much a son to me as you were for those years I fostered you, and I know you mean well. I couldn't let you ride away into danger without your knowing that and havin' my blessing."

She raised her arms and he gave her a warm hug. Then she patted his arm lightly as she said in a scolding, motherly way:

"You come back to us safely now. Never forget what I've taught you. And don't forget to eat enough!"

He smiled at her. "I will. And, Taillta, you'll always be a mother to me as well."

This was too much for the tough and seemingly stoic woman. To hide the starting tears she turned quickly away and moved to join the others.

Lugh mounted and settled himself well into the saddle, knowing the speed with which they would move. He lifted a hand in a parting wave and gave the Riders the command to leave.

With a sudden roar and a sharp blast of wind, the silver company was off. The grey-white horse went with them, sweeping Lugh along in their midst.

The Dagda's party watched the glowing stream rush away. They would delay no longer themselves. Climbing onto their own, earthly mounts, they turned across the hillside into the rising sun and headed away from Tara.

On the smooth hillside only two figures were left, looking very lonely now as they stared after the rapidly disappearing company. The younger woman's face was still sternly set, but a single, betraying tear traced a bright path on the white cheek.

The departing horsemen moved at a good pace, anxious to reach the sea in three days. Soon they were far out from Tara and confident that at this rate, they would make their goal well ahead of time.

Morrigan took on her raven form and flew out far ahead of the rest to spy their route in case they should encounter Fomor parties. She kept up a sharp observation, sweeping back and forth across their path. Below her, the company continued to move at a good pace.

"It's a fine day for traveling, it is that," said Gilla, bouncing along awkwardly on a horse as lanky as he, beaming with a child's simple joy as he admired the scene.

The Dagda looked down from the heights of his great horse at the clown and shook his head in disbelief.

"You have a truly amazing view of things," he said with heavy sarcasm. "Here it is, a fall day where the sun is never warm, where a cold wind nips at us with the sharp whelp's teeth of the coming winter wolf and smells of a storm coming off the sea, and you say that it's fine!"

"It could always be worse, surely," Gilla countered. "And we're off on a fine adventure. That's enough to raise the spirits, so it is."

"An adventure?" the Dagda said. "Is that what you call this mission of ours?"

"Of course!" the other replied brightly. "And think what life would be without it."

"I'm not seeking any excitement on this trip," Findgoll said, pulling his horse up on the other side of Gilla's to join the conversation. "I'm only hoping that we'll return in time to save our people from the Fomor."

"We will," the Dagda assured him, "if this Manannan fellow cooperates."

"And if we don't run upon some Fomor patrol," Angus Og added from beyond his father.

"Ah, there'll be no danger of that!" Gilla declared heartily. "The Morrigan will give us plenty of warning. Getting the cauldron back safely from the isle will be the tricky bit."

"You're certain of that?" the Dagda asked doubtfully.

The clown beamed assurance. "Of course. This little ride to the sea, why it'll be no trouble at all!"

A dull grey metal spade chunked softly into the damp earth. The man in the ragged dress of a Fomor warrior heaved out the shovelful of moist, black soil and paused to get a breath and examine his trench.

It was waist deep now and long and wide enough to contain a lying human form. He nodded with satisfaction and looked along the ridge of the low hill. A score of other warriors worked away at like tasks, cutting out a line of small trenches.

He looked up at the sky, half covered with a front of grey clouds sliding across from the east. He pulled down the filthy scarf that covered the lower half of his face so that he could sniff the air for the scent of rain. He revealed a nose and mouth free of such deformities as the Fomor used the scarves to hide. In fact, nothing about the warrior seemed marked by the grotesque abnormalities of the island Fomor. And the same was true of the others along the ridge.

One of the warriors was striding briskly along the line. As he moved he repeated the same orders in crisp, curt tones.

"Hurry up and finish, all of you. Hurry up! As soon as you're finished with your trench, gather brush to cover it. Be certain you can't be seen from below or from above." He stopped and raised his eyes to scan the sky. "We must be under cover before we come within that bloody raven-woman's range."

"How much longer do you think it'll be, Captain?" the first warrior asked.

The officer shook his head. "There's no way to tell how far ahead of their party she may fly. We can't take any risks."

"There's no chance that they won't come this way?"

"It's the fastest route to the coast," he said, "and it's the way they've marked on their own charts." He pulled out a small packet and unfolded it into a large sheet of thin material marked by a detailed map of the countryside. He held it for the warrior to see, placing a finger on a line marked in red. "You see, they'll move down this way, and then they'll come right here." He smiled and placed a finger on the valley.

Gilla Decaire put a long finger on the valley marked on his map and then checked the spot against the countryside.

Ahead the road dipped down into a cleft. The smooth hills they had been crossing since leaving Tara had become a bit more steep, and here they rose up to form a deeper valley, one side rising in a rocky, sheer face where it formed its narrowest point below them. But beyond that the land seemed to open up, and wide, flat country was visible.

Gilla nodded with satisfaction.

"This is the last of this rugged bit," he told the others grouped around his horse. "It gets much smoother beyond that cleft."

"It can't be soon enough for me," the Dagda said, looking up with distaste at the hills bunched like great, lurking beasts. "This countryside is too confining. Too many chances of surprises."

"Well then, let's get ourselves out of it with no delay," Gilla urged.

The Dagda gave the order and they started forward, moving into the valley and down toward the narrow cleft. The escorting de Danann warriors rode in a tight wedge, point forward, sides forming a sheltered pocket for the Dagda and his companions.

It was a cool afternoon, and still, as before a storm. The overcast was complete now. A low, even, rippling sheet of clouds masked the sun, softening the countryside with a haze of grey.

Gilla and Findgoll rode side by side, discussing their route beyond the valley, making pleased noises over their fine progress so far. Angus rode easily, engaged in light banter with two young warriors in the company. Overhead Morrigan swept easily, lightly, almost playing on the faint currents of air, as if even the tough and wily bird-woman had succumbed to the quiet and ease of the journey.

Only the Dagda remained wary, the old veteran's sense of the dangerous that had kept him alive so long preventing him from relaxing. They passed deeper into the valley that rose higher and higher. As they neared the bottom end, his eyes swung ever more restlessly back and forth, searching the hills on either side.

He had just completed a probing examination of the ridge on his right and was swinging his head to the left when, in the tail of his eyes, he caught the flicker of something bright.

Immediately he jerked his gaze back toward it. It had been the briefest of glimmers, but he had seen it, he was sure. Somewhere up there, along that hill's crest. But there was no sign of it now, no movement, nothing at all on the bare hillside save for that row of brush along the very top.

They were entering the deepest point of the valley, just before the cleft. A steep wall of bare rock rose on their left, the high slope on the hillside on their right. In moments they would be through and into open country once again.

It could have been stray sunlight on a piece of shiny stone or a pool, he told himself. But his battle instincts told him it was not. It was the glint of metal, and that meant a weapon. Something was wrong.

He opened his mouth to call a warning to Angus. But even as the first words started from him, the warrior riding beside his son jerked sideways and toppled heavily from his mount.

There was no sound. The warrior gave no cry. The rest of the party continued on, not even aware. But Angus pulled up his horse in shock and stared down at the body crumpled below him, stared without comprehension at the thin shaft of grey that stuck from the chest.

Only the Dagda realized what was happening.

"Everyone look out!" he bellowed. "We're in a trap!"

And as he spoke, death began to rain upon them.

Half a dozen of their warriors were struck at once. Some fell or were knocked from their horses by the force of the impact. One slumped forward while another maintained his seat, clutching the shaft imbedded in his thigh.

A horse was hit, staggering and falling sideways to roll its rider under. Another reared up, shrieking in its pain, and then dropped down. Other horses began to panic and there was instant confusion in the company.

A young warrior right in front of Gilla took a bolt through his neck and it tore out, spraying his lifeblood with it. The disguised Sea-God searched around him, at a loss to know where these silent messengers of death were coming from.

But the Dagda knew. He understood the meaning of the glimmer of light.

"It's bowmen, on the ridge!" he shouted. "Angus, get the others out of this. I'm going after them!"

Gilla now grasped what was happening. He, too, recognized the weapons being used against them and understood that the Dagda meant to stop them alone. As the champion turned his mount out of the press and started up the slope, Gilla shouted a desperate warning.

"That's madness! You can't make it up that hill!"

But the Dagda was already far up the slope, urging his horse ahead ever faster, charging directly toward the ridge as he lifted his huge battle-ax to swing in one hand above his head.

Then the hidden bowmen realized what he meant to do and more of the lethal darts began to fly toward him. The Dagda's horse was struck in the chest. It shuddered and its forelegs

collapsed under it at full gallop. Its momentum drove it forward, pulling the Dagda over and crashing heavily atop him.
Neither of them moved again.

Down below, the rest of the party looked up toward the
downed man, momentarily stunned by the swift and total defeat of the giant they thought of as invincible.

"By all the powers!" Findgoll cried. "Is he dead?"

"Never mind!" Angus shouted. "Come on! We must get
away from here!"

It was true. The brief respite the Dagda's lone attack had
afforded the rest of them was now over. The darts were again
all being directed into the defenseless group.

But they quickly realized that getting away was impossible.
Most of the horses were already dead or wounded. The tangle
of their bodies blocked the narrow way for those remaining.
They were trapped there against the steep backdrop of rock
and left with nowhere to go. Their only chance was to scramble
for cover behind the few scattered rocks and bushes and the
carcasses of the dead animals.

"If the Dagda's not dead, I hope the fool giant's stunned,"
Gilla said as he and Findgoll dove into the shelter of a fallen
horse. "He'd be prickled like a hedgehog if he went up that
slope."

"What kind of weapon are they using on us?" Findgoll
asked.

"It's a bow of a marvelous kind," Gilla told him. "I've seen
them used before. They can shoot twice the distance of any
other bow, and with twice the force and accuracy."

"Look!" cried Angus, pointing up. "There's Morrigan!"

The black figure sailed above them, then banked and began
a tight spiral as she dropped toward them.

"She's coming down!" Findgoll cried in alarm. "If she
doesn't see those bowmen and comes too close . . ."

"Then we may lose her as well," Angus finished grimly.

And they watched helplessly as the great bird swooped
steadily lower, into the range of the deadly bolts.

VIII

FINDGOLL'S MIST

WHEN MORRIGAN HAD flown back from her advance scouting to check on the party's progress, she had seen them under attack. She started down to try to discover what was happening to them.

The arrows moved with such speed that she was at a loss to discover their source until she saw a figure rise from the screening shrubbery on the hill's crest to get a better shot. She saw him lift some curious device and look along it, then saw the bow at its front snap forward, sending a shaft toward her companions huddled below.

Without hesitation, she furled her wings and dropped, shooting downward like an arrow herself, talons and beak ready for an attack.

The captain of the hidden bowmen had seen her soaring above and saw her speeding down. He called a warning to his men.

"There's that blasted crow-woman now. Shoot her!"

A flock of arrows sang upward to meet her descending flight. She saw them coming and, in a desperate move, she tucked herself into a ball and fell like a stone, barely dropping out of the darts' path in time. As they whistled harmlessly over her, she pulled herself from the plummet with an effort, turned and flapped away, zigzagging in her flight to avoid further shots.

Once beyond their easy range, she circled back and swooped down to land amongst the fallen horses and men. Hopping into the shelter of a downed horse, she effected her transformation and looked about her at those left. Her eyes narrowed.

"Where's the Dagda?" she rasped.

"He's up there," Angus told her, pointing to the still figure on the slope. "We don't know if he is alive or not."

She looked toward the fallen man. For an instant, worry soft-

63

ened the harshness of her face. Then rage hardened it again
and she drew her weapons.

"Not much use in having those out," Gilla remarked. "You
aren't going to be gettin' close enough to use them."

She gave him a hard look. "Then what do we do?" Her dry
voice crackled.

A warrior, hidden behind a nearby horse carcass, suddenly
jerked backward and fell, a shaft through his shoulder.

"Looks to me as if we sit here and wait for them to hit us,
one by one," Angus said angrily.

"They are very good," Gilla remarked. He looked over at
Findgoll, crouching next to him. He was sheltered except for
his rump, sticking up above him and looking rather exposed.
The clown shoved it down. "Careless, leaving that out," he said
affably, then looked up toward the sky. "A pity it's so early in
the day. If we could survive until nightfall, we might sneak
away."

"They're not going to give us the time for that," Angus said,
"Look there."

On the hillside above, a score of figures had suddenly become visible. The Fomor warriors, each carrying a strange-
looking bow, were moving boldly down the slope toward them.

"What are they about now?" Findgoll asked, peeking out at
them.

"I'd say they're tired of us not obligin' them and allowing
ourselves to be shot," Gilla casually remarked. "They're simply
going to stroll down here and move into positions where they
can hit us. And there's really not much we can do about it."

The descending bowmen moved past the Dagda's body, ignoring the still figure as dead. Then they began to spread out,
some coming straight in, others angling off to the left and
right.

"See there?" Gilla said brightly, as if he'd won a bet. "What
did I tell you? They'll surround us and leave us no place at all to
hide."

"I wish you'd stop being so damnably cheerful about it,"
Angus said irritably. "They're going to kill us."

"Oh, I don't think so," Gilla replied. "No, there's always
some way to make things work out. I mean, it's not going to be
night soon, but darkness is something any good sorcerer can
create." He patted his Druid companion on the seat.

"Of course!" the little man cried, sitting up. "What a fool I
am. I can lay a blanket over us that they can't see through."

"Can you make it an illusion for them and not for us?" Gilla asked.

"Certainly," Findgoll assured him. "But it will only last a short while."

"It'll have to be long enough," said Gilla.

"All right, then. Just help me get my things!"

He began crawling for a downed horse nearby. Gilla followed. When they reached it, the two men pulled loose a basket strapped to the animal's back. The Druid began to rummage within it.

Another of the remaining de Danann warriors clutched suddenly at a shaft in his throat and fell.

"Best hurry, Findgoll," Gilla said. "They're already too close."

But the little Druid could not be rushed. With some twigs of yew and oak pulled from the basket he built a small fire. It took precious moments to start it with flint and steel and to blow it to life.

"Try to move a bit faster, Findgoll." Gilla urged.

The Druid selected certain phials from his basket carefully.

"Faster, Findgoll," said Gilla, watching the bowmen advance.

He painstakingly mixed the assorted elements from the phials in a small silver bowl.

"Hurry, Findgoll!" Gilla urged again, a bit more desperately.

The Druid muttered an incantation over his concoction. The bowmen were now close on three sides, their weapons rising to fire at the unprotected de Dananns.

"They're going to shoot!" Gilla called and squeezed his eyes closed to wait for the impact of the bolt.

Findgoll tossed the potion on the fire.

With a rush of flame, a fat billow of grey-black smoke puffed up and out.

It gushed like a spouting geyser from its source in the fire, rolling out in a wave in all directions.

At the sound Gilla opened his eyes and grinned. "Good work. Now everyone get down. Lie flat and lie still."

The survivors obediently lay down, weapons out and ready at hand.

The attackers moved up to the edge of the cloud and hesitated there, unwilling to enter this eerie, unnatural mist. But their captain was impatient and shouted angrily.

"What are you waiting for? It's only some foolish Druid trick.

Now get in there and finish them. We can't leave any of them alive."

Reluctantly the circle of men moved forward, into the enveloping shroud of grey mist. It was cool and damp within, the drifting tendrils of the cloud clinging, coiling about them as they moved. Its thickness obscured everything, draining all color, leaving only vague shapes that seemed to glide forward from the swirling void.

The bowmen crept along, slowly, eyes searching around them, loaded weapons ready. The survivors waited silently, motionlessly, for them to come.

Angus lay on his stomach, hearing his own heart, trying not to breathe. Something crunched not far from his feet. He fought his impulse to roll over and look and lay still, feeling the skin of his shoulders prickle at the expectation of a metal shaft sinking home there. But the crunching of the footsteps moved on by.

He risked lifting his head. The mist seemed only a faint haze to him. He could clearly see a bowman only a few feet away, stopped, back to him.

Silently he levered himself up, lifted his sword, and lunged. The weapon, skillfully aimed, drove through the Fomor's back, skewering the heart. The man made only a brief grunt of pained surprise and fell. He thudded down softly, but his falling weapon clattered to the rocks. It was loud in the muffled silence.

"What was that?" another Fomor cried aloud, his voice betraying his nervousness.

"Quiet!" the captain ordered sharply from outside the cloud, trying to catch some glimpse of his invisible men.

The Fomor moved on, but now more cautiously. One came upon a form lying face down, one arm outflung, the other beneath it.

"I found one!" he called into the void. "He looks dead!"

He leaned down over it, gripped the shoulder, and rolled the figure back. As it came over he saw the cadaverous face and shouted in surprise, "Why, it's the Mor—"

But he got no further. For the raven-woman's free arm had shot up, locking onto his neck with taloned fingers of enormous strength. With one move she jerked him down toward her while the concealed hand whipped out, revealing a dagger that slashed up and across the man's exposed throat. His words were cut off in a gurgling cry. Then there was only silence again in the drifting haze.

"Nolick? Was that you?" another of the bowmen called.

"I said quiet!" the captain shouted angrily, straining his eyes into the darkness for any movement.

Inside the mist, another bowman crept along, gripping his weapon tightly in unsteady hands. This uncanny silence and fog, these strange shadows and noises were quickly unnerving him. Now every rock, every shadow, seemed alive.

He heard a noise before him and began to back away, peering ahead for some sign of what had made it. An arm shot from the swirling gray behind him, encircled him, jerked him back into the blade of a short dagger. He slumped. Gilla Decaire lowered him softly to the ground and wiped the blade on the Fomor rags. His usually amiable face was hard and held nothing but grim intent.

As he straightened, he saw another bowman moving some distance away. Silently he blessed the magic of Findgoll and prayed to Danu the power of it would last a bit longer.

He straightened fully, drawing up his lanky form to make it fully visible to the groping Fomor. Then he called out cheerfully:

"Hello there! Are you looking for me?"

The man jerked around toward him, in his alarm letting off his bolt too soon. It went far wide of its mark. Gilla clucked with regret.

"Oh, bad luck," he said. "Care to try again?"

The man slammed another bolt into his weapon and cocked the bow back again. He started after the taunting clown.

The lean form flitted before him, now here, now there, in the shifting clouds, like a hare in the underbrush. The bowman's irritation and his unsteadiness grew.

Gilla, meantime, was on a hunt of his own. Very soon, he saw what he sought just ahead, the stalking figure of another bowman. Skillfully he led the first closer until he felt the two must be visible to one another as moving shapes. He stood still and upright between them and shouted:

"Say! Here I am!"

As the two men wheeled toward the sound of his voice, bows rising to fire, he dropped to the ground. Both men fired at the first shadow in the mist they saw. Each was knocked off his feet by the solid blow of the other's arrow.

Gilla stood up and looked from one of them to the other.

"They really are very good shots," he said, and shook his head. "Too bad."

By now, the remaining Fomor were near panic. Others of them began to loose their arrows at anything moving. Shots zipped through the roiling mist wildly. Another and then another of the bowmen dropped, his own fellow's bolt in him.

Outside the mist, the captain heard the telltale sound of the bowstrings. One arrow flew from the cloud and past his head. Then one of his men, mortally wounded by an arrow through his side, staggered from the bank of mist and collapsed.

"Stop! Stop firing!" the captain shouted. "You're hitting each other! Stop where you are. Move toward the sound of my voice. Come out here and we'll form a line to sweep through. Do you hear?"

There was no sign of movement, no sound from the mist.

"Answer me!" he called louder. "Let me hear you each respond."

Still nothing.

"What's wrong?" A note of desperation had entered his voice. "Neid! Seanchab! Ingol! Answer me!"

There was no reply. He stared into the fog, trying to penetrate its mysterious depths. And he found, suddenly, that it seemed to be giving way before his gaze. It was rolling back and up as if a wind had risen to push it away. The spell had run its course. The darkness of Findgoll was dispersing.

He could see figures now. But there were only two. Where were the rest? The last vestiges of the haze lifted, and he saw at last who the figures were.

It was the gawky clown who stood facing him, grinning. Not far from him was the grim black Morrigan. And as the captain watched in shock, Findgoll, Angus, and four other warriors stood up from their hiding spots amongst the rocks and brush and dead horses.

Then the captain saw his men, scattered about on the ground, dying or dead. Four lay at Morrigan's feet, throats neatly slit. She bared her teeth, showing him her thirst had been fully slaked in their hot blood.

"Why you—" he cried out, lifting his own bow to fire at her.

But a sound from behind distracted him and he swung around. He was in time to see the descending blade of a giant ax before it struck home. Split nearly to the waist, he was driven to the ground. A groggy but angry Dagda looked down in grim satisfaction at his work.

"You couldn't have picked a finer moment to come back to life," Gilla told the giant with enthusiasm.

"Father!" Angus cried happily. "Thank the powers. We thought that you were dead!"

"Not very likely," the champion growled, planting a broad foot on the carcass of the officer to help him lever out the deeply embedded weapon.

"They very nearly had us all," said Findgoll with relief. "What were our losses?"

Angus was moving through the area, checking on the the de Danann warriors. "Twelve of our people are dead," he announced. "Four more are too badly wounded to go on with us."

"Four left then, and the four of us," said the Dagda, walking down to join the others. He added as an afterthought, "Oh, and Findgoll."

"It was Findgoll who saved your own son and the rest, you great, hulking ox!" the little Druid retorted heatedly. "Your 'strong arms and true blades' did you little enough good. Don't be forgetting that."

"I will not," said the Dagda, with regret. "And I'm quite certain you'll not be letting me."

"Can we still go on?" asked Angus. "There are so few of us, and we've no animals left to carry us."

"There's little choice in that," the Dagda answered. "Those of our escort who escaped can take the wounded back to Tara, but there'll be no time for us to return for more horses. We can reach the coast more quickly if we continue on foot. And once we've brought the cauldron to Eire, we'll have Lugh and his Riders to help us carry the thing safely back."

"We can make it in time if there's nothing else to interfere," said Gilla in an unusually thoughtful tone.

"What do you mean?" asked a puzzled Angus. "We can surely be watching out for any more chance patrols like this one."

"This was no chance patrol," said the Morrigan's rasping voice. "Those men were hiding in trenches on the hill. They were waiting for us."

"Maybe they were waiting to ambush any de Dananns who came this way," Angus suggested.

"No," said Gilla. "It's much worse than that. Look here."

He pulled the masking scarf from the face of one of the dead bowmen. The others looked down at it.

"See there. There's no deformity at all on him. And it's the same with the rest of them." He looked around at the others. "You know what that means."

"They can't be from the Tower!" Angus said in disbelief.

"Aye. And this is more proof of that," said the Dagda, lifting one of the strange weapons. It was a short bow fixed at right angles to a metal stock fitted with a complex mechanism to hold the arrow and release it. "I've seen these before. They're from the Tower too." He examined an arrow, a short, thick metal rod trimmed at one end with tapered feathers and at the other with a sharp, barbed head. "Nasty weapons they are. Like the bloody Fomor."

"My friends," Gilla said with great solemnity, "we know that Balor would never send his precious warriors and weapons into Eire just to ambush anyone who came along. No, only a very, very special purpose could bring them. He must know what we're about. And, more than that, he knows the exact route we are taking."

He looked up at the surrounding hills and down through the cleft toward the open country beyond. Suddenly it didn't seem so inviting to him. It was too smooth, too lacking in convenient places where they could hide.

"I'm thinking that this isn't the end of it," he said, the carefree tones of the clown touched with doubt for the first time. "Something has gone wrong. Very, very wrong. There's no way of telling now what else may be waiting out there for us."

And as he scanned the countryside again, his eyes turned toward the west. Was something, he wondered, waiting out there for Lugh as well?

IX

LUGH'S RIDE

LUGH LAMFADA STOOD on the low mound, looking off across the meadows toward the great hill thrusting up abruptly against the sky.

The hill was steep-sided and rocky, rising almost sheer to a flat, grassy top. At its base, just before him, were clustered uncountable small, neat mounds, like the brood of the mother hill nestling for warmth close to its body.

The setting sun struck across the top of the mound in a blaze of golden light that made the isolated place seem the more separate, aloof and grand, a fitting spot for some god to dwell and look out over his lands.

Lugh moved back to his tiny fire, built as much for comfort against the coming night as for cooking or warmth. There was very little else to raise his spirits. The Riders of the Sidhe certainly offered no companionship, drawn up like the walls of a palisade around his mound, spears up, silent and motionless as always when at rest. And his own muscles were no help, screaming out at him with their pains from the long ride.

How far had he come that day? It still seemed incredible to him. He laid himself in the most comfortable position he could and unrolled the parchment map Gilla had given him to trace the route he'd followed.

It may have been wearying, but it had been exhilarating as well. The pace of the Riders had been breathtaking at first, like standing on a cliff and catching the full force of a sea storm square in the face. He'd clung on that plunging horse that had never seemed to touch the ground, and he had been carried along in the midst of that unnatural company as if he'd been as much a wraith, a being of streaming cloud, as they.

The country had flowed past, forests, meadows, hills, all blending into a blurred rush of green-grey. They had covered impossible distances, and he had seen by the movement of the sun—the only firm object in his cosmos then—that the time it had taken was very short. In one day they had swung in a great curve through much of Eire.

The only respite from the dizzying pace had been when a new settlement was reached. The reception Lugh had received at each had quickly taken on a monotonous similarity. The folk of the ringfort or hilltop dwelling had come forth to stare in awe at these mystical beings who had swept upon them like some great wind. Most of those Lugh had seen were a worn and hungry lot, but all were still willing to share their meager supplies with a stranger.

When Lugh had announced his mission to them, their responses had been the same as well. Bobd Derg had been proven wrong. Manannan had as well. The de Dananns had needed no urging to fight. Their will had not been destroyed by their oppressors. They had been willing, often eager, to unite behind Nuada, their old warlord. They had been ready to join a rising, no matter what the cost.

Ironically, he had sensed that few of them had real hope. They had said they would fight and likely die because they had nothing more to lose, and dying in battle was the only dignity left. Still, they had been prepared to march at once for Tara, and this had been enough for Lugh. Only the will to fight needed to be theirs. With luck, he and his companions would supply them with the rest.

As he and the Riders had progressed, Lugh had checked each settlement against his chart. Now he examined the full distance with some awe. They had swept a vast curve around Eire, north from Tara and then far west to the sea, turning south to this spot. He had visited more than twenty villages. He had repeated his plea for help so often that he wasn't surprised at the soreness of his throat.

He rolled up the map and sat looking across at the hill. The sun had dropped lower behind it now, lighting only the top in one last, bright flare of parting. It threw the clustered mounds into deeper shadow and increased the sense of mystery surrounding them.

He looked over the scores upon scores of them more closely. They looked like the burial mounds he had seen near Tara, but here there were so many scattered across the meadows. Hundreds of people would have found resting places there. Who had built them? Even the de Dananns didn't know. Their builders had come and left these time-eroded mounds long before the first of Lugh's people had come to Eire. And where had they gone? Had they been driven out or destroyed, as the de Dananns had done to the Firbolgs, as the Fomor were trying to do to them? He wondered if, when the de Dananns did succeed in becoming the true masters of Eire, they would, one day, only be deposed themselves or simply vanish into some mysterious mounds of their own.

Alone, he felt the spirit of the country strongly there. It was a presence around him, pervasive and demanding, like the presence of the sea. It was a harsh and an independent spirit, like that of the people who lived in it. It inspired love somehow in its rugged beauty, but it gave no compromise. It would never be held or conquered, only coveted. And he knew, as if he could see it himself, that many peoples would come and go, would battle and love and rage and die here. They, all of them, would go one day and be forgotten, like the rest. And what value would all their struggling and dying have then?

He realized that his thoughts had turned dark with the

dying sun. A sense of profound loneliness came upon him like a weight. He understood just how much he missed the company and the support of Aine.

To escape his melancholy turn of mind, he rolled himself in his cloak and lay down by the fire to sleep. He heard the wind, sharp with the fresh tang of coming fall, whistle through the drying grass and leaves. He slept, but he couldn't escape his thoughts. He dreamed of Aine, of her warm body lying close against his, of the smooth texture of her skin, of her eyes smiling into his.

But in the dream she turned to a column of ice within his arms. He started awake to find a dawn of chill, white frost tingeing the grass tips and glinting on the meadows around, a foretaste of winter's snows. He was stiff and arose feeling tired, groggy, and still depressed.

But once on the road, his spirits lifted again.

The sun was bright and soon burned off the frost. It was a fine, fresh day and he was free, really on his own, for the first time. He was doing a fine, important job, and very capably indeed, he told himself. He actually began to feel the Champion for once, and really worthy of the responsibility given him.

Their direction was more southerly now. The settlements they visited were on the fringes of the de Dananns' western lands. They were scattered and most were very small. He noted that his company covered more distance between stops, and that the countryside through which they moved became increasingly more barren, rocky, harsh.

In the afternoon of the second day, they came out of their supernatural ride near a good-sized settlement. As usual, the blur of passing scenery began to slow until things took on a recognizable form. The wail and whoosh of their movement faded away, and Lugh found that they were on the upper edge of a wide valley.

The ground was high there, and the view was good. The valley swooped down gently toward a distant haze of sea. On either side, high hills of a pale rock rose steeply, shining golden in the afternoon sun.

The lower ground was of the same light rock, and the little vegetation there was clung tenuously in the narrow crevices that cut through them.

The stone walls of the ringfort were quite near. He had seen many like it in these last stops, for the country had become quite barren and lacked the soft earth or timber to build ramparts. Loose rock, however, was in abundance.

Still, this fort was larger than any he'd seen yet. The wall was twice his height and looked quite thick. Its circle was large enough to enclose a dozen homes.

The Riders had drawn up on either side of him just before the main entrance—doors of heavy wickerwork closing a wide cut in the wall. There was no one visible about the dun or on the ramparts. A small cattle herd was browsing in the valley below, but there were no herdsmen.

It wasn't an unusual situation to Lugh. The Riders had often frightened the weak and naturally suspicious villagers into hiding. He had been forced to coax them out several times.

He did as he had done then. He rode up to the gateway and stopped at the edge of the shallow defensive trench that circled the wall.

"Hello!" he called to the fort. "I am from Tara. My name is Lugh Lamfada, a warrior to Nuada, High-King of the Tuatha de Danann!"

That usually was enough to bring them forth. But here there was no response. No curious heads popped above the wall to look. No answering calls were lifted from inside.

He tried again. "Bres has been deposed. The de Dananns are joining in a rising against Fomor. I've come to ask you to join in it."

Still there was no answer, no signs of life at all from the ring of stone.

A vague worry began to rise in Lugh. Usually that last bit was enough to draw the most reluctant out. What was wrong here?

He turned and trotted back to the Riders to issue a brief order.

"I'm going to the gates. Stand here and wait."

There was no need to tell them to keep watch or be prepared. Those things they always did.

Lugh turned back and rode boldly up toward the gate. He knew that if the villagers were truly frightened and huddling inside, he might be inviting a thrown spear with this move.

But there was no spear, no challenge, no sound from inside. He stopped at the doors and shouted through the wickerwork.

"Hello inside! What's wrong with you? Why don't you answer me?"

When there was still no answer, he tried the gates, very gingerly at first. He put a hand against one of the sections and pushed, just a little. The door swung easily on its wooden posts, opening half an arm's length. It was not locked.

He tried to peek through the narrow crack, but he could see only the corner of two houses and the beaten earth of one side of the yard. No people were visible.

His puzzlement increased. He dismounted and drew out the Answerer, some instinct telling him to take no chances here. These villagers might believe him to be a lying enemy. A trap might await him just inside. So with the gleaming blade ready in one hand, he pushed the door fully open and walked through.

Beyond the gateway was a large yard. Beyond it, in a rough semicircle, were the dwellings. Nowhere was there any sign of life.

Lugh stood for a time looking searchingly, warily, around the fort's interior. He saw no movements, heard no tiny sounds. If someone was hiding there, they were very good at it. The fort seemed totally deserted.

But he would go no further without support. He turned back to the doors and called to the waiting Riders.

"Come inside! Spread out and circle the yard!"

Immediately they obeyed, gliding forward through the gates, parting inside and turning in two directions, one column circling left, the other right. They moved around the inside of the circling wall, one by one dropping off and taking positions at neat intervals until they were spaced around the entire yard.

When they had halted, Lugh stepped forward into the center, examining the dwellings more critically. Most were homes of the familiar circular type with thatched roofs rising up into sharp cones. But like most of those he'd seen in these barren western lands, the lower walls were of neatly piled stones, not wicker and plaster. There were two sheds as well, square structures with flat roofs, meant for storage of livestock, tools, or food.

One of the structures squatting in the center of the others was much larger. Its circle was stretched into an oval. It had to be the main hall.

He moved across the yard to it, looking about him constantly, seeking any sign of the fifty or more people who would inhabit a place this size.

He stopped at the doorway to the hall and peered into its shadows. It seemed empty. He stepped cautiously within and stood, guard up, waiting for his eyes to adjust.

The interior was one oval room. The earthen floor was scattered with rush—fresh rush, he judged, by the strong scent of it in the air. The central fire pit was circled with low tables for eating. Here his wandering gaze fixed and curiosity pulled him forward. For the tables were set with plates and food.

He looked at the food more closely. There were bits of bread and cheese, some scraps of meat, some fish, some vegetables. The bread was stale, but showed no signs of mold. It had been sitting there less than a day.

He moved around the tables, past the central fire pit. He paused there and squatted down beside it. Heat was rising from the ash piles. He lifted an iron spit to stir them. Beneath the grey he found the glowing red of several coals. He dug further and uncovered several of the rugged chunks of black peat still unburned. The fire had been newly laid the night before, he judged.

He walked back to the doorway and paused there, looking around the compound once again. The total silence was a bit unnerving. In the sunny, still fall afternoon it was as if the world were holding its breath, as if time had stopped here. He stepped forward and hit something with his foot. He looked down to find a rag doll, worn from some child's constant love, its crude wooden head smiling up at him with a faded mouth of paint. He reached down for it, then stood to gaze around at the high ridges of the hills, puzzlement creasing his young face.

Where had they gone? What could have made them abandon this place so abruptly, leaving belongings, leaving food on their plates, not stopping even to retrieve a fallen toy?

It couldn't have been some Fomor raid. There would have been signs of the fight. The Fomor would have left this place a slaughterhouse, bodies unburied, houses ripped apart.

Had some magic been used on them? Some trick? Some enchantment? Or were they still here somewhere, hiding?

He wheeled about in a circle, running his gaze over the whole compound again. Someone was here. He knew it. He could feel eyes upon him.

"If you're hiding, please come out!" he shouted. "I'm a friend."

That gained him nothing. He shook his head. The eeriness of the place was bewildering. He had an impulse to leave. He had no time for such delays in any case. But his stubbornness and youthful curiosity kept him there. He had to know what was happening.

Then he remembered the souterrain.

Most of the ringforts had them. That hidden underground room where things could be stored, where inhabitants could hide from enemies. And a tunnel that led out beyond the walls to some sheltered spot to allow an escape. There had to be one here.

The main hall was the likeliest place to look. He went back into it. He set the doll down carefully on a table where its wide, painted eyes watched him scrape at the floor rushes with his feet.

He was seeking the covered entrance and he found it quickly. He lifted an earth-covered square of slate to expose a hole and a crude ladder leading down to darkness. Lighting a small torch from the fire's embers, he started down, very slowly, still wary of some trap.

At the bottom of the ladder he stopped, holding the torch up ahead of him. Its reflected glow ran unevenly away along walls and ceiling lined with grey-black slate. The flat slabs formed a neat, square tunnel high enough so he could stand nearly erect.

The air was cool and damp, and the stone glistened with moisture. There was a strong scent of moist earth and another odor too—one that he couldn't identify but found familiar, and unpleasantly so. It aroused a sharp fear in him for the first time, and he found himself suddenly reluctant to force himself ahead.

But he did move ahead, moving slowly along the tunnel, peering ahead into the gloom that the torch's light did little to dispel. The passage ran straight along for some way. Then it abruptly forked. A second passage turned off at a sharp angle from the first.

He paused at the corner and then eased cautiously around it to look down the side passage. It was short and seemed to open into some larger space, some blackness that swallowed the faint rays of his light.

He moved toward it, fighting to control the breathing that increased along with his rising sense of dread. He came into the opening to the room and lifted the torch high. It nearly dropped from his hand as he recoiled.

He had found the inhabitants of the ringfort.

They were piled neatly, row upon row of them—men, women, children, all stacked together like cut wood. Many stared up blankly at the roof, their eyes gleaming with false life in the wavering torch light.

He understood what that other odor was now. It was blood. They were awash with it. It flooded the floor in a great pool that had only begun to dry around the edges at Lugh's feet.

It seemed to his horrified gaze that all had had their throats neatly slit, like animals slaughtered in some ritual. They showed no signs of struggle and few looked afraid. Their frozen expressions were mostly of surprise.

He turned away, sickened by the sight. It wasn't only the dead or the wounds or the blood. He had seen those in abundance before. It was the methodical way these poor people had been butchered and piled there, killed without any chance, without even knowing why.

And then the why of it suddenly hit him like a physical blow. This was no Fomor raid. They had been killed to get them out of the way quickly, to make the village seem deserted. And there was only one reason to do that—to draw him inside.

He ran for the ladder, driven by a single, urgent need. He had to get to the Riders, get out of that ringfort.

He scrambled up the ladder, threw down the torch, and rushed to the doorway. As he reached it, he could see the yard and some of the waiting horsemen. He raised his voice and shouted to them.

"Riders! Riders!"

He stepped into the yard as they started toward him. But as he did, the earth shuddered, and all before him seemed to rise up in a searing column of flame as a massive explosion wracked the interior of the tiny fort.

X

INTO THE BURREN

LUGH WAS KNOCKED backward by the force of the blast. He fell heavily to the floor of the hall and lay stunned. When he finally staggered to his feet, he found that everything beyond the doorway was trapped in a ring of rising flames.

Within the circle of the stone wall, it formed a solid screen, blocking all view of the country beyond, arching up above into a dome that obscured the sky. Where the Riders of the Sidhe had stood, there was no sign of anything but fire. Lugh assumed they had been caught by the full force of the blast, enveloped by the flames. The power of it had apparently swept the beings away. Whether it had destroyed them or not, he had no way of knowing. But he couldn't believe that even they could have survived this.

The intense heat was nearly unbearable. His skin felt tightly stretched across his face. His body and clothes were scorched from the first explosion, and he realized that only the stout rock walls of the hall had kept him from being killed.

Several of the structures had survived, he saw, but their end was fast creeping upon them. Their thatched roofs were all ablaze, forming cones of fire that sent tight spirals of flame and smoke up to join the thick column rising above the fort. He looked at the roof of his own shelter. It was clearly afire, too, the inside surface streaming with smoke and raining burning splinters upon the room's interior. He knew that he couldn't last long there.

Already the smoke was starting to choke him, crawling deeper into his lungs at every cough. He dropped down to the floor where some fresh air was left, but it was rapidly being sucked away by the inferno surrounding him.

He had nowhere to go, nothing to do. The fire burned on with no sign of abating, fueled by someone or something he couldn't understand or act against. He couldn't break through the wall of it. He was a captive of its circle. And now the flames above began to swirl. The rising heat had created a whirlpool in the currents of air. It began to spin faster, faster, pulling up the fire, drawing in more air and making it burn all the hotter, raising the temperature in its heart, in its trapped little huddle of doomed huts, to a height which nothing could survive.

It would not be much longer, Lugh knew. The roof above was ready to collapse upon him. His bare arms and legs and face were singed in a score of spots. His cloak smoldered.

He threw a wild, despairing glance around the room, and his gaze was met by the wide painted eyes of a forlorn, drooping figure, already smoking itself, but still smiling at him courageously. The little doll. Soon, thought Lugh, it and he would join its owner. And he found himself almost envying her quick death over the one he was about to experience.

But that fatalistic thought took his smoke-numbed mind to another. He saw the bodies in the souterrain, and he saw that other passage. That passage might take him out of this stricken fort!

He took a last breath and crawled for the tunnel entrance, dodging the falling pieces. He was nearly there when a loud, rending crack came from above. He glanced up to see the whole structure of the roof collapsing. He dove for the entrance and toppled into the tunnel as the flaming debris crashed down, burying the interior of the hall.

He dragged himself along the tunnel away from the entrance and got to his feet. The air here was still fresh, and the heat of the fire raging above much reduced. A stiff breeze was blowing up the tunnel past him, drawn by the heat. That meant the tunnel did open out somewhere ahead. He hesitated no longer but began to run along the passageway, past the turning where the bodies lay, for such a distance along the darkened way that it had to be passing well beyond the outer walls of the ringfort.

It made a sharp curve, and as he rounded it, he saw light ahead. The soft light of day shimmering along the smooth, damp tunnel walls.

He charged to the tunnel's edge and pushed through a screening wall of brush to the outside. He found himself far down the valley below the fort, and he climbed a small slope to look back up toward it. It was lost in fire and smoke that rose high up in a spinning column toward the clouds. The Riders were gone, his own horse gone with them. He was on foot in this barren land and totally alone now.

And then he realized he was not alone.

"Well, mates, it was a good thing we came to check here. I told you he might be smart enough to find that escape tunnel."

Lugh whirled about to see three figures rise from their hiding places in the rocks and close in around him. They were Fomor warriors, clad in the filthy rags of their breed. One was a true horror, his head disfigured like something of wax that had melted and sagged, carrying eyes down to one side, dragging over the nose in a thick flow, leaving the mouth slack, hanging, and constantly adrool. The second was more like something that had crawled from the sea. It was a Fomor aberrant Lugh had become familiar with. His eyes popped, fish-like. Folds of skin, like gills, fluttered on the sides of his neck as he breathed. His mouth was tiny and pursed and he seemed lacking in nostrils, ears, or hair. The short hands that gripped his heavy lance were webbed.

The third man, and their leader, was normal by comparison. The only flaw in his crude, swarthy looks was a great leather patch covering one side of his face. And one of his hands ended in a stump fitted with a heavy iron cap.

"You are a clever one, you are," the fish-face chortled happily. "I'll go and get the others now, right?"

He started to turn away, but a sharp word from the leader stopped him.

"Hold on! Why share this prize with them? It was we who thought to come here. Think of the prize from that fancy cap'n if we take him to the ship ourselves!"

"I don't know," the one with the sagging head said in a slow, doubtful voice. "He might put up a fight. I don't like that sword."

Hearing his words, Lugh realized for the first time since the explosion that he still held the Answerer in his hand. In all the confusion, his warrior instincts had seen that he kept a grip upon it. Now, feeling its weight in his hand, he was aware of the blade's power coursing into him, filling him with new vitality, pushing out the despair. If these animals weren't going to call their friends, he had some chance. They had made a mistake that might be fatal.

"Look, he's just a pup," the leader was reasoning to his friends. "Havin' a hound's teeth won't do him any good." He looked to Lugh and spoke in what he must have thought a cajoling voice. "Now, lad, you don't want to be killed here, do you? We won't harm you. I promise that. Them Fomor dandies from the Tower said that if you was to be captured, they'd want you alive. So, be a sensible boy. Drop that sword."

The three started to edge forward, and Lugh waited no longer. He dove forward, making a lightning attack on the closest first.

His speed took the leader by surprise. He wasn't even able to raise the sword in his good hand as the bright Answerer swept across his chest, the razor edge laying him open and slashing the ribs like dried twigs. He fell back and Lugh's blade reversed its swing, leaping like a coiled serpent's strike toward the attacking soft-faced one.

He lifted the sword and shield he carried, but it did little good. Lugh's sword stroke slammed both down, and the point flicked deftly, lightly, back up, catching the Fomor under the chin and cleaving the face as if it were wet clay.

The third Fomor, the fish-headed one, stared in terror at his comrades' sudden end, then heaved his lance wildly at Lugh and turned to run. As he did, he began to scream shrilly:

"He's here! The boy escaped! Help!"

The being was too far for Lugh to strike at. In a desperate move he cast the Answerer, hoping to silence the cries. The weapon, fashioned, honed, and balanced by the magical hands of master smiths in Tir-na-nog, flew unerringly to its mark. It buried its length in his back, severing the spine. His voice was cut off and he collapsed in a heap.

Thanking Danu, Lugh ran to the body and wrenched the blade out. But he had stopped the man too late. There were answering shouts from the valley around him. He saw many figures rising from positions in the rocky fields around the blazing fort and starting toward him. There seemed to be scores of them. Too many to fight. If he meant to survive, his only choice now was to try to escape.

On this open ground, the only promising hiding spots seemed to be the hills rising on either side. The scattered Fomor were between him and the western hills. He turned away and headed toward the east.

He started off at the best speed he could manage on the hard, rugged ground. A misstep here would mean delay at best, a broken leg at worst. Fortunately, the same terrain hampered the Fomor, who now spotted him and started in pursuit. They were all afoot, as no horses could cross such treacherous fields without taking a fall. Unfortunately, without large rocks or stands of brush and trees, those after Lugh could spot him and follow easily. He could only hope that he could lose them on the hill.

He reached its base far ahead of the pursuers. A backward glance told him many of the deformed creatures were having hard going here. Those in the lead were spreading out to prevent him from turning along the hill's base. His only choice was straight up.

The rough hillside was even tougher going than the valley. The slope was steep and the rock much decayed by erosion, crumbling out from under him. He scrambled upward over it, sliding back at times, body scraping cruelly on the sharper rubble. But the top was in sight, and the Fomor falling further behind, and he pushed himself to struggle up the last distance to a high ridge.

He paused there, standing up to look back down. The valley and the sea at its base were spread out before him now. Far down there, little more than an elongated speck, an object sat against the shore. As tiny as it was, Lugh knew it. A black warship of the Tower. He remembered the words of the Fomor with the patch. Of course Balor's men were behind this attack! Only they would have the unknown means to engineer the explosion of the fort.

He looked down at the warriors climbing slowly up behind him. He would be far away before they reached the top, and on this ground they could never discover which way he had gone.

He turned to face the land beyond the crest. It was a flat, bleak, rippling sea of grey-white stone as far as he could see. It offered no shelter, no comfort, and no sign of life. His heart sank again.

Escape he might, he thought, but what did that mean? Where would he go? What could he do to continue with his mission? He didn't know. He only knew that for now he simply needed to survive, to keep on. His map was lost with his food and other clothing, on the horse of the Riders. To the south and east seemed the most promising to him. With what optimism he could muster, he set out at a brisk pace across the field of rock.

Far below him, at the black ship, a messenger of the Fomor band arrived breathless from his run.

The warship's captain, sallow-featured, tall, and arrogant, looked down from the vessel's side at his wretched island cousin and smirked in satisfaction as he anticipated the report.

"I see our little trap was a success," he said.

"It was, Captain. It wiped them horsemen right away, it did," the messenger agreed eagerly. Then he hesitated before adding timidly, "But, I'm afraid I've got to tell you that . . . ah . . . the boy escaped."

The captain's smile was wiped away as by a slap.

"He what!"

"He got out of the fort," the messenger went on. "He got up that eastern hill"—he waved vaguely toward it—"and he's well out into the Burren now."

"You can't let him get away," the captain shouted. "Balor will see you all lose your lives if he does." He well knew that his own life might be forfeited too. "Your people are supposed to know this area. Get after him."

The messenger looked out across the sea to the western horizon. The sun was dropping toward it now with seeming speed.

"Don't know, Cap'n," he said doubtfully. "It'll be night 'fore too long. Hard to be trackin' him then."

"We'll see to that," the officer told him curtly. "You just see that he's found, whatever the cost. He can't escape."

"Oh, there's not much fear o' that," the other said with a shrewd smile. He looked up toward the stark, forbidding hills. "Even if we don't get him, not many survive crossin' them Burrens alone, not with what's livin' in there, they don't. Your lad isn't likely to make it through the night."

The coming of night was not far away when the Dagda's party finally left the hilly country and moved down from the last valley mouth into the open, rolling grasslands of the east. Even on foot, the going was easy here. The hills were low and soft, the terrain a lush, thick fur of grass, ruffled by the sea breezes. They plowed along through it, Dagda in the lead to break a wide path, and moved quite rapidly.

Morrigan, as usual, drifted above and ahead, on scout. Gilla strode along, swinging his long legs, whistling merry tunes. Angus and his father marched with apparent tirelessness, eager to reach the ocean. Only the little Druid complained at the pace.

"Is it really necessary to be going so fast?" he asked of no one in particular. "I thought we were well able to reach the coast soon enough."

"There may be other delays," the Dagda told him tersely. "We may need this extra time then."

"We may need our strength then too," Findgoll retorted. "And I'll not be likely to have any."

"You asked to come," the Dagda reminded him. "If your legs are too short, why don't you use that magic of yours to lengthen them?" He laughed heartily at his joke, winking at his son.

The little Druid gave him a very hard look at that. He might have made a caustic reply, but he had no chance. For the Morrigan cut off one of her lazy sweeps abruptly and dove down toward them. She swooped in to a landing on one of the giant champion's shoulders and began a lengthy series of harsh squawks and cackles. The Dagda translated for the rest.

"She says a man is hiding on the hilltop just ahead."

"Only one?" asked Gilla.

"She saw only one. But she didn't go too close after what happened the last time."

"Could be a Fomor lookout," said Gilla, "watching for us in case we escaped their trap above."

"That means there might be larger parties of them nearby," said the Dagda. "We can't afford to let this one warn them." He patted his ax. "Let's be sure he doesn't get away."

"Let's divide," Gilla suggested. "You to the left, Angus and I to the right. Come in behind him."

"What about me?" Findgoll asked.

"Stay with me and stay out of the way," the big man ordered.

They separated and the two parties moved in wide arcs out and around the low hill far ahead. They crept up toward it through the grass. Morrigan stayed with the Dagda, riding on his broad shoulder, ready to act if needed. The Druid moved behind, wishing he could supply more help in such a situation.

They were close to the hill when it went wrong. Gilla, lifting his head cautiously from the grass to peer ahead, saw a movement on the hilltop. Then he saw their quarry rise up from his own hiding spot and lift a long, tube-shaped device to his eye. It swung around toward Gilla. The clown saw a glint of something at its end. Before he could duck down it had pointed directly at him.

The man acted instantly. He leaped to his feet, dropping the tube, and shouted: "They're here! They're on us!" Then he turned and ran from the hill. Beside him, a second man, unseen before, also jumped to his feet to run after the first.

Across the hill, the Dagda saw them run. The two had to be stopped.

"Get after them, Morrigan," he growled. "Slow them down."

As he and his comrades set out in pursuit, the raven flapped its wings and flew ahead, skimming the grass tips as she streaked toward the Fomor scouts.

She caught the trailing runner first, her claws raking his head and neck, the force of her strike bowling him over. As he fell, she was on him, going directly for the eyes. He had no chance, and in seconds she left him, blinded and wallowing in his blood, as she started after the second.

But her delay had given the other quite a lead. It would take her longer to get him, and he was running toward another hill some distance farther on.

The three other pursuers reached the downed man and paused to dispatch him. Angus looked after the other.

"He may get away," he said with concern.

"Morrigan'll catch him," the Dagda said confidently.

"Where's he makin' for?" asked Gilla. "That little hill?"

"Looks like there's some kind of hut on it," said Angus. "Suppose his friends are there?"

"He won't make it," said the Dagda. "She's nearly on him."

"Wait!" said the clown, pulling to a sudden stop. "That's no hut!" And he shouted after the others, "No! Don't go on!"

Angus and Findgoll stopped, and then the Dagda, looking back at Gilla in disbelief.

"Are you mad?" the Dagda shouted. "Morrigan may need help!"

The object on the distant hill suddenly gave out a deep-throated, coughing roar, like some enormous beast abruptly awakened from sleep. This roar lifted, but quickly settled into a low rumble. Then the thing began to move.

"It's coming toward us!" cried Angus. "What is it? Is it alive?"

It was too far to see any details of its form. It was large and grey, and it seemed to have legs, but it glided forward, down the slope, moving smoothly and with increasing speed.

"I don't know what it is, but I don't think it's friendly," Gilla said. "Run. We'll discuss it later."

There was no argument. All four turned and headed away across the meadows.

"Angle to the east!" Gilla told the others. "We can't let that thing come between us and the sea."

They all complied, heading in a long sweep around the advancing unknown.

Morrigan, meanwhile, was still in heated pursuit of the second Fomor scout. Her attention totally fixed on him, she was unaware of his goal, the thing that was now on its way toward her.

Unaware, that is, until the approaching rumble of it drew her attention up and she saw a looming mass of grey descending upon her from the hillside.

She had a quick impression of it—a great object swarming with Fomor warriors—and then she was breaking off her attack, wheeling sharply up and away, expecting to be fired on again.

But she lifted away safely, soaring up and around to spot her comrades in full retreat. She looped down to them and glided in beside the Dagda, chattering noisily at him.

"She says there are men on it," he told the others.

"What is it?" Angus asked.

"She didn't wait to see."

"Something else sent against us by the Tower Fomor, you can be certain," Gilla said. "They're very clever, they are."

The fugitives had managed to get past the thing and head on to the east, but they had lost some distance in doing it. The grey monster was observably closer now, gliding along through the tall grasses like a ship on a calm sea.

"Let's stand and fight it," the Dagda said angrily, hating to run from anything.

"We can't risk that," Gilla said. "Our mission is first. We'll simply have to escape it."

The Dagda eyed him skeptically.

"And how are we to do that? We can't run on forever."

"Only until dark," the clown assured him breezily. "We'll just keep ahead until dark. Then it won't be able to follow. I'm sure of it." He grinned around at them all. "Trust me!"

XI

THE SACRED HILL

THROUGHOUT THE AFTERNOON, Lugh Lamfada pushed doggedly into the heart of the dismal waste of stone, searching for signs of other de Danann habitations.

He saw some strange formations that had to be man-made. They were always constructed of enormous slabs of rock set on end to form simple walls and a flat capstone to form a roof. But they were clearly not living places, and they seemed very old. Seeing the odd structures, thrusting up so starkly from the flat fields of rock, only served to emphasize how isolated he was in this alien place.

The only positive aspect of the landscape's emptiness was that it meant the Fomor had been left far behind. He gained at least a bit of comfort from the hope that they had been lost for good.

Late in the afternoon, he came to the foot of a high ridge that blocked his way. To bypass it meant to turn at a right angle to his present course. He decided to go up.

He found a rough path that zigzagged up the rocky face. It was difficult and tiring going, with no place to stop and rest until he was two-thirds of the way to the top. Here there was a wide, flat ledge, and he paused to look back on the way he'd come.

The view from this height was magnificent. The land of smooth stone seemed to tumble away in a downhill flood like a bubbling, swift stream. The afternoon skies were clearing, as they often did in Eire before the brilliant gold of sunsets. Only a few fat clouds of luminescent white drifted lazily, almost hanging still.

There it was again, he thought. The harshness and the beauty of that land juxtaposed. The wild, rough land that had plagued him through the afternoon now lifted his heart with its grandness. He could not hate it, no matter how unhospitable it had been. Part of its own spirit was in him.

He turned to continue his climbing, and it was then he noticed a wider path, a real path if he was any judge at all. It went off from one side of the little plateau, running at a slant along the face. It was free of vegetation and looked as if it were used regularly, but whether by men or animals he couldn't say.

Still, it offered more possibility than he had at present, and it was certainly an easier route. He followed it.

Higher it went, changing to a sort of crude stairway in the rocks, climbing now right up the rugged face. Though it was much steeper, the many footholds in the rock made it quite easy for him. He soon found himself coming onto another flat area, but much larger, and very near the top.

It was a roughly circular area, its back hemmed by a curve of the hill that rose a bit higher behind it. In the center of this space was a crude ring of widely spaced, upright stones.

He felt some hope rising in him at this sign of human presence, but it sank quickly enough when he moved closer to them. The rugged slabs of rock upended there were well rounded at their tops, weathered by uncountable years of Eire's rains and scouring sea winds. Like those strange constructions he had passed, this ring was the product of hands long turned to the sod of Eire.

Then a vagrant sound came drifting to him. It sounded like the wind, like a bird's call—or like the voice of a human raised in song.

Telling himself that was madness, he moved toward the sound. It had come, he judged, from the topmost part of the hill, above that last rise.

A deeper depression in the flat rock, like another worn path, offered him a way, leading from the ring right up the incline. He followed it, finally reaching the highest level.

The hilltop was an enormous plain of its own, stretching far away before it dropped again to the surrounding sea of rock. It was quite flat, and the objects that dotted it were sharply outlined by the bright rays of the late sun. The slanting light threw long, sharp shadows from them, exaggerating their size and emphatic shape.

Scattered before him were several of the massive structures of stone. One near him was a neat box formed of five slabs, two at the sides, two across them for a roof, the last closing one end. The end facing toward the country spreading out below the hill was open, as if whatever being might have dwelt or been laid to rest there might have wished to admire it.

He listened again for the scrap of song without success. But he did become aware of a constant, meandering hum in the air, like the sound of a thousand softly playing pipers, intertwining a thousand airy tunes, creating an eerie sort of lamenting harmony. He tried to locate the source of this and discovered it was all around him, coming from the rocks themselves. The evening breezes from the sea, much stiffer on this exposed high ground, were sweeping through the heaps and walls of loose rock, playing their tunes on the many openings.

He moved ahead, across the high plateau, passing more of the stone structures and other rings and scores upon scores of strangely shaped rocks upended in cracks or piled in cairns. Whatever the purpose of all this was, he knew that this site had been important to some race, or many races, for a very long time.

Abruptly he stopped again, catching sight of the most striking object in this peculiar collection. Some distance ahead, on a slightly higher, open spot of ground, there rose a large, rounded mound. From its high, neat, smoothly formed swell, it was clear that this was no natural formation. Save for the fact that it seemed less worn by time, it was much like the mounds Lugh had seen before.

But here, thrusting up alone on this high, sacred place, it had an unnatural aura about it that made him feel all the more strange. And as the late sun began to lose its fragile fall warmth, he felt the breezes take on a sudden, unpleasant chill.

This place, he felt, had nothing to do with life. It was all to do with death. The cold of death would come sweeping across it with the darkness. He did not want to be here in the darkness.

He turned to make his way back down the hill, but then jerked back. He had heard that fluttering fragment of song again. This time he knew it was a human voice. A chant. There were people somewhere up here.

They could be Fomor, of course, but he doubted that. Findgoll had once told him that the superstitious Eireland Fomor avoided the "haunted" spots. On the other hand, that same fact might mean it was de Dananns living here, for often the fugitives from the Fomor used such places to escape the raiders.

With this idea, he decided to investigate further. The mound itself was the only likely spot for a hidden camp, so he headed purposefully toward it. His earlier fear was forgotten. He only wished to do his searching before full darkness came upon him and he lost his way.

He reached the mound's base as the sun slipped down, leaving only the halo of its light in the sky, letting the shadows take lordship of the hill. The sound of the chanting was definite now, though he couldn't discern words. There seemed to be several voices. They were coming from beyond the mound.

He eased cautiously around it. He could take no chances, even if these were de Dananns. On his first meeting with Findgoll, the little Druid—who had been protecting a hidden de Danann camp—had thought Lugh an enemy and tried very hard to frighten him to death.

He began to see light behind the mound. The source of the glow came gradually into view. A large space before the mound was lit by many torches and a great bonfire. A crowd of people were grouped around this fire, and Lugh peeped out from the shelter of the hill to have a clear look at them.

When he got it, he ducked back into the shelter at once,

heart pumping wildly. For the people gathered there weren't Fomor, but they were just as certainly not de Dananns.

He decided he had to get away from there before he was seen. He started to slip cautiously back into the shadows, but a noise behind him brought him whirling around, his sword rising in defense.

He wasn't quick enough. Something solid descended on his skull and he dropped heavily to the ground, sinking into a darkness.

In the darkness the two white lights glowed steadily, like the glinting stare of an unblinking cat.

"So, they won't be able to follow us in the dark?" the Dagda said with heavy sarcasm. "And just what do you call that?"

The night was fully upon his party now, and they lay panting with their long exertion atop a low hill, looking back toward the west. A low ridge there showed, for the most part, as only a darker line against the softer black of a moonlit sky. Except in one spot. There the twin beams of light made the grassy meadows as bright as a clear noon day.

For a brief time after nightfall, the exhausted fugitives had believed the thing pursuing them had been lost, unable to follow their trail in the grasses without light. Finally they had decided it was safe to pause for a rest upon the little hill. But then, from the vast silence of the night, the sound that had plagued them through the long afternoon had arisen again. The distant thunder of the grey monster had returned.

They had turned in shock to gaze back along their path. At first that distant rise had been all dark. Soon, however, a glow, like the first showing of a rising sun, had appeared. It had lifted in a great halo above the rise, and then the two sharp points of light had winked suddenly into sight. They had moved swiftly forward across the rise and changed as they came, growing to form long cones that threw a wide patch of light across the hillside, making the tall, thick grass glow an intense green against the surrounding black.

"Are those that monster's eyes?" Angus asked, awed by the unknown powers of the thing.

"That's no monster," Gilla scoffed. "It's some infernal device of the Fomor again."

"Then what are those blazing lights?" asked Findgoll. "No powers of mine could create their like."

"I've seen something like it, in my traveling," Gilla mused.

"In the eastern lands. A special glass could magnify the light of a single candle or concentrate a sunbeam to a burning dot!"

"There's no sun now," the Dagda pointed out tersely, "and no candle could be made to shine like that!"

"True enough," Gilla agreed. "But, remember, the Fomor have the use of many forces we don't understand."

"The question is, what do we do about it now?" the big warrior said. "With those lights it can surely follow our path through the night. It seems to me that we'll have to stand and fight."

"Not so hasty, my friend," Gilla said soothingly. "We can still escape."

"You said that the last time," the Dagda reminded him.

But Gilla's bright optimism was not to be dulled. "I wasn't wholly wrong. It's not stopped by the night, but it's clearly slowed. Look there. Even with those lights it's got to feel the way."

They looked. The thing was moving slowly across the far hillside, the twin beams sweeping back and forth before it, crisscrossing as it searched for signs of their passage through the grass.

"You see? While it's feeling its way along, we'll easily be able to get far ahead of it. By dawn we'll be nearly to the sea and it'll have no chance to catch up to us."

The confidence the clown exuded did not convince the Dagda. He looked skeptically at the face smiling amiably at him and thought of a poor half-wit he had known who never saw ill in anything.

He examined his other companions. They seemed able to continue for a time, if the pace was slowed. He himself felt strong and Gilla never seemed to tire. Angus looked weary but able, and Morrigan, who had only changed back to human form after darkness made it hard for her to see, was fresh. The little Druid, however, looked near exhaustion, and that gave him some doubts.

"Seems we've little other choice," he said. "Still, I'd like to find some way of finishing that beast. Findgoll, haven't you some magic to throw against it?"

"And if I had, don't you think I'd be using it?" he replied irritably. "I lost the goods I'd need for that in our first little encounter. My own powers aren't up to raising any spell that great now."

"I thought as much," said the Dagda heavily, shaking his head. "Useless to us again."

"As useless as your great ax and your bull's strength," the Druid countered angrily. "Don't be making those pitying noises over me!"

"And what about your going on, then?" asked the champion. "You look done in!"

"You never mind my going on!" Findgoll said, climbing to his feet and facing the big man challengingly. "I'll match my stride to yours on any day. If we mean to go on, let's do it."

The Dagda eyed the little man facing him like a feisty pup and supressed a grin. He'd known challenging the Druid's strength would help put new energy into him.

"Right, then!" he said, getting up himself and looking at Gilla. "We'll follow your advice once more, clown. But Danu herself won't save you if you're not right this time!"

"I've always been right before, haven't I?" Gilla asked him, grinning widely. Then he considered and shrugged. "Well, near enough to right, anyway. Just trust me!"

He jumped to his feet and started off again, leading the way down the far side of the hill away from the tracking beast, toward the east as before.

It was smooth ground, and seemingly not dangerous to traverse in the darkness. But that fact could help their pursuers to move more quickly too. Still, Gilla's optimism stayed unbridled, and he encouraged the others in bright tones.

"We've only got to keep on at our best pace. We'll soon leave that thing far behind."

However, the smoothness of the ground was deceptive. The flowing waves of grass concealed its dangers. Findgoll suddenly cried out sharply and plunged forward, disappearing momentarily into the tall stalks.

Fearing some trap, the others rushed to him. They were reassured to hear the little Druid cursing fluidly.

He sat up in the grass, grimacing with pain, clutching his left ankle with both hands.

"Some foolish, bloody mole has carelessly left its burrow hole here open!" he explained in agony. "I've put my foot in it!"

"You surely have done that!" the Dagda agreed, not too patiently. "Well, come on then. Get up. We can't be resting any longer with that Fomor monster about to pounce on us."

Findgoll tried to rise but fell back, exclaiming anew with the sharp pains.

"Can't do it," he gasped. "Think I've broken it."

"Oh, by Queen Danu!" the Dagda cried irritably.

He reached down and unceremoniously lifted the protesting Druid like a child. Tossing the small man casually across one shoulder, he started off again.

"I told you that you'd only be an extra weight," he reminded the Druid sardonically.

The lightweight Findgoll didn't have any discernible effect on the giant's speed. He led the way as they started up another low hill. But the Druid found it far less than satisfying as a way to travel.

"Oh . . . you're . . . going . . . oof . . . too fast!" he said brokenly as he bounced helplessly against the hard mass of the Dagda's shoulder. "Can't you . . . ow . . . jolt . . . a bit . . . less?"

"No complaints from you, or I'll leave you behind," the Dagda told him firmly.

"Best make a comfortable place for yourself, Findgoll," Gilla advised cheerfully. "It's going to be a long, long night."

"Aine!" Taillta called urgently to the girl, rousing her from sleep.

The voice cut through her confused and troubling dream of Lugh battling shadowy figures for his life. She sat up groggily on her bed of skins and looked into the worried face of her friend.

"What's the matter?" she asked. Then she saw Taillta's expression. Alarm sharpened her words. "Something's wrong! What is it? Is it Lugh?"

"The Riders of the Sidhe—they've come back alone."

Aine understood at once the gravity of this. The whole existence of the Riders revolved around Lugh. They would never return without him unless . . .

The awful possibilities drove Aine hurriedly from bed. She slipped on her tunic, belted her sword about her waist, and grabbed her cloak.

"All right, Taillta, take me to them."

The older woman led the way from the sleeping quarters of the fortress and into the darkness of Tara's training grounds. It was very quiet, most of the population asleep. But in the center of the compound a pale light, like a full autumn moon, glowed around the double column of the Riders of the Sidhe and illuminated the small group of de Dananns standing beside them.

As the two women approached, High-King Nuada moved from this group to meet them, his expression drawn with concern.

"I am glad to see you," he said with evident relief, leading them to the Riders. "They appeared here suddenly from nowhere a short while ago. We've tried to communicate with them, but they won't speak." He shook his head in perplexity. "They just sit there like graven images and take no note of us. Even the Druids have had no success."

They stopped at the head of the column, looking up toward the tall, staring figures. Only one of the two lead horses was occupied. The other was the riderless white mount meant for Lugh.

"That riderless horse was an ominous sign," said Nuada. "But we hoped that you, as one of Lugh's friends, might have the magic of these beings and be able to speak with them."

"You are right, Nuada," Aine told him. "I'll find out what's happened."

She steppd toward the lead figure, lifted a hand to rest on the being's arm. The odd aura of light flooded from him to encompass her as well. The mystical warrior inclined his head and dropped his sparkling gaze to meet hers.

"Something has happened to Lugh?" she asked.

He nodded.

"Is he dead?"

From the gleaming eyes an image seemed to flash down and fill her mind. She saw Lugh entering the stone hut of an empty village and saw an explosion of flame that devoured everything instantly.

She cringed inwardly at the image, but then another came, of blasted ruins, of debris, but no charred bodies.

"You returned to the place after the fire and Lugh was gone," she said.

Another nod.

She turned to the others with some relief.

"He doesn't know if Lugh is dead. The Riders were temporarily dispersed by some kind of powerful force at a village far to the west, in a rocky, desolate place near the sea."

"The Burren," Taillta said.

"When the Riders were able to re-form and returned, they

could find no sign of Lugh's body in the burned ruins," Aine
continued. "He may have escaped. But without him to command them, there was nothing else for them to do but return
here."

"But what happened?" asked Nuada. "Who attacked them?"

"They don't know. The attack was a surprise."

Bobd Derg moved forward from the group to confront
Nuada.

"So, High-King, already your little missions have come to an
end." His grim words were tinged with satisfaction.

"They are not at an end," came Nuada's sharp retort.

"Of course they are. Don't you see what this means? The
Fomor must have done this. And they must have had help from
the Tower of Glass."

"We don't know that."

"Come now, Nuada. Who else would have the power to attack these beings successfully?"

"He is right," agreed High-Druid Meglin. "The Eireland
Fomor could not do it alone."

"You would love to spread that idea through our people,
wouldn't you, Bobd Derg?" the High-King accused. "It would
surely help you convince them to flee Eire."

"Why not?" the other challenged. "There's no chance for
Lugh's mission to be completed now. We'll have too few warriors to face Bres even if this supposed magic cauldron does
arrive to strengthen them."

Aine had been considering the situation during their argument. Now she made her decision.

"Can you show me where this happened?" she asked the
leader of the horsemen.

The head nodded again.

"All right. Then we'll go now." She moved to the riderless
horse, gripped its reins, and pulled herself lightly onto its
back. The horse gave no sign of protest.

Nuada did. "Hold on! What is it you're planning to do?"

"I'm going to find out if Lugh is alive," she said. She hesitated, then went on firmly. "If he is not, then I will complete
his mission myself."

"I agree that someone must go," he said, "but why you?"

"Because, High-King, I am the only other one here who can
command these Riders. With them, I can sweep through Eire
before the night is ended if I must. But, more than that, I'm

going because Lugh's success, his mission, his life, are as much my responsibility as his. Nothing will keep me from it anymore."

"All right," Nuada said, not really understanding her need to act, but feeling the emotion that drove her. "Then the Powers of Danu go with you."

"I hope so," Aine said sincerely.

"Wait, Aine. I'm going as well," Taillta said with force. "I know those lands. I can help you. And I'll not be left behind again either. Lugh means as much to me."

Aine saw the plea in the woman's face. She understood. She put out a hand.

"Join me then. The great white horse can carry us both."

She pulled the other woman up behind her. Without further delay she lifted a hand to gesture sharply forward and gave a curt command to the Riders.

At once the company lifted and swept away, a river of flowing silver in the moonlight, gliding out of the fortress and into the blackness of the sleeping countryside.

Once they had gone, Nuada turned his attention back to Bobd Derg.

"You will speak no more of this!" he commanded the bard. "Two days only have passed. There's no reason yet for you to be composing poems of defeat. No one but ourselves shall know of this, or the speaker will face my wrath!" He glared around him to take in the others in the group as well. "We've made a bond to wait, and we will wait!"

From the shelter of a corner of the hall, Ruadan watched these events carefully. He had returned to Tara to learn if the Fomor plans were succeeding. But these events were troubling to him. The deep shadows masked the grim expression that hardened the look of his innocent young face.

Astride the powerful horse that now flew across the darkened earth amidst the Riders, Aine spoke urgently to her companion.

"We must move quickly to find him, Taillta. My heart and my mind tell me he's alive. But I also feel he's in danger he can't survive alone."

She turned to meet the older woman's eyes, her own filled with anguish. "Oh, Taillta, if he dies alone, it'll be because we sent him out so coldly to it. I don't think I could bear that."

"You're speaking nonsense," Taillta assured her. "Lugh did

what he wanted to do. And he's not going to die. He's too strong and too clever. We'll find him. We just have to keep our heads."

She spoke with confidence to bolster the girl, but she felt grave fears herself. She knew the Burren lands. She knew them well. She would find it a miracle indeed if their young warrior really was still alive.

XII

THE SACRIFICE

LUGH WAS ALIVE, but he was wondering how long he would remain so.

He had awakened to find himself surrounded by hundreds of grinning skulls. Many were piled in mounds. Some sat in the niches of small structures of rock. And some two dozen crowned waist-high columns of stone set upright in a circle around him.

This collection place of skulls was in the smooth area before an entrance to the giant mound. A square opening into the pile of earth was framed by massive stones carved with crude spirals and interwoven curves. Even larger stones with similar carving set off the outer limits of the sacred space and its massed death heads. There was something about those carvings he found familiar, but he couldn't focus on exactly what it was. He was rather distracted.

For not all the faces staring at him now were of the dead. There were quite a number of living ones gathered as well. The large bonfire near Lugh in the center of the ring and the many flaring torches revealed them quite clearly. In fact, they were rather more clear than Lugh really felt necessary. For the appearance of the group that surrounded him brought very little hope or comfort to his mind.

He'd never seen men like them yet in Eire. They were much shorter than the de Dananns, but this was more than compensated for by their thick and powerful builds. Massive shoulders, arms, and legs were more like those of bulls than men, some even worthy of comparison with the Dagda's frame. Yet they were certainly not Fomor, having no physical deformities, at least so far as Lugh could see. They were all heavily clothed in tunics and trousers of animal skins, and their wide faces were largely masked by long, wavy masses of dark hair and beard.

There were more than fifty of them, he estimated, all heavily armed with axes, spears, swords, and shields, but of a much cruder make than those of the skilled de Dananns. Still, they looked just as effective for all that.

The warriors formed a solid circle, all well outside the ring of standing stones, watching him curiously, warily, and silently.

Lugh shifted uneasily within the tight leather thongs that bound him to the tall pillar of stone. He had no idea why he was here. He had the impression, as he met the stolid gazes of the encircling men, that it was not for anything pleasant. He had tried several times to speak to them, to ask them who they were and what they wanted. He had met only silence and the dark, chill looks.

He hadn't long to wait to discover what they meant for him, however. For soon after his awakening, several of the warriors took up tiompan—large hoops of wood stretched over with tanned hide—and began to beat upon them with pieces of carved bone. To the slow, hollow, rhythmic tones, a group of figures emerged from the entrance to the mound and strode in ceremonial pride toward the stone ring.

There were four figures in the group, and two of them seized the young warrior's attention at once. For they were young women of large and sturdy but well-structured frame, this last point made quite obvious by the fact that even in the chill night, they wore no clothes at all.

Yet their bodies were not uncovered, for every bit of their flesh was covered with elaborate tatoos that colored their skin a deep blue. The detailed designs of stylized animals, serpents, and birds flowed and intertwined in graceful curves along their limbs, across the rounded curves of their supple forms. Even in his dangerous situation, Lugh found himself quite intrigued, and examined the fine artistry very carefully.

But then his attention was drawn to the two male figures that followed the women out.

First came a man he guessed was the tribal Druid or shaman. He was shorter and much stouter than the rest, moving with a rolling sort of stride like the waddle of a rather obese

goose. His shape was exaggerated to near ridiculous size by the
massive cloak of bird feathers that almost engulfed him. His
head, with its round pink face, flowing white hair and beard,
seemed like a decoration set upon this moving mound.

The last man to emerge was a warrior, the largest and the
thickest of the lot. Once he might have been the most powerful
as well, but he was now running toward fat and he was getting
old. Lugh guessed he hadn't many years of fighting life left to
him. But for now he appeared to be the chieftain of this clan.
He wore an elaborate gold torc at his throat, and the hilts of his
sword were banded in silver and set with rough-cut jewels.
Moreover, he had that arrogant stride of a long-time and long-
assured leader.

The two women led the way past the ring of stones into the
circle, stopping on either side of Lugh. The feathered shaman
moved boldly forward, as well, to stop just before the bound
warrior. But the chieftain stopped outside the ring, joining his
warriors to look into the sacred space.

The man before Lugh eyed him gravely. Lugh tried to smile
his most ingratiating smile and spoke with as much warmth as
he could raise.

"Hello, there. You seem an intelligent man. I want you to
know that I'm not here to harm you. I'm not your enemy."

Not a flicker of emotion indicated that the man had even
heard. He turned away from Lugh and the two women moved
up on either side, raising objects that they carried in offering to
him.

"Look, I'm just a lone warrior," Lugh persisted, a little more
urgently. "I'm a messenger . . . from Tara . . . from the High-
King himself."

That had no greater impact on any of them. The shaman took
from one woman a small cup of beaten bronze. The other held
out a short, wide dagger, but he shook his head and she
stepped back.

"I'm all alone and lost," said Lugh. "I really could use some
help."

The shaman turned back toward Lugh, the cup in one hand.
The other hand, so far concealed beneath the bulky cloak, now
lifted into view. It held the Answerer in its scabbard.

"I don't know what you want, but I'm not your enemy," said
Lugh, trying to keep the desperation from his voice. He told
himself a real hero would never show his fear. "I'm on a mission

to help Eire. I'm raising the de Dananns to war against the Fomor. You know the Fomor? The raiders?"

But Lugh might as well have been talking to himself for all the response his words drew. The beat of the tiompan became more intense and, as it did, the shaman turned the Answerer point down, letting the sheath slide off to reveal the gleaming blade.

Lugh watched this ritual with growing alarm. He began to throw his weight against the binding with greater force.

"What are you doing?" he demanded. "Let me free! I've done nothing to you!"

The shaman looked into Lugh's eyes directly for the first time.

"It'll do you no good, struggling," he said in a surprisingly gentle voice. "Please, lad, be calm. It will go much easier for you."

Startled by the voice, Lugh did cease his struggles to stare at the old man.

"So, you do speak!" he said. "I was beginning to believe you didn't understand me."

Faint puzzlement drew deep creases around the shaman's eyes. "And why would I not? You know that both our languages are one."

"I don't know anything about you!" Lugh protested. "I don't know why you're doing this to me."

"It's a great honor, really," the old magician said with an attempt at cheer. "You'll be the instrument in my foretelling the future for our tribe!" But his tone became more dismal as he added, "Of course, you'll not survive the ritual."

"Not survive?" said Lugh, understandably taken aback by this. "Why not? What are you going to do?"

The old man shook his head. "You're better off not to know."

He lifted the Answerer and slowly began to pour the thick red-gold liquid from the cup along the edge of the blade. It clung to the metal, tingeing it like blood in the firelight. As he began, the tempo of the drums increased again. The two women began a sinuous dance, moving slowly about the circle in opposite directions to the rhythm.

"I want to know," Lugh insisted courageously. "If I'm going to be killed, you have to tell me how."

The old shaman sighed. "Very well," he said heavily, continuing carefully to pour the liquid all along the edge. "I will

read the omens of the future in your convulsions and the spurt-
ing of your blood as you die." He looked up toward the young
prisoner, seeing the dismay in his eyes. "You see? You didn't
really want to know."

"Go on," Lugh asked stoutly.

The magician carefully set down the empty cup and held the
Answerer out in both hands. He moved toward Lugh, the keen
point of the weapon forward. Lifting it, he touched Lugh on
the belly lightly.

"The blade must be inserted with proper care, to make it
certain you'll die most slowly and in greatest agony." He
moved the blade to touch the warrior's forehead and, finally,
his lips. Lugh tasted the liquid. It was a sweet honey-mead. Its
pleasant flavor was a sharp contrast to the harshness of the
shaman's words, though they were cloaked with the old man's
obvious regret.

"Sorry, lad," he said, backing away again. "It wasn't my wish
that this be done to you."

"Shaman!" the chieftain called gruffly. "Why is it you're
speaking to him? Get on with the rite."

"Why?" Lugh asked once more. "I told you I'm no enemy to
you. I don't even know you. Why are you going to do this to
me?"

"You are a de Danann," came the chieftain's curt reply. "That
is enough."

Now it was the old magician's turn to protest. He turned to
look at the chieftain, asking plaintively: "Sreng, must this be
done? He is so young, and he's done us no harm."

"This has been decided, old one," the chieftain told the old
man with impatience. "Do as I command, quickly, and with no
more talk."

Wearily, sorrowfully, the aging shaman turned his gaze back
toward Lugh.

"Please!" Lugh appealed to him. "You at least have to tell me
why I'm going to die."

Lugh could see the anguish in the old man's eyes, but he
didn't speak again. Clearly he had no choice but to obey the
cruel warlord. He lifted the sword aloft in both hands, closed
his eyes, dropped his head back, and muttered an incantation
to the skies.

The rhythm of the drums rose to a driving height, making a
nearly continuous roll of thunder. The dance of the two women
grew wilder, more abandoned, more sensuous, as they worked

themselves into a frenzied state, their tatooed bodies glisten-
ing with sweat in the cool air, weaving closer about the fire and
the bound victim.

Then the drums stopped suddenly. The women, very near to
Lugh now, leaped to his sides, each seizing a bound arm to
hold him tightly. Their strength in the height of their ritual
fervor was tremendous, and he found himself unable to move.

The shaman opened his eyes and slowly lowered his gaze to
meet Lugh's. He brought the Answerer down and held it before him. He started toward the young warrior, bringing the
point of the slender blade against his belly again.

"By every power," Lugh shouted at the circling warriors,
"you can't kill me without telling me why!"

"You sound a madman, surely, not to know," the chieftain
said. "After your people defeated us, took our lands, and drove
us into the wilds to live like animals, you don't know why you
are our enemy? No more lies before you die. Show us whether
the de Dananns have the courage to die without complaint."

At these words, Lugh's mind began to work furiously. They
recalled to him the tales he had been told of the de Danann's
first coming to Eire and their battles to take control. He looked
around at the squat, dark warriors. He looked up at the carvings on the portal stones and understood why they seemed so
familiar to him.

"You are the Firbolgs!" he cried.

The point of the sword began to press inward as the shaman
began to apply weight. A bit more and it would penetrate.

"Wait!" said Lugh urgently. "Listen to me! I was raised by
Firbolgs. My foster mother was Taillta, daughter of MacErc!"

The pressure eased. Astounded by this news, the aging magician looked back toward his chief, his expression questioning.

"He lies," Sreng said heatedly. "On with the sacrifice!"

"No!" Lugh cried. "Look at my brooch. Taillta gave it to me
years ago. She called it her clan sign!"

The shaman released one hand from the sword and lifted it
to pull back Lugh's heavy cloak, revealing the large ornament that fastened the garment at his throat. It was a spiral of
copper, its pin a dagger-shaped line piercing the center. It was
a match for the central carving on the top portal stone.

"I know this piece," said the old shaman. "MacErc himself
wore it. It *is* his clan sign."

"It proves nothing," Sreng retorted. "MacErc is dead. His

daughter and his clan disappeared long ago. Massacred by the de Dananns, most likely, and this boy's ornament was stolen from our dead."

The shaman turned completely away from Lugh to face his chief now, lowering the sword.

"This boy wears the symbol of a Firbolg clan. It gives him protection from harm by any of us. It is not for us to question where it came from, only to obey our own rules."

"This is a de Danann!" the chieftain cried. "Our tribal laws aren't to protect the likes of him."

The warriors around the circle, bewildered by this strange turn of events, were shaken from their ritual silence and now muttered amongst themselves. There seemed some disagreement in their views, and the voices began to grow louder in dispute.

"I was always against sacrificing him, Sreng," the shaman admitted boldly. "And now I know that I was right. To destroy one who is under protection of our laws would be to bring the wrath of every power upon us. I thank them that we were saved in time!"

His voice was rising, booming dramatically across the silent, barren hilltop with a vitality that surprised Lugh. He realized the old man was fighting desperately to convince the Firbolgs to let him go, using superstition as his only weapon.

It seemed to have some effect. He heard supporting shouts from the warriors. But the battle-hardened Sreng was not to be convinced so easily by threats of mystic retribution.

"You'll not frighten us that way, magician," he countered, trying to restore courage to his men. "You only mean to save him. Nothing will happen."

"Are you so certain, Sreng?" the shaman asked. "There is a power in this boy. I felt it from the start. If you doubt that, look upon this sword!"

He held the Answerer aloft. It caught the fire and gleamed with an intense golden light. All felt the tremor of the force coursing within it.

"Perhaps you are right," the old man told his chieftain with final cunning, "but do you really wish to risk destruction of our whole tribe, of all of us, just to see the end of one lost boy?"

Sreng saw the worried looks passing amongst his men. He knew the hold that the superstitions had on them. They were afraid now, and to disregard it would be to invite rebellion. *That* the wily veteran could not have.

"Release him," he said tersely.

Quickly the shaman used the Answerer to cut Lugh's bonds. He picked up the scabbard and handed both to the young warrior.

"Here," he said. "Fortune has saved you. I am glad of it. Now leave this place."

"I can't," Lugh said. "I need your help."

He stepped past the shaman and addressed the warriors.

"I'm afoot in this wilderness. I'm lost. I must complete my mission or the Fomor will destroy the de Dananns. Please help me. Join me. Lead me from here."

"The brooch has saved your life," the chieftain growled darkly, "but only this time. No one believes your lie. You are no Firbolg. You are de Danann. Listen to the shaman and leave our sacred place, and pray to your gods we never meet again."

The old man moved up close behind Lugh, murmuring urgently: "You must go. And quickly. If Sreng has his way, they may yet change their minds. Run from this place. Run now!"

Lugh realized the truth in what he said, seeing the hostility in the encircling eyes. Without another word he walked from the ring. The warriors parted to let him through and he strode into the shadows beyond the fire's light. No one moved to stop him.

He made his way back toward the pathway that had brought him to this hilltop, planning to climb down and be away quickly in case their minds should change.

He passed the scattered stones and rings, looming shadows in the night, and reached the lower plateau above the steeper drop to the countryside spreading out below. But as he moved to the edge and looked downward, he received a shock of surprise.

An uneven row of lights—more than fifty he guessed—stretched across the ground along the base of the hill.

As he watched, the line crawled nearer, and in the reflected glow of the strange lights, he finally understood what he was seeing. A large band of Fomor were moving across the Burren, searching the ground before them with the aid of a miraculous device each one carried. It was a small box from which a circle of yellow light projected a powerful beam that lit the ground before it for some distance. Clearly, more of the Tower's marvels had been supplied to let the hunt for him continue even in the darkness.

Wearily, desperately, he turned away and moved along the hill's edge, cutting down and across the slope to head away from the Fomor and into the desolate Burren once again.

XIII

STALKED

THE NIGHT WAS becoming a very long one for Lugh.

The moon rose and lit his way, as he plodded on through the empty lands, but it only served to emphasize how treacherous the ground he crossed was. The white light made the weather-smoothed surfaces of rock glow palely, and threw the many rifts into deeper shadow so the whole vast plain before him looked like a rolling sea of deep troughs and foamy peaks.

Since leaving the Firbolgs, his desperation had slowly increased. He had moved as rapidly as he could to keep ahead of the Fomor, trailing somewhere behind him in the darkness. He had to keep going in hopes of finding some help, some way of continuing his mission. But he couldn't ignore the fact that he had no idea which way help might be.

Never before had he felt so alone. Even the Riders had given him some sense of company. But in this alien place, he felt removed from all help, all warmth, all life. He looked around him at the hostile landscape. He wondered if any other life even existed out here.

As if in answer to him, a shadow flitted across a distant spot of moonlit rock.

It was too far for him to detect its shape, but from its speed he guessed it was a hare. The thought of that reminded him how hungry he was, and he longed to stop and set a snare. But that was impossible.

He caught another movement, off to one side, and peered out toward it. Another rabbit? He watched, and then he saw the thing again, slipping across a brighter spot and back into the shadows.

He saw enough this time to make him begin to watch more closely. That thing had been no rabbit. He scanned the jumbled landscape as he went on, waiting to catch another look at it.

When he did, his hand went to his sword hilt and gripped it tightly. The shadow he'd seen was as large as that of a man. But it was no man. It was too low to the ground and moved with too much speed. Even more disturbing was the fact that the thing seemed to be keeping pace with him.

There was nothing to do about it but to keep on. But he'd gone only a little farther when a movement on his other side caught his eye. He watched there and again saw a slinking form.

Was it the same beast, or another? Soon that was answered too. The shadows began to show themselves more boldly, crossing the spots of light, even pausing in them as if to let him know that they were there.

There were several of them, he could see now. They were on all sides of him, moving with him. And they were gradually, carefully closing in.

One of them paused upon a higher rock, fully exposed under the glowing moon. He recognized the sinewy, gaunt form, the massive head, the glinting fangs in the smiling mouth. He knew it was a pack of cunning, deadly wolves that stalked him.

He kept panic in check by an effort of will. Wolves, unless starving, weren't really eager for a fight. They wouldn't attack him unless they felt confident of an easy victim. All he had to do was keep moving on, calmly, steadily, showing them no fear.

He tried to ignore the shadows as he went on. He couldn't let the presence of them force him to run. That would trigger an attack. For a time it seemed his reasoning was right. He went on for some way with the wolves escorting him and making no moves to close farther in.

Then, suddenly, they stopped.

He realized this when he saw the forms of three wolves standing in full view not far ahead, blocking his path.

He pulled up and, very, very cautiously, turned to look around him. On all sides were the other forms of wolves, all standing ready, creating a full ring. He understood now why they had decided to challenge him. From the first half-dozen he had noted, their numbers had swelled to around a score. To such a company, a single victim, even a dangerous human one, was no real threat.

They began to creep in, all at once, as if some silent command had gone out. They would come from all sides, giving him no chance, dragging him down. He could hear the low growl from the many throats. He could see the glinting circle of their eyes, like stones in a necklace.

He drew the Answerer from its sheath. The gleaming blade surprised them, stopped them. Some shied back in fear. But the effect was only momentary. They had faced warriors before, and this one was alone, despite his strange weapon.

Once more they began to close in.

Lugh knew that to stay in their ring would be fatal. Some way ahead he saw a larger standing rock. He waited no longer. Swinging the sword around him to drive the pack back, he charged through one side of their ring. One wolf ducked away. Another leaped toward him and then crumpled as the weapon sliced through its neck. A back swing severed the front paw of a third who had ducked in for Lugh's ankle, and it yowled its pain. Then he was out of the ring and leaping recklessly over the uneven rocks.

His attack had taken the animals by surprise. In the moments it took for them to react, he had gained a slight lead in his race for that stone.

He didn't pause or look around. He could hear the sounds of his pursuers close behind. With every stride he expected a heavy body to crash against his back and teeth to fasten in his neck or leg.

But he reached the upright stone ahead of them, whirling at bay there to face the snarling pack. Now, back to the stone, he could swing the Answerer before him and hold them off.

It was a wild and desperate battle he fought for his life against the blood-maddened pack. They all seemed to be upon him at once, like a single beast with a score of snapping heads, several always driving in as he swept the blade constantly to force them back, to ward off the ripping teeth.

One of them managed to slip beneath his guard to fasten its jaws on his ankle. He staggered and dropped down and several more were on him. He was certain that he was finished, but he used his fists, his feet, even his teeth, in a grappling, clawing struggle to wrench himself free. He heaved up, throwing them off, the great sword wheeling in glowing arcs that cleared a space before him again.

He threw himself back against the rock and faced them, panting hard, looking into that half circle of baleful eyes and glinting teeth. Although three more of them were down, those left seemed little inclined to end the fight. He was getting weaker, his sword arm aching from the constant effort. He was torn in a dozen places, streaming with his own blood. Once more and they would have him. He knew it.

Still, as they started in again, he raised his weapon, determined to keep at it until the last, take every one of them he could. In a snarling wave they struck him together, jaws going for the legs to pull him down, for the sword arm, for the vulnerable face and neck.

Then something plunged downward upon the mass from above, landed between him and the pack and brought them down in a sprawling pile.

Surprised, Lugh pulled back against the rock, staring in bewilderment at this unexpected addition to the fray. He peered intently into the mass convulsing before him in the moonlight, trying to see what was happening. It seemed a tangled pile of legs and tails and teeth, a noisy brawl, punctuated by snarls and occasional howls of pain.

He couldn't tell what it was that had plunged into their midst, but it was certainly large, and it was some kind of beast. At first the battle seemed equal. The wolves were smaller but far outnumbered it and were relentless in their savage attack. Then one was tossed from the writhing mass, falling heavily to the ground with a sharp yelp. It rose and quit the fight. Another was caught in the thing's enormous jaws and a quick shake broke its neck. It dropped, lifeless. The claws and teeth of the unknown beast seemed everywhere at once. It moved with a speed even the wolves couldn't match.

Another wolf was tossed away and slunk off, limping. A fourth staggered away with its bowels trailing and fell. Then, in a body, the pack gave it up. They broke away suddenly and scattered, speeding away into the night, leaving their vanquisher and the battered Lugh alone.

Now it occurred to Lugh to wonder what was next. Had he been rescued, or had this beast only saved him for itself? He lifted his weapon defensively and looked at the figure standing there, revealed clearly under the moon.

It was in some respects quite like a dog itself, he thought, or perhaps a cat. It was, in either case, quite furry. Its body was long and slim and sinewy, its neck muscled and as thick as a pony's. The enormous feet were clawed, or were those a bird's talons? He couldn't be sure. The whole animal was too confusing. But he could be sure of the large and deadly teeth, for the beast seemed to grin at him with a wide mouth that split a long, square nose.

It stepped toward him, its movements lithe and graceful, a long cordlike tail whipping nervously behind it. The huge mouth parted, the lips curling back from the front tearing fangs. Lugh readied for its spring as it crouched down.

"You look nearly done in, you do," it said in a soft and sympathetic voice. "Don't worry. I won't hurt you."

He lowered his sword, flabbergasted by the voice.

"You talk?" he asked it, not believing he had really heard.

"It's certain that I do, for you must have understood it yourself, young fellow," it answered, clearly amused by its effect on him.

Suddenly drained of all his energy, Lugh sank down against the rock. "Well, whatever you are, I've no strength to fight you," he said. "So I hope it is the truth you're telling me."

"It's a great many things I've been, but never a liar," it told him sincerely, dropping down on its haunches, like a hound. "It's the Pooka I'm called."

"Pooka?" Lugh repeated vaguely.

"Ah, you've never heard tell of me?" it said, sounding a bit disappointed. "I thought the tales of the Pooka were told about every fire in the west of Eire."

"I'm new to Eire," Lugh explained. "And new to the west."

"That explains it then," the beast said, brightening. "But I should have known you were new here, to be wandering on the Burren alone, and in the night."

"I'm lost," Lugh said. "And I'm being hunted—chased—by the Fomor."

"The Fomor, is it?" the thing said, interested. "You have got yourself in a mess then, haven't you?"

"I've got to keep going," Lugh said. "Can't delay anymore." He pushed himself to his feet again. He was unsteady, weak from fatigue and hunger and loss of blood. He felt groggy.

"You'll not go far in your state," the Pooka said. "You need a bit of rest. Come with me, now. I know a safe place where you can go. I'll even carry you there."

"Carry me?" Lugh said. "How will you do that?"

"Like this," it said.

Lugh decided he must be weaker than he thought. His vision was failing him. The figure in the dark seemed to be growing soft, swelling, bulging, wavering, in peculiar ways and growing larger.

"There!" the Pooka announced with satisfaction. "Climb on!"

Lugh found himself looking at a tall, sleek horse!

"How . . . how did you do that?" he asked in wonder.

"I'll tell you later. Come on now, get on, before your Fomor friends catch up to you."

He went to the animal, too weary and too weak to argue. With an effort he pulled himself onto its broad back and sank forward, head against the neck, arms encircling it.

"Hold tight," the animal advised and started off, trotting as gently as it could across the moonlit waves of stone.

It made its way toward the south, and after a time the nature of the land began to change. They were coming out of the Burren, into a country where more trees grew and the rocky ground turned to meadows.

The magical horse came at last to a large grove of trees and found its way into the thick growth along a nearly invisible path. It wound past the massive trunks of great gnarled oaks to a small clearing hidden deep within.

When it stopped, the exhausted young man, now nearly unconscious from his loss of blood, slid down from its back. He tried to stand, but the effort was too much. He sank down on the earth and fell at once into a heavy sleep.

Predawn mists clung thickly around the hilltops and above the tiny lake. They slowed the progress of the line of Firbolg warriors who were making their way from the sacred hill back toward their home. They had completed their ritual with a sacrificial bull to replace Lugh. Now they wanted only the comfort of a meal, the warmth of their own fires.

Home was a short distance ahead of them. Across a last plain was the lake and the small island fortress they had built of woven saplings. Their crannog.

But as they came in sight of the structures looming up as dark shapes in the grey, they stopped in alarm. For between them and their home sat a line of glowing silver horsemen.

The Firbolgs bunched together, weapons coming up defensively. Their concern was for their families behind the walls. Their superstitious fears were fired by the strange appearance of the grim, shining warriors.

Sreng ordered them to maintain control and hastily spread them into an opposing line. He eyed the waiting riders narrowly, himself not sure what action to take next.

But the next action came from the other side. The rank of horsemen parted and two riders moved forward from the rest. They dismounted, moving toward the Firbolgs on foot. Midway they stopped and waited, clearly expecting a like response from Sreng's force.

"They expect us to meet them," the shaman said.

"I see that," Sreng said irritably. He had no real desire to confront these beings, whatever they were. But he couldn't look the coward to his men. "All right, then. You and I will go."

Cautiously, he and the shaman made their way toward the two figures. As they neared, and the shrouding mist between grew thinner, he began to see them more clearly. His sense of wonder grew and his fear declined. It was two women who faced them there!

He stopped before them, openly appraising them. Both were handsome, and one was very young. They were well armed, but neither had the hard look or massive body of the great women warriors he had known.

"Who are you, then?" he demanded with renewed arrogance. "What do you mean blockin' our way?"

"We've no idea of keeping you from your homes," the younger woman said with politeness. "We're searching for someone, and yours is the first dwelling place we've found. We want to know if you've seen a young warrior alone, lost in the barren lands."

"We know nothing," he answered curtly. "Be out of our way!"

This time the older woman spoke, and with a great deal less friendliness.

"It's not a hospitable man you are, though Firbolg chieftains have always been known for such. We're not leaving this place until you speak with us."

"Are you not?" he said. "And are your score of bright, slender warriors with their thin lances to stop us? Are they even really men? Shaman, what do you say?"

"They seem more like shapes made of the sunlit mists," he said. "Some magic forms, and not solid at all."

"These two women shaped them to frighten us," Sreng said with confidence. "Shaman, use your own powers to sweep them from our way."

The old man shook his head doubtfully. "I don't know. I feel great forces coursing in them. I think that we should talk."

"You've challenged me once tonight," the chieftain bellowed. "Don't do it again for your life. Do as I say if your failing magic is still enough."

With an expression of great unhappiness, the shaman moved forward. Neither of the women moved to interfere.

"Pardon this," he told them. "I've really no choice." And he raised his arms, beginning an incantation.

As he did, the lances of the Riders dropped forward as one, forming a line of bright points aimed at the feather-cloaked magician.

Each flared with blue-white light that jumped from one to another, joining them in a single, crackling line of energy that shot forward like a lightning bolt, slamming against the shaman and casting him backward. He fell nearly at the feet of the gathered Firbolgs, who recoiled in terror, looking down at the sprawled figure whose cloak smoked from the scorching blast.

"He's not dead," Aine assured the chieftain, who gaped, open-mouthed. "The Riders of the Sidhe only act in our defense. They'll kill only if you try to kill us."

"Now," said the older woman, "will you tell us what we want to know, Sreng?"

He jerked his gaze back to her from the fallen magician, yet more amazed.

"How do you know me?" he asked, clearly afraid. "More magic?"

"I know you, Sreng. I saw you when I was a young girl. You were a chieftain of my father." She stepped toward the other warriors and spoke loudly so all could hear. "I am Taillta, daughter of MacErc!"

Voices exclaimed in surprise amongst the Firbolgs. The dumbfounded chieftain replied before he thought.

"So he spoke the truth! You are his—" He choked this off.

But not before Taillta heard and understood. She rounded on him sharply.

"So, you have seen him! Tell us quickly, where?"

"Why should we help?" Sreng challenged, trying to reassert himself. "Why should we believe your tale any more than his?"

"She is Taillta," gasped a voice. It came from the poor, aging shaman, now being helped to his feet by the tatooed women. He drew himself up weakly and forced out the halting words. "I remember her from those days. As you should, Sreng."

The chieftain eyed her more closely. Then he nodded, reluctantly.

"Perhaps you are MacErc's daughter," he said. "What kind

of traitor is it you've become, returning to us to ask help for a de Danann enemy?"

"Lugh is not an enemy of the Firbolgs," she told all of them. "He means to help destroy the Fomor."

"The Fomor are not our enemies," Sreng argued.

"It was the leader of the Fomor—Balor One-Eye himself— who killed MacErc," she said.

A cry of outrage arose amongst the gathered warriors.

"My father knew it was the Fomor who were forcing us to war against the de Dananns for control of Eire," she continued forcefully. "He meant to make a peace with them and share Eire. But the Fomor wanted us to fight, to ravage one another, to make each other weak."

"That's all lies," Sreng shouted. "When we came to Eire, the Fomor gave the land to us! They let us live here in peace! But when the de Dananns came, they challenged us. They wanted Eire for themselves and they warred against us. It was the de Dananns who destroyed us and stole the land."

"The de Dananns would have shared Eire with us," she countered fiercely. "You know they offered that. But the treacherous Fomor convinced us we must fear them and made us go to war. My father knew that, and he died. My clan knew that, and the Fomor slaughtered them." She was looking past Sreng now, her voice raised to address the warriors. "Hundreds of Firbolgs were tortured and killed because Balor One-Eye wanted the boy we had hidden. Scores of MacErc's warriors died bravely to protect him and help him escape."

Sreng looked around at his men and saw in their expressions that Taillta's words were reaching them. They listened and they believed. With more desperation, he tried to counter her effect.

"The boy!" he said sardonically. "Always it comes back to him. What madness is it that would make you give up your lives for him?"

"A prophecy," she tersely responded. "It said that Lugh, the son of the Champion Cian, would bring about the destruction of the Fomor. I helped him. The warriors of MacErc helped him. Because through him will come the vengeance for my father's death and for the wrongs the Fomor have done us!"

"This is some private vengeance of your own you're seekin', not ours," Sreng said stubbornly. "And don't be thinkin' we're fools enough to be swayed by it. We know well enough what the de Dananns did to us."

He turned then to speak to his warriors, his voice heavy with emotion as he appealed to them.

"You all remember how they crushed our batallions at the battle of Magh Turiedh. It was little enough mercy they showed us that day! They drove us back, tearing at us the while, until there were only three hundred warriors left in all our eleven batallions. That night the keenin' for the dead came so loud from every Firbolg hut that the roarin' wind itself was drowned out by the dreadful sound of it.

"And you remember how they forced us to a peace and took Eire from us, took our homes and herds and fine green fields and left us this barren land. They forced us here, to freeze and starve and live like animals!"

"They didn't force us to come here," she said. "The Firbolgs chose to retreat into the farthest corners of Eire and scorn the de Danann's offer of friendship. But we had no need to be their enemies then, and we've no need now."

"She is right," the old shaman said courageously. "We have kept our hatred alive for too long. It is time truly to make our peace. We must help her."

There were murmurs of agreement from the Firbolg warriors. Clearly many of them had seen the truth in Taillta's words. Sreng saw they were wavering. He reacted angrily.

"No!" he cried. "My brothers died in that battle. My wife died of cold and hunger our first winter here. The de Dananns must pay for that. The Fomor will make them pay. They'll catch that boy of yours. They'll destroy all the de Dananns."

"What do you mean?" Aine demanded anxiously.

The chieftain smiled, enjoying her discomfort. He answered her with savage satisfaction.

"We saw this Lugh. We let him go alive. And after he departed, the Fomors hunting for him came to us. I sent them after him."

Taillta advanced upon him threateningly, her face hard with anger.

"You sent them after him? I might have known you would. Your hatred of the de Dananns has made you mad."

His face grew flushed and he laid his hand upon his sword.

"You'll not give me such insult, woman. Leave here or I'll kill you, magic warriors or not!"

"You'll help us find Lugh before the Fomor do," she retorted in her own rage. "If you'll not do it, your warriors will."

"Not while I am chieftain," he said with massive arrogance.

"Then that," Taillta said decisively, "is what I'm going to change."

At those words the chieftain appeared surprised, and then greatly pleased. He smiled.

"Are you meaning to give me challenge?" he asked.

"I am," she told him, drawing herself up and meeting his gaze boldly.

"By our Firbolg codes? Without the help of your silver warriors?"

"Alone," she agreed.

"Done, then," he said heartily. He began at once to pull off his heavy cloak. Taillta began to do the same.

Aine, alarmed by this sudden challenge, moved close to her friend to murmur anxiously:

"What is happening? What are you going to do?"

"I've challenged him for the right of leadership," Taillta explained, casually, as if it were an everyday ritual. "If I win, I'll take control of the clan. Then they will have to help us."

"And what is it you have to do to win?" asked Aine.

Taillta shrugged. "I have to kill him."

Aine looked across at the burly chieftain. He had now stripped himself to the waist, defying the chill dawn. Though heavy, he was a strongly built man, with a massive chest thickly furred with hair, short, powerful arms, sloping shoulders, and a thick neck. He looked more like a standing bear than a human. He took up his broad-bladed sword and his round shield edged with thick iron and looked across at them.

"Kill him?" Aine asked in disbelief. "He's twice your size!"

"He's old, and fat, and likely getting slow," Taillta countered with great bravado, returning his look with a bold glare. "My father taught me a warrior's skills to match any man's."

"Taillta, I can't let you take this risk!" Aine told her forcefully.

The older woman met her eyes. "This is my choice. We must have their help to find Lugh. This is how I have to get it. It's for Lugh, and that's all you should think about."

"I don't want you to die," Aine said, her usual reserve gone in her fears for her friend.

Taillta smiled. "You're making me the victim, girl. I don't intend to lose. And you'd best pray I don't, or there'll be no finding Lugh in this great Burren before the Fomor do."

With that she took up her weapons and moved forward,

ready to close with the chieftain, who already grinned in victory.

XIV

THE IRON MONSTER

THE FIGURES RAN wearily on through a darkness that was now beginning to give way to dawn. Ahead of them, the sky was filled with a soft, rising glow that promised the coming sun. No group of people were more unhappy to see it.

"Now that bloody thing will be after us at its full pace again," gasped out the weary Angus.

"It'll make no difference," said Gilla, still loping along quite easily, still smiling his usual inane smile. "We're far ahead of it by now. We'll easily be able to reach the sea before it catches us."

Even the mighty Dagda was moving with more effort after a night of running. He looked in amazement at the clown as the growing light revealed him.

"How can you still be so fresh?" he asked.

"Weariness is only in the mind," Gilla answered brightly.

"And, since you've little of that . . ." the Dagda added irritably.

"None . . . of you . . . oof . . . has any . . . reason . . . umpf . . . for complaint!" said Findgoll, who had suffered through a night of shaking on the Dagda's shoulder. "I believe . . . ooh . . . that all my bones . . . have been knocked . . . ahhh . . . loose!"

"Findgoll, you are ungrateful," the Dagda said. "Be quiet or you'll be walking, ankle or no." He shook his head and went on in an angry growl, "But it galls me to have to run. I wish we had stayed to fight the thing."

"We couldn't risk our mission," Gilla reminded him. "And you see that I was right."

"Very well, so you were right," the Dagda admitted grudgingly. "But you'd best not let me see you gloating over it with that foolish grin or it's you that'll carry the little wretch."

"Little wretch?" Findgoll cried indignantly. "Why . . . you great . . . stone-headed—"

His voice cut off in midtirade. He listened. They all did. They had reached the center of an enormous plain of tall grasses, beginning to dry and yellow in the autumn's sun and winds. They were alone on the vast, level expanse. Alone until, from the silence, a roar arose, and from a hidden low spot ahead of them a massive shape leaped suddenly into view.

"Oh, by the powers," Findgoll wailed in despair. "There it is!"

"Down. Quick!" ordered Gilla, and the company dropped into the tall grass out of sight.

"So, we're far ahead of it by now, are we?" the Dagda said with heavy sarcasm. "Now it's between us and the sea!"

"What do we do?" Angus asked. "We can't get around it, and we can't outrun it much longer."

Gilla peeped out of the grass toward the thing.

"What's it doing?" Morrigan asked.

"Just sitting there," the clown answered.

The others joined him in peering cautiously out at the beast. It was sitting motionless, like an enormous grey animal squatting on four legs. It was much closer than ever before, and for the first time the fugitives were able to have a good look at it.

It appeared to be a wheeled vehicle of a smooth metal. Its wheels were not the thin, iron-shod wood of the de Dananns' carts, but taller than two men and thick and made of some black material deeply grooved all around the outer edge. They were fixed to the ends of stalklike axles that extended from its body. This body was a rectangular metal box that rose high above the ground. Its front and sides were studded with a complex array of objects, many busily engaged in movements— wheels spinning, levers rising and falling, hinged bits opening and closing—whose purpose the watchers couldn't even guess.

Atop this structure was a flat deck, much like a ship's, pointed at the prow. At the back, the deck rose in two stairs to a higher quarterdeck. Centered there was a sort of cage formed of metal rods arching over the head of a man seated before a long, altarlike metal object. But he was not bent over it to worship, the disguised Sea-God knew. This protected man was the driver of the beast, and that altar held the secret to its control.

There were over a dozen men aboard it, all in the tight-fitting grey uniforms of the Tower Fomor. They had clearly decided it was useless to hide their presence in Eire anymore. Two of them flanked the driver's cage. The others were clustered at the prow. There were also mounted two barrel-shaped objects with circles of polished glass set in the forward ends. These, the watchers guessed, had to be the source of the lights that had plagued them through the night.

The lights were set on tall poles, and looked like the stalked eyes of a sea crab. In fact, save for the squareness of its lines, the machine's whole effect was that of some monstrous shellfish, even to its having a set of rather crablike appendages.

These massive limbs were hinged to the middle of its front near the ground. Their bottom edges were lined with scores of closely set, well-honed metal scythes. Each arm was jointed at its center and folded inward to meet the other just below the prow, as if the thing were now in prayer.

"It's a kind of great cart!" Angus said, struggling to relate the awesome vehicle to something he understood. "But how can it move without horses to pull it?"

"How can the Fomor move their ships without any sails?" Gilla returned and shrugged. "Who knows? Let's hope they've no other little surprises like it with them."

"Do you think it's seen us?" asked Findgoll.

As if in answer, the roaring of the vehicle rose in volume and it started forward again, rolling through the tall grasses directly toward them.

"That decides it, then," the Dagda announced decisively. "We'll have to fight it."

He hefted his ax meaningfully and started to rise, but Gilla pulled him down.

"Not so hasty," he cautioned. "Look there!"

As the metal beast sped toward them, the huge arms began to open. They swung out to the sides and then dropped on the hinges until they came in contact with the ground. At once the sharp scythes cut in, churning up the grass and soil, slicing easily through the sod and turning it in a hundred furrows. The two limbs now formed a single, lethal wall across the front of the machine.

"You see? The thing has teeth. Those warriors aren't meaning to fight us. They'll simply mow us like the grass. It will take some trickery to get aboard that beast."

The Dagda gave Gilla a disbelieving look. "Don't tell me you have another mad idea."

"It's a simple one. You'll lead the thing away. I'll get aboard and stop it. Then you'll be free to deal with the Fomor."

"You'll stop it. Just like that," the Dagda said doubtfully. "You can do that?"

"The simplest part!" Gilla answered with breezy assurance. He grinned. "Unless you'd like to make a try."

"For the sake of Danu," Morrigan said sharply, "there's no time for this. We have to act now!"

The Dagda looked out again at the approaching vehicle. He nodded. "All right, clown. We'll do it."

"Good," Gilla said happily. "You and Angus lead the thing away. Findgoll, with your leg you'd best stay here. I'll wait for it to turn and go in behind it. Morrigan, become a raven and follow me. Raise a diversion when I get ready to go after the driver. See him? Inside that cage."

"I see," she croaked, and at once went into her transformation.

"Ready, then?" Gilla asked as the familiar shape of the black bird appeared.

His comrades nodded. The vast metal thing was nearly upon them.

"Then, go!" he cried.

Angus and the Dagda rose up and darted away through the grass like startled hares, cutting directly across the path of the thing.

Gilla watched, praying to Danu the vehicle would turn to follow them.

It did, reacting with amazing speed, its enormous front wheels pivoting under the urging of the complex, jointed arrangement beneath. It swung around, turning its back on those still hiding in the grass.

"We've got to be quick now, Morrigan!" Gilla told the raven. "Those two won't be able to outrun that thing for long!"

He leaped up and ran for the rear of the rolling beast as it sped away. It had quite a lead on him, and he had to move at his best speed.

None of the Fomor warriors on the deck above noticed him. Their attention was fixed on the figures running desperately ahead. The fact that three of the fugitive band were missing seemed not to have registered yet.

Gilla reached the stern of the vast machine. It rose up, a sheer wall of flat grey metal, to that rear platform where the driver sat in his cage. Around the base of the stern ran a narrow ledge, waist-high from the ground. From there a narrow ladder of metal bands led up the side.

He got a grip on the ledge. But the machine's rear wheel bounded over a mound and jerked upward, shaking him loose and nearly knocking him off his feet. He knew that if he fell he wouldn't have another chance to catch up to the machine. He staggered but managed to stay upright. Still, the vehicle had now gained on him again. He forced himself to his full speed once more.

He concentrated his last power and dove forward. One lean but strong hand gripped the edge. He pulled closer and caught at the metal with the other. Then, with a great heave, he launched himself onto the ledge.

He seesawed there for an instant, body aboard, legs swinging down to drag his flapping shoes in the grass. He reached up and managed to grip the lowest rung of the ladder and, with another effort, hauled his lower half to safety. Clambering to his feet, he started quickly upward.

He reached the upper deck and stopped just below it, peeking over the edge to scout his way. The driver of the mechanical beast was absorbed by the array of devices within his cage. On either side the Fomor soldiers stood, watching the pursuit.

Morrigan, who had flown up from the grass to circle over the rolling vehicle, now saw that it was her time to act. To divert attention from Gilla, she swooped boldly down and into the faces of the Fomor in the prow.

She took the first one totally by surprise, her strong talons gripping his face, her beating wings knocking him off balance. He flailed out wildly and toppled forward off the edge, down in front of the rows of sweeping blades.

Like the jaws of some rapacious creature, the blades seemed to suck him in. He was pulled through sideways, run over by a dozen of the razor-edged scythes. In an instant they had chewed him and driven the remains into the earth, tingeing the dark, plowed soil red in a swath behind.

Not pausing, Morrigan attacked the others, swooping here and there to strike them. They drew swords in a desperate attempt to beat the raven off, but were so busy cowering and protecting their vulnerable eyes that their blows went wild.

"Go help them get that bird!" the driver irritably commanded the soldiers on either side of him. "Keep it away from me!"

Obediently the two drew weapons and started forward, leaving the driver alone. When Gilla saw this, he attacked.

He jumped onto the platform and, in a single, powerful move, seized the startled driver by the throat of his tunic and yanked him bodily from his seat. Before the man could shout, the clown swung him around toward the edge. The man flew off head first, diving almost gracefully to the ground below, ramming his head deeply into the soft, turned earth. His body slammed down heavily atop it and he was still.

Gilla didn't pause to admire the effect. He hopped into the vacated seat, unnoticed by the soldiers engaged forward. He looked for the first time at the devices that controlled the vast machine—and he found himself at a complete loss!

He stared in bewilderment at the myriad of strange contrivances before him. He had traveled and he had seen much, but none of it had prepared him for this. There were levery things and jointed things and tiny lights that blinked. There were bumps and holes and engraved devices and bits that slid and bits that turned and bits that didn't seem to do anything at all. And he couldn't even begin to guess what the purpose of any of them was.

But there really wasn't time for casual pondering. The Dagda and his son were nearly beneath the blades. He began flipping and shoving and banging everything, working—quite systematically he thought—from left to right.

The first effect of this was that the beast gave out a loud, pained snort, jerked forward, and began to roll even faster.

The Dagda and Angus, seeing the thing all but leaping after them, forced yet more speed out of their own weakening legs.

"What is that madman doing?" the Dagda bellowed. "I knew we shouldn't have trusted him again!"

"What shall we do?" cried Angus. "Shall we separate?"

"No," said the Dagda fiercely. "I've my own idea this time. You go and help!"

"Go aboard it? How?"

"I'll show you," the Dagda told him and, without warning, he swept up his son and lifted the astonished warrior above his head. He turned to face the oncoming machine.

"No! What are you doing?" Angus shouted.

"Quiet!" his father commanded. "Just be ready to grab a hold!"

And with that, he launched Angus up in a high arc.

Understanding what his father intended, the warrior prepared himself. His father's power was enough to lift him easily above the cutting blades. He came down atop the wide arm that held them, slamming hard against the metal, scrambling for a hold on a row of large knobs where the scythes fastened to the support. He got a grip and pulled himself up astride the arm.

As the Dagda saw him land safely, he turned and ran again, now only paces ahead of the rending teeth of the beast.

Angus climbed to his feet and ran boldly along the arm to the side of the machine. Just above his head was the edge of the forward deck. He jumped up and grabbed it, pulling himself up to peek over the edge.

Directly before him, Morrigan was still in a brawl with the Fomor soldiers, sweeping amongst them, beating at them with her great wings, tearing with beak and claws. Gilla was at the controls, engaged now in a nearly frantic effort to slow it down, to turn it, to make it do anything helpful.

Unfortunately, his efforts had drawn the attention of one of the soldiers. As Angus watched, he pulled another aside and pointed to the driver's cage. The two men left the fight with the raven and headed toward the rear. Angus realized he had come just in time. Gilla was going to need more help.

He wasted no time entering the fray. As one of the soldiers dodging Morrigan moved close to him, he reached up and grabbed the man's ankle, yanking him over the side. The Fomor fell, striking the arm below and bouncing forward in front of the blades. His last cry was sliced off sharply and another trail of red stained Eire's dark soil.

Quickly Angus hauled himself up onto the deck and drew his sword and dagger to face the rest.

As the soldiers turned toward this new attacker in surprise, Morrigan used the respite to flutter down behind them and transform. Suddenly the astonished Fomor found themselves between two formidable opponents.

"Kill them quickly!" Angus told her. "Gilla needs help!"

Indeed he did. For the clown had given over his tampering with the controls to defend himself from the attack of the two soldiers. One came at him from either side of the cage, and he was forced to shift constantly back and forth to parry the swords jabbing in at him.

"I'm really very busy here, you know," he told them. "Couldn't this wait for just a bit?"

But the soldiers didn't seem inclined to listen to reason.

He was hampered by his position behind the controls, although the bars of the cage were providing some protection. The two couldn't easily get at him and couldn't swing at him. They were forced to make thrusts between the metal bands. Then one drove his blade forward just too far and Gilla brought his own weapon down on it with full force. He drove the Fomor weapon against a bar and it snapped off just above the hilt.

The other soldier, however, used this chance to get around the side of the cage and come directly in at the clown. Gilla threw himself back and the man's thrust slipped past, but the momentum brought him in to collide and grapple with the clown.

They twisted around in their struggle and fell against the panel of controls, shifting half of them at once.

This had an effect. The machine bucked, shuddered, slowed somewhat, and then began to make a long, easy turn.

Out in front, the Dagda suddenly realized the thing was falling away behind him. He stopped in amazement to watch it make a curve and circle back the way it had come. Noting the struggle on the deck, he headed after the now departing vehicle, intending to join the fight. Then a more urgent concern filled him as he saw the direction that the beast was taking.

In its wide circle, it was heading back toward where the crippled, helpless Findgoll lay.

He began to run faster, this time in a desperate attempt to pull Findgoll from its path.

Aboard, the fight was nearly over. Morrigan and Angus were forcing the last three warriors against the side. Angus disarmed one of them with a skillful thrust. The Fomor looked fearfully at their adversaries, at the ruthless gleam in Morrigan's bright eyes. Then they exchanged a look of agreement and turned together to leap over the side.

They landed in the plowed earth behind the blades, alive but unlikely to do any moving for some time.

At the controls, Gilla had finally managed to shove his assailant back and disable him with a blow of his fist. But the one he had disarmed now came leaping upon him, knocking Gilla completely from the seat. Locked together, the two rolled to the edge of the deck. There the Fomor got a firm grip on the clown's thin throat and began to push him over the side.

One of the immense rear wheels was turning right below his

head. He could feel it brushing the ends of his long, tangled hair.

He looked into the face of his adversary. The fellow looked very determined, and he had the muscles to accomplish his intent. Gilla found his will to succeed distressingly excessive.

"You're . . . making it . . . very hard . . . for me to breathe," he pointed out in a choked voice. "I'd be grateful if you'd let go."

The man only tightened his grip, forcing Gilla back, back, until the clown thought his spine would crack. The top of the wheel was nearly touching his head now. The deep grooves caught and pulled at his dangling hair.

"You Fomor . . . aren't much . . . for listenin', are you?" he gasped out.

He was nearly over now, his consciousness fading. The man grinned in victory.

Then the grin froze on his face and he straightened stiffly upright, hands dropping away from Gilla's throat. The eyes went blank and he toppled forward, falling over Gilla, his weight carrying him over the side.

Gilla saw the metal bolt protruding from his back as he landed upon the wheel and was rolled down and under it, to be pressed into the soft, turned soil.

The rescued clown sat up to see Angus standing on the lower deck, holding one of the Fomor bows.

"Look what I found!" he said, grinning.

"Thank you for that!" Gilla said warmly, climbing up and grimacing at his wrenched back. "But what about your father?"

"He's behind us," Morrigan crackled, moving to the prow. "But look there!" She pointed ahead.

They could see Findgoll now. And the Druid had seen them. He was waving, apparently unaware of his danger.

"We'll run right over him!" Angus cried. "Gilla, I thought you could stop this thing!"

"I'm trying," the clown assured him. "But you could help. See if you can find out what makes it run. Try to turn it off!"

He climbed back behind the controls, and they began a search of the machine for some way to bring it to a halt.

The Dagda, meantime, had caught up with them from behind. He realized there was no time to get around the moving thing and reach Findgoll. He had to find a way to stop it, or at least slow it until those above could act. And he only knew of one way he might do that himself. He moved up to the long axle that connected the rear wheels, took a firm grip on the heavy metal cylinder, and dug in.

Instantly he was making his own deep furrow in the earth as his braced legs were dragged along. He set himself, threw back against the forward pull, and tensed. He pitted his entire strength, called upon every bit of will, every trick of mystical control that he had learned in the Magic Isles. He shut his eyes, focused his mind and body, and challenged the mechanical force of the metal beast with his own powers.

Slowly, slowly, his will began to tell. The thing began to lose speed. It balked and roared in complaint, lumbering along sluggishly. Still, it crawled forward, across the unmarked grass, cutting its way toward the place where Findgoll lay.

The Druid, finally understanding his peril, began his own crawling, but he was too late and his effort too slow to save him.

The Dagda's effort, however, was giving the others more time. Gilla prodded and flicked at the controls. Morrigan and Angus probed everywhere for some vulnerable spot in the monster's iron hide. Their efforts were in vain.

"There's nothing!" Angus said despairingly. He and Morrigan moved back to join the clown.

Below, the Dagda strained, ignoring the screaming pain in his muscles.

Findgoll looked up at the thing looming above him and froze in fear.

Gilla jerked and prodded at the controls.

"There's nothing else to do!" cried Angus. He seized a large heavy tool set in brackets on the panel's side and wrenched it free. He swung it up over the controls, to strike. "We've got to smash them all!"

"No! No!" Gilla protested, working faster. "I can find the way!"

The Dagda was near exhaustion, his muscles tearing as if the arms would be pulled from their sockets. He set his teeth and hung grimly on.

"It's too late!" Angus shouted at the clown. "Move back!"

He tensed himself to slam the metal tool against the panel.

The shadow of the machine fell upon the Druid. The gleaming teeth slid forward to rend him.

Morrigan's long, bony hand shot forward, gripped a tiny lever in one corner of the panel, and twisted it.

The vehicle's powerful roar died instantly. It rolled quietly, gently, to a halt, its scythes just cutting into the sod before Findgoll's feet.

Angus and Gilla looked up in astonishment at the raven-woman. An uncharacteristic little smile lit her gaunt face and she shrugged.

"It was the only thing you hadn't touched," she said casually.

"About time!" Findgoll called in a shrill, scolding voice, having recovered his senses.

"I'll certainly agree with that!" the Dagda added sincerely, moving out from under the machine and flexing his sore arms.

"Thank you for your help," the little Druid told the giant champion. "I'd no idea you cared so much for my life."

"Not your life," the Dagda said gruffly. "It's your foolish tricks I'd miss."

"But what'll we do now?" Angus asked his comrades. "It's still a way to the sea, and there may be more Fomor seeking us."

"We've none of that to be fearin' anymore," Gilla said with his usual glee, patting the controls in front of him. "From here on, we ride!"

XV

TO THE SEA

IN THE LITTLE cove, one of the sleek black ships of the Tower Fomor sat drawn up on the shore. Nearby it on the beach, its crewmen were camped around several cooking fires. And not far away from them, like a giant sea creature that had crawled from the water to feed, sat another of the metal vehicles.

Safely hidden on a hill above the cove, Gilla and his party stared down on this unpleasant company for a time, in unhappy silence.

"Well, they've certainly managed to block our way again," Angus said at length.

"Are you certain it's here we're to find the ship that will take us to Manannan's Isle?" the Dagda asked the clown.

"I am that!" Gilla cheerfully replied. He was the only one

not touched by the gloom. "Our boat is hidden in the little thumb of rocks that juts out just beyond them, there." He pointed. "It's the way that we must go."

"Just how is it you know all these things, clown?" Morrigan rattled curiously.

"Lugh gave me fine instructions, that he did!" he assured her. "Now all we've a need to do is get it and be off. We've plenty of time."

"All we've a need to do!" Angus repeated scornfully. "Why not? There are only a hundred men down there. And another of those bleeding iron beasts."

"It does make me wonder just a bit how they always seem to know exactly where we'll go," Gilla said with unusual gravity.

"If they know we're coming here, maybe they've found the boat too," Findgoll suggested.

"Ah, no," Gilla assured him. "The boat's hidden so only we can find it. Lugh told me that Manannan's seen to that." He smiled and added with great awe, "He must truly be an amazin' man!"

"Never mind him," the Dagda said sharply, unimpressed. "What about us? How will we get to it? Those Fomor aren't likely just to sit and watch us putting out to sea."

"We'll have to take them unawares," said Gilla. "By good fortune, we've got the perfect thing for doing that."

He gestured back over his shoulder at the machine they had captured and driven here.

"What, use that thing?" the Dagda asked skeptically.

"We'll ride it right down upon them," Gilla said with savage delight. "They'll not know it's us until we're amongst them."

"Can you control the thing that well?"

"I brought us here, didn't I, now?" the clown said, sounding hurt that the big man would doubt his skill.

"You nearly killed us doing it," the Dagda reminded him.

"Just a bit of experimenting. I'm fully master of it now."

"And what about that other little piece of metal?" Angus wondered. "They could use it to stop us."

"Trust me," said Gilla, smiling his broadest smile. "I have a plan."

"That I should have guessed," the Dagda groaned.

It was not long after that the Fomor gathered below heard the rising sound of something growling, and looked up to see one of their own machines roll over the rise behind the shore and start down toward them.

The captain in charge of the waiting men eyed it thoughtfully.

"I wonder what it's doing back here so soon?" he asked.

"Maybe it's finished off the de Dananns," a nearby lieutenant suggested.

"It certainly better have if it's returning," he said sharply.

He and the others stood watching it come without any sense of alarm. As it came closer, the captain did note that there seemed to be very few men on its superstructure. He wondered if they had run into more resistance than expected. Still, if they had succeeded, Balor would be pleased, no matter what the cost.

He climbed the gangway into his ship and gave orders to the crew there. The well-disciplined sailors acted swiftly, swinging out a huge crane. He would have both machines loaded at once and be off back to the Tower.

Meanwhile, on the approaching vehicle, the passengers scanned the scene ahead with growing tension. Except, of course, for Gilla. He sat back at the controls, lazily manipulating the vast machine, humming a merry little air and enjoying himself.

At the prow stood Angus and the Dagda. Morrigan, again in her raven guise, perched on the cage above Gilla while Findgoll, still nursing his ankle, sat on the platform nearby.

"No signs of alarm there yet," the Dagda remarked. "They seem to be making some preparations about the ship."

"To welcome us home, no doubt," the clown said with a satisfied grin. "Keep steady, you two. Angus, keep that thing ready. You're certain you can hit something with it now?"

Angus hefted the Fomor crossbow and answered with what assurance he could. "I hope so. I've been practicing with it all day."

"Good enough. But don't fire until you're sure."

They kept on steadily, slowly, directly toward their monster's twin. Only a few soldiers were lounging upon it, watching them come. It was silent, and no one manned its controls. Gilla knew it would take some time to bring it into action now.

As they drew yet nearer to the Fomor camp, the captain paused to look again, noting something puzzling. The cutting arms were out. That was very odd. They were to be kept in except in an attack. What was that driver thinking about?

"Bring me a glass!" he ordered his lieutenant.

Instantly the man brought one of the tubular devices to him.

He peered through it, seeing the machine and its riders twice as large as before. His sweeping gaze lit on the two at the prow. As he focused on them, he realized with a shock that that giant figure could not be one of his men!

"The thing's been captured!" he bellowed. He ran to the ship's side, shouting across to the men at the second machine. "Quickly, get that vehicle manned! Stop them! They are de Dananns!"

Soldiers scrambled for the vehicle. Those already aboard it rushed for their positions.

"They're going to get that thing moving," said the Dagda. "They must have spotted us!"

"Shall I fire?" said Angus, lifting the bow.

"Steady!" Gilla said calmly. "Just a bit farther."

The driver of the other machine was now at its controls. They heard the preliminary coughing and whining of the forces within it as they began to awaken.

"They're starting it," said the Dagda.

"A little bit more," said Gilla.

Soldiers were gathering on the forward platform. Some were moving to the prow, seizing bows of their own. The man at the controls was manipulating them frantically to ready the monster for movement. The scythe arms began to unfold.

"Now!" Gilla said.

Angus fired. With a sharp, metallic snap, the bow sent its bolt speeding to the target.

It was a hit. The driver was knocked backward completely from his seat by the impact of the bolt that transfixed his chest. At the same moment, Gilla wheeled his vehicle sharply away and headed it straight in toward the Fomor encampment and the beached ship.

The Fomor captain watched in growing horror as the vast thing turned toward him, the cutting blades ready to tear through scores of men at once. And if it struck the ship . . .

"Aboard!" he screamed at the panicking men below. "Get aboard! Cast off at once!"

The Fomor on the other vehicle were still trying to act. A new driver was climbing behind the controls. But it was already too late. The rolling machine was past and heading with increasing speed toward the shore.

Gilla now climbed from behind his own controls and shouted to his comrades.

"Let's go now! Climb off this way! Off the back!"

They all headed toward the stern of the vehicle. Morrigan flapped away as the rest started down the ladder.

"Roll as you hit," Gilla advised. "Then head at an angle toward that rock spit to the north. Get under cover there."

As they were climbing down, the Fomor were clambering madly into their ship. Their captain was giving orders in a shrill, desperate voice and casting ever more fearful glances at the descending behemoth that was about to ravage his precious vessel.

"Get this ship off!" he shouted to the crew already aboard. "Forget the rest. Cut loose! Cut loose!"

Axes were seized and wielded against the mooring cables. Powerful forces deep within the ship rumbled to life. With agonizing slowness it began dragging itself from the sucking grip of the sand. The gangways fell, splashing into the water. Men still climbing up them were dropped into the sea. Those left on the shore began to run into the surf, crying out for rescue, begging not to be abandoned there.

And behind the desperate Fomor, the brutal thing bore down, its glinting teeth ready to devour them.

Some dove into the water to escape. Others tried to run out of the way. Many did escape, but many were caught, chewed up, their shredded bodies spewed out the back or plowed into the furrows in the sandy soil. The pale grey beach was turned rust in a wide swath.

The machine plunged into the sea in a great wallop and swoosh of water. The pressure of the water slowed its forward motion as it drove on in, giving the ship added time to slip away. Its sleek bow just cleared the shallows and the metal beast's scythe arm only nicked its side. Then the ship was out of reach and the vehicle sank to rest in water that came up nearly to its deck.

Under the surface, the flooded insides of the thing began a coughing sound like that of a drowning man. It spluttered instead of roaring steadily. Then it began to grumble in a low and ominous voice and the whole structure started shuddering as the sound built to a nearly deafening pitch.

"Full back!" the captain ordered as he saw the thing convulsing in its death throes.

The forces powering the black ship raised their own loud thunder and the lean hull sliced back through the waves at an increasing speed, opening a wider space between the two.

The de Danann adventurers had by this time reached the

rocks unnoticed. They climbed into their shelter to watch with glee the havoc they had created. The ship was pulling desperately away. The dozens still stranded on the beach were fleeing in all directions from the stricken machine. Those Fomor crewing its twin were abandoning it to run as well.

"I think we should take shelter," Gilla suggested to the rest.

"Why?" asked the Dagda.

A vast explosion rocked the shore, knocking them off their feet into the rocks as debris flew over them. The shaking continued for long moments, accompanied by secondary explosions like the crack of recurrent lightning. It deafened them, showered them with sand and flying metal bits. Finally the sound rolled away and they ventured a cautious look out at the scene.

The machine had largely disappeared, leaving a hole in the seabed just offshore that was already filling with incoming waves. Above, a great grey-white cloud puffed up and spread into the sky. Around the hole for some distance the flying remains had created a fan of deep marks in the sand.

The second machine had been overturned by the blast. It lay, wheels moving slowly, like a beetle flipped onto its back. The few men who had survived were struggling to rise or lying hurt and moaning along the shore.

The ship had escaped, but barely. Its side was marked by the impact of flying wreckage and most of its crew had been thrown to the decks, stunned. The vessel wallowed in the heavy waves the blast had made, apparently not under anyone's control.

"Now's the time to go," Gilla said. "Quick, now. While that ship's helpless."

He urged his comrades, themselves somewhat stunned by the incredible force of the explosion, toward the sea end of the natural rock jetty. He led them over the larger rocks and down to the water. There, with a triumphant wave, he showed them a hidden cave beneath the overhanging boulders where a small vessel lay.

It was a curragh, made of many hides stretched over a frame of supple branches. It had a sail fixed to a slender mast. It was a light and fragile-looking craft and the Dagda eyed it critically.

"Is that to carry all of us?"

"It is," Gilla replied. "Get in. There's little time."

The big man hesitated. "It won't hold even the likes of me! Can't this great Sea-God do any better for us?"

"He's a man of simple tastes," Gilla said, a touch impatient. "This boat will be enough. Please, just get in!"

Reluctantly, the Dagda climbed down and into it. Miraculously, the little vessel seemed unaffected by his formidable weight.

"You see?" said Gilla, smiling in a superior way. "Will the rest of you get in now? And quickly!"

The others clambered in at once. Morrigan fluttered down to land atop a seat. Gilla moved to the stern and seized the tiller while Angus hauled up the sail.

The small spread billowed at once, and the boat responded smartly, scooting out of the hidden slot into the open sea and away.

She was well out before there was any sign of life from the black ship. Then a cry went up from the recovering crew. The Fomor captain stumbled to his feet and moved to the side, realizing that their quarry had somehow gotten to a boat and were sailing away under his very nose.

Visions of having to face Balor with that news flashed through his mind. He bellowed commands to his still groggy crew.

"Get this vessel underway! Put about!"

Sluggishly, the black ship turned out to sea. The internal forces that powered her began to propel her forward in the wake of the little craft.

"To the sail!" he ordered.

Hands scrambled for the tall mast, and soon the glowing white sail blossomed, its massive spread ballooning out to catch the breezes and thrust the vessel forward at greater speed.

"They're after us now!" Angus announced.

"Nothing to fear," Gilla assured him. "There's no ship fast enough to catch us!"

He seemed to be right. Although the sleek metal ship traveled with marvelous speed, some greater magic seemed to carry the smaller craft flying across the water like a wave-skimming bird.

"We're free of them, then!" Findgoll said with relief.

"Well, not quite," Gilla answered lightly, as if it were a matter of no great note. "The Fomor aren't going to be makin' it quite so easy for us."

"So easy!" Angus repeated in disbelief. "You call what we've been through so far easy?"

"Still, it's not ended yet," said the clown, pointing forward. "Look there."

Directly ahead of them, a long, dark shape topped by a cloud of iridescent white hove into view on the rim of the sea.

"Another ship?" the Dagda said heavily.

"The Fomor from the Tower are thorough, that they are," said Gilla. "I thought they might try to block us should we get out to sea."

"We can run past her," the Dagda said. "Turn north."

"And then what?" Gilla inquired pleasantly, pointing again.

From the north a third ship had appeared and was sweeping toward them.

"There's always the south," Angus suggested.

"Not anymore," said Findgoll. For yet another ship had now topped the horizon there, headed their way.

"They've caught us in a box!" the Dagda cried angrily, looking around. From the tip of the mast on each a tiny light was visible, blinking wildly. "What are they doing with those lights?"

"Telling one another that we're here," Gilla replied. "Likely they're deciding a plan of attack."

"Whichever way we run, they'll cut us off," Angus said in a defeated voice. "They've caught us surely this time."

"Nothing like it," Gilla said with no lessening of his merry assurance. "This only adds a bit of fun to the chase, it does."

And with that, he pointed the little boat toward the ship coming in from the east.

"You can't just sail straight along as if nothing were wrong," the Dagda protested. "What about all your grand planning?"

"I've a plan," Gilla told him. "But let them close their trap a bit. Then we'll wiggle out."

As the disguised Sea-God Manannan himself, Gilla might have used his enormous powers over the sea to disable, delay, or even destroy the Fomor. But his orders from his Queen Danu withheld him from wanton destruction unless he had no choice. Besides, he thought, there would be great fun and satisfaction in toying with these arrogant Fomor and then making fools of them.

Not sharing his thoughts, his companions did not share his carefree manner as he steered them in toward seemingly certain doom.

The ship before them was now quite close. The de Dananns could see its details and see the sailors swarming on its deck.

The other ships were drawing closer, too, tightening the sides of the box, closing their trap.

But Gilla let the box grow smaller, smaller, until it seemed he meant to ram the ship sweeping toward them head on. Its bow loomed over them when he finally pulled the craft sharply about.

It heeled far over, nearly launching the Dagda over the side. As it turned away, the Fomor ship was taken off guard and sailed past, unable to turn in time. When it finally did respond, the small craft was away, driving toward the south.

But the southern ship was slashing through the waves into a blocking position. Quicker to respond to Gilla's move, its captain put his helm hard over, cutting in front of the new course.

Gilla turned sharply the opposite way, catching the Dagda off balance once more and sending him reeling across to the boat's other side. He bellowed his anger, clutching wildly at the mast to save himself.

The tiny ship was now running parallel to the Fomor warship. It was only yards away, and its sailors were lining the bulwarks, training weapons on them. They included a crossbow of enormous size carrying a bolt larger than a man's leg and fitted with a barbed head of iron. Attached to it was a cable, and it was clear they intended to try a grapple.

"Gilla, they're going to spear us like a fish!" Angus warned.

"Not really," the unflappable clown called back. For, coming at them from the front was the northern ship, also speeding to cut them off. It was now on a collision course with the ship beside them.

Neither captain had realized until now the situation the tiny craft was drawing them into. Finally seeing the other bearing down at full speed, each frantically moved to alter course. Gilla veered hard left away from them as they tried to swerve apart.

They managed to miss striking, their sides scraping against one another with a rending shriek of metal. But by now the ship that had come in from the east had made a sharp turn of its own and was heading toward the other two. As this third ship drove in, its captain saw the others locked together, barely moving. He tried to reverse his power, but it was far too late. His prow rammed directly into the starboard prow of the southbound ship and slammed it against the one on the far side.

All three were jerked violently to a dead stop, throwing the crews from their feet. The slender mast of the ramming ship shivered in the impact, cracked near its base, and toppled forward, bringing down its sail in a graceful billow into the cables of the others' sails, creating a magnificent tangle.

Gilla looked back at the carnage as the little boat shot away, laughing in his delight. Then a shouted warning from the Dagda, who still clung tightly to the mast, brought his gaze back to the front. He realized that they were nearly under the bow of the last ship, the one that had pursued them from Eire.

It had come up on them in the confusion. Its captain was gloating. He was going to drive their frail boat under.

He was mistaken. With a careless flip of the tiller, Gilla sent the boat around in another tight turn. It shot across the big ship's bow and away.

The despairing captain of the final boat, seeing his quarry slip away a second time, was not ready to give up. He screamed orders at his crew to maintain the pursuit. But in his rage he failed to note the three ships stopped ahead. He crashed into them at full speed, wracking them again, driving his sharp bow deep into the hull of the northbound ship.

For moments the four captains were busily engaged in shouting accusations and threats at one another, each trying to place the blame on someone else. Then a lowly and courageous sailor pointed out to them that while they argued, their quarry had escaped.

In hopeless dismay, they watched the tiny boat flit away across the sea until it was lost in the haze of the earth's rim.

All four men knew that long before they could sort out this chaos and start in pursuit, the de Danann craft would be entering the band of mists that surrounded Manannan's Isle. And none of them, even if it meant facing Balor's wrath, would take their ship into that terrible white void. For only death lurked there.

Nuada forced himself to watch the warriors practicing with their spears. It was painfully slow progress they showed. But at least, he thought, it was progress.

A more pleasing development was the speed with which their ranks had begun to swell. Already Lugh's early success in contacting the settlements was having its effect. He only hoped that Lugh—or Aine if it came to that—would be able to complete the mission.

His thoughts were interrupted by the approach of Captain Niet.

"My King, our scouts intercepted a party of men coming back toward Tara."

"Coming back?" Nuada repeated in puzzlement. "From where?"

Niet looked carefully around. No one was nearby save young Ruadan, busily honing the edges of his spearpoint. The boy was loyal to the High-King, an adoring puppy constantly following him around. Niet disregarded his presence and continued, but dropped his voice to a confidential tone.

"They were the men escorting the Dagda's party. They were ambushed by Tower Fomor."

"By the powers!" Nuada said in shock.

"It's all right," Niet hastily went on. "The Dagda and the others escaped and went ahead. But they sent those of the escort who weren't hurt back here with the wounded. Knowing Bobd Derg's feelings, I thought it best just to tuck them quietly away."

"Good man," said Nuada. "Yes, our Bard would do a great deal of ranting if he heard about this." He shook his head. "But it looks worse and worse, Niet. If the Tower really is involved . . ."

"Even its powers can't stop the likes of the Dagda and Morrigan, My King," the captain said with conviction. "They told the men to say that they'll still return here in good time."

Nuada hoped so. These ominous events troubled him deeply. But he told himself it was still too soon to begin fearing the worst.

"Supply those men with whatever they need," he told Niet, and dismissed him. Turning back to the spear throwers, he noted Ruadan, apparently still hard at work, tongue tip sticking from the side of his mouth in concentration.

"My boy, you'll keep to yourself anything you've heard, won't you?" he asked.

The young warrior looked up, his guileless face filled with obvious bewilderment at this question.

"My King, I was so busy here, I wasn't even aware you were speaking to someone."

Satisfied with that, Nuada smiled. "Never mind then. Get on with your work. You'll yet be a de Danann champion yourself."

Ruadan beamed at this and obediently got back to his job. But his mind was working even more furiously. Here was another bit of unsettling news. It must, he decided, be carried to his father at once.

He began to devise a scheme to slip away from Tara that night and make a visit to the Fomor camp.

XVI

THE POOKA

WHEN LUGH AWOKE from his long slumber, it was to a very peculiar sight indeed.

An enormous set of haunches filled his view. Startled, he sat up and stared around him, momentarily confused.

He realized that what was before him was a large black horse. But the animal was crouched down on all fours, for all the world like a man, neck stretched out, huge lips pursed absurdly as it gently puffed on a tiny fire.

The thing really wasn't a horse, he decided as he considered it more closely. It had clawed feet, or paws, more like those of a cat. And it seemed much too hairy for a horse. More woolly, in fact, like a sheep.

Then the fog of his heavy sleep cleared, and he understood that it was the Pooka he saw. He looked around him at the tiny clearing in the woods and recalled how it had brought him here. When? The night before? That fact shocked him and he looked up to the sky. It was full daylight now. The sun was high. How much precious time had he lost here?

"How long have I been asleep?" he asked aloud.

The animal started and jumped to its feet at the sound, swinging its head around on the long neck. Large brown eyes regarded him and the creature visibly relaxed.

"Ah, so you're awake, are you?" it said, baring wide, flat teeth in what Lugh guessed was meant for a smile. "Well, I hope your feeling better. You were well out when I finally got you here. It's been all the night you slept."

"And half the morning, too, it seems," Lugh added. "I can't stay here any longer. I've got to get on."

He tried to rise from the bed of leaves, but his wounds and his stiffened limbs rebelled in their agony and he fell back.

"Wait on," the Pooka advised, shifting around toward him. "You'll not be moving so quickly. You were badly used. Rest a bit more. Regain some of your strength."

"But the Fomor!" Lugh protested.

"We left your Fomor wandering in the Burren. There's no sign of them about. But, tell me now, why is it that race of mongrels is chasing after you?"

"I'm on a mission to call every de Danann to a hosting against them," Lugh said. "They mean to keep me from doing that."

"So, the de Dananns are finally going to rise against them!" the being said with great interest. "I thought that might never come."

Lugh eyed the Pooka with greater curiosity. "You know about it?"

"It's certain that I do," it assured him gravely. "In my wanderings I learn all the happenings and see what the Fomor have done. I hope the de Dananns can crush them."

"They'll have little chance of that unless I can complete my task," Lugh said glumly. "The Fomor have managed to destroy my escort and leave me afoot and lost. I'll never be able to contact the last settlements in time. I've half of Eire yet to reach."

At that the Pooka brightened, pulling itself up. "But you can, with my help!" it announced.

"You? How can you do that?" the young warrior asked in puzzlement.

"I can fly you anywhere you're needing to go."

"Fly me?" Lugh repeated, doubtfully. He examined the Pooka's large and decidedly earthbound form.

It smiled again. "Well, not like this, surely. You've forgotten that I can shift my shape whenever I please. I can become the greatest, grandest bird you ever saw. Strong enough to carry you easily."

The being proclaimed this with a ringing note of pride. Lugh believed that it could do what it said. He had seen with his own eyes that it was capable of radical changes in form. Still, though he sensed the Pooka was good-hearted and sincerely wanted to help, the young warrior was a stranger to it.

"Why is it you're so willing to help me?" he asked it with open curiosity. "First you risked your own life against the wolves, and now this."

"Last night I helped you because you were needing help," it answered simply. "Today, knowing of your mission, I want to help you complete it. I've reasons for wishing to see the de Dananns win. So, will you let me help?" The voice became cajoling. The liquid brown eyes pleaded.

"You've little need to convince me," Lugh said. "I've no other chance of finishing my task. I need your help. Of course I'll accept your offer, and gladly!"

"Ah, that's fine then!" it said with great delight. It nodded toward a small pile of fur by the little fire. "I've some game here. I'll leave you to clean and cook it. Eat and begin restoring the strength you've lost. After that, we can be off."

Lugh agreed readily. His stomach was crying out in its hunger. He took the brace of rabbits the Pooka had caught, skinned them with his dagger, and spitted them on long sticks to prop over the fire. As he worked, the beast dropped down nearby and watched him, clearly fascinated by everything the young warrior did.

In turn, Lugh considered the amazing being. Its gentle, pleasant manner seemed a sharp contrast to the savagery with which it had fallen upon the wolves. He wondered if its nature changed to fit the type of beast that it became. He rather hoped not.

"Hands are truly wonderful things, that they are," the Pooka said in a thoughtful voice. "It was the most terrible time I had starting up that fire. I never build them for myself, you know. The best of paws or claws are almost useless, clumsy things. Yes, I do miss hands."

"Miss them?" asked Lugh. He had learned in Eire that one didn't pry into another's life uninvited. Still, the peculiar nature of the Pooka made it very hard for a curious young man. Unable to restrain himself, he asked: "Did you have hands once?"

"Hands, arms, feet, legs—oh, yes. All of that. All the normal parts." His voice grew quite wistful, almost sorrowful. The eyes grew darker and the large nose even seemed to droop.

"Look here," Lugh ventured after some further hesitation, "would you mind telling me about yourself? I mean, I'm really going mad with questions about who you are and how it is you speak."

The thing cheered at Lugh's interest. "No. I'd not mind telling you at all."

It drew itself up into a resemblance of a sitting posture, back legs pulled up like a dog's, front legs crossed casually before it.

"Long ago," it began, "those of my clan were men, like you, before we lost the power to take on that form. My own father was of the Sons of Nemed who went to live in the Isles of the Blessed."

"You mean, you're of the Tuatha de Danann yourself?" interrupted the astonished Lugh.

"That we were," it confirmed. "And like the others who dwelt in Tir-na-nog, we learned something of the arts of magic from the people of Queen Danu. Many of the de Dananns developed their own skills. My father's was the skill of shifting shape. Ah, he was a master of that one. And there must have been something of the natural ability for it in his blood, you know, for he had no trouble teaching the magic to us, and we all had a mastery of it that no other of the de Dananns could match. Why, from the time we were babes we were playing about with our forms. Drove our mothers mad, it did!"

As it spoke, Lugh began to notice that the form of the being was altering right then. Not having seen this happen clearly before, Lugh observed the transformation, much intrigued.

It was a very peculiar sort of shifting process, as if the Pooka were formed of some thick fluid or soft clay. The body bulged and shrank and stretched as if it were undecided as to what animal shape to take. The head altered most radically, the nose swelling out or deflating, the eyes growing or shrinking to glowing dots, the mouth stretching to alarming size or drawing in to a thin line.

This created outrageous and often grotesque combinations as fleetingly as the shifting of a cloud's shape in the wind.

The fascination quickly wore thin for Lugh. It was too bewildering.

"Excuse me," he said as politely as he could, "but did you know that your body had become a bit . . . ah . . ."—he searched for the right word—". . . loose?"

"Ah, I'm sorry about that!" the Pooka said apologetically. "I let it go when I'm not thinking about it."

"Well, if you'd not mind, I'd find it easier if you could keep one shape. It's hard to listen to you when you're changing about like that. And it's not that pleasant to watch, you know."

"I suppose not," it agreed. The being settled back into a

roughly horselike shape again, though its feet were those of a dog and its body was small and round and very fuzzy, like a sheep's. It was strange, Lugh thought, but certainly not alarming.

"Tell me more about this skill of yours," the warrior said. "Is it like what the Morrigan can do?"

It snorted derisively. "The Morrigan. She's mastered only the single shape of the raven. We can be anything. Our clan was quite proud of that. Too proud, in fact. Our troubles started because of it."

"You mean that's why you lost the power to become men?" Lugh asked.

The creature nodded, its large eyes sad again. "Aye. It was our own weakness did it. You see, we began to use our power for trickery. Some of my brothers liked nothing more than to take a form and cause some mischief. And I did a share of it myself. It was especially good sport to play our little pranks upon the ladies."

The creature smiled and its voice took on a nostalgic note as it continued. "I remember a time when five of them were bathing in a pond. We turned to great, handsome swans and glided out toward them. And them, all unaware . . ." It looked at the young warrior, who was listening quite attentively, and quickly shook itself from this dubious reverie. "Never mind that. The thing was, none of our trickery was meant to do any harm, nasty though some thought it. We did no evil until we were drawn into it by that Druid Mathgen." The name was spat out like something obscene.

"Mathgen?" said Lugh. "I've never heard of him. Was he a de Danann?"

"He was. But he's long since been destroyed. You see, he plotted to overthrow Danu and to seize the Four Cities for himself. But to capture Danu, he needed help to sneak into her palace and surprise her. Well, for that he used his powers to convince some of my poor, weak brothers to join him. Just a bit of sport, he told them. A great joke on Danu it was to be.

"And so they took on the shape of birds to carry the man and his brigands into the sacred inner courts of Danu. When they realized what he was truly about, it was too late. And when the de Dananns managed to defeat his scheme, my brothers were named traitors right along with him."

He shook his head in sorrow at the painful memory before going on heavily.

"The rest of the de Dananns had been putting up with our pranks for years, and many of them already distrusted us. So they weren't inclined to give us much sympathy, you can be sure of that! They decreed that the whole tribe of the Pookas was not to be trusted again by them, and they appealed to Danu to inflict a fitting punishment on us so that neither we nor they would ever forget our terrible crime.

"'Since you love so much to take the shapes of creatures,' she said, 'your fate will be to do so always, for it's never the shape of men you'll wear again.'"

"That sounds a bit hard," the fair-minded young warrior remarked, feeling sorry for the poor, cursed animal.

"To me it's always seemed what we deserved," it said. "In any case, when the rest of the de Dananns returned to Eire from the Blessed Isles, my clan chose to come too. Now we make our homes in the lonely places, outcast by our own people, ashamed of and avoiding the sight of man. Though some of my brothers still like to play their tricks on de Dananns or Fomor or Firbolgs, or anyone wearing the human form."

The Pooka sighed again, the round sides heaving with it, and shook its great head.

"But, for myself, I've missed the company of men," it went on dismally. "It's why I've drifted away from the rest and wander alone. It's why I came to help you. I'd come to the aid of any of my old race. And now," it added more hopefully, "maybe you've given me a chance to earn some forgiveness and at least regain the friendship of the de Dananns."

"Well, Pooka, you've already earned the friendship of one," Lugh told it heartily. "And I promise you my friendship and my help for as long as I may live."

The being's mood lightened with these words. The big lips drew up, forming a wide, if peculiar, grin once more.

"Young warrior, I've not heard fairer words from a man in many years. I thank you. Now, tell me your name."

"I am called Lugh Lamfada."

"And I am Shaglan," it returned, thrusting out a forepaw. Lugh saw the intent and clasped it with his hand. "Now we are bound, and I promise you that I'll serve you as faithfully." It nodded toward the skewered rabbits. "But for now, you'd best see to your food."

The meat was nearly done, and Lugh pulled one of the carcasses from the fire.

"We'll be needing to discuss which way you want to go," the

Pooka said. "I've learned the country well in my wanderings, and I think I know most of the de Danann settlements."

"I'm glad of that," Lugh said, greatly thankful for meeting this wondrous creature. "I lost my own charts when I was attacked."

"Then, if you'll leave it to me, I'd say we should—"

The Pooka's words were cut off abruptly as it jerked its head up, cocking the pointed ears forward to listen.

"Did you hear that?" it asked.

"I didn't hear anything," said Lugh. To him, the morning woods were silent except for the normal calls of birds.

"Odd," said the Pooka in a distracted way. "I was certain I heard it. Almost as if someone were calling me. But faint and far away." It shrugged the narrow shoulders in a very human gesture. "Ah well, no matter."

"I don't know," said Lugh, not willing to take any more risks. "The Fomor are still after me, you know."

"They're not clever enough to follow us here," Shaglan assured him.

"Not the Eirelanders maybe, but they've the help of those from the Tower of Glass."

"Have they?" the Pooka said, impressed. "Well then, maybe I should do a bit of scouting to be certain they're nowhere about." It climbed to its feet. "You finish that food and rest a bit more. When I return, we can be off."

It rose and headed into the trees. Even in its strange form, it moved with grace and silence, Lugh noted. He pulled himself more upright against a tree bole and began to gnaw on the roasted rabbit. It was tough and lean and stringy, but to the famished lad it tasted marvelous.

He allowed himself a few moments of complete relaxation as he ate. For the first time since losing the Riders, things seemed to be going his way. He actually felt hopeful again. He hadn't really done so badly, after all. He had been scorched and battered and torn and nearly killed three times, but he had survived. He had found help and a way to continue his mission. He didn't feel much the Champion, but at least he wouldn't fail in the task Manannan and his destiny had set for him.

He finished both the rabbits and rested a bit. But soon he found himself fretting about the Pooka. It certainly was taking a long time getting back.

Then he sat up abruptly, listening intently. This time he,

too, had heard a distant cry. But it was a sound that he recognized. It was the shrill neigh of a frightened horse.

Ignoring his stiffness and soreness in his alarm, he jumped to his feet, drew the Answerer, and ran through the woods toward the sound. It changed its nature as he went, from neigh to bellow to shrill scream to roar, each a bit louder and more desperate than the last.

The sound was just ahead of him now, and he burst through a last screen of brush into a tiny open spot on the trail. Across it, tangled in a snare of heavy ropes, hung the form of a bedraggled animal that looked somewhat like a lion. It was spinning slowly in the tangle its struggles had created. And as it swung toward him and he saw its eyes, he realized it was the Pooka caught there.

Without considering further, he ran forward to give the being his aid. But as it saw him it cried out in warning:

"Lugh, get back! It's a trap for you!"

The warrior leaped away as another snare was triggered beneath his feet, yanking up the net of ropes that would have caught him as surely as it had the Pooka. He moved to the center of the open space and swung around to see scores of figures burst from the woods on every side.

He was surrounded by the horrible, grinning faces of the Fomor.

"This time we'll be taking no chances with you," one of them announced. Fifty spear and sword points were directed toward Lugh, forming a solid, bristling ring. "You'll surrender to us now, or you will die."

Lugh turned, casting his gaze around him as the circle began slowly to close in. He saw no chances of escape this time. His new hopes were gone. Still, he would never let them take him to Balor any way but dead.

As he lifted his glowing sword and set himself for his last battle, his final thoughts were of Aine. He would have wished to see her once again, he told himself regretfully. What a fool he had been!

Then, at a sharp command, the Fomor drove forward together in attack.

XVII

MANANNAN'S ISLE

THE TINY CRAFT of Lugh's comrades flitted through the heavy mysterious fog.

Gilla, as usual, was humming merrily, but the Dagda watched around him constantly, warily. He didn't like this fog at all.

"There's things living in here, I've heard," he said. "How do you know they'll not attack us?"

"Manannan will see to that," Gilla assured him.

"And just how will he do that?" the Dagda challenged. "It's not likely he even knows we're here. He can't see us, can he?"

"He knows," said Gilla. "He's a most powerful man. It's hard to believe anyone could be quite so amazing, really!"

"I can hardly wait to meet this being," the Dagda said with some sarcasm.

"Well, I'm anxious to meet him," Findgoll said. "I've many questions to ask him. Why, just take this boat!" He had been examining the little vessel carefully for some time, shaking his head and muttering in awed tones. "It looks very plain, but for it to sail so swiftly, to carry our weight so easily, and to turn with such agility must take great magic indeed."

"You could credit my marvelous steering just a bit," Gilla said, pretending to be hurt.

"What was that?" the Dagda said suddenly, shifting forward to peer out into the curling white. There had been a brief splash of water there, like a wave striking against something.

"Just a fish leapin'" the clown said.

"Look there!" cried Angus, pointing past the stern.

A great hump had popped to the surface there and a long neck, like a serpent thicker than a man, had risen, lifting a flat head. It gazed on them with tiny, glinting eyes for an instant and then, as silently and swiftly as it had come, slid back beneath the waves.

"That was no fish," the Dagda stated boldly.

146

"I'll agree to that, right enough," said Gilla. "Some pet of the great Sea-God's, no doubt. Harmless to us."

There was a soft bump against the right side of the bow, shifting the course of the small boat slightly.

"What struck us?" Findgoll wondered. He peered over the side.

"Careful, there," warned the suspicious Dagda. "Something may leap up and snap off your head!"

A second bump on the right shifted the craft again. The fearless little Druid leaned across that side to look.

"Why, there's a large fish of some kind down there," he said. "It's swimming right along with us, bold as you please."

"There's another here," said Angus, on the left. "It looks as if it's escorting us along, swimming at the surface."

"They may be planning an attack on us," the Dagda said with some concern, lifting his war-ax.

"Ah, they're only friendly dolphins," Gilla said, laughing at the big man's alarm. "They're pilots for us, using those great, flat noses of theirs to put our boat on the right course through this fog. They're helping us. Can't I convince you that we're safe here? Manannan will see nothing happens to us."

"Clown, I don't see what it is that gives you such great confidence in him."

"He's promised to help us," was the clown's simple answer.

"That may be enough for you, but not for me," the wily old veteran said darkly. "I don't know him or why he should help us. Until I see his cauldron and hear him tell us to take it along with his good wishes, I'll keep myself on guard, if you don't mind." And to make his point more clear, he laid his massive war-ax across his knees.

"Do as you wish," Gilla said, grinning, "but, believe me, what I've said is as true as if you'd heard it from Manannan himself."

To that the champion only grunted in reply.

"If you're so knowing of this Sea-God's realm," said Angus, "how much longer is it to his isle?"

"Look ahead," Gilla advised.

There was a sudden brightening of the mist from grey-white to luminescent pearl, and then it was gone, the little boat tearing through the final layer of it like a fine blade cutting through a filmy cotton shroud. In an instant they were in the open sea, and the band of fog was rising up behind them in a high, solid barrier wall.

Before them was a low, sun-flooded isle, a soft green land
with slopes rising in lush swells to restful blue-grey hills, for-
ested and rich.

"There it is," Gilla announced triumphantly. "Manannan's
Isle. And, thanks to our pilots, I think the landing place is right
ahead."

The little ship swept them smoothly in through the shore
waves to a lazy curve of beach nestled between widespread,
welcoming arms of land. The vessel ran up onto the smooth
shore and grounded gently, with only a whispering hiss. Angus
leaped out first and drew the vessel above the inward rushing
of the waves. Then the others climbed out.

"There," said Gilla. "Now, didn't I tell you we'd come here
safe, and with almost no trouble at all!"

"I'm still waiting until it's all ended," the Dagda told him
stubbornly. He retained a ready grip upon his weapon as he
looked around him carefully.

Morrigan, who had not spoken once during the voyage, now
took a breath of air and spread wide her arms, lifting up the
dark cloak in a gesture of freedom and obvious relief. It was the
most expressive sign of human frailty that Gilla had ever seen
the raven-woman show.

"Are you certain this is the right place?" the Dagda asked. "I
don't see any signs of life. Where does this Sea-God live?"

"His home is that way," said Gilla, waving ahead. "Lugh
showed me when I visited here with him. That's where we'll
find the cauldron."

"Lead on, then," the champion ordered. "The sooner I see
this being, the sooner I'll feel better about all this."

Obediently, Gilla led them up a narrow pathway that went
inland from the shore. It crossed a low ridge of hills that
opened beyond into broad, flat plains of grass flowing away in
their own sea to the misty hills.

Gilla pointed ahead, toward the middle of the plains.

"There it is," he said. "Manannan's Sidhe."

"Sidhe?" Angus repeated.

"That's the name of the place where the Sea-God dwells,"
the clown explained.

The de Dananns looked ahead in puzzlement. They didn't
understand at first what they were seeing. In the center of the
level plain was only a large, smooth swell of grass-covered hill.

"What is it you're telling us, fool?" the Dagda said irritably.
"There's nothing there. Only that hill."

"The Sidhe *is* that hill," Gilla told him. "Come on."

As they moved closer to it, they recognized that what had seemed a natural hill was far too even, too rounded. They were looking at an artificial mound, but one of enormous size.

"Those strange warriors who came to Eire with Lugh," said Findgoll thoughtfully, "they are called Riders of the Sidhe. Was it from this place, from Manannan that they came?"

"They did," Gilla admitted. "I told you that Manannan meant to give you aid."

"But why didn't Lugh, or you, tell us before?" said the Dagda.

"It wasn't meant to be revealed then," Gilla answered simply. "But now there are many things you will have to discover." Including, he thought, the true identity of your foolish companion. He smiled inwardly, anticipating the effect this would have on them, especially the Dagda.

They continued along the path to the hill and up the side into an opening, a square passageway that led them into the dim interior of the mound. As the sunlight faded behind them, the darkness grew, along with the Dagda's wariness. It was too good a place for them to be taken in ambush again.

Then, with an abruptness that did take the visitors by surprise, the tunnel opened into an enormous space.

The company found itself looking down on and across the inside of a vast room with a dome-shaped roof. Clearly the interior of the hollow hill. Some lightweight construction unknown to them formed a sweeping curve of latticework to support the outer skin of earth. It was so large—actually, it seemed to them somehow much larger within than without— that it encompassed an entire countryside. Spreading out before them were rolling meadows, lakes, streams, woods, a whole complex landscape. It was, in fact, its own tiny world enclosed, complete with growing crops and grazing herds of sheep and cows.

Light was admitted through the highest point of the dome, which from the inside looked open to the sky.

"This . . . is his home?" asked the Dagda, openly stunned.

"It is all a bit much, don't you think?" said Gilla critically. "It's never seemed very comfortable to me. Not like a real home at all. Wants a few cozy places, it does. A fireplace and a few pieces of furniture. Maybe a tapestry or two. Still, I suppose it's shelter from the rain and snow."

"I think it's magnificent," said Findgoll, delighted. "But it's clearly not a real place. I mean, it must be magic that created it. A very powerful magic. A nature-controlling magic."

He looked around him and considered, his little face puckering with his thoughtfulness.

"And it's very familiar, somehow," he went on, sensing something in the aura of the place he couldn't define. "I feel a sort of comfort here that I've felt before." He looked to his comrades. "Don't you feel it?"

Angus shrugged, but Morrigan nodded sharply.

"As if we'd been here before," she rasped in an oddly softened voice, peering around her with glittering eyes.

The suspicious Dagda was too busy examining the place for dangers to let such ephemeral notions interest him.

"Where is Manannan?" he asked impatiently. "Where is the cauldron? We must be hurrying."

"I think that they'll be showing us from here," said the clown.

For, out of the country below them, a strange party of beings was now moving up to meet them.

Although they appeared to be human women, they resembled more a gathering of butterflies around autumn flowers. They drifted, floated, almost seemed to glide upward, on the gentle slope that led to the visitors' high point of entrance. All were in light, flowing gowns of warm, rich browns and reds and golds that shifted constantly, like fall leaves rustling in a breeze.

From somewhere music drifted upward with them, too, a light and cheerful air, filling the watchers with a sense of ease and a renewed vitality, washing away their weariness and care. The women moved to its rhythms with an extraordinary grace, a youthful litheness that combined a dance and a natural exuberance for life.

Angus found it quite sensual, and watched the approaching company with intense interest. He noted the women were all quite beautiful, with elegantly sculptured features, high foreheads, and large, luminous eyes. Their hair was mostly very fair, unbound in great waves about their shoulders.

The young warrior had never seen their like before, never heard such music. But this was not true of his father and the other de Dananns.

"Now I understand why I found the aura of this place familiar," Findgoll said in amazement. "These women are of the

Blessed Isles." He looked around him again. "This place is a home of Queen Danu's people!"

"But here?" asked the Dagda, himself bewildered by this discovery. "Why? Is Manannan MacLir from the Four Cities as well?"

All the visitors looked at Gilla at once. The clown only shrugged and grinned in his familiar, silly way.

"My friends, I think it's soon enough that you'll have the answers to all those questions," he promised.

The Dagda was about to demand to know how the clown was so certain about that, but he had no chance. The crowd of women came around them then, caught them up, and softly engulfed them in a warm, welcoming wave.

Angus looked around, falling quickly within the sensuous spell they cast. Smiling faces swirled around him. Light hands brushed his cheek, bodies and flowing gowns caressed his, and a captivating scent surrounded him.

"These are the people of Tir-na-nog?" he said in a dreamy way. "I'm sorry now I wasn't born before we left there."

"Easy, lad," Findgoll warned. "The people of Danu are lovers of all the pleasures of life, but it can become a bit heady for us mortal beings. Like too much of even the finest ale can."

Angus shook off the trance that had nearly claimed him and took a firmer hold upon his wits.

Though the visitors noted nothing odd in the behavior of the women, the disguised Guardian of the Sidhe did. There was something stiff in their movements, something frozen and fixed in the wide smiles and the bright eyes.

And there were rather fewer welcomers than he'd expected. His faithful followers normally swarmed to greet him on his returns, nearly drowning him in lavish affection. Of course, he had always found all that quite an irritant—rather like being assaulted by a pack of exuberant puppies—and had often been harsh in telling them to leave off such embarassing displays.

Apparently his warnings had worked . . . perhaps too well. These few women now seemed to be going through the motions without any real enthusiasm. He wondered if he had gone too far. He actually missed the rampant joy.

With gentle pressure, the bright company began to direct the visitors forward. Looking rather like a bull surrounded by a flock of birds, the Dagda glowered around him.

"What is this? Where are they wanting us to go?"

"To where your questions will be answered, I'd say," Gilla replied.

So, reluctantly, the big man allowed them to herd him along.

From the entrance to the mound, they moved down into the heart of the enclosed realm. They passed fields of plants of vivid colors and exotic shapes unknown in the colder climes of Eire. They moved through a grove of trees with smooth, limb-less boles and leaves like crowns of sharp spikes. Marvelous and varied types of beasts moved all about them. Gaudily plumaged birds swooped above, creatures in fur or scales scampered from their path. From one tree a being like a tiny and very hairy human hung by its tail and jabbered at them.

To the companions of Angus, these sights were only more reminders of the mystical land where they had once dwelt for a time. But to him, they were fabulous things that he had only heard about in childhood tales, not really believing. Now he believed. He sensed that, in such a magical place, anything was possible.

It was the people here who intrigued the young warrior the most. He saw more women, and men as well, playing in the fields, minding the grazing herds, tending the gardens and the planted areas. Along the edge of a small, clear pond, a group played at musical instruments—pipes and harps and some pieces he didn't know. It was they who created the melodies that filled the air.

"Everyone here seems so content," he remarked.

"Oh, that they are," Findgoll told him. "They laugh, love, enjoy, care for the living things, and draw their own powers from nature itself. Violence and hatred, fear and pain, are un-known to them."

"Now you can see why we had to leave them," the Dagda put in gruffly. "In time all our own people would have become like them."

"Would that have been so bad?" Angus wondered, again fall-ing under the seductive charms of the Sidhe.

"Wake up, boy!" the Dagda said sharply. "You sound like Bobd Derg! This isn't the way for us. It's their way. We must make our own."

Shocked back to reality, Angus understood. Still he sighed in regret. "It would be nice, though, to want only peace."

"Someday we may have it," his father said. "But we must

earn it. For now, in our world, the lack of a fighting spirit is deadly."

"Too much peace can be deadly in its way too," Gilla added. "For a man like you, Angus, this life would become boring very soon."

"I'd like to find that out myself," the young warrior responded with a smile.

By now the company had nearly reached the center of the Sidhe. As they came around a final grove of strange trees, they could see ahead a small, neatly rounded mound, a miniature of the outside of the Sidhe itself.

It was in the very center of the circular space, directly beneath the opening of the dome. Atop its smooth surface was a circle of upright stones. It was clearly toward this spot that they were making their way.

"It must be there that we'll meet Manannan," said Findgoll with growing excitement.

"That you will," Gilla assured him.

They splashed across a last, shallow brook and mounted the gentle slope to the top. The standing stones were shoulder-high pillars spaced evenly in a large ring, encompassing most of the level space. In a tight cluster near the center of this ring were another group of the Sidhe's inhabitants. Men this time, dressed in simple white tunics and trousers edged with silver design.

As the visitors came up to the stones, this party moved forward to meet them. The Dagda eyed them narrowly, wondering which of these fresh, boyish-faced men could be the great Manannan.

"Welcome," a tall, slender, golden-haired youth amongst them said. "Please come forward, into our sacred ring."

The men moved back to let the visitors pass through them. The company of women remained outside the stones.

Gilla led the others forward, but as he passed the men, he stopped in puzzlement. Before him, in the center of the circle, were only the burned-out remains of a fire.

He whirled about to look at the gathered people of the Sidhe, now bunched at the edge of the ring, watching them with those fixed, bright smiles.

"The cauldron!" he said sharply. "The spear! They're gone!"

Their smiles faded at that. They exchanged fearful glances. Then the same young man spoke.

"I am sorry," he said with welling sadness. "We had no choice."

"No choice at all!" another, iron voice suddenly clanged out in the vast silence of the Sidhe.

And from beyond the sheltering mound, a vast dark figure rose suddenly into view, fixing upon them the searing red light of the single, blazing eye.

BOOK III
BATTLE FOR THE SIDHE

XVIII

BALOR'S SURPRISE

FROM HIDING PLACES in the Sidhe all around the mound, scores of grey-clad Fomor soldiers, led by Balor's chief officer, Sital Salmhor, charged forth to encircle the little band.

But even those brief seconds were enough for Morrigan to begin her transformation.

"Stop her!" Salmhor yelled as he saw the shimmering light envelop her. "Seize her before she changes!"

His soldiers tried, but they met the weapons of Gilla, Angus, and the Dagda, who had formed a defensive triangle around Morrigan and Findgoll.

The swift movement of thier weapons knitted a fence of iron that kept the attackers back and gave Morrigan the extra time she needed to complete her change and lift upward, powerful black wings pumping to pull her clear.

The soldiers looked up helplessly as she rose far above their heads and began a straight climb upward, laboring toward the opening at the top of the dome.

"She'll try to fly out!" the officer shouted. "Bowmen, take positions. Shoot her down."

Two dozen bowmen moved from the lower ground onto the clear area on the mound's side. Two dozen of the lethal crossbows lifted upward to take careful aim at the large black bird slowly, desperately, fighting its way toward that high circle of light that meant freedom.

She was nearly to it now. The officer below lifted his hand and prepared to give the order to fire.

She glanced down and saw them. Knowing what to expect, she waited until the bolts were released and then she veered sharply aside. The bolts whooshed by her in a flock. Then, before they could reload, she had swept back upward toward the top of the dome.

Sital Salmhor watched in frustration as the great raven reached the opening and glided through, banking quickly away out of sight beyond.

Balor had kept his attention on the others of the party still holding his soldiers at bay on the mound. He swept his deadly eye across them again, lifting the lid the slightest fraction. The increase of heat was like a column of red-hot metal thrusting at them. The Fomor pulled back away from it.

"Now, the rest of you, surrender to me immediately, or I'll destroy you where you stand!"

Gilla and his comrades tried to glare boldly into the intense light, unafraid, but their bodies were already soaked with sweat.

"Why should we give up?" the Dagda challenged. "You'll kill us anyway."

"I see your point," Balor agreed. The eye shifted again, bringing the crimson beam to rest on the knot of Manannan's people. They faced it stolidly, but it was clear the heat was painful to them.

"Would you rather watch them flare up one by one, like moths caught in a flame?" the dark giant asked without emotion.

"I think he's got us," the disguised Sea-God said resignedly. "We can't let him destroy these people."

"You're right," the Dagda said. He dropped his war-ax to the ground. "You've won, Balor."

The lid dropped to a hairline slit, cutting off the heat. The gaze came back to the little band from Eire.

"Predictable," Balor commented. "Your own foolish codes of honor defeat you. Salmhor, have their weapons gathered."

The Fomor officer directed his men to take up the weapons dropped by the prisoners. The soldiers formed a bristling wall around them.

"You must think of us as very dangerous men," Gilla commented dryly.

"I will admit," said the Commander's hollow, clanging voice, "that you must be more tenacious then I believed. I never thought you would get this far."

"Sorry to say, we had to break two of your iron playthings

while we were about it," the clown said, grinning up at the looming figure.

"They can be replaced," Balor replied with no faint note of interest. "And it does appear that all your bravery was for nothing."

"What do you mean?" the Dagda asked. "We only came here to do a bit of visiting with the Sea-God."

"You came here to fetch a magical cauldron from this 'Sea-God' and take it back to save your people," Balor replied, each word a hammer stroke. "You have failed. Your warriors will remain starved and weak, easy prey to the forces of Bres. He will at last have his way—the final, total annihilation of the de Danann race."

"How do you know our mission, Balor?" Findgoll asked boldly. "How did you learn about Manannan's Isle?"

"I have my own methods," the giant answered. "They told me that Manannan was helping you. It was then I decided to visit this little isle. It has plagued my ships long enough. I discovered that the great terrors that guard his domain were no match for my powers." The eye flared wickedly. "It took only a day to burn our path through his band of mists. Though—how did you put it?—I'm afraid the 'Sea-God' will have several less playthings himself. The absurd sea creatures were too stubborn to run."

The disguised "Sea-God" opened his mouth to reply, but held himself back.

"It took two days of searching to discover this mound was a dwelling and to find a way in," the Commander went on. "The absurdity of his creatures and his mists are matched only by the complete idiocy of this place." The massive head swung slowly, sweeping the red gaze around the vast space. "It is totally impractical, defenseless, useless, filled with these unnecessary plants and these poor, childlike beings!" The gaze flicked across the huddled inhabitants again. "They ran like frightened does when we arrived. We'd managed to gather up only a few of them when you were seen arriving. These captives were told that they and you would die immediately if they failed to act normally when you entered. I wanted no chance of your escaping again. It worked quite well too. They're very docile."

The crimson eye moved back to the adventurers. "You know,

your journey here was futile from the start. This Manannan's powers are so weak, they would have been little use to you."

Stung by this harsh criticism, the clown-dressed Manannan was forced to a response.

"Maybe this Manannan hasn't really used his powers on you," he suggested.

"And why not?" Balor countered. "No, fool, he has no powers. He has run away with the others."

"You mean, you haven't captured him?" Findgoll asked.

"It is only a matter of time," the giant replied without concern in the booming voice. "We'll search him out and discover this cauldron, if it truly exists."

Manannan's heart lifted with new hope at these words. So they had not found the cauldron! That meant his own people had managed to spirit it and the magic spear away to some hiding place. There was still hope.

"I'm surprised you don't know where they are," he said mockingly to the threatening dark figure in the foolish manner of Gilla. "I thought the mighty Balor knew everything!"

"Your obvious madness is all that saves you from my wrath, clown," Balor clanged, his eye bathing the lanky figure with the red glow. "I know it was you who invaded my Tower with young Lugh. You will yet pay for that. For now, be silent."

"But, what about us, Balor?" the Dagda demanded. "Why are you keeping us alive?"

"You may have your uses," he said. "But we'll have to deal with them later. I've wasted enough time on you now."

He looked toward the Fomor officer. "Salmhor, have the guard take them all away and keep a watch on them. Especially our visitors from Eire."

"At once, Commander."

Salmhor signaled and a troop of men appeared from behind Balor, moving around him to the mound's crest. They were clothed in the same uniforms, but wore tight skullcaps of silver. Instead of the regular Fomor weapons, each carried a thick, lance-shaped device with a round, shining ball fitted to the head. The men looked hard and strong and disciplined, but their weapons seemed very little threat.

As they circled the prisoners, the regular Fomor troops withdrew to the bottom of the hill. These guards numbered only a score. Half of them surrounded the band from Eire while the others moved in around the inhabitants of the Sidhe.

They began to herd the people of Manannan away. They did it quite roughly, with shoves and blows from the butt ends of thier strange weapons. One of the slender young women was actually knocked from her feet by this harsh treatment. When Angus saw this, he reacted angrily, charging forward to her aid.

"Let her alone, you—"

One of the guards moved in, thrusting forward with the ball end of his lance. Angus ducked away, bringing up his arm to deflect the weapon. The ball touched him lightly on his shoulder.

There was a sharp crackle, and he was jerked violently backward, thudding heavily to the ground.

The Dagda bellowed in rage and advanced, but three more soldiers surrounded him and threatened him with their weapons. He stopped, eyeing them uncertainly. Meanwhile, Findgoll moved to Angus, kneeling at his side to examine the young man. He was awake, his eyes glazed by the energy that had stunned him.

"He's alive," the little Druid announced.

"Certainly," Balor remarked tonelessly. "The prods are only to encourage obedience, unless I order them used to kill. But I advise you not to challenge these men. They are my private guard. You'll find them to be highly trained."

Angus shook his head to bring himself back to full consciousness and climbed to his feet, determined not to show his pain. He eyed Balor stolidly, forcing back the urge to clutch his tingling arm.

"Now, if you're finished with your futile gestures of bravery, you will go with my guards."

The little group exchanged looks of agreement. There was nothing else they could do now. They moved away at the direction of the guards without further argument.

The glowing red eye of Balor followed them off the mound. Then it swiveled to Sital Salmhor.

"And you, get those other troops back at the search," the hard voice ordered. "I want this entire area covered and all its inhabitants brought to me! Do it if you have to tear everything apart. I want that cauldron and I want Manannan MacLir!"

Lugh's battle was savage, desperate, and final.

Knowing he couldn't win, the young warrior fought wildly,

swinging the great Answerer in both hands, making bold, deadly sweeps about him at the circle of nightmare faces.

The very numbers of the Fomor horde told against them, for they were pressed in tightly, and it hampered their movement and use of weapons. But their thick, bunched bodies were easy marks for the gleaming blade hewing through them, carving trails of blood. Around the swiftly moving champion, the bodies piled up.

Still, Lugh knew it was only a matter of time. He was already weak. The surge of energy that had carried him into this fight was ebbing away. He had a score of new wounds, minor but all draining his blood until his body shone pinkly with the crimson mixed in his sweat.

Above him, the Pooka itself was struggling desperately to tear free of the woven strands. But its efforts only entangled it further. Seeing Lugh's strength waning, his swings growing more labored, it shouted encouragement to him.

"Don't give up, Lugh. Hold on! Help is coming!"

Lugh didn't think the Pooka was going to free itself in time to help him. And if it did, it would only be killed itself. Yet he fought on, putting his will into holding the Fomor off just another moment. It was a game, his weary mind thought. A final and very deadly game for him.

The end came suddenly. A Fomor dove forward, impaling himself on the Answerer which tore out through his back. He fell, his heavy body dragging the weapon down. Lugh yanked back on it, but in the brief movement, his guard was down. A second Fomor drove in, his blade plunging deeply into Lugh's side.

Lugh freed his sword and staggered back, pulling himself off the point with a grunt of pain. He managed to sweep the Answerer up, slicing the Fomor's boar face across the snout. But still off balance, badly slowed, he couldn't turn fast enough to parry another assault from the rear. A short, burly, sluglike warrior leaped upon his back, striking downward with a dagger.

It hit the shoulder blade and glanced off, slipping sideways instead of sinking straight in. It didn't kill Lugh outright, but it finished him. He shuddered and all his strength went from him. As the Fomor dropped back, he fell forward, thudding to his knees, then toppled face down onto the blood-soaked earth.

He lay there, eyes open, conscious, but no longer able to move. Resigned to death, he passively awaited the final blow.

It didn't come.

There was some confusion around him. There were shouts and a loud clashing of arms and the screams of men. He grew impatient waiting for his death. With the strength of his left arm—his right seemed not to work—he rolled himself onto his side and managed to lift his head to see just what was holding these incompetent beings up.

He discovered that they were all facing away from him now, apparently engaged in some confused and violent struggle with another force more deadly than themselves. He saw the glint of weapons rise and fall, saw bodies crashing down in the packed mass. An arm, severed above the elbow, fell before his face, fingers still working to grasp a vanished sword.

Finally one Fomor detached itself from the rest and turned toward him. He looked up into a grinning shark-face and watched with calm detachment as the warrior lifted an already bloodied longsword to make the final stroke.

At last, Lugh thought with a certain relief. The release from all this pain. And just in time. He needed a good rest.

But then that face was swept away by the blow of a battle-ax that dissolved it in a spray of red. Another face loomed up instead, a very peculiar sort of face, not human, yet not monstrous. A friendly face. A face he knew.

The Pooka!

Curious, Lugh thought. It couldn't be here. It was some kind of fancy his dying was causing him.

"I told you help would come," it said, its voice a wavering, distant blur of sound.

Now Lugh knew he was in some final dream, for up beside the Pooka's broad face rose two others, bright and hazy like full moons rising on a misty night. The faces of Taillta and Aine.

XIX

DANU

THE OLD FIRBOLG shaman tightened the binding about Lugh's waist. The young warrior moaned softly with the pain of movement. Already his blood was soaking through the linen in a bright stain against the white.

They were back within the tiny clearing where the Pooka made his home. It was dark now, and above, the thick, arching branches of the encircling gnarled oaks seemed to form a solid roof lit to golden by many torches and a great fire.

Around the edge of the circular clearing, like silver idols set in the niches of some temple, the Riders of the Sidhe were spaced precisely, motionless, lances up, glowing with their own soft white radiance. Around them were grouped the warriors of the Firbolg tribe, the braver within the Riders' circle, the more timid well behind them in the more sheltered, more familiar surroundings of the trees.

Across the fire from Lugh and the shaman sat the Pooka, back now in a roughly ponylike form, sitting on its haunches and watching its new friend being treated, great concern clear in its liquid brown eyes. Beside it stood Taillta and Aine, their faces betraying their own anxiety.

His ministrations completed, the shaman sat back on his heels and smiled down at the young man.

"There, lad," he said soothingly. "I've done all that I can for you."

"I know you have," Lugh told him graciously. His voice was irritatingly weak to him, and even forcing this much out was an effort. "I thank you for what you've done, here and before."

"Well, you rest now," the man said, putting as much encouragement into his tone as he could summon. "You'll be feeling much better soon."

But as he rose and turned away toward the two women his smile disappeared and he shook his head.

164

He passed around the fire to them, his face now registering a deep gloom.

"What is it?" Aine demanded, not wanting to accept the facts she had already guessed.

"The wounds are very bad. Neither one nor both would kill him. But he was already weakened, and he has suffered a great deal." He looked regretfully toward Lugh. "I'm afraid that what I can do for him is much too little."

"Too little?" Taillta repeated sharply. "I can remember your healing powers from my youth. It was said you could save any warrior not already in his grave!"

"My powers can't overcome those of life and death. Not even those of the greatest de Danann physicians can do that. Perhaps I can heal his wounds, but only if he wills it. Only his own spirit can help him to live."

"Well, he's certainly not going to die!" Aine told him firmly. "That I'll not allow."

She and Taillta went to Lugh's side, kneeling down beside the silent form. He seemed asleep, and Aine was struck by how young he seemed, his face relaxed, the marks of weariness and wear softened by the fire's light. He looked like the innocent and frightened boy she had first seen in Tara's hall, boldly facing the treacherous Bres. How much had happened to them since!

His eyes fluttered open as he sensed the presences near him. He looked toward the two women and his face lit with his joy.

"Ah, it's very glad I am to be seeing you again," he said with such great depth of feeling that Aine felt the tears welling into her eyes. She blinked them back, putting on a hearty, matter-of-fact manner.

"You look well enough, considering your adventures," she told him. "You'll have to be getting up soon. There's a mission you've got to complete, and there's little time."

He smiled faintly at this but didn't reply. Instead he asked: "But how did you find me?"

"It was the Pooka," Taillta said. "Aine used her powers over the animals to call them and have them help us search for you. The Pooka heard her call and came to us. He told us where you were. We sent him back to tell you we were on our way to you. That's when he was caught. But we arrived soon after. My Firbolgs destroyed the whole Fomor band."

"How did you get their help?" Lugh wondered.

"Taillta is now the chieftain of their tribe!" Aine announced proudly. "She killed their old leader. He'd betrayed her father to the Fomor long ago."

"I remember him," said Lugh. "And I know the skill of the woman who taught me to fight. I would like to have wagered on that match."

He laughed at this, but he started coughing. The strain on his back wound drew him up sharply with the pain. His smile vanished and he sank back, paler, weaker, more of his vital spirit drained away.

Anguished, helpless, the two women could only watch. After a few moments, he found the energy to speak again.

"Aine," he said, lifting a hand to her. She grasped it in both of hers. It was very cold. "Aine, I'm happy you found me. I'm happy that the Riders weren't destroyed. Now I'll know that the mission can still go on, even though I've failed in it."

"You haven't failed," she told him firmly. "You couldn't have avoided this. It wasn't your fault."

"It was. I was a fool. I shouldn't have gone into that ringfort like some curious young pup. I let myself be trapped."

"If anyone is a fool, it's Manannan. He shouldn't have made you go alone. I should have been with you."

"No!" he said. "In that he was right. Better that you were safe, that you could go on. If he was wrong, it was in thinking me a champion."

"You are," she insisted.

"No, Aine. I don't believe that. I never have. It was my wanting to help the de Dananns, my thinking that I really was meant to succeed that made me go on. Now I see that my destiny was false. It was luck that got me as far as it did. That and your help. Now I've no luck left. I've made the de Dananns' defeat the more certain. They need no more of such a champion as that."

"I've never heard you talk like this before," she said in despair.

"Too much has happened to me, Aine. It's worn me out. I don't want to try to fight it anymore. I only want to rest."

She looked into that pale face, aged by the marks of pain as he forced himself to speak. She knew that it was her own brother's use of him that had finally broken his courageous heart. This time she couldn't stop the tears that rose in her eyes, slipping down to draw their gleaming trails across her cheeks.

He lifted up his hand and touched the softness of one cheek, gently wiping away the tear with his caress.

"The only regret I had in dying here was that we'd last parted in anger, and that I'd not see you again to ask if you forgive me."

"You know I do," she said. "And nothing will ever keep me from your side again."

He shook his head. "No. That can't be. You have to go on from here. Take the Riders. Complete the mission or the de Dananns will be destroyed. Promise me you will. Promise . . ."

The hand slid away. The eyes dropped closed and the face relaxed into lines of painless repose.

"No, Lugh!" Aine cried out in her agony. "Don't die. I love you!"

She dropped her head forward, pressing her lips to his with such intensity it seemed she meant to will her own life force into him.

But there was no response.

She looked up wildly at Taillta, who gazed helplessly, tearfully, down at the boy she had raised. She was a hard and practical woman who had defied death all of her years, but in the face of this, she too was stricken with despair.

"Taillta, we can't be too late!" said Aine. "Not after all this! We can't just watch him die!"

"He is in his last sleep now," the old shaman said gently, moving up beside them. "At least his end will be a peaceful one."

Aine looked around at the Firbolgs gathered, hushed by the scene, at Taillta and the shaman, at the Pooka, its ungainly head hung in sorrow. She looked at the circling Riders and a new determination rose in her.

"No!" she said fiercely. "It is not the end! I will not let this be the end!"

Wiping the streaming tears savagely from her face, she rose to her feet. She lifted her head toward the canopy of trees and held up her arms. Her voice, fired by her will, rang out commandingly.

"Mother Danu!" she called. "By all the powers you have given us, by the task you have set for us, by the forces of Tir-na-nog, I call you here to me."

The occupants of the clearing watched her with curiosity, bewildered by her strange action, but caught up by the intensity of it. They all stood frozen, waiting.

Nothing happened.

"Danu!" Aine cried more stridently. "You cannot desert us now. You will hear me and you will answer me. I demand it!"

A sudden wind swept upon them from the west, soaring through the wood, yanking the treetops with a brutal force as it boomed through them.

The Firbolgs looked up fearfully toward the sound. Their torches flapped sharply in the gust, flickering out. Seized by feelings of terror, the warriors crouched down, pulling their cloaks tightly about them. In the rising wail of the great wind sweeping above, they heard the keening voices of their spirits all loosed upon them at once.

Only Aine and the Riders defied the blast. The shining horsemen sat unmoved, untouched. Aine turned directly into the wind, letting it pull her cloak away from her slender body, letting it turn her long hair to a shimmering stream behind her as she set her youthful face in defiant lines. For she knew that her plea had been heard and answered.

Above the trees now, the torrent of wind was drawing with it a line of heavy clouds, forming a dense, dark ceiling that blinked out the points of starlight as it came and pulled a cover across the moon that even its bright glow couldn't penetrate.

A darkness like a thick black liquid poured into the surrounding woods and filled them up. The gnarled boles of the encircling trees seemed to melt into a single, solid wall. The branches interlacing high above seemed to blend into one great dome of blackness. Soon the dark had made a huge cylinder of the clearing, sealing all the occupants within.

Once it had formed, the wind died abruptly, cut off as if a door had been swung closed. An ominous silence fell upon the clearing. It was not a natural silence, not just the silence of stilled animals and hushed men, but something more profound. A barrier created by some enormous power had isolated this place from the realms of mortal men. Contact with another, secret realm could now safely be made.

Only a single source of light was left within the space. It

came from the Riders of the Sidhe. At first it was a pale silver shimmering, like a winter's full moon reflecting from a pond, its flickering fragments of brightness providing an eerie illumination for the scene. But it began to increase swiftly. The fitful glow became a steady one. The Riders radiated an energy that seemed generated within, blooming outward, suffusing their forms, turning their outlines hazy. Then it concentrated, drawing together and floating upward, climbing from each Rider's body along his slender lance to its point.

There the energy formed into a ball of iridescent light, so intense that it was nearly blinding, forcing the awed watchers to turn away or shield their eyes. The terror-stricken Firbolgs trapped within the cylinder of blackness cowered deeper beneath their cloaks, recalling the last time such a light had appeared.

As the luminous bubbles swelled to a bursting point, each one erupted with a bolt of silver lightning that arced across to the lance beside it, then on around the circle, leaping from point to point. The crackling streaks of energy left behind slender, glowing tendrils, like threads of finely drawn silver. They intertwined as they danced about the ring, weaving an intricate pattern that rested upon the upraised lance points. White radiance flooded the enclosed space, banishing all shadows, washing away all color, drowning everything in a shining pool.

But once the circuits were all completed and the circle closed, the ring of light began to rise upward. It lifted slowly, forming a silver wall. Just below the black canopy of trees it began to curve inward gracefully, the circle shrinking toward the center like the contracting pupil of an eye. Finally it closed completely and a dome of brightness had been created high above.

Aine looked up toward it, preparing for what she knew would be coming now. For, in the center of that glowing dome, the enormous image of a human face was beginning to take form.

It was a woman's face, of simple, subtle lines, beautiful in a familiar, comforting way, like a bright spring afternoon, but awesome, too, like the marvel of a sunset striking through towering banks of clouds. The staring old shaman had never seen a face like it. But Taillta and Aine knew it, and so did the disbelieving Pooka who breathed the name in awe:

"Queen Danu!"

The expression of the face was marked by worry now. The soothing, smooth voice was rippled with concern.

"Aine, what is wrong? Why have you summoned me here?"

"I need you help, Danu," Aine told her tersely, having no time for graciousness. "Without it, Lugh will die."

The voice and the lustrous golden eyes filled with great sorrow. "I am sorry for that. But you know I am not able to give you help. My powers to act in Eire are limited. I am bound by our laws not to interfere. I have already done everything I can. You know that, Aine. The rest must be done by you and by the de Dananns alone."

Aine was not to be convinced. Her chin set stubbornly.

"Lugh is dying," she replied forcefully, her passion making her bold. "It is our fault that he is. We caused him to be here."

"We gave him only the chance to act," Danu reasoned gently. "The choice was his."

"No!" Aine countered with heat. "The choice was never really his. We've never truly given him one. From his birth we've manipulated him to bring him to the point where he had to act. We've made him a tool to serve our own purposes. It's our fault."

Danu seemed to take no offense at this. The soft, amiable voice continued in regretful and reasonable tones.

"I understand why you feel this way, but it is destiny working here, not us. We are only the instruments of Fate. No act of ours can change it. It will happen as it must. I am truly sorry, my dear girl. It pains me to be so cruel in this, but I have no other choice. I cannot directly interfere."

"You must," Aine pleaded, desperate now to find some way of convincing her queen that she could help. "This isn't direct interference, Danu. The de Dananns must still choose to fight themselves. Lugh can only help them if they find the will. And, it is the Prophecy that declared he would help them destroy the Fomor power. The Prophecy has set this fate for him. So, if you act to make it happen as it is meant to, aren't you only playing out your proper part?"

The face of the being above was still for a long moment, clearly absorbed in thought. Aine held her breath, feeling the racing of her heart.

Then, slowly, a smile dawned on the Queen's face, like the sun gliding from behind its masking cloud, bathing all below in its warming light. And as she spoke again, her voice was also warm with amusement.

"You are a very clever woman, Aine. I understand more clearly why Manannan treasures you. You've reasoned very well. All right, then. I will help you with my powers."

The smile faded, and the Queen's expression turned grave.

"But, believe this: I can heal his wounds, restore the strength to him, but I cannot save his life despite himself. His spirit is as weakened as his body. His hope is gone. Without them, the rest is of no worth at all. We must see if we can reach his inner will and give new life to it."

Her lustrous eyes turned their light upon Lugh. Her voice addressed him in gently coaxing tones.

"Listen to me, Lugh of the Long Arm. You have chosen to be our Champion. You cannot desert us now. All Eire is in danger. You must help to save it. You must give the de Danann people the will to fight. Only you can do it. Only you!"

The young warrior lay unmoving, his pale, lifeless face not showing the slightest sign that he had heard.

"Now, Aine," Danu said, "kneel down by him. Place your hands upon his chest, flat, side by side."

The girl did as she was commanded.

"Through you will go the powers. If he wills them to work, he will be restored. If not, he will die. In the end, no one can make another's fate for him. No power is that strong. Do you understand, Aine?"

"Yes, my Queen," she answered.

"Then, good luck to you. I will not be able to give you such help again!"

The face faded, leaving behind the bright dome of glowing light. Then it fell back, the pupil opening wide again, the ring spreading out as it sank down upon the Riders of the Sidhe.

As it did, the mystic warriors dropped their lances forward in one movement. The silver rings about their hafts jingled with a high, clear music. The shining lance heads, carrying down their wreath of interweaving lights, were all pointed toward Aine. She braced herself, ready for the transfer of magic power. The Riders' glow increased, once more filling the black cylinder. New strands of light arched out from each spear, joining at the girl. She felt the energy crackle across her body, tingling her flesh. She pulsed with it. It flooded over her, drenching her like hot liquid. It coursed down her bare white arms and they were afire. It collected at her hands, where they pressed to the chest of the dying Lugh, and made them luminous.

But the force stayed there. It wasn't being absorbed by the young warrior, as if something in his body were blocking it. She felt it vibrating in her palms as it pooled and increased there, the light building to a near-blinding intensity.

"Lugh," she said urgently, leaning closer to him, "it is up to you! Remember what the Dagda told us once. The de Dananns must prove their desire to earn their place, or they will never be anything on their own. If you give up now, the same will be true of you! You said that you only wanted to be free to discover your own self. Maybe you aren't a champion, but you'll never have a chance to discover who you are until you've finished this. Please, for yourself, fight! Fight!"

The young champion's body began to convulse and he moaned in agony. He jerked violently back and forth, head twitching as if he were in a frantic struggle with some unseen force. This ended in an abrupt stiffening as he thrust his legs out rigidly, clenched his fists, drawing tight his muscles until the tendons in his neck and limbs stood out sharply, quivering in their tautness. It seemed the last, grim stage of his inner struggle, his spirit locked in a final death grip with his own weakness, every faculty left to him concentrated in the battle.

Then something within him gave way with the suddenness of a dam's bursting apart under enormous pressure. The pent-up energy pooled around Aine's hands gushed forth, sinking down, pouring into his body, filling it up with such radiance that it shone out from him, turning his flesh a translucent red through which his bones, his veins, showed as dark lines.

He convulsed again, uttering a sharp cry of pain as if some real fire were coursing inside him. But this torture was mercifully brief. Soon his body ceased its thrashing and began to relax. His breathing slowly returned to a steadier, more normal rate. The light within him faded gradually away and his color returned to a warm, healthy hue.

Finally his eyes opened. They focused, fixing a gaze of remarkably mild surprise upon the anxious face of Aine.

He smiled.

"Hello!" he said. "What's wrong? Have I been asleep?"

XX

MANANNAN'S SECRET

LUGH SLID THE Answerer into its sheath and buckled the weapon on.

"Are you certain you're feeling well?" the old shaman asked.

"It's amazing," replied the youth. He gingerly touched the wound in his side. "It's still a bit tender there, but it's nearly healed. I'll have quite a scar, though, to show the others."

Aine smiled. His spirits had been revived along with his strength. He was anxious to get on now that the Riders had been restored to him.

"We can't be wasting any more time," he said. "We'll have to rush to reach the other settlements, and even so we'll be late to meet the others returning with the cauldron. Shall we be going?"

He looked around at them, and then was struck by some factors he'd overlooked in his renewed enthusiasm to be off.

"Oh," he said, looking from his companions to the grey horse, "I just realized. Can the Riders carry all of us?"

"They won't need to, Lugh," said Taillta gravely.

He looked quizzically at her. "Why not? I want you all with me."

The older woman hesitated, then spoke out straightforwardly. "I've decided that I'll be staying here."

Lugh looked around at the Firbolgs gathered in the clearing. "What, stay here?" he asked. "With them?"

"They're my own people, Lugh," she told him. "It's time I was back with them. I've been away a very long time."

Lugh's youthful face registered his dismay. "But Taillta, we need you. I need you. All my life you've been by me, giving your help to me."

"You don't need my help anymore. I know that's true, even if you don't believe it yet yourself. Besides, I've done what I was

173

meant to do in this. The rest of it is up to you. My part is ended. I've got to be taking up my own life again."

"Not until the Fomor are destroyed," he argued stubbornly. "You have to help me get the vengeance for your people."

"I can help more by staying with them." She placed her hands upon his arms and spoke firmly. "You must see what it is I'm saying, Lugh. It was the hope of my father and of yours that the de Dananns live and share Eire in peace. They both died for that hope. If I stay here, maybe I can bring the Firbolgs to accept it now. Maybe I can bring them to believe that it is the Fomor who are our enemies. Then we will join you in seeing them destroyed. But no matter what happens, I am where I belong."

He looked into her eyes and understood that there would be no argument with her. She had always been determined, and always right as well. Reluctantly he nodded his assent. He even managed a smile.

"I will see you again, though," he said. "You will promise me that."

"Of course I will," she assured him. "Now, get yourself ready to go. You must hurry."

He nodded and moved away from her, leaving Aine to say her own good-byes. He noticed the Pooka and approached it.

The creature was standing at the side of the clearing, well removed from the others, looking a bit neglected and forlorn. The Firbolgs, harboring their own superstitious fears of the strange beings, stayed very far from it.

As it saw Lugh coming toward it, it brightened visibly.

"I thought you'd forgotten me," it said, "seeing as how you've no need of me anymore."

"Well, it is true that I don't need your help," Lugh admitted.

Its rising cheer sank again. Its huge, soft nose drooped.

"Oh," it said dismally, "I was expecting as much."

"And it would be dangerous for you if you did go with me," Lugh continued.

The whole body sagged in defeat now, the great head hanging forward.

"I suppose that's true," it said dejectedly.

"Still," Lugh went on matter-of-factly, "if you'd like to go, I'd certainly welcome your companionship."

The head lifted, the nose springing back.

"Really? Do you mean that? You'd not be tricking a trickster now?"

"I would not," Lugh said heartily. "I've pledged my friendship to you. I won't break that pledge."

"Then I would like to go with you. I'd be most proud to go!"

"Wait, now!" Aine protested. "You can't take this"—she eyed it critically—"this thing along with us."

"Why not?" Lugh asked, somewhat shocked by her harsh tone.

"Because he's a Pooka!" Aine exclaimed. "A Pooka's never to be trusted!"

"This one is," Lugh said stoutly.

The Pooka drew itself up and used its wide mouth to flash what it must have thought a winning smile at her.

"Just look at the evil expression on it," she said. "That's the face of a deceiver if I've ever seen one."

Lugh examined the Pooka's broad, inane grin and shrugged.

"I don't know," he said. "He rather reminds me of your own brother."

"Manannan's not to be trusted either," she shot back. "Lugh, we're taking enough risks without having him along with us. What use can he be?"

"You can never tell," Lugh replied. "He does have a talent that might be useful. He's very anxious to prove himself. And I've a feeling we just may need him."

She shook her head. "Well, this is all time wasted in our arguing, as there's no way it can really go with us. It can't ride the grey with us, and it can't keep up with the Riders on its own."

"But there is a way!" the being enthusiastically added. "Just watch!"

And before their startled gaze, it dwindled suddenly away, shrinking and altering radically as it did, until, in moments, it was so tiny its exact nature was impossible to define.

"Pick me up!" a faint, high voice called to them.

Lugh looked toward Aine.

"Go ahead," she offered. "I'm certainly not touching it."

He leaned down and extended a palm. The animal crawled quickly onto it. He saw that it was a round and furry mouselike being with a pointed pink snout well equipped with bristling whiskers.

"There!" it announced with a certain pride in its equally tiny voice. "I'll not be any burden to you this way."

Lugh held it out toward Aine. She glanced from the harmless-looking little beast to him, clearly wavering. Lugh made his final plea.

"Aine, he's saved me twice. He could have left me to die. He could have abandoned me instead of bringing you. I think he's earned our trust."

She sighed. "All right. All right," she said resignedly. "It can come. But you'd better see it doesn't come near me!"

"You'll not be disappointed in me," it told her, "that I promise."

Lugh carried it to the waiting horse and opened one of the carrying pouches slung across its back. He pulled it open and set the small animal carefully upon the supplies inside.

"You can ride in here comfortably, I think," he said.

"Just don't be nibbling at the food!" Aine warned it, swinging herself lightly onto the mount.

Lugh turned for a final good-bye to Taillta. She saw the look on his face as he approached and knew what he intended. As he raised his arms she put up a staying hand and spoke firmly.

"None of that, my boy. I'm a chieftain now. How would it seem to these hard warriors of mine to see me being hugged by you?"

He stopped, abashed by this. But she smiled at him warmly.

"I know what you feel," she said. "I'll always know that. So, no more sorrow or farewells. Just be off with you. Time's flyin' like the wind itself."

"All right, then," he said, smiling in return. "But I'll be seeing you soon."

He went to the horse and climbed on, settling himself behind Aine for the swift journey. Both of them lifted hands in a parting wave to Taillta, then Lugh gave the Riders the command to go.

Taillta moved to the head of the warrior band she now commanded and watched as the horsemen flowed away in a silver stream through the dark trees. As they passed from sight, she turned to the old shaman and spoke with authority.

"I'll want the other chieftains gathered for a talk," she told him. "They're all to know that the daughter of MacErc has returned."

He smiled, anticipating their reactions. "There may be those not so happy at that news."

"Just as well," she answered with satisfaction. "There's little I love so much as a good fight."

"My father, it may be that the Fomor will fail," Ruadan said earnestly.

Bres looked up from his eating. He and his son were in a small pavilion, erected for his personal comforts, quite separate from the growing Fomor army.

"What have you heard that makes you believe so?" the former High-King of Eire demanded. He had been expecting more positive news from his spy.

"The Riders of the Sidhe returned to Tara unharmed. Lugh was separated from them, but there is no way to know if he is dead. The girl, Aine, has taken the Riders. She can complete the mission, call the de Dananns to host."

"Aine!" Bres said angrily. "She has helped Lugh to thwart me before."

"These special Tower forces may have failed to stop the Dagda's party too," Ruadan added. "The survivors of their escort returned to Tara to say they had been ambushed, but that the Dagda was going on with Morrigan, Findgoll, Angus, and this clown called Gilla."

"They all escaped?" said Bres in disbelief. "It's as if some charm protected them!" He slammed a fist to the tabletop in his frustration. "The powers blast that arrogant Tower lot. A great help all their forces have been to us."

"Be easy, Father," Ruadan said soothingly. "They may yet succeed. And, in the meantime, they have at least delayed the de Dananns in restoring their army."

"Perhaps, boy," he said. "Perhaps that will be enough. Our own forces are gathering faster than I expected. As soon as enough have gathered to overwhelm the de Dananns, we will march. For you, return to Tara. Keep up your watch. Play the innocent servant to Nuada until the very end. When it is over, you can come and take your proper place at my side."

"Too bad about Mother," the boy said.

"What do you mean?" asked Bres.

The boy fixed his father with a hard, cruel look that nakedly revealed the Fomor heart behind the puppylike façade.

"She is a de Danann," he said flatly. "She will have to die with the rest."

Axes chunked rhythmically into the trunks of the strange trees, cutting easily into their soft, stringy wood. The party of Fomor soldiers were wielding their tools with tireless efficiency, methodically working their way through the little grove. One by one the exotic, graceful trees fell with a soft whisper of regret, crackling down upon their piled fellows.

The captives watched this razing helplessly.

"Such beautiful trees," Findgoll said in despair. "How can those animals destroy them so wantonly?"

"The Fomor care nothing for beauty," the Dagda said, striding back and forth in his frustration. "Their minds are ice and iron. They'll find what Balor wants, no matter what they have to do. Before they're finished, there'll likely be little left of this place."

It certainly seemed as though he was right. More parties of Fomor were busily scouring the Sidhe, seeking any place that might hide objects or men. They were probing the streams with poles, turning up rocks, trampling fields and gardens, tearing out foliage. The whole bright, gentle world within the Sidhe was being ravaged brutally. And Balor, from his throne atop the mound, oversaw it like the graven image of some ancient god of death, dark and grim and terrible.

From their own position, the captives could see only a little of the activity within the Sidhe. They were being held in a hollow some distance from the mound. There the special guards of Balor could keep them easily penned. They patrolled in watches, changing at regular intervals. Always a third of them kept up the guard, unceasingly circling their prisoners, constantly on the alert.

The Dagda snorted at them as he made his own restless circuit, but paused as he noticed Gilla, lying back on the grass, lanky form spread comfortably, apparently quite at ease.

"Well, it's certain you don't seem much distressed by this," he said accusingly, stopping beside the being to glare down, hands on hips.

The clown lifted his shaggy brows to peer up at the figure looming over him. His eyes showed his amusement as he lightly replied: "There really isn't much that we can do about it, is there, now?"

"You can't be so indifferent to this . . . this violation of such a marvelous place," Findgoll said, his tone one of shock. "Look what those awful Fomor are doing!"

Gilla Decaire glanced about him and nodded. "They seem to be having a good time at it. Do you think it's something in their natures?"

"Ah, can you never be serious, fool?" the Dagda said in disgust and wheeled away to resume stalking.

"I'll admit, I've trouble understanding you myself," Findgoll remarked to Gilla. "Only a madman could watch this happening without feeling anger in his heart. And I've known you long enough to be certain you're no madman."

The look of amusement died in the clownish face.

"I don't like seeing the waste, really, old friend," he replied with more gravity. "And someday they will surely pay for it." He shrugged then, and the more frivolous tone returned. "Meanwhile, it's harmless enough violence they're doing, and it's certainly a good waste of their time. That gives more to us."

"Time?" the Dagda growled as he passed on another circuit. "Time for what?"

"Time for Morrigan to bring some help to us."

"And what help can she bring us in time?" he asked derisively. "Tara is too far."

"You've forgotten Lugh," said Gilla. "He should be waiting for us on Eire's shore right now. I'm certain Morrigan's thinking that same thing. With his help, we might still find a way of completing our little task."

"You've some mad vision of your own that's made you believe this can happen," the scornful champion declared. He waved a hand around at the searching Fomor. "But I've the cold reality before me. Look at them. How much longer do you think it'll be takin' that lot of bloody scavengers to find your cauldron and your precious Manannan?"

"Oh, as to that, they can look just as long as they don't get tired of it," the clown told him. "Forever, in fact. It's possible they might come across the cauldron, though I doubt it, but I can say for certain that they'll never find Manannan MacLir out there." He waved about at the vastness of the Sidhe.

"What do you mean?" the Dagda demanded, eyeing the lanky man narrowly. "Why not?"

"Because he isn't out there."

"He's left the Sidhe then?" asked Findgoll.

"Not exactly," the one called Gilla answered in a coy way. He looked around him carefully to be certain no guards were close by. Then he gestured the two closer. Doubtful but curious, they moved in. He sat up and they both bent down to him.

"You see," he said in a confidential tone, "I'm Manannan MacLir."

The Dagda straightened up, hooting with laughter.

"Ha! That's a fine one, that is! You, Manannan!"

"Quiet now," the man in the clown disguise cautioned. "Let's not announce that bit of news to Balor. I knew you'd react that way, but it's the truth."

"You finally, actually, have gone fully mad," the big man said with emphasis. "I'll have no more of you." And with that, he turned his back in a gesture of finality.

But Findgoll stayed where he was, eyeing the clownish figure uncertainly. Manannan turned his attention there.

"You see," he said, dropping the affected tones of Gilla, "I was going to have to reveal myself to you anyway, once we came here."

"You'd not jest with us?" the little Druid asked. "Not on a thing like that? You really are this Sea-God?"

"Of course," he said heartily, but then added, more modestly, "well, not a Sea-God actually. Although I do have some very interesting powers."

Findgoll looked into those clear, light eyes. He felt the power there, noticed an aura with his own druidic powers that he had never sensed before in the clown. He considered, analyzed, and then nodded.

"I believe you," he said with assurance.

Not believing his ears, the Dagda spun around to them again.

"Findgoll! You're not letting him pull you into this? You're ravin' too!"

"I said I'd always known Gilla wasn't mad. And if you'd think, you great lump, instead of bellowing, you'd see that it explains a great deal about our strange comrade. Like why he was so close to Lugh, and how he brought us here and got us through the fog safely."

The Dagda wasn't convinced. "If he's this 'Sea-God,' why doesn't he use his powers to help us now? Answer that!"

"I'm supplied only with powers over the sea," Manannan explained pleasantly.

"Mighty poor ones if they let Balor walk in here."

"If I'd been here, he wouldn't have," Manannan assured him. "At least I'd have given him a tussle for it. It was a great surprise to me that Balor thought to strike here. I would never have guessed he had the ability to anticipate our moves the way he's done or to discover the link between me and your uprising. I made a mistake in underestimating him." He fixed them with a hard gaze. "I don't ordinarily make mistakes."

He looked up toward the black figure and went on more thoughtfully.

"No. There must be something more to our Balor that I didn't take into account. Something very deep and dangerous, I think. Even more dangerous than he is. I'd surely like to find out what it is."

He shrugged and his mood lightened again. "Anyway, that's for later. For now, we must keep my identity a secret, if we can. That way I may yet get a chance to use my powers against him."

"Balor will give up the hunt sooner or later," Findgoll noted.

"But maybe before that, we'll have a chance to escape."

"If you are Manannan," the Dagda said, very guardedly, "why have you kept it a secret from us all this time?"

"I had to be able to work in Eire unknown to you," he answered simply.

Findgoll was more interested in another point.

"Then you are from Queen Danu, like this Sidhe and these people?" was his question.

"I am."

"If that's so, I demand that you explain to us just what it is you and this Sidhe of yours are doing here!"

"You've certainly earned the right to know it," the tall man answered with real gravity. "And it was something I was going to tell you anyway. This isn't quite the way I'd planned on doing it, but I do think it's time that I revealed everything to you."

XXI
QUEEN DANU'S PLAN

"I THINK WE should talk someplace where we can't be overheard," Manannan recommended. "Over here."

He led them to the gathered inhabitants of the Sidhe, who had all bunched into the center of the circular hollow, farthest from the patrolling guards.

"Where's Angus?" Manannan asked. "He should hear this too."

"From the look I saw in his eye, I'd say he was up to a bit of dalliance," his father said. "I'll get him."

He moved into the group, most of whom were seated on the ground, talking in soft tones or watching their home being systematically destroyed. Their faces mirrored their total dismay at this, and the Dagda guessed it likely that most of these young people, protected all their lives, had never experienced such savagery, indeed, probably had no way to comprehend it. He noticed that here and there, some were putting on a braver front, even playing at harps or pipes in an attempt to ease the atmosphere of fear.

He called to Angus as he moved through them, still feeling rather like a great bull amongst a flock of birds from the fluttering, half-frightened looks he drew. He recalled that he had always felt that way amongst the people of Danu. To his relief, Angus finally responded and rose from where he had been seated, comforting with all the fervor of his young soul a gathering of the women of the Sidhe.

"Not too busy, I hope?" his father asked dryly.

Angus colored with embarassment. "I was . . . ah . . . trying to keep them from being so afraid."

The Dagda glanced around at the collection of exceptionally beautiful young faces looking up toward his son with warm smiles and ardent expressions.

"I think you've succeeded," he said. "Now, come with me."

"Do you have to leave us?" one asked, her caressing voice tinged with disappointment.

"I'll be back," he promised as he moved away, very reluctantly, at his father's side.

"They think I'm a great warrior!" he said, in a distant, happy way.

"A good thing they don't know the truth," the Dagda answered tersely. "Shake loose of your dreaming, boy. There's no place for it now!"

The effect of that voice on Angus was like that of a sudden dunk in a winter sea.

They rejoined the others and moved farther into the midst of the company. Manannan spoke quietly to several as they went, and they began to pass his words along. A general murmuring of talk began around them, and more instruments were lifted in light melodies. By the time the four had reached the center, they were surrounded by a soft but constant haze of sound.

"That'll keep any unwanted ears from listening in," the disguised Sea-God said. "Let's sit here."

He dropped down on a small, clear patch of grass and the others joined him. Not knowing what this sudden meeting was all about, Angus looked puzzled.

"The clown here has told us he's really Manannan," his father explained, his voice still reflecting his own doubt.

"Gilla? Manannan?" Angus said, and his expression as he looked at the long, ragged personage indicated he shared his father's doubts.

"It doesn't really matter whether you believe me or not," Manannan told them. "I owe an explanation of all this to you, and I'm going to give it. All right?"

They agreed to listen, however skeptical.

"Once you saw the Sidhe, you'd have to know of Danu's involvement here. My concern is to make you see why it was necessary."

"True enough," Findgoll agreed. "When we left Tir-na-nog to return to Eire, she promised us that she would not interfere in our winning our own place there."

"And so she has not," he insisted. "Everything the Tuatha de Danann have done has been by their own will. But, you see, she knew that you would face some difficulties in Eire, and she at least wanted you to have a"—he hesitated over the exact word—"well, a sort of guardian."

"A guardian!" the Dagda repeated indignantly.

"She knew you might resent that," Manannan said quickly. "She understood that you had to leave Tir-na-nog and return to Eire to prove yourselves. But that didn't mean she wasn't going to try to help you in any way she could. You wouldn't expect that, would you?"

"Of course not!" Angus heartily agreed, and received a cold glance from his father, who wasn't quite so easily convinced.

"So, Danu sent me here to do whatever I could," the man went on brightly. "But what I do is governed by some very strict conditions. I'm never to influence or interfere in any decisions you might make. And none of the magic of Tir-na-nog is to be used in Eire except by the free choice of your people."

He gestured around him at the enormous room. "This Sidhe was established as a link between Eire and Tir-na-nog. It was protected by the fog and by the rumors of the monstrous 'Sea-God' that I spread personally." He grinned in the old, Gillaish way. "From here I was to keep watch on Eire, reporting back to Danu on events."

"You've done much more than that," Findgoll pointed out. "You helped us for years in that clown disguise."

"I did," he openly agreed, "and it was great fun. But, I was using none of the powers of Danu. I have only the abilities of an ordinary man in Eire. My powers are good only upon the sea. Another of the conditions set by my Queen."

"Why is it you were the one sent?" the little Druid inquired. "I don't remember seeing you during our time in Tir-na-nog."

"Because I was never there," he answered. "I'm a bit of an outcast to my people. I never could adjust to their quiet life. So, I've wandered most of my days, seeking adventure of some kind."

"I can understand that well enough," said the Dagda, unbending a little. He had to admit to himself that no matter how strange the clown had been, he and the champion shared a love of action.

"Thank you," the tall man responded graciously. "In any case, my talents have never been appreciated there, until this need arose. I was the only one of Tir-na-nog at all suited for Danu's mission. So I was chosen by her, with a certain distaste, I'm afraid. I don't think even she really understands me.

"Of course I took the job at once, thinking what marvelous

adventure it would be! But most of it has been quite boring, until recently. Most of the time I just waited."

"Waited?" Findgoll repeated. "For what?"

"For the time when your rising would come. Oh, Danu knew all about that. When Lugh was born, she'd forseen that he would be the one to lead you against the Fomor. Unfortunately, Balor also learned of the Prophecy. So, it became part of my task to see that Lugh survived to play his role. I managed to keep him hidden until he'd reached manhood, then sent him back to Eire."

"So that's were he was for all these years!" said Findgoll.

"But, what about this magical cauldron?" the Dagda wanted to know.

"That? Oh, that's one of the Four Gifts," Manannan said. "Each of the Four Cities provided one, to be used by the de Dananns, should they choose to use them. Of course, since Danu cannot take her magic into Eire, these objects must be taken there by de Dananns themselves. That's why you had to fetch the cauldron. Two other gifts Lugh took there. One was his own sword, the Answerer. The other was the Stone of Truth he used to prove Nuada the rightful king."

"The Lia Fail!" Findgoll exclaimed. "Of course. We wondered how it had come there from Tir-na-nog."

"You said four gifts," put in Angus. "What is the fourth?"

"A spear with a point blazing with such energy that it has to be contained by a special liquid. My people must have managed to hide it with the cauldron. And it seems that it's one thing, at least, our one-eyed Commander doesn't know about."

"When will it be used?" the young warrior asked.

The tall man shrugged. "I don't know. When the time comes for it, I suppose, as with the other gifts. The High-Druids of each city used their powers to decide on a gift. So far they seem to have chosen well." He looked around at his companions, adding with emphasis, "But understand me, none of these gifts, or any of the things I've done, has interfered with what you've done in Eire. Your choices to act and your own will have brought you here."

Plagued by doubts, the Dagda shook his head.

"I don't know. In taking any of her help, aren't we saying that we can't win Eire by ourselves?"

"And if this cauldron didn't come from Danu, wouldn't we use it without this foolish worry?" Findgoll countered. "Didn't we come here for it freely enough?"

"He's right, Father," Angus added. "This cauldron will only help restore the strength the Fomor stole from us. It won't win the battle. We'll have to do it. This may be the only way we can give ourselves even a fighting chance."

"Your warrior pride can be put aside for now, at least," Findgoll said. "It's the survival of all our people that's important."

The champion looked from one to another of them, his face clouded with his indecision. But at last he knew there was only one choice to make.

"All right," he said heavily. "We'll take Danu's gift, and we'll keep your secret, Sea-God. At least for now." He gave a short, humorless laugh, glancing up toward Balor. "Of course, it's a fine thing for us to say all this, sitting in the shadow of that thing."

"Don't give up yet," Manannan told him. "There's still a chance. Remember the Morrigan."

Lugh threw another stick of bleached wood onto the little fire. There was a sharp, chill wind off the night sea, but here, sheltered in a little nest of rocks above the shore, the fire created a cozy pocket of warmth.

Around it in the open, oblivious to the wind and cold, the shimmering Riders sat, forming their protective ring, lances up, spear points glowing faintly with their energy.

The young warrior and his companions had completed their circuit of Eire and arrived at the rendezvous destination nearly two days late. Lugh had expected to find the others waiting there—probably impatiently, knowing the Dagda—with the cauldron. But they had seen no sign of life anywhere along the rugged coast. He and Aine had checked their chart many times to insure that this was, indeed, the proper place.

"I wonder if anything's happened to them," Lugh brooded, staring into the fire.

"I suppose it's possible," said Aine, seated close beside him, her cloak pulled about her legs for extra warmth. "If Balor knew about your mission, it's likely he knew about theirs. But, I can't believe he could do more than delay them. They're too clever and too hard. And they have Manannan with them."

"Your brother is not perfect, you know," Lugh remarked critically. "I've learned that, and you've said it yourself. And he's got no special powers in Eire."

"I know. And he is a great fool sometimes. But he does have a special talent for making things work out." She looked up thoughtfully into the night sky. "I wonder, sometimes, if Danu hasn't put some special, protective cloak on him. She acts as if she doesn't approve of him, but I think she secretly likes him."

"Queen Danu," Lugh said, remembering. "Did she really save me?"

"You saved yourself," she said emphatically. "Remember that."

He smiled. "All right. But you know what I mean. Did she really appear?"

"She did. And she gave me the power to heal you."

Lugh closed his eyes. "You know, I can almost see her, that face above me, but only as if it were some dream." He opened his eyes and looked at her. "The whole thing was a dream, and not very clear."

"It's just as well," Aine told him, with more sincerity than he knew. She was relieved to discover that he remembered so little of her own part.

"Do you think I could ever see Danu?" Lugh asked. "All of her, that is?"

"I'm certain she would like to meet you," Aine said. "But, it would mean you would have to go to Tir-na-nog with me."

He looked into her eyes, thinking he saw in their clear, bright depths an invitation, and a promise.

He leaned toward her, his arm sliding forward, around the slender waist.

"There is nowhere that I wouldn't go with you," he said.

He started to pull her toward him, but she pushed him away, casting her gaze across the fire meaningfully.

There, on a small rock close to the warmth, the tiny, mouselike being sat, busily nibbling at a crust of bread. It stopped when it noted her looking toward it.

"Pay no mind to me at all," the Pooka said politely.

She looked at it with some distaste. "Do you have to stay like that?"

It shrugged its small shoulders in a very human manner. "I never thought of it. I eat much less this way."

"Never mind! Just change into some other form. Something a bit less disagreeable."

"Certainly!" It agreed amicably. "And just what form would that be?"

"How about a dog?" she suggested. "Something with a good, big head."

It began the change at once. The head came first, a broad, square-muzzled head with pointed ears and large, dark eyes. The body filled out behind it, but stopped far short of matching the great head. It made an absurd sight, that massive, grinning face haphazardly attached to that small form.

"That's not right," she told it irritably.

"You wanted a big head," it answered innocently.

"Only on a body it fits. No more tricks. Finish it properly."

The body grew, finally reaching proportions suited for the head, about the size and look of a wolfhound.

Satisfied, Aine nodded at the beast.

"That's quite nice. Now, if you can keep from your foolery, I might decide I don't mind you at all."

"Why, thank you!" it told her, obviously pleased. It looked from her to Lugh who was, unseen by Aine, making desperate signals with his face for the Pooka to depart.

It considered the meaning of this, then understood.

"You know, I think I ought to take a little walk around this area," it suggested casually. "I'd like to be certain there are no Fomor sneaking about."

"A good idea," Lugh quickly agreed. "Take a nice, long look. But stay in sight of the fire. And don't fall into any traps this time."

"I won't," it promised. It looked from Lugh to Aine with a knowing grin. "The same to you!"

It rose up languidly, stretched the new, long body, and sauntered off into the surrounding night.

"What did it mean by that?" Aine asked.

"I've no idea," said Lugh. His arm stole out again, encircling her waist, this time pulling her toward him. "Never mind that. Do you know how long it's been since we were alone?"

She put up her hands, pushing against his chest. "Stop, Lugh. Please don't try any of that with me. Not now!"

He pulled back to look at her in puzzlement. "But I thought our argument was finished."

"It is. We are friends," she said very properly. "But our relationship will not go beyond that. Remember what my brother said. Now that we are together, I don't want to give him any reason to believe that he was right. Nothing between us will interfere with what we have to do."

"But there is something between us," he said. "We can't pretend there isn't."

"That's only in your own mind," she said, looking toward the fire to avoid his searching gaze. "I like you a great deal. But as a comrade first, or perhaps a brother. If you've decided there's something else—"

"Wait!" he said sharply, seizing her arms tightly and pulling her around so that he could look directly into her eyes. "Don't expect me to believe that again. I know . . ." He paused, faint images clearing in his mind as he stared at her, faint words strengthening in his memory. "I remember!" he said more positively. "I was nearly dead. I thought it was more of some dream, but it wasn't. It was you! You said you loved me!"

She hesitated, wanting to deny it, but seeing in his face that she would never convince him of that. Finally, in a tightly controlled voice, she replied:

"I said it to save you. It was meant to help you want to stay alive."

"Because you love me," he insisted.

"Because you are important to Eire, and it is my task to help you stay alive," she answered with cool preciseness.

"That's always your argument to hide behind," he said. "But there is more. There's more and you know it."

She tried to twist away, but he stubbornly held on, keeping her there as he went on in uncompromising tones.

"It's not your brother you're afraid of, is it? You're afraid of yourself! You think he might be right, that you do have deeper feelings for me than you'll admit."

"No!" she protested, but a tinge of uncertainty appeared in her voice.

"Yes," he countered with force. "You told me once you didn't like feeling that you weren't in control. But this is something you can't control. So you hide it, fighting to stay the cold, hard warrior, the great adventuress. But when you thought I was dying, you let it show. You can't hide it from me anymore. Don't try!"

He pulled her to him. His sudden move took her by surprise, and she was unable to resist. He pressed his lips to hers, bringing her body tightly against his.

She felt the warmth of him, felt it building within herself. Her own control was slipping. She realized that her fear for his life really had loosed her inner feelings. Now they confused her, left her open to contending forces of emotion and logic, love and duty.

Perhaps she was foolish to hold back. One or both of them might die yet, and soon. Should she deny any chance for themselves?

In this bewildering and rebellious state of mind, her passions soon began to dominate. She began to return his kiss with her own ardor, encircling him with her arms.

Together they sank down to lie on the soft, sandy earth warmed by the fire. It seemed to them the heat had grown unbearable, and they pulled away the hampering cloaks, unaware of everything now but one another's bodies.

Lugh's hand slid down the smooth curve of her side, over her hip, past the hem of the short tunic to lie caressingly on the bare, hot flesh of her thigh. Then it began a slow move upward again, dragging the garment with it.

Her own hands slid lingeringly from his back across his chest. They met at the buckle of his sword belt, began to unfasten it.

A piercing, high-pitched shriek rose suddenly, stabbing through the night.

XXII

BALOR'S RAGE

THE TWO SAT up as if they had been jabbed by the sound.

They pulled apart and looked out into the night where a series of loud squawks and rattling noises could now be heard.

"Something must have happened to the Pooka!" Aine said.

"Oh, no!" Lugh cried irritably, slamming a fist to the ground in frustration. "I should have expected something."

To him, this was another untimely interruption. But to Aine, it was a welcome rescue. It gave her a chance to gather the shattered forces of her will and re-form a rational front again. She quickly rearranged her clothes, seized her cloak, and jumped to her feet.

"Come on," she told him briskly, once more a warrior. "We've got to see what's wrong."

Lugh knew she was right. Pushing back his disappointment once again, he rose and drew out the Answerer.

But they had no chance to go to the rescue. From the darkness a form appeared, striding into the light. It was a large black cat with glowing eyes, and it gripped a struggling raven in its jaws.

Stopping by the fire, the animal spat the bird out on the ground.

"I saw this raven out there creeping up on you," came the Pooka's voice from the cat. "I took on the proper form to deal with it."

The bedraggled bird, most of its feathers askew, lay upon the ground, body heaving with its labored breathing, sharp black eyes glaring up at them.

Then it began to glow with a blue-white light, like a dark sapphire lit from within.

"Oh, no," Lugh said in dismay. "This is no bird."

The light bloomed outward, swallowing up the raven, stretching out along the ground, then fading away. A familiar, bony form was now visible lying by the fire.

Once her own form had been regained, she wasted no time. With an angry caw, she sprang up, charging toward the Pooka, her hands grabbing for her sword hilts.

The animal crouched back defensively, snarling.

"Wait, Morrigan!" Lugh cried, jumping between the two with his sword raised. "It's our friend! It thought it was helping us!"

She hesitated, looking narrowly from the beast toward Lugh.

"Your friend?" she asked in a voice that rattled like dry bones. "He is a Pooka. No friend to us. They are traitors! Lying tricksters!"

"Not this one," Lugh said soothingly. "He saved my life. He wants to help us. Please, Morrigan, leave him be."

She made a harsh, angry sound and released her weapons.

"All right, Lugh. I've no time for it anyway. You must start back to Manannan's Isle with me at once!"

"Why?" Aine asked. "What's wrong?"

The raven-woman answered in a single word. "Balor!"

The sun was just breasting the curved rim of the sea when the immense, eaglelike bird began its long, sweeping descent from the sky.

Lugh looked down from its back to the slate-grey ocean surface now visible far below and squeezed his eyes shut, tightening his grip on the bird's long neck.

"Let up there just a bit," it said in the Pooka's familiar voice. "You're cutting off my breathing."

"Sorry," Lugh said, relaxing his hold a little. "I hate admitting it, but I have a great fear of heights."

"I used to have it," the being answered lightly. "But flying cured me. When you're cut off totally from the earth this way, you feel completely free. Take a look. It's beautiful."

"I'll take your word for it," he said, keeping his eyes shut.

But Lugh's torture was nearly over. The green-grey jewel of Manannan's Isle was now visible below, and the Pooka spiraled in, seeking its landing spot, finally drifting softly down into a glade sheltered by a band of trees and a low ridge of hills.

"We're here," it told Lugh, who gratefully released his hold and slid from the bird's back onto the ground. He was never more glad of feeling it beneath his feet.

From the nearby ridge, Aine and Morrigan descended, running across the glade to meet the arrivals.

"Are you all right?" Aine asked Lugh, noting his rather pale look.

"I wish there had been another way to come," he answered honestly.

But there had been none. The Riders of the Sidhe had been unable to take them across. Their only way of reaching the isle was for Lugh to order them dissolved back into the atmosphere and then recall them once he reached the place. So the willing Pooka had volunteered its talents to their cause. And, despite Morrigan's open distrust and Aine's more veiled doubts, its help had been accepted. As Lugh had pointed out to his skeptical friends, they really had no choice.

The bird form it took, though huge, hadn't been able to carry both Aine and Lugh at once. It had made two trips during the night, not complaining of the tremendous effort this required. Aine, over Lugh's protest, had gone first. Knowing the isle, she had argued that she could best scout the situation there. Morrigan had agreed.

Now, recovering from his harrowing ride, Lugh asked what she had found.

"Come with us," she said.

She and Morrigan led the way toward the nearby woods. The Pooka transformed himself as they went, resuming the hound shape that had pleased Aine.

The trees of the woods were tall pines, widely spaced. Their slender trunks rose up to an intricate lace of greenery far above, where slender branches seemed woven together by their thick fringe of needles. Through gaps in this fabric, bolts of white morning light shot down at sharp angles to throw bright patches on the ground.

The forest floor was level, carpeted thickly with brown needles glowing golden where the sun struck them. The four moved easily, threading through the trees after Aine, the soft ground deadening the sounds of their footsteps.

It was certainly beautiful and very peaceful, Lugh thought. Like the rest of Manannan's Isle. But what was Aine about bringing them here?

A tune began to sound softly through the quiet woods. It was a light air played on a flute or pipes, he thought. And with its rising notes, the trees around them were suddenly populated.

The figures seemed to materialize from the air, they slipped so gently into view from their hiding places. So at one with nature were they that, until now, they had remained invisible.

Lugh's recent experiences had made him understandably skittish when suddenly confronted, and he had his sword half-way out before recognizing these slender, beautiful people as inhabitants of Manannan's Sidhe. His gesture alarmed them, and they started back, eyes wide like startled fawns. Aine quickly lifted a staying hand and spoke in soothing tones to them.

"It's all right. This is Lugh. You know him. And this is the Pooka. He is our friend too."

At this they moved forward again, still somewhat warily. It was clear to Lugh that their own first experience with the Fomor had left them much frightened and unsure. But a few of the young women he had met on his earlier visits to the Sidhe ventured timid smiles. He returned them warmly, and this seemed, at last, to return their confidence. They crowded in around the four now, as if their presence provided some security.

"What is it all of you are doing here?" Lugh asked them.

"They escaped the Sidhe when Balor's men came in," Aine explained. "They came to hide here, not knowing what else to do. I came on them while I was scouting the area." She smiled around at them. "They've never really been in a violent situation like this in their lives. But they did quite well. They managed to get the Spear of Gorias and the cauldron out while the Fomor were capturing their friends inside."

"You mean the cauldron's safe?" Lugh said with delight.

"It is," a young man assured him, proudly. "It is hidden here, in these woods. Those soldiers will never find it, the spear, or us. They think we are all inside the Sidhe."

"The main entrance is heavily guarded," Aine explained. "They must believe that's enough to trap everyone inside. They don't realize that there are other ways in and out of the mound."

"Why didn't the Fomor discover them?" Lugh asked.

"The Sidhe makes them invisible to anyone but its own people," she said. "And it protects them so no one can chance into them."

"How does it do that?" Morrigan wanted to know.

"Any outsider is misdirected," Aine told her. "Manannan calls it 'Being Lead Astray.' If someone comes too close, he suddenly finds himself across a meadow, heading another way."

"Then if Balor believes no one can have escaped," Lugh said thoughtfully, "the cauldron will be safe here. Still, that leaves the rest of these people and our friends trapped inside. We have to get them out."

"We do not have to get them out," Morrigan said in a low rattle.

"What?" Lugh asked sharply, not understanding.

"We have the cauldron," she said. "Our mission is to take it back to Tara. We can go now. The others would understand."

He was shocked by that. "What, leave them here? You know what that would mean!"

"I know," she answered flatly. "But to risk ourselves to save them is to risk the entire de Danann race."

He stared into the chill depths of those dark eyes, trying to fathom them. He looked at the expressionless death's head face. Was this strange being whose life was warfare and blood telling him he must abandon his comrades and her own, or was she merely pointing out the potential hazards of their actions?

He didn't know, and it didn't matter. He knew that the others must be saved if it was possible. Reasonable or not, he knew he had to act.

"I am going in there, Morrigan," he said. "I'm going to see what can be done. If there's any way they can be rescued, I'm going to try it. Stay out here with the cauldron if you want. Then you can take it back if something happens to me."

He was surprised when he detected the hint of a smile thaw the icy sheen of her eyes for an instant and heard a certain satisfaction in her creaking voice as she replied.

"You'll go nowhere without me."

He nodded and looked at Aine. "What about you? You'll have to lead us into the Sidhe. Will you do it?"

"They may be dead already, Lugh," she said reluctantly.

"I know. Will you take us in?"

"You know I will. It's my own brother in there."

"And you?" he said to Shaglan. "There'll be more danger in this than you bargained for. You owe nothing to me. You've already done more than you needed."

"I owe the de Dananns," it said. "This may be some little payment for that."

"You'll not buy forgiveness from us, Pooka," Morrigan told it darkly. And, to Lugh: "It'll betray us. Mark what I'm saying to you now."

"It will go, and welcome," Lugh said staunchly. "Thank you, Shaglan."

He turned toward the people of the Sidhe.

"As for all of you, get back into your hiding places and wait for us. Keep that spear and cauldron out of sight."

The young man nodded. He gestured toward the rest. Like sunbeams fading with a passing cloud, they swiftly disappeared amongst the trees again. The woods seemed empty.

"Let's go then, shall we?" Lugh asked his companions briskly. "Aine, you're certain you can get us in unseen?"

"Of course!" she answered with some indignation. "For years I've prowled this place when I was bored. Follow me!"

She led the way again, out of the woods and across the meadows toward the giant mound. It looked to the others as if she were headed toward a blank hillside. But as they entered an area covered with heavy brush, Lugh, Morrigan, and the Pooka found themselves suddenly feeling quite disoriented. It appeared to them that they were headed away from the mound, the ground shifting about them. It was a dizzying sensation. But they followed close to Aine, carefully keeping an eye on her, and soon experienced another peculiar phenomenon that Lugh recalled from his past visits there. One moment they were outside, and the next they realized they were not. The Sidhe seemed gently to envelop them, draw them in, and they were suddenly looking up at the interior of the mound, not the sky.

"What an extraordinary feeling," the Pooka said with awe.

"Shhh!" Aine warned, and pulled them into the shelter of a brightly flowering thicket.

Ahead of them appeared a Fomor patrol in a straggling line. As they moved along, they looked searchingly around, their expressions clearly showing grave concern. Just past where the four were hiding, they stopped in a bunch and stood, staring about them in a hopeless sort of way. Then, at the angry-sounding orders of a young officer, they turned and started wearily back the way they'd come.

"They look a little lost, don't they?" Lugh remarked softly when they were out of sight.

"I'm not surprised," said Aine. "The inside of this place is as bewildering as the out. Come on. We'll try to work our way closer to the central mound."

"Hold on," said the Pooka. They looked toward it and found it in a state of flux. Soon it settled into the large, catlike form. "I thought this might be more useful for sneaking about," it said.

The Morrigan fixed it with a glittering eye, its form recalling her recent indignity.

"That's something a Pooka would know all about," she crackled nastily.

"Jealous because you can do only that dusty crow, are you?" the animal shot back.

She hissed, drawing back her thin lips to reveal the sharp, tearing teeth. Lugh stepped quickly in again.

"Now look, the both of you, this has got to stop! You'll have to get along for now. Morrigan, please believe that the Pooka wants to help!"

She shook her head. "No. And I'll not turn my back to it."
Then she added, reluctantly, "But I'll not argue with it anymore."

"And you, Shaglan," Lugh said to the animal, "watch your
tongue as well."

It smiled back. "I will do that," it promised.

"Then, can we be going on now?" Aine asked, made impatient by this childish exchange. "We've got to keep moving
with all these Fomor wandering about."

They agreed, and then began a cautious movement through
the vast countryside contained within the Sidhe, moving ever
closer to the central mound.

The red gaze turned from its constant, slow scanning of the
Sidhe to rest upon the Fomor officer.

"Yes, Salmhor?" Balor asked.

"My Commander," the other began cautiously, not relishing
the report he was about to make, "the patrols have encoun-
tered some difficulties. They have captured only a few more
inhabitants. The rest . . . they seem to have disappeared."

"Disappeared?" The iron voice clanged. "Within the con-
fines of this mound? How could they?"

"The interior of this place is very . . . confusing, Commander," Sital Salmhor began, uncertain how to explain. "The
more the patrols search, the larger it seems to become. They
discover more fields, more streams, more woods, many more
than this space could possibly contain. Some of them have become disoriented, even lost. They've had to abandon searching
and find their way back. The men are growing frightened by it,
Commander." He looked around the Sidhe nervously. "And, I
must confess to a growing unease myself."

"I've sensed it too," Balor responded. "There is some kind of
force at work here, some peculiar power."

"I'm afraid that continuing the search is useless, Commander," Salmhor told him. "It might prove dangerous as
well."

"I agree. This mound is protecting its secrets from us. We'll
waste no more time. I think we will try a more direct means of
finding what we want. Salmhor, select a group from our prisoners. And bring our visitors from Eire back to me."

The officer went down from the mound at once, gathering a

party of Balor's personal guard and marching purposefully into the hollow.

They spread into a line as they neared the gathering there. Alarmed by their approach, Manannan's people rose and drew together. The lanky guardian and his comrades moved forward in a protective way, boldly confronting the officer.

"What's happening now?" demanded the Dagda.

"That is not for you to ask," Salmhor answered haughtily. "Balor wants you brought to him. Come along!"

Some of the guards moved to circle them. Reluctantly they started off, following the officer's lead. As they did, Angus looked back toward the other prisoners, noting that more guards were now approaching them and pushing some of them out of the group with the strange power lances, as if they were cutting cattle from a herd.

He paused, asking sharply, "Wait! What are they doing?"

"Never mind, lad," said Manannan, urging him on. "Nothing you can do now. No need for getting yourself hurt again."

Angus looked around at the shining lanceheads, recalling the stinging pain. He did as he was told.

They were led back up the mound to the dark giant waiting by the ring of stones. The four were lined up before him, each with a guard standing close behind.

Once more the crimson eye rested upon them, bathed them with its unpleasant warmth.

"I have lost patience with these beings," the flat, metallic voice announced. "My troops have searched this place to no avail. What has been hidden has been hidden too well for us to find. That fact is very unfortunate, but for them, not for me."

"What do you mean, Balor?" the Dagda asked.

"Only that now I must use less pleasant means to discover where this cauldron and Manannan are."

"None of them will tell you anything, you great heap of rustin' iron," Manannan told him, again using Gilla's voice.

"I warned you before, fool," the dark giant said in an ominous rumble.

"Warn me all you like," he replied carelessly, "but they'll not talk to you."

"I think they will. At least, they will after they see what happens to those who refuse. It should not take long. They seem as frivolous as this ridiculous dwelling place. Breaking them should take no more effort than breaking this Sea-God's power."

"They aren't so frail as you think, Balor," the disguised Manannan warned. "Believe me, you won't learn anything from them."

The eye intensified its light a fraction, pouring more heat upon them. "Perhaps from you, then."

"From us?" said Findgoll. "We know no more than you."

"That may be true. But I sense that you could save me all this unnecessary effort . . . and pain. I kept you alive for that reason. So, if you know anything, it would be better for you to tell me."

"Why?" Manannan demanded. "We surely won't be saving ourselves to give you what you want. And we're no more likely to tell you anything than they are!"

"You may think differently after you've watched some of these pretty young bodies turned to piles of blackened sticks," Balor coldly announced.

XXIII

A DESPERATE DELAY

"SALMHOR! BRING THE first ones up!" Balor commanded.

"I'm afraid this might be it," Manannan softly told his companions as the officer went to do his Commander's bidding.

"And no sign of help," the Dagda murmured back.

"Don't give up yet. There's still some time."

The Dagda shook his head. He couldn't believe there was any hope.

A dozen of Manannan's people appeared on the crest of the mound, herded along by more of Balor's guards. They were pushed forward into the ring of stones where they stood, huddled together, staring up toward the giant figure like small children facing an angry teacher.

"Now," said Balor slowly, heavily, "I will ask each one of you where Manannan and this cauldron are. I will ask you only once, and if I do not receive the answer that I want, you will feel the power of my eye. It will not be quick, and it will be very painful. Do you understand?"

"You can't do that!" Angus cried out angrily.

"You'd prefer to tell me what I want to know?" Balor said to him. "Tell me and you can stop this."

"I can't!" Angus said in frustration. "I don't know anything."

"Too bad," said Balor, and the red gaze slid away, moving across the hilltop to the knot of captives.

The crimson light flitted across them, resting here, then there, finally stopping on a slender, finely boned young woman with a billowing flow of silver-blond hair.

"You will be the first." Balor declared.

The rest were moved back from her by the guards. She was clearly frightened, but courageous in the face of her own death, standing motionless, head up, returning the hot gaze of Balor unflinchingly.

"Will you tell me what I want to know?" the giant asked.

She remained silent, staring upward at him.

"Very well, then," he said, the words clanging like a death knell.

With an agonizing slowness, the lid of the great eye began to lift.

"All right. Enough!" said the figure in the clown's dress loudly. "The game's gone far enough, Balor."

The eye ceased to open further. The gaze swung back to him.

"What are you saying, fool?" the giant demanded.

"Just that I really can't let you go through with harming any of these people," he said calmly, dropping Gilla's manner of speech abruptly. "To be quite honest, I had hoped you'd keep up your searching a bit longer. But since you clearly intend to become nasty about it, I'll have to reveal the truth."

"What truth is that?" the voice asked sharply. "Quickly!"

"You must promise that if I reveal Manannan's whereabouts to you, you'll not harm these people anymore."

"I will promise, if you reveal him to me," Balor said.

"Good enough," the other responded easily. "You see, you really don't need to ask any of them where this Manannan is. He is standing before you!"

"Where?" Balor asked, the flat voice marked by confusion.

"Right here!" the tall, ragged man declared, lifting his arms to present himself. "I am Manannan MacLir!"

"I will tolerate no more of your mad talk, clown," the Commander warned.

"It's true!" the other insisted. "I've been traveling Eire in disguise! Look!"

With a swift, flamboyant gesture, Gilla seized the long, ragged beard and tore it from his face. His comrades watched in horror as the beard seemed to pull the flesh of the face away with it. But from beneath it, another face appeared. It was a bolder but still pleasant-featured face, set now in an expression of challenge to the metal giant. In another move, the man swept off the straggling head of hair, revealing thick, curling locks of silver-grey.

"There!" he declared triumphantly. "Now you're facing the real Guardian of the Sidhe. And it's your good fortune that I was gone from here when you came, or I'd have given you and that bloody eye something to deal with!"

Though his companions were amazed by this sudden transformation, it seemed to have little effect on Balor.

"Don't think that you can frighten me with your foolish boasting," the flat voice replied. "If you are Manannan, your little games have been no threat to me. You're as harmless as this absurd dwelling of yours. Your disguise of a clown is a perfect one for you, for that is all your are."

"Just give me a chance with you on the sea," Manannan challenged, somewhat irritated by this scorn, "and we'll see whose powers are greater."

"We can see that here," Balor told him, "You are finished, 'Sea-God.' Give up your allegiance with the de Dananns, turn this cauldron over to me, and you may save your little isle."

"And if I refuse to tell you where it is?"

"Then I will take a great pleasure in extracting that information from you."

"Your will against mine, eh?" Manannan said courageously. "A sort of contest between us. Well, I warn you, you red-eyed mountain of metal scrap, you can't do anything that will make you the master of Manannan MacLir!"

"Salmhor, take the others back below!" Balor thundered.

As guards came forward and herded the other captives away, Dagda leaned toward his lanky companion to mutter darkly:

"Manannan, why are you doing this?"

The other shrugged. "To delay him longer. Every moment might count for us."

"And just how is it you're planning to delay?"

"Well, it'll take some time for him to torture me."

"Oh, well, that's marvelous, that is!" the Dagda said irritably.

"Sorry," Manannan told him. "It's the only plan I could come up with this time."

From the remnants of a grove of trees half ravaged by Fomor axes, the little rescue party peered cautiously out toward the nearby mound. Using Aine's knowledge of the Sidhe, they had managed to work their way this close. Now they assessed the situation there critically.

It was not especially good.

Their companions could be seen clearly atop the mound, standing beneath the deadly eye of the black giant, surrounded by most of Balor's personal guards. The rest of the Fomor soldiers, having been recalled from searching, were forming up below the mound. Lugh estimated that there were nearly a hundred men, all told, many armed with the familiar crossbows.

"They are not going to be easy to get to, there," Aine remarked, quite unnecessarily, Lugh thought.

They watched as the group of Sidhe inhabitants was moved from the hill and returned to the hollow.

"Well, there's something, at least," he said. "Only four or five men are guarding Manannan's people. And nobody else is paying any attention to them. Let's try to get them free first."

"And then what?" Aine asked.

He shrugged. "I've no idea. One step at a time, I think."

They moved stealthily around the mound at a safe distance, making their way through the ravaged underbrush and trees and gardens until they were close to the little hollow where the inhabitants of the Sidhe were being held. Taking up a vantage point behind a battered but still thick hedge, they made another survey.

Four guards were pacing the perimeter about the captives now. Two other Fomor soldiers were standing a little distance from them, watching the activities on the mound and speaking in low tones. One of them carried a crossbow slung across his shoulder.

"We've got to deal with those two first," Lugh whispered. "If we could get them over here somehow . . ."

"Leave that to me," the Pooka said, winking.

And moments later, one of the two Fomor stopped in mid-sentence to stare past his companion's shoulder toward the row of bushes in complete surprise.

"What's wrong, mate?" the other soldier asked.

"There! Look!" the first cried.

The second whirled toward the bushes. Nothing was visible.

"There's nothing there!" he said, confused. "What was it?"

"It was a duck . . . or, a rabbit," the first said, still staring at the spot where the thing had briefly appeared.

"It can't be both!"

"But it was," the soldier insisted, looking at his fellow. "It had enormous webbed feet. And it had ears. Long ones!" He raised a hand high above his head to demonstrate. Then he pointed toward a gap in the row of bushes. "He popped right out of there. Then"—he hesitated before going on—"then he smiled . . . and he waved at me."

His companion gave him a very curious look. "This strange place is affecting your mind, Eab. That's what it is."

"No!" Eab said hotly, angered by his comrade's disbelief. "I saw it. And look! There it is again!"

Once more the other soldier spun around. Once more he saw only empty bushes. He turned back toward Eab, smiling understandingly.

"It's all right," he said in a soothing voice. "We've all been feeling a bit confused. Try to ignore it."

Eab did not like his fellow's patronizing tone. Indignantly he replied: "I'm not confused. There is something there, and I am going to show you."

With that, he marched right to the gap in the bushes, un-slung the crossbow he carried, and stepped into the foliage, disappearing from sight.

The other soldier heard some crackling sounds as his comrade advanced. Then, abruptly, there was silence.

"Eab?" he called.

When he received no answer, he moved cautiously toward the gap. He leaned forward, peering into the tangle of branches. Faster than he could react, a long arm shot out, snaked about his neck, and jerked him out of sight.

There was more rustling deep within the bushes, and soon two figures in the close-fitting grey uniforms reappeared. But in the interim, something about the shape of one had drastically changed. The stocky Fomor figure had become quite lean and so tall the pants legs barely reached the calf.

Casually, these two moved toward the patrolling guards. As they did, two other figures slid cautiously through the surrounding screen of bushes, taking up their own positions.

The uniformed pair parted, each heading toward a guard. None of the Fomor took notice of them until one, turning at the end of his walk, looked toward the approaching figure, expecting to see a familiar face.

What he saw was a sleek, skull-like head and dark eyes glittering at him with a hungry light.

Shocked, he hesitated just an instant in bringing up his power spear in defense. It was an instant too much. Morrigan was upon him, driving her sword upward under his ribs into his heart.

As Lugh saw Morrigan move, he struck as well, leaping upon the back of his guard, driving him down, slamming his head against the ground. The man went limp.

Across the hollow, an enormous catlike beast sprang down from a low tree limb upon its chosen victim, bearing him down and cutting off his cries with a quick nip of its jaws. The last guard, seeing his fellows attacked, turned to run but stopped, surprised, as a slender and beautiful young girl stepped from cover to block his way. Growling, he stepped forward to sweep her from his path. She raised a crossbow and sent its metal bolt flying. She had fired the bows before. Her aim was deadly. The bolt struck his forehead squarely, burying itself in his brain, the force of the blow snapping his head back and throwing him from his feet.

Dealing with the four guards had taken only seconds and made no noise. Now the rescuers quickly seized their victims and dragged them into the hollow, out of sight of those at the mound.

The group of captives huddled there cowered back from them in fear. They had witnessed the savage killing of the guards in horror, watched now with a mixture of alarm and bewilderment as the four laid out the bloody bodies and approached them.

Aine quickly moved ahead of her companions, addressing the inhabitants of the Sidhe in soothing, friendly tones.

"It's all right. You all know me. I'm Aine. We've come to set you free."

The gathering took heart as they recognized her and saw Lugh and Morrigan strip off their uniforms.

"That's right," Lugh said. "You're going to have to leave here, escape into the Sidhe and hide. Do you understand?"

Some of them nodded, but he could tell by their expressions that most of them were too confused or too stunned by recent events to be trusted to act alone. They were like a flock of sheep caught in a violent storm, bunched together, not wanting to move.

"Aine," he said, "someone is going to have to take them in hand or they'll never get away."

"I know," she agreed. "Poor things. It was never intended that they should have to deal with anything like this."

Morrigan, meanwhile, had been examining one of the strange weapons of the guards. The gleaming silver ball fascinated the raven in her, held her eye. Curious, she reached out a bony finger to touch it.

"Don't do that!" a young man in the group warned her.

She jerked back the finger, her head snapping around to him.

"What do you mean?" she rasped.

"That globe holds some kind of power. It was strong enough to knock one of your friends down. It only has to touch your body lightly to work."

She nodded a curt thanks. Then, still curious, she lifted the spear by the thick shaft and examined it more closely. She could feel a vibration through it, presumably from this power that it held. Halfway down the shaft were some odd indentations and a small knob. This she experimentally turned, first left, then right. The vibration increased one way, faded nearly away the other. She returned it to the original point and, feeling it was nothing to play about with, set it carefully back upon the ground.

"All right," Aine said to the others. "We've gotten this far. What will we do next?"

"Let's see what's happening," Lugh suggested.

Carefully they climbed back to the rim of the hollow, just high enough so that the mound was visible. Nothing there had changed. Their friends were still gathered before Balor. The soldiers were still gathering below. No one was moving their way or taking note of them. So far they were safe.

Aine considered the situation upon the mound and shook her head.

"There is no possible way for us to get to them. Not with Balor and all those Fomor there."

"There is one," Lugh said, trying to sound determined. "But I'm afraid it calls for me to attack Balor head-on."

"Attack him?" Aine said in disbelief. "How can you do that?"

"Very simple. I'll summon the Riders of the Sidhe and we'll go in at him. Those soldiers of his won't be able to stop them."

"And what about that eye?" she pointed out.

"Oh, the eye," he said lightly, as if it were unimportant. "The Riders should be able to counter that." He smiled with what he intended to be confidence. It didn't quite work. "Our power against theirs, eh? Should be exciting."

"Lugh, you don't know how powerful Balor is," she argued. "Some kind of Fomor energy has already scattered the Riders once!"

He looked at her, his attempt at assurance gone, his voice grim. "I'm not fond of this myself. But I'm afraid we're out of alternatives. If I'm not mistaken, they're preparing to do something unpleasant to your brother. We're nearly out of time."

She looked up toward the mound. It did look as if the familiar lanky figure was being tied to one of the stone pillars.

"All right," she said. "Send the Riders. But you don't have to lead them."

He met her eyes. "You know I do. Balor is away from his Tower and his ships. He may never be this vulnerable again. If there's a chance to destroy him, this is it. I've got to try."

She knew that he was right. She wanted to say more, but she held back. Her own feelings couldn't interfere. This was what he had to do. She nodded.

He smiled. "I was rather hoping you'd talk me out of it."

"I'm going with you," she said.

He shook his head. "You can't. You've got to get up on that mound while I've got their attention and try to set the others free. Otherwise, if I do fail . . ." He stopped, not wanting to complete the thought.

"We'll be no better off," she finished for him. "I understand." Her emotions now in rigid check, she was the experienced fighter again, considering the strategy with cold practicality.

"Be careful," he told her. "We can't risk everyone being caught. Someone's got to take that cauldron back to Tara."

"We all will," she told him with certainty.

"All right. I'm off then," he said briskly. "I'll work my way around to the far side of the mound and call the Riders there. That'll draw their attention away from you. As soon as you see the Riders coming, send these people out and come ahead."

She nodded again. Without more words, Lugh started away, heading into the foliage and out of sight. As soon as he was gone, Aine, the Pooka, and Morrigan gathered the captives and prepared them to make their own escape.

Meanwhile, the young warrior made his way in a wide circuit about the mound. He was not hindered this time by having to avoid Fomor patrols. Nearly all the soldiers were now gathered in neat ranks below the mound. He moved quickly to a point directly opposite the hollow and separated from the mound by a wide, open, and nearly level meadow. Perfect for an attack, he thought. Though it would make the Riders, and himself, easy marks for the power of that blasted eye.

He stared for a moment at the black giant. As before, he felt a deep fear of the strange being. But he felt an anger too. It had destroyed his home, killed his father, and was trying to wipe out the de Danann race. Champion of the Sidhe or not, he had his own reasons for wanting to make a try at Balor of the One Eye.

The crimson eye was opening a fraction wider now, he noted. Its beam was falling upon the bound form of Manannan. Lugh realized that it was time to act, and quickly, or it might be too late for the Master of the Sidhe. He closed his eyes and began the incantation that would, once more, summon the Riders to him.

XXIV

CLASH OF POWERS

MANANNAN WAS TRYING very hard not to scream. He had decided early on that he was not going to give this collection of iron junk the satisfaction of seeing him in pain. Just now he was wishing he had not made such a rash promise to himself. A scream or two might be somewhat relieving.

He wondered why his clothes didn't burst into flames from the heat playing over him. The ruby beam must certainly be that hot. He recalled a day in his youth when he had played on the beach under a rare, bright sun and spent the next days lying motionless, in agony. His skin must look as burned now.

He wondered if he would swell up, his skin crackling and bursting like a roasted pig's. He didn't much like that picture and hurriedly pushed it from his mind. He went back to concentrating on keeping the careless grin upon his face.

The light snapped off abruptly, and cooling air rushed in, feeling nearly frigid in its contrast. He opened his eyes and peered upward, blinking to clear the afterglow.

"You are a stubborn man"—the metallic voice clattered sharply—"or a totally mad one."

"That's been suggested before," Manannan managed to respond cheerily.

"Why are you enduring this suffering for the de Dananns?" the giant demanded. "What do they mean to you that you should want to help them?"

The tall man shrugged as best he could, bound as he was to the standing stone. "It's something to occupy my free time."

"I ask you again: Abandon them. Promise you'll give no more help to them and give the cauldron to me. Then you may stay on your isle and play your games of Sea-God all you wish."

"No," Manannan said regretfully. "I'm sorry, but that's really not possible."

208

"You'll die, you know. And it won't save anything. The cauldron will never reach Tara now."

Manannan grinned up at the inhuman face. "Maybe."

There was a silence. The shuttered eye that rested upon him was so unmoving, he began to think Balor had fallen asleep. Then the voice came again, in ringing, measured tones.

"You will die before you tell me anything. I see that. To inflict further pain upon you would be a waste of time. Salmhor, release him."

At the officer's gesture, a guard stepped forward and cut the lanky guardian's bonds. He stepped back toward his companions, trying to ignore the pain of his raw skin as he moved.

"Admitting you're beaten, are you?" he inquired lightly.

"I am changing my method, that is all!" Balor flatly replied. "If your own pain will not force you to help me, perhaps the pain of others will."

A shadow of alarm crossed Manannan's face.

"You promised not to harm my people again," he reminded Balor. He sensed what was coming next.

"Your people, yes. But not your companions. Your good de Danann friends whose welfare concerns you so much."

The gaze moved slowly from one of them to another as the iron voice went on.

"Which one? Not the Dagda, I think, though I would like to see what would break him. And young Angus will quite likely prove stubborn as well. But the old Druid—"

"You'll not be harming him, One-Eye," the Dagda shouted angrily at the giant, moving in front of the little man. "Try your burning look on me!"

"I don't need the likes of you protecting me," Findgoll said with indignation. He pushed past the bulk of the warrior to look up challengingly at the towering figure, hands on hips and pointed chin thrust out in a defiant gesture. "Do what you can to me, Balor. I'm not afraid of you."

"You will both have your chance," the being assured them. "At least, you will if your 'Sea-God' refuses to help me."

"You surely do have a nasty turn of mind, Balor," Manannan said, his thoughts working desperately. He had done everything he could to delay this inevitable moment. "Would my giving you the cauldron save them?"

"It would," came the flat reply.

"No!" the Dagda protested. "You can't give in!"

"Quiet!" Manannan retorted with some heat. "Bargaining is all I've got left now."

"Very reasonable," said Balor.

"The Dagda and these others will be set free, allowed to return to Eire?" he asked.

"Once I have the cauldron, they are no threat to me."

"You'd go away, leave my people and my Sidhe unharmed?"

"You would never be disturbed by us again."

"And all I have to do for this is to betray the de Dananns and allow them to be slaughtered by Bres. Is that it?"

The massive barrel head inclined slightly in affirmation.

"That's a very generous offer," Manannan said with apparent seriousness. "Would you mind if I took a bit of time to think it over?"

"Time?" asked Balor. "How much time?"

"Oh, I don't know," Manannan said, considering. "It's a very crucial thing, isn't it? I mean, it's not to be taken lightly. It requires a great deal of good, hard, careful thought. A day, perhaps?"

The answer came in an echoing clang of sound.

"You have no intention of accepting this bargain!"

Manannan grinned ruefully. "I didn't really think you'd go along. I took a chance on it anyway."

"You're only trying to delay, aren't you?" Balor demanded. "Why? What are you waiting for?"

A faint rushing sound came to Manannan's ears. It was like the sound of wind, but he knew it was something else. As it grew louder, he looked toward its source.

"For that!" he said, and lifted an arm to gesture toward a distant edge of the vast Sidhe.

As Balor and the others looked toward it, a stream of light, like molten silver, flowed into view. Sinuously it wound through the foliage, rocks, and hills, making its way swiftly toward the mound. At the far edge of the wide meadows that lay below one side of the mound, the silver stream slowed, spread, pouring forward into a glowing line that came finally to a halt.

As it did, the bright aura about it faded away, revealing the figures of mounted warriors, slender lances set forward for the attack.

Balor recalled them from the vague images projected by Mathgen's mind. He knew they were the Riders of the Sidhe. And he also knew the youthful warrior who now appeared from the shelter of a shrub and ran to the Riders. His cold, echoing voice could not disguise the astonishment he felt.

"Lugh!"

The captives on the mound were surprised as well, save for Manannan. They watched, amazed, as Lugh reached a riderless horse—a tall, aristocratic grey—at the center of the line of Riders and leaped agilely onto the animal's back.

"The clown was right!" the Dagda said.

"Again," Findgoll added pointedly.

As Lugh joined the Riders' company, they began to move, beginning a charge directly across the meadows toward the mound. Balor's head swiveled toward his officer and his orders rattled out.

"Salmhor, send our whole force against them now! Quickly! Don't let them near this hill!"

The officer headed away at a run, crying out commands to the Fomor grouped below. The disciplined veterans formed up in moments and headed forward to engage the advancing horsemen.

"You'll not find these beings so useless or so frail, Balor," Manannan said, smiling with satisfaction. "Or so easy to kill."

"That we will see," the Commander replied, no flutter of concern in the cold drone of his voice.

The two lines closed, a hundred Fomor engaging twenty Riders. But the plunging rank of shining horsemen never slowed, driving into the attacking men, the gleaming spear points thrusting through the Fomor like a ray of light striking through a pane of glass. Impaled on the weapons, the soldiers were lifted from their feet and thrown back into their fellows. As they fell, the lances slipped free of them at once and rose, ready to strike again.

The Fomor ranks were thrown into confusion. They scattered before the attackers and a confused melee began. When the Fomor tried to get in behind the horsemen to strike at them, the Riders wheeled their lithe, quick mounts around to drive their bright spears home. Lugh moved amongst them, using his own Answerer with as much skill, slashing through the Fomor ranks.

Back in the hollow, the watching Pooka signaled to his companions that the battle had been joined. Aine and Morrigan began to direct and shoo the people of Manannan out.

"Keep going!" Aine admonished them. "And don't stay in the Sidhe! Get out of it as quickly as you can!"

Frightened, uncertain of what to do, they moved slowly at first. But finally they got the idea and began scampering away like rabbits released from a pen, bursting from the hollow and scattering in all directions. Soon the vast countryside of the Sidhe had swallowed them up.

As soon as they were all safely away, the three companions drew together and left the hollow themselves. But their way was directly toward the mound. Time had come for them to make their own attempt.

With great caution they moved up toward the little hill, taking advantage of what cover they could find. But they were in little danger of being noticed. All the attention of those on the mound was directed toward the fight on the far side.

They reached its slopes, crept up them, lying down to crawl the last distance to the top. Lifting their heads just far enough to peep over the crest, they surveyed the scene before them.

Balor had now moved his huge, wheeled throne across the mound's top to the opposite side to observe the battle more closely. Slightly behind him, within the circle of standing stones, the prisoners stood surrounded by a dozen of the helmeted guards. Most of them, too, were more interested in the battle raging below than in their charges.

It was clear to the three watchers that if they struck quickly, they had a good chance of getting their companions safely away before anyone could stop them. Save for Balor.

If Lugh could draw the power of Balor's eye to him and keep it there, even for a few moments, they could move. Aine only wished she could be certain that Lugh and the Riders could survive that power.

For now, the towering figure was sitting motionless, the deadly eye nearly closed, its power contained behind the heavy lid. Balor watched the forces contending on the meadows below him impassively, like a chess player examining his board.

Soon, however, it became evident that the Fomor would not win this fight. Even when a soldier did manage to get close enough to strike at a Rider, his weapon seemed to encounter only air, sliding through the horseman as if he were made of mist. Yet the spears of the Riders and Lugh's Answerer were solid and deadly enough in their turn, inflicting great slaughter on the hapless troops.

The Fomor withdrew, trying to regroup, but Lugh led the Riders against them again at once, allowing them no rest, driving the panicking soldiers back toward the mound in a retreat that turned quickly to a rout. The Fomor began fleeing to escape the gleaming lance points of the charging Riders.

"You see, Balor," Manannan said with some pride. "We aren't as powerless as you think. Release us before they reach you or you will be destroyed."

If the guardian was hoping to frighten Balor to surrender, he was quickly disappointed. The dark figure's reply came in heavy hammer strokes.

"They will be the ones destroyed, you fool. Watch!"

The lid of the eye began to lift, the hairline slit widened to a narrow crack. The power of the eye, still only a fraction of its full potential, streamed out in a hard, clear ruby beam, shooting toward the horsemen.

But Lugh had anticipated this. As soon as he saw the eye begin to widen, he ordered the Riders together. Swiftly they gathered into a tight circle around him. As one, they raised their lances to point at Balor. At each weapon's tip appeared the intense white glow. The tendrils of light leaped quickly around the circle, intertwining to form the ring of light. As the last link joined, the energy leaped outward from the Riders, blazing toward Balor in a thick silver column.

Midway between the two, the ruby beam met it. They slammed together with a thunderclap and flash of lightning explosion. Then they held there, the two forces—mystic and mechanical—pouring against one another like jets of water, flattening against one another while their edges curled back, shredded, flickered away.

They crackled with the contending energies. The air around them was charged with tingling electricity. The whole Sidhe vibrated from the enormous power being expended in a duel that seemed to match opponents of equal strength.

As soon as this struggle joined, the three began to launch their rescue attempt.

They left the edge of the hill, creeping forward to the shelter of the nearest standing stones. Aine peered cautiously around hers. The prisoners were only a few paces away now. Their guards were all looking the other way.

Aine took up a pebble and tossed it against the tall man's back. At first she thought Manannan hadn't felt it. But then he turned very slightly and cast a quick look toward his sister. His face registered no surprise at seeing her. One eye gave only the briefest of winks to show that he acknowledged her presence.

On the field beyond the mound, the contest between the Riders and Balor continued. But after an initial balance of the two powers, the crimson beam of the giant's energy was beginning to push back the shield of silver light.

Aine realized that the Riders were going to lose. It would be only moments until the red light reached the Riders themselves, and there was no way to know what would happen then. If she and her companions meant to act, they had to do it now.

Praying that Lugh would manage to escape, she drew her sword, signaled the others, and leaped to the attack.

The three drove into the guards with speed and ferocity, ruthlessly cutting down the first ones before they could defend themselves. The rest turned, startled to find themselves confronted by two armed and deadly women and a very large, very savage cat.

The captives reacted instantly, charging forward to join the fight, unarmed as they were. As Angus saw his friends begin to close with the guards, he wondered if they knew of the danger of the strange power-spears.

"Don't let them touch you with the silver globes!" he called to the three, and launched himself at a guard about to swing at Aine.

The man was knocked forward by the weight of Angus and thudded down. As he tried to roll over, Angus struck out with his fist. He knocked the man unconscious, wrenched the power-spear from him, and got up.

"My turn!" he said with a savage glee and swung the weapon toward another charging guard.

The globe slammed into the man's stomach. Its released energy doubled him up and threw him backward. He dropped to the ground like bundled rags, sizzling from the power that had coursed through him. Startled by the effect, Angus looked down at the weapon. He realized that its energy had now been increased to a level meant to kill.

By this time the Dagda, too, had snatched up one of the

weapons from a fallen guard and taken on a pair of attackers. He had no time or use for the fine points of parry and thrust, instead using his spear as a club, smashing the guards' weapons away, felling them with tremendous, swinging blows.

Minding Angus's warning, the others engaged in careful fights with the remaining guards. Aine and Morrigan found that the heavy spears were cumbersome to wield, and the Fomor had little chance against their rapid, skillful swordplay. The Pooka darted here and there about them, throwing its sinewy body upon any enemy it could get behind, dragging him down, and finishing him quickly.

It was a brief, bloody struggle. In moments all the guards were beaten. The Dagda looked down at a fallen opponent and shook his head.

"So these are Balor's best warriors," he said with disgust. "Phaw!"

"All right!" Manannan told the others briskly. "Off the mound. Hurry! There's not much time."

He was certainly right. The ruby beam was drawing ever closer to the Riders, its light beginning to bleed into the silver glow, tingeing it with rose. Lugh had already realized that Balor's power was too strong. Still, he couldn't break off the fight now. If he couldn't defeat Balor, he had to at least be certain his friends had a chance to escape. So, instead of withdrawing the Riders, he sent them forward, directly into the beam of crimson light. He would see to it that Balor was fully occupied.

They pressed forward against the energy driving upon them. Balor increased it, using the full force of the eye in an attempt to reach them. It blazed from the hilltop like a red sun. It beat upon the shrinking silver shield. Behind it, Lugh felt the heat begin to build.

"Can't we help him?" Aine asked her brother urgently.

He shrugged. "We can always try. You come with me. You others, get off this mound now."

"But we can help too!" the Dagda argued. "We'll all attack that monster!"

"And we'll all be killed. A direct attack won't harm that pile of iron. Remember the cauldron, man! Someone's got to escape. So get away! Quickly!"

Reluctantly, the Dagda and the others agreed. The big man lifted the little Druid and they moved down the slope and away into the foliage. Manannan and his sister charged across the hilltop boldly, coming right up beneath Balor's back.

They stared up at the being. The massive, square-cornered throne rose to twice their height, and the broad back of Balor himself that much higher again. Both throne and giant hummed with the force being generated inside to power the eye.

Manannan looked desperately for some way the being might be attacked. But the smooth metal surface of the back offered no vulnerable spots.

"Give me a boost up," he told his sister.

"What?"

"A boost. Up there. I've got to get closer."

"Closer! You can't climb right on him!" she protested.

"It's all right. He's busy. Now hurry up!"

She made a stirrup with her hands. He put a foot in it. There was great strength in the slender girl. She lifted her lanky brother high. He stretched, gripped the top edge of the throne, and hauled himself up.

The barrel head was still far above him. No way to reach it. But this close to the surface of the back, he could discern a fine, hairline crack. If he could get his sword . . .

"Look out!" Aine cried from below.

He looked up as one of Balor's huge hands swept down at him and ducked away as it swished past his head. In his absorption he hadn't noticed the arm swing up and back to strike at him. Only the awkward position had saved him.

But Manannan's presence had clearly attracted the attention of the being, despite its occupation with the Riders. Balor had now become aware of what had happened behind him, and his massive voice boomed out hollowly.

"Salmhor! The guards are dead! I'm being attacked!"

Salmhor and his remaining, exhausted troops were scattered in the meadows below the mound, awaiting the outcome of the contest. But at his commander's orders, the officer obediently gathered some soldiers and headed at a run for the mound.

Manannan gave up his attempt and dropped from the throne to land beside Aine.

"Run!" he said. "Sorry. There's nothing we can do."

"But Lugh!" she said despairingly.

"We can't help him. We've got to save ourselves. Come on!"

And they ran back across the hilltop, down the far slope, heading for shelter in the vast landscape.

Through the nearly blinding glare, Lugh saw his comrades run from the hilltop. At least, he thought, he had the satisfaction of knowing that Balor had been thwarted in this much.

For him, the battle was nearly over. The ruby light had pressed the silver back into a thin, curved shield above the circle of Riders. It blasted against the surface, a jet of energy building in intensity to a blazing peak.

The beam suddenly broke through the shield. The whole of the thin defense of shimmering white gave way, shattering like ice. In a last gesture of defense, Lugh lifted his sword before him. The Riders, seeking in their last instant to protect him, cast the final measure of their power inward, their glow joining within the circle, forming a hazy globe that enveloped the young champion.

The full force of the crimson beam fell directly upon it, turning the silver to a bloody hue for an instant before it swallowed Lugh and the Riders in a single, swelling burst of radiance.

XXV

SAVING THE SIDHE

SHAKEN BUT UNHARMED, Lugh staggered to his feet. He realized that the last power of the Riders had protected him. But of those warriors, or of his own grey horse, there was no sign. Balor's force had snuffed them out as one would a candle.

He realized the Answerer was gone, too, and looked about for it. It lay some distance away. He stepped toward it, but a hard voice stopped him.

"If you move any farther, you will die."

He looked up to see the red glow of the single eye fixed steadily upon him, its destructive energy now lowered. It bathed him with a nearly scorching heat.

"You see now that your power is nothing against mine," the

giant said. "Your mystic energy has no real strength. It is no equal to what the science of the Fomor has created."

Salmhor and his men had now reached the mound's top. They were in time to see Aine and her brother disappear into the cover of a thick wall of bushes.

"Manannan is escaping, Commander!" the officer cried. "Shall we go after him?"

"No," Balor ordered. "It's of no purpose now."

"I don't understand, Commander," the bewildered officer said. "What about the Sea-God . . . and the cauldron?"

"They will be taken care of. And we have a much more valuable prize in exchange. See that our new captive is secured at once. And re-form your troops."

Salmhor gave orders. Soldiers moved quickly to bind Lugh and bring him to the mound. The remainder of the badly decimated Fomor company re-formed again below the mound.

"Commander," the officer said hesitantly as this was done, "if we don't act, these de Dananns will be free to take their cauldron back to Eire. We could begin the search again—"

"No," Balor said sharply, cutting him off. The eye lifted to scan the vast interior of the Sidhe as he went on. "I'm certain that searching further would be a waste of time. Those silver horsemen entered the mound through some hidden passage. It's likely the cauldron and this Manannan's little group have escaped the same way. And now that he is loose, he may have some other surprises for us. It is possible that this 'Sea-God' has more powers than I believed."

The eye came back to Salmhor. "In any event, we'll take no chances. Once the troops have gathered, we'll start back to the ship. As soon as we are far enough out to sea, I'll see to it that nothing on this isle survives!"

Lugh heard these last words as he reached the mound.

"You can't do that!" he cried in protest.

"But you know I can, young Lugh," the hard voice replied, the shuttered red glare falling upon him. "You have seen the full power of this eye yourself."

Lugh knew that he was right. He had witnessed the tremendous force of the eye blasting apart a massive fortress and the high cliff on which it sat like a boy destroying a sand building with a kick of the foot.

"Why not destroy me too?" Lugh asked angrily.

"Because your appearance here, your survival of the trap set for you, has proven something to me that I'd never really believed," the giant replied. "Mathgen thought his own powers might not destroy you. He was right."

The name of Mathgen struck a faintly familiar chord in Lugh's mind. But he had no time to consider its importance now. Too much else was happening that he needed to understand.

"You've the power to destroy me," Lugh said. "Why not use it?"

"Because I now believe that this Prophecy cannot be denied. Manannan, the cauldron, the de Dananns, are all unimportant. You are the key to the destruction of the Fomor race. You are the one who will see that the Prophecy is fulfilled."

"Then kill me."

"The Prophecy does not say you will be killed. It may be that such a thing is not possible. Perhaps it is dangerous even to try. It may be that so long as you choose freely to fulfill the Prophecy, it will be your destiny to do so, and nothing can stop it."

"That's nonsense," Lugh said harshly. "You beat me this time. I couldn't destroy you."

"This time!" Balor repeated. "Yet you survived. As you have survived so often before—at the Tower, against Bres, against Mathgen's power. No, there is some force in you. A dangerous force. My people have none of the de Dananns' belief in magic, but there is something in you that I have no wish to challenge. It must be you who ends this Prophecy. You must choose not to be the Champion. You must choose not to fulfill this destiny and it will have no more hold upon you."

Once Lugh had wished to be free of the destiny Manannan had thrust upon him. On the point of death he had seen it as false. Now he considered Balor's words. Was there a truth in them? Did he have a force within him? Was he, indeed, the key to the destruction of the Fomor and of this metal monster towering above him?

These thoughts gave him new courage to boldly look up into the glowing eye.

"You think I would choose to abandon the de Dananns?" He managed a scornful smile at this notion. "And why would I do that? I am one of them. My father was their champion, killed by you!"

"You are much more than a de Danann, Lugh," the low, ringing voice tolled out. "You are also the son of Ethlinn, my own daughter!"

From their shelter in the thickets some distance from the mound, Manannan and his reunited company watched the Fomor and Lugh upon the hill.

"That young fool," the lanky guardian said with unaccustomed heat. "Why did he have to lead the Riders against Balor that way? We could have escaped without him taking that chance. Besides, we're the ones who can be sacrificed. Not him!"

"You made him the Champion," Aine shot back angrily. "You can't be upset with him if he acts like one. He was only doing what he thought he had to do!"

Abashed by the truth of this, he smiled sheepishly. "I'm sorry. You're absolutely right. He was very courageous to go at Balor like that. It just leaves us in a very awkward spot, that's all."

"I still say we didn't have to run," the Dagda said. "We could have stayed behind and made a real attack on Balor!"

"And gotten ourselves reduced to lumps of ash?" said Manannan. "Fine help that would have been. This way we might get another chance at him at least. If I could only use my powers . . ."

"Your powers!" the Dagda said in derisive tones. "We've seen precious little of those!"

"Can't the Riders of the Sidhe be re-formed?" Findgoll asked.

The guardian shook his head. "If they weren't destroyed completely by that energy of Balor's, it'll likely be a great while before they can recover. I'm afraid we're on our own, as usual."

He peered out cautiously again from cover, toward the gathering troops.

"It looks as if they've given up on us," he commented. "Balor must have realized by now that it's useless to try finding us again."

"Do you think they'll leave the isle?" Angus asked.

"It may be. If they do, I might be able to use my powers"— he threw the Dagda a smile—"regardless of what anyone thinks of them, and rescue Lugh."

"You might, might you?" the Dagda said, his disdain still

very evident. "Well, if your powers are so great as all that, there should be no question of the thing."

"I suppose I could simply destroy them all," Manannan replied dryly. "But I really don't think we want that, at least so long as Lugh is with them. Our concern is somehow to get him away from them, under the eye of that cursed heap of iron."

Across the Sidhe, the Fomor had now formed up in their well-ordered columns. Lugh, under a heavy guard, was placed in their center, and the march back toward the entrance was begun. Behind them, Balor rolled smoothly along on the massive, wheeled throne, his head pivoting constantly back and forth, scanning the interior for any movement.

"There they go!" Manannan announced. "We'd better follow them. But I suggest we let them get well ahead. We don't want to be caught in the gaze of that flaming eye."

They waited impatiently as the Fomor party climbed the slope to the tunnel entrance and finally left the Sidhe. Only then did they decide that it was safe to follow. Still, they moved to the tunnel and through it with great cautiousness, mindful that the wily Balor might have left a trap behind.

By the time they finally reached the outside of the mound, the metal giant's force was far ahead, moving across the meadows toward the sea.

"Their ship is in the southwest cove," Aine told her brother. "They really must be planning to leave."

"Let's go and watch," Manannan said, with more of his usual buoyant nature returned to him. "We can wave good-bye."

The little band made quite a peculiar sight as it stealthily pursued the Fomor troops across the fields. Their adventures had left all of them looking as ragged as Manannan was in his clown dress. With his gawky figure, massive Dagda, cadaverous Morrigan, tiny Findgoll, and the lion-shaped Pooka together, they looked more like a party of traveling entertainers than of determined rescuers.

When the Fomor reached the cove, Manannan led his comrades to a vantage point where they could safely watch the activity below. They saw, drawn up close to the shore, a familiar black ship of the Tower fleet, but half again as large as the others. A wide bridge of flat metal sheets had been built from it up across the rocky beach to the smooth ground above. The soldiers had already marched down it, taking their prisoner to the waiting ship. Balor was in the process of descending now, the wheeled contraption inching slowly but steadily down the steep incline.

Once he had reached the bottom and was alongside the ship, a massive crane was swung out on a boom. Men scurried to affix its cables to protrusions on Balor's throne. Then, with a loud and labored groaning sound, like some great beast straining under the immense load, the crane rose up, lifting the Commander, swinging him aboard, lowering him to rest in the ship's stern. There, the base of the throne was settled by more men into grooves in the metal deck, and heavy latches were forced into place, locking it firmly down.

"Fascinating," Manannan remarked, honestly intrigued. "They actually attach him to the ship. Couldn't have him just rolling about, I guess."

With Balor settled, Lugh was brought to stand by him, under a heavy guard. Many of the soldiers went below deck while the Fomor sailors took their stations. From his own position just beside his commander, Sital Salmhor gave the final orders to depart. At once the ship's forces boomed to life, settling quickly to a deep, steady, throbbing sound. The sleek vessel backed away from the shore and turned its sharp prow toward the sea.

"Right!" Manannan said with satisfaction. "Now all we have to do is let them get out a bit, and we can act."

"I'm not certain that I really want to know," the Dagda said warily, "but does that mean you have another plan?"

"I do," the tall man said, grinning with his old charm. "And better than the last."

"I surely hope it is," the other replied.

The black ship was well out into the sea by now, slashing through the waves toward the bank of fog lining the horizon.

Manannan was expecting to see it continue on. He was surprised when its forward speed was reduced and it fell away from its course, swinging around to run slowly, parallel to the coast.

The ship was still only a short distance out, and close enough for Manannan's party to see clearly, when the barrel head of Balor began swiveling toward them. As it did, the glitter of the eye, at first only a bright red point of light, began to grow sharply in intensity.

Manannan was the first to grasp the ominous significance in this.

"Balor's not leaving!" he cried. "He's going to destroy the isle from there!"

He leaped boldly up onto the rocks above the sea and stretched out his arms toward the waves. Almost at once, the sea made its response. There began a roaring sound, distant but growing rapidly, like constant rolling thunder sweeping in. Aboard the Fomor ship, the alarmed sailors turned to look out toward it. They saw a line of high, sharp waves sweep from the fog band and descend upon them with incredible speed.

Unaware of this, Balor was steadying his gaze upon the isle, focusing his power upon the peak of the mound visible above the shore. The destructive beam shone out as the first wave struck the ship sideways on. It heeled the vessel over suddenly, jerking down the crimson gaze. The force of it struck the rocky shore near the company of heroes, shaking the island with the force of its explosion, blasting out a cavern that would have held Tara's central hall.

The little company was knocked down, showered with the fine fragments of the rock. As they staggered up again, the Dagda called out warningly to the guardian:

"Let's not just get him pointing that eye at us, shall we?"

On the ship, Sital Salmhor gave orders to his helmsmen to quickly turn the bow into the new, incoming line of waves. Balor, trying to hold his aim upon the Sidhe, bellowed in his anger.

"Salmhor, what are you doing? Hold this ship steady!"

"We cannot, Commander!" the officer protested desperately. "We'll be swamped!"

The ship came about quickly enough to take the next waves three-quarters across the bow. It rocked dangerously, but managed to crash through. Now realizing that something strange was happening, Balor swung his massive head around to see the lines of waves, one close upon another, rolling out from the fog toward them. He understood.

"All right. Turn into them. But keep this ship as steady as you can! I'm not leaving here without wiping away that mound!"

He turned his gaze once more toward the peaceful green isle. This time he noted the tiny group of figures clustered on the rocks above the shore. Even at that distance he recognized the "Sea-God's" lanky form.

"Manannan," the voice clanged out. "This is some trick of his."

"But, Commander, you said he had no powers you couldn't defeat," Salmhor reminded him.

"Never mind!" Balor said sharply. "Hold steady!"

The giant tried once more to fix his gaze upon the shore, this time aiming at the Guardian of the Isle himself. But the next incoming wave struck the ship, sweeping under it, lifting it high, dropping it forward into the trough beyond where yet another wave swooped it up almost at once. The dizzying rise and fall made it impossible to direct a beam from the eye.

"Please, Commander," Salmhor said desperately, "we must put on some forward speed or the waves will drive us under. They are coming faster every moment!"

Balor considered. If this sudden attack of the sea was caused by Manannan, then the being did have enormous and dangerous powers. He might even use them to try destroying the ship if he thought it would save his isle. A strategic retreat for now seemed the most sensible course.

"Very well, Salmhor," he agreed. "We can see to Manannan's Isle later. Head out to sea. Full speed!"

When the guardian realized that the black ship was headed away and that Balor had given up the attack, he ceased his own at once. He dropped his arms and jumped down from the rocks. The sea waves died immediately and the water returned to a gently rippling calm.

"What are you doing?" Aine protested. "You'll let them get away!"

"If I tried to use the waves to hold them, I might sink the craft," he told her reasonably. "It wouldn't save Lugh for us. He's bound and under guard. No, we've got to find a way to free him and somehow get him off before I unleash my real force on that monster's ship."

He began a rapid descent to the beach, whistling loudly as he went. Puzzled, the others scrambled after him.

By the time they reached the edge of the sea, a very peculiar craft had appeared around the northern point of the cove, moving briskly toward them in answer to the master's call.

It was a large and very ornate chariot-of-war pulled by a prancing team of graceful white horses. They glided across the wavetops, wheels churning up a frothy wake, horses' hooves planting firmly on the water's surface as if it were solid earth.

Manannan realized with amusement that his companions from Eire were staring rather openmouthed at this incredible sight. The Dagda looked at him and spoke, this time with genuine awe.

"You really are the Sea-God!"

"Please, don't say it with such reverence," Manannan protested. "I'm a man with a certain amount of magical power. Incredibly handsome, yes. Brilliant, witty, bold, all of that. But still a man, and your friend. Don't let that change."

"How can those horses do that?" Angus asked. "They act as if they were trotting across a field!"

"It seems that way to them," Manannan explained. "To their eyes, they're on the most normal and solid of meadows. They'd balk if they thought they were walking on the sea. Actually, it's a fairly simple bit of magic to harden up briefly the waves just in the chariot's path. I've found it a most effective device for frightening away fishermen who happen too close to the isle. A sword-waving man in a chariot on the sea sends them into a panic! And, of course, it helps build up the Sea-God image."

"I've seen Danu's High-Druids use the spell," said Findgoll, more impressed than ever by Manannan's power. "Of course, they wouldn't teach its use to us. They said we could never control it."

"Look, could you two carry on your little talk some other time?" the Dagda injected with some irritation. "That ship is carrying Lugh farther away every moment. We've got to do something."

"Nothing can really be done quite yet," Manannan told him placidly. "I want to give them time to get well into the fog band first. They can't think anyone is coming after them."

The chariot had now reached them, the team trotting up upon the shore, pulling to a halt right beside the little band. Manannan hopped into the car.

"What are you going to do?" asked Aine.

"Only surprise can save Lugh," he explained. "Someone has got to sneak aboard and free Lugh." He looked at the raven-woman. "Morrigan, I'm afraid it's got to be you. Will you come?"

Without a word, the black-cloaked warrior climbed into the chariot beside him. Knowing her dislike of the sea, Manannan's admiration for her increased.

"What about the rest of us?" the Dagda asked.

"Force will gain us nothing this time," he replied. "One person alone may have a chance to get to Lugh with my help."

Each of the others demanded that they be the one allowed to take this risk, Aine most stridently. But Manannan held up a silencing hand.

"I know how you all feel, but you've got to trust me again in this. I can't get close enough for you to climb aboard, and none of you can fly there."

"I can," said a quiet voice.

Manannan looked toward it, seeing the curious lion-beast who had accompanied them from the Sidhe.

"Oh, hello," he said politely. "I'd quite forgotten you. You're a Pooka, aren't you?"

It nodded. "My name is Shaglan."

"I've been meaning to ask how it was you joined our little band."

"It saved Lugh in Eire," Aine hastened to explain. "It's been very helpful to us since."

"Yes," Manannan agreed. "I saw it on the mound. Most effective."

"It's still not to be trusted." Morrigan cawed harshly.

At this the Pooka looked hurt.

"I know their reputation," the tall man said, "but if he's a friend to Lugh, he's welcome with us!"

The Pooka smiled with renewed confidence. "And I could help you now," he offered earnestly. "I could fly to the ship as well."

"I'll take no help from the likes of it," Morrigan said, fixing the animal with her sharp gaze. "Neither Lugh nor I would survive."

"Morrigan could be right," the Dagda put in. "I don't know what this one's done, but nothing would convince me of their good intent. They've betrayed us before, and this one may just be waiting to do it again. This is Lugh's life we're talking about. We surely can't be risking it with a Pooka!"

The faces of Angus and Findgoll mirrored the suspicion and hostility their friends had voiced. Shaglan looked around at them despairingly, finally meeting the eyes of Aine.

"Aine, please tell them," it implored her. "You know me. You know I'd not betray Lugh. Tell them I only want to help."

She looked into the large, dark, soulful eyes. She wanted to support the poor beast, but she couldn't. Her heart told her to trust it, but her mind was still clouded with the old distrust of its treacherous family. There was too much uncertainty, and she couldn't allow that to endanger Lugh.

She shook her head slowly. "I'm sorry, Shaglan," she said with great regret. "I just cannot take the chance. Please understand."

Crushed by this rejection, the whole animal wilted before their eyes. Its spirit gone, it let its form go, too, and lost all definition, becoming a vague, shifting conglomeration of animal parts, all sagging together in a poignant image of dejection.

It turned without another word and slunk away, climbing up from the beach and vanishing from sight.

Manannan shook his head. "Too bad. But, you may have acted for the best. And Morrigan can likely do this better alone."

He looked back out to sea. The Fomor vessel had by now reached the band of fog, and its sleek hull sliced into the thick grey like a knife into a loaf of bread, slipping quickly out of sight.

"Ah, time to go!" he announced. "Hang on, Morrigan."

With that he took up the reins and, with a brief farewell wave to the others, ordered the team away. The horses swiftly pulled the chariot to sea, and in moments it was far out in the cove, skimming away at an increasing speed.

Behind him on the shore he left a collection of very worried faces.

"What if they fail?" the Dagda asked bluntly.

"If anyone can succeed in this, it is Manannan," Aine replied with what assurance she could raise.

"What if they fail?" he asked again, more insistently.

XXVI

THE BLACK SHIP

WITHIN THE FOG, Manannan was urging the team forward, but at a much slower pace. The great wheels softly rolled across the waves. The fog that enveloped them was like a muffler, deadening all noise.

"I wanted Balor's ship well into the fog before we came too close," he whispered to Morrigan. "As soon as we're in sight of it, you only have to fly to it without being seen, release Lugh, and get over the side with him. Then I'll sweep in and pick you up." He grinned. "It's quite simple, really."

"I cannot swim," the low, hoarse voice croaked out.

"Lugh can," he replied reassuringly. "And I'll be close by. It'll work out. Just trust me."

She gave him a chill, glittering look but didn't reply. She stood stiffly, furled in her cloak, her hand clutching the rail of the chariot, her skull-like face an emotionless mask. Only the white knuckles of her bony hand upon the rail revealed her inner tension. Manannan noted it, amused but unconcerned. No matter what her fears, he knew that when the time for action came, she would be wholly the fearless warrior.

"As soon as you have Lugh off that ship, I can turn my powers fully against it," he told her with anticipation. "Then we can see who really is the stronger here." Something in the fog ahead caught his attention then, and he peered toward it.

"Ah, there it is!" he said, pointing.

Faintly, at first only a grey shape floating in the clouds, the Fomor ship came into view.

"We'll have to move in closer," he said softly. "We have to be able to see what's happening on the deck."

"It would help if something could distract the Fomor," she said.

"That," he replied, "will be taken care of soon."

Aboard the black ship, the giant figure of Balor had just

finished scanning the fog-shrouded seas behind. His metallic voice held a distinct note of satisfaction as he spoke to Lugh, under guard before him.

"Your 'Sea-God' has clearly given up any other attempts to stop me. I'll return later to finish our little contest. But he is of no matter now. Returning to the Tower with you is our only concern. Once you see that you are wrong to help the de Dananns against us, their foolish little rebellion will come to nothing, even if your companions do succeed in returning that cauldron to Eire."

"Dragging me to your iceberg is a waste of your time, Balor," Lugh said fiercely. "You'll never convince me that I'm your grandson. My mother could never have been the daughter to a monstrous thing like you!"

"I will not explain the ways of it to you," the voice rumbled slowly. "But you know the truth of it in your heart and in the deepest part of your mind. Think! Feel! Then deny it."

With a growing sense of unease, Lugh considered Balor's words. Were they the truth? Was that why he had felt that strange sense of kinship with the traitorous Bres? Was it because they were alike in this, both half-breeds, the blood of two races flowing in their veins?

He pushed the idea away. No, it was impossible. It was a trick by this ruthless being to confuse him, to convince him to withdraw his help from the de Dananns.

"You'll never get me to change my mind, Balor," he said with determination. "I know what you are and what you've done. So you'd best destroy me right now if you can, because I'll do all I can to destroy you!"

"Sooner or later, you will come to believe," the giant said. His gaze shifted to his officer. "Salmhor, take him below and secure him there. As soon as we are clear of this fog, get the sail up and set a course directly for the Tower."

Salmhor and an escort of soldiers took Lugh forward. As they walked, the young warrior looked around him in curiosity. He had never seen one of the great black ships of the Tower so closely. Despite his perilous situation, he found himself fascinated.

Just forward of the stern where Balor's throne sat was a small, square structure with open doors on either side. As they moved past it, Lugh glanced inside, noting a Fomor busy over a complex array of gadgets, levers, and wheels. These, he as-

sumed, were the mechanisms that somehow controlled the
huge vessel.

Just beyond this structure, the deck opened up, a wide, flat
expanse of dark metal whose surface was patterned with small,
raised diamonds. Along the sides, waist-high rails prevented
anyone's falling overboard. Fomor now lined those rails, peering with great interest and a bit of concern into the rolling
banks of fog. Far ahead, at the sharply pointed prow, there was
a raised platform. More Fomor were clustered there, several
busy around an enormous crossbow, like ones Lugh had seen
before but many times larger. They were cranking back its
thick string, setting in its firing channel a bolt thicker than his
leg.

Clearly they were preparing for something, waiting for
something. He wondered what? And then he realized. They
still had to contend with the weird and often deadly menagerie
of sea creatures that inhabited Manannan's protective fog.

In the center of the deck, just before the towering mast,
they reached a large, rectangular opening. A set of metal stairs
led down from there into the dim interior of the ship. With
Salmhor leading the way, they descended below the main
deck, into a narrow corridor. Small, glowing squares set at regular intervals along the corridor ceiling coldly lit the blank grey
metal walls. They revealed doors, widely spaced along either
side.

At the first door on their right, Salmhor stopped, turning a
latch and swinging the heavy panel back. He stepped aside,
directing the soldiers to take Lugh through. The room beyond
was long but narrow, the outer wall formed by the ship's hull,
curving out and up. It was a storage room, Lugh judged, with
tiers of kegs stacked and roped against the inner wall, and
other types of equipment—boxes, barrels, covered lumps of no
recognizable shape—all securely tied to heavy cleats in the
deck to prevent their shifting.

Salmhor had the soldiers fasten Lugh to one of these cleats
set in the outer hull. They used a heavy chain with shackles
that clamped tightly about his ankles, the sharp edges pressing
into the flesh. Boltlike objects locked them securely.

Salmhor ordered the guards back to the door and stood looking at Lugh, an arrogant smirk of triumph on his lips.

From his belt he pulled the sheathed Answerer, which he

had carried aboard. He stepped toward Lugh, holding it up temptingly.

"I thought you might wish to look at this, at least," he taunted.

Lugh made a sudden leap forward, reaching out in a desperate attempt to grasp the blade. It was just the move Salmhor had hoped for. He had carefully stayed just outside Lugh's short reach. Now he stepped back as the shackles at the warrior's ankles tripped him up. Lugh fell forward, crashing heavily to the hard deck. As he did, Salmhor stepped forward, swinging his heavily booted foot into Lugh's ribs.

The young man grunted at the blow, rolling onto his side. He looked up into the grinning face of the officer.

"Just too far," Salmhor said with mock regret. "How sad."

Carefully tugging his pristine uniform down smoothly again, he went to the door and hung the Answerer on a hook beside it.

"There," he said. "Now you'll have something to think about during our voyage. You'll never have another chance to use this weapon to humiliate soldiers of the Tower."

He strode haughtily from the room, slamming the metal door behind him.

Lugh sat up, pressing a hand to his bruised side. He found that the skin of his ankles had been cut by the shackles, and blood oozed around the edges of the metal. He examined his prison more carefully, noting a row of cleats along the outer wall. From each one chains like his own were hung, and the rust-brown stains upon their heavy cuffs told him that they had been used. Clearly, the ship had carried captives before.

He sat back against the chill wall in despair, looking at the Answerer, so maddeningly close. If he could only reach it, he was certain that even these chains couldn't withstand its magically tempered blade. He looked about him, but nothing he might use to help him was within his reach. Was he really doomed to be carried off to Balor's fortress of glass?

Something heavy struck the vessel from below, making the hull vibrate. For a moment he was puzzled by this, but then he understood. The creatures of the fog had begun their attack upon the ship.

Perhaps none of them would ever reach the Tower.

On the deck above, Balor was already bellowing out his commands.

"Salmhor, see that we keep a straight heading. Ready the men to repel any attack."

The officer set the helmsman to a steady course, and the black ship knifed on through the fog. Balor turned his crimson eye toward the sea ahead, waiting for some form to show itself. Fomor armed with spears and long pikes and crossbows took positions at points along the bulwarks, prepared in case some creature should manage to reach the vessel's side.

Another hard bump came against the hull. This he ignored. The ship was too large, its surface too hard for any blow to damage it seriously. And if anything did become visible, even for a moment, Balor would have his chance.

There was a long pause. The ship glided on in silence save for the soft gurgle of water under the sleek keel. Then, in the fog ahead, something dark and massive suddenly loomed up. In panic, the helmsman jerked the vessel aside to avoid collision. The beam of energy Balor fired went wide, exploding on the surface of the sea, sending up a geyser of spray.

"Turn from the course again, and you will die!" Balor warned the helmsman.

The black spear of the ship tore on through the shrouding grey. Another form rose up before it, a smooth, rounded hump of back and a slender neck topped by a snakelike head. In bold challenge to the ship, it held position dead ahead. This time, however, the ship did not swerve away.

Balor's eye lifted, and a ruby beam of light shot through the swirling clouds like red-hot iron thrust through a bank of snow, melting it away. It struck the unprotected body of the beast, burning a tunnel into the flesh. The animal convulsed in its death agony, rolling over, switching violently across the surface, large flippers, neck, and tail creating a maelstrom about it before it sank from sight.

But this single defeat did not frighten away the creatures inhabiting the fog. Things of many kinds, some impossible to define in the roiling grey, now came against the Fomor ship in a more unified attack. Other long-necked beings popped up here and there, only to glide away. A group of Usiage Baugh—green-grey water horses with webbed hands for hooves and manes like flowing seaweed—charged out of the clouds, darted at the ship, and dove beneath it. Thick, sucker-coated tentacles crawled over the sides to grab for the Fomor, and massive fish leaped from the water to strike the vessel's sides. The assault was continuous and determined. It kept the crew and soldiers of the ship in constant readiness to fend something off, and it kept Balor's eye in constant movement, swinging from side to side to send out its deadly beam.

But these creatures had tasted the sting of Balor's eye before. This time they moved more quickly, stayed farther away, teasing and nagging at the Fomor, but with some safety. Still, the beam struck home at times, killing or badly wounding every being it touched.

From the chariot hovering behind and to one side of the black ship, Morrigan and Manannan watched this struggle begin. They had been close enough to see Lugh moved below, and now, with the commencement of this attack, it was time to act.

"All right, Morrigan," Manannan said softly. "We don't dare move closer or they may take note of us, even busy as they are. Lugh's somewhere inside that ship. Find him and get him overboard. And remember to go off on this side so I'll be sure to see you."

"As you said, simple," she hissed.

She made her transformation and rose up, the black form sailing into the banks of fog. Manannan kept his eyes fixed upon the Fomor ship, holding the chariot carefully at a constant distance, ready to dart in.

The raven glided silently through the billowing grey to the ship. She made two high passes above the deck before she identified the opening that led below. Then, picking a moment when the Fomor seemed fully occupied by the menacing creatures, she swooped directly in, arrowing down from the fog in a black streak, aiming skillfully for the dark rectangle. She went unobserved by the Fomor along the rails, shooting down the stairway out of sight.

But her passage was not totally unnoticed. Sital Salmhor, keeping an officer's eye on the performance of his men, saw the bird flash past. He knew that black shape, had seen it soaring safely away from him in the Sidhe. He knew where the ravenwoman was heading now.

Balor was occupied, loosing scorching blasts of light at a hovering band of water horses. The arrogant Salmhor chose to deal with this himself. He called to three nearby soldiers.

"Come with me quickly," he ordered. "Morrigan has just gone to free Lugh."

Down below, Morrigan had landed in the corridor and, finding it empty, had made her transformation. Now, sword in hand, she threw open the first door she reached and leaped inside.

"Morrigan!" Lugh exclaimed with surprise and delight.

She stepped forward, stopping at the sight of his shackles. "What about those?" she asked sharply.

"Get me the Answerer!" he told her, pointing to it. "There!"

She turned and saw it, moved quickly to it and lifted it from the hook.

Behind her, in the doorway, Lugh saw the movements and the flicker of light on a keen blade. He shouted a warning as the soldiers burst through.

She had just enough time to launch the sheathed sword toward Lugh before they were upon her, the three men driving her back along the room. But she drew her other weapon and their advance was stopped by her furious counterattack.

Lugh, meanwhile, had leaped to his feet and caught the thrown Answerer's hilt in both hands. Sital Salmhor, coming through the doorway on the heels of his men, saw Lugh regain the weapon and rushed upon him, drawing his own sword.

In a swift move, Lugh shook the bright blade free of its sheath, raised it above his head, and brought the edge—hardened by the magic of Tir-na-nog—down in a well-aimed blow against the chain linking the shackles.

The sword cut through them as if they were of wood, setting Lugh free. Salmhor cried out in rage and launched a flat swing of his weapon at Lugh's neck. The warrior jerked back and the blade whisked harmlessly past. He swept the Answerer upward, its fine point just touching the tunic front of Salmhor's uniform, tearing the material and scratching a line of blood across his chest.

The officer staggered back. He glanced down, horrified not at his minor wound, but at the damage to his perfect uniform. He drove in again, this time with a precise flurry of blows calculated to beat down his opponent's guard. As a swordsman, Lugh found him well-disciplined and fast. But his methodical style of fighting proved his weakness. Lugh quickly saw where each blow would come from and began easily to counter them. He drove Salmhor back across the room with a flamboyant series of parries and thrusts that threw a sudden fear into the officer.

Lugh began to regret that he would have to kill the man. To humiliate him would be much more satisfying. Then he saw his chance. He backed Salmhor against the tiers of barrels along the wall and, swinging a high blow that made the man duck down, he deftly cut through the ropes holding the cargo in place.

The whole wall toppled forward, the avalanche of barrels catching Salmor beneath and bearing him to the floor, stunned and pinned by the weight. Several barrels, Lugh noted with pleasure, had been filled with food supplies, and various types of liquid were now oozing out to cover the man and his neat grey uniform.

"How sad," said Lugh, turning away to aid Morrigan.

He saw at once that she needed none. Two of the Fomor were already down, and she was in the act of finishing the third. One sword pushed up the man's long pike, the other dove in beneath, slipping through his rib cage.

She joined Lugh and they rushed to the door expecting other soldiers. But the corridor was empty.

"What now?" he whispered.

"We get over the side into the sea," she told him. "Hurry!"

They moved along the corridor to the stairs and crept upward, weapons ready. Crouching at the top, they peered out on deck. Beyond and high above the square structure where the helmsman worked, Balor's barrel head was visible, swiveling constantly from side to side, the slit of red eye ready to flash its beam. The rest of the Fomor were at their positions along the bulwarks.

Morrigan pointed to a section of the nearby rail that held no soldiers.

"We must go over there," she whispered. "Don't be stopped by anything."

He nodded. Together they leaped from the stairwell and ran for the rail.

None of the Fomor took note of them until they reached it. Lugh knew that they were safe. No one could stop them from vaulting the rail now. He grabbed its upper rung, prepared to leap over, then paused. Morrigan, beside him, had ceased to move.

He looked at her. She was frozen, her hands gripping the rail tightly, her body stiff, her gaze fixed on the water gushing past below. He saw something showing in her face that he had never seen before—stark fear! He realized that for some reason she was unable to jump into the sea.

The Fomor were now beginning to move toward them, brandishing their pikes and spears. The crossbows were coming up.

"We've got to jump, Morrigan!" he pleaded.

No response.

He knew he had to take her over the side, but there was no time. The Fomor were nearly upon them.

A huge form with outspread wings swooped down from the fog above the ship upon the advancing soldiers. Its clawed feet raked across the first ones, driving them back into their fellows. As this unexpected savior wheeled up and around to dive back, Lugh recognized a familiar shape. It was the Pooka.

"Get over!" it cried to him as it swept in again. "I'll keep them off."

Lugh obeyed. He pried Morrigan's strong grip from the rail, threw an arm about her bony waist.

The bird swooped down upon the Fomor, forcing them to duck. But now Balor's attention had been drawn to the events upon his own deck. His massive head swiveled back, and, as the bird turned and shot up before his eye, the ruby light flashed out.

The beam seemed to blast right through the Pooka, crumpling it into a bundle of feathers and knocking it aside. It plunged downward, crashing into the sea.

Lugh had no time to mourn his friend's loss. As the Fomor charged in, he dove forward, taking Morrigan across the rail with him.

XXVII

REUNION

MANANNAN SAW LUGH and Morrigan go over the ship's side and drop into the sea. He also saw Balor's head swinging around to bring the crimson eye to bear on them.

Now was his time to act, and to act quickly. He raised his arms and called upon his powers to strike.

The sea's answer came at once.

From the softly eddying fog a gale rose with a great roar, lifting up from the sea like some monster rising from the depths. It blasted through the greyness, spinning back the clouds in swirling columns on either side. The sea creatures swarming about heard it come and vanished in an instant from its path as the towering force slammed itself against the Fomor ship.

The vessel was caught broadside, unprepared. It heeled far over under the staggering blow, catapulting many of its startled crew far out into the waves. Its slender mast and sails were torn savagely away and cast overboard, where they trailed by the tangled rigging. The swift tilting of the stricken ship caught Balor by surprise as well. His massive upper body was jerked to one side. His arm and shoulder crashed into the sea. The side of the ship was driven underwater, held there by the dragging anchor of his overbalanced weight, and water poured in.

Balor thrashed out with his free arm, trying to throw himself back upright. Though taken off guard, he was still not beaten. He meant to use every means left him to survive.

"Cut loose the mast!" he bellowed through the shrieking winds. "Helmsman, turn the bow into this! Turn the bow!"

The Fomor struggled to obey. Men clambered along the tilted deck to reach the dragging wreckage and began to hack at the lines with their weapons. The helmsman, thrown from the little wheelroom by the first blow of the gale, pulled himself back to the controls. With desperate efforts he tried to throw the rudder over and bring the foundering ship about.

Manannan watched these desperate measures, watched the men thrashing wildly in the sea, and there was no pity in him. He remembered only what these cruel beings had so casually done to his innocent people and his bright Sidhe. He was not going to let them escape his revenge now.

He lifted his arms and shouted his command to the savage winds: "Strike them with your fury! Throw your full wrath upon them. Destroy that ship!"

And, with redoubled force, the gale threw itself again against the vessel. The sleek craft, seeming so vast and powerful before, was now no more than a bit of leaf, caught in a fall breeze and whisked away across the waves. The frantic attempts of its crew to right it were useless against such a punishing blast.

Manannan's last view was of a battered, mastless vessel, listing ever more badly from shipped water and the dragging weight of Balor. He was now heeled over so far that his entire side and one arm trailed in the water, while the other arm still flailed as he struggled vainly to throw himself back.

Then the swirling banks of fog swallowed up the scene. Balor and his ship were gone, and with their disappearance, the wind died too.

Manannan regretted that he couldn't follow after and watch the monster's final descent into the depths, but he had another matter more pressing at the moment. He urged the team quickly toward the place where Lugh and Morrigan struggled in the water.

They were not having an easy time of it. Morrigan's dread fear of the sea had turned her to a statue, a sinking deadweight that Lugh was desperately trying to buoy while he stayed afloat himself. But the Answerer was hanging from his waist, and the heavy shackles were still about his ankles, and their combined weight was trying very hard to pull him down.

He saw the chariot rushing through the waves toward them, but it was still so far away. Could he keep both of them from going under until it arrived? The waves were already washing against his face, filling his mouth and nose with their harshness, nearly gagging him.

Then something pushed up under him. Something large and

hard and smooth. He remembered the sea creatures. Had they come back?

The thing rose, lifting him higher, allowing him to keep his own head and Morrigan's above the surface. But something else came above the surface too—a large and sharp-edged fin. A shark of enormous size was beneath them.

Lugh considered panicking, but there was little he could do. He sat still, holding the raven-woman tightly, riding the creature's back, hoping Manannan would reach them before it decided to do anything irreparable.

The huge fish lay placidly beneath them as the chariot pulled beside them. Manannan leaned over the side and Lugh passed Morrigan to him.

"Quickly," he said. "There's a shark right under me."

The tall man looked down and glimpsed the sleek, giant shape beneath the waves. He hurried to haul Morrigan safely inside, then grabbed Lugh's hands and helped him aboard.

But as soon as they were off the shark moved, turning swiftly toward them and lifting from the water to reveal its wide, flat head and open jaws.

"It's coming for us," Lugh said, gripping his sword hilt.

"I nearly drowned myself there, holding you two up," it said affably in a familiar voice. "Did you know sharks have to keep swimming to breathe?"

"Shaglan!" Lugh cried in astonishment. "I thought that you were dead!"

"Just scorched a bit. Balor's eye really missed me."

"We'll discuss it later," Manannan advised, peering around into the fog. "Some real sea creatures may return to visit soon. And few of them are friendly, even to me."

So he turned the chariot back toward the isle and urged the team to a gallop. Shaglan, reveling in the speed of his new form, swam merrily about them on their way, insuring that nothing else would dare to do them harm.

"It would seem to me that you might owe this Pooka your life," Manannan commented in a casual way, looking at Morrigan.

They and the rest of their finally reunited band were back in the Sidhe now, seated around a large and cheering fire upon the central mound. Manannan's people, their normal bright spirits restored to them, hovered about, giving the heroes food and tending to various minor wounds. The Dagda constantly shooed them away, finding their attentions an irritant. Angus and Lugh seemed to find them a delight.

The young champion and Morrigan were bundled in heavy blankets, and huddled close to the flames. The hardy Lugh was already recovered from his soaking, but the raven-woman still shivered.

Even so, she was alert, fixing Manannan with a sharp eye as he spoke, and nodding in agreement with his words.

"I distrusted the Pooka. I was wrong," she rasped out. She looked toward it where it sat beside the fire, returned now to a large doglike form that Aine liked. "I will repay you."

"Just be my friend," it told her hopefully. "All I ask is to be a part of the de Danann race again, to talk to human beings, to be welcomed by them."

"You will be," the Dagda said heartily, "that I promise you. So far as we are concerned, you have redeemed yourself for the traitorous act of your family. You, at least, will no longer be cast out by our people."

The being smiled happily at this, and Lugh smiled with it, glad it had fulfilled part of its desires.

"He's a worthy addition to our little band," Manannan pronounced with enthusiasm. "Lugh, I'm glad you brought him with you."

"You should be thanking Danu that we came here at all!" Aine said with some irritation. "You know, the Fomor nearly killed Lugh in Eire. If they had, what would have happened to you then, my clever brother?"

"Ah, I knew you'd come," he said lightly, grinning. "I never had any doubt."

"Never any doubt?" she said in disbelief. "You should have been out there in the Burren with us. There would have been plenty of doubt then!"

"I had complete confidence in you," he told her. "Why do you think I kept you behind at Tara?"

"You told me why!" She glanced at Lugh. "You said that I . . . that we . . ."

He waved that away. "I only said that to make you stay. I needed someone held in reserve in case things did go wrong. I knew that if something happened to Lugh, you'd rush to help him or carry on for him. The Riders were ordered to return to you in such events. Well, I couldn't tell you that, could I? If you'd thought Lugh was in danger, you'd have insisted on going along with him. So I used the easiest means I could to separate you. It worked out quite well. Just as I planned."

"Why . . . you . . . hound!" she said, each word an explosion of rage. "You took advantage of my feelings for Lugh to make me do your will. You couldn't trust me to see the sense of it myself. Lugh is right. You are a manipulator, and a treacherous one. From now on, I'll do exactly as I please."

With that, she got up and moved to Lugh. She knelt by him, grabbed his face in both hands, pulled the astonished young man toward her, and planted squarely on his lips a long, hard, and very ardent kiss, to the vast interest and amusement of the others.

When she finally pulled away, it was to enthusiastic cheers from Findgoll, the Dagda, Shaglan, and her own brother.

"Fine work, Aine," he congratulated, not the least contrite.

"It's certainly warmed me up!" Lugh remarked, recovering from his surprise to smile at her.

"Me as well," Angus said with feeling.

From across the Sidhe there came a faint rumbling sound, and the gathering upon the mound turned toward it. From the distant trees a cart had emerged, pulled by scores of the inhabitants and carrying a large, dark object.

"Ah, they've brought the cauldron back," Manannan announced with satisfaction. "Good. Now we can prepare to get on our way."

"Do you think the Fomor will try to stop us going back?" asked Lugh.

"Maybe," the guardian answered. "But their ships can't stop me, and we'll choose a different route to Tara. One they'll hopefully not know." He grew thoughtful. "I will admit, though, that I'd feel better if I knew how they'd anticipated our moves."

A memory returned to Lugh at that.

"Balor said that he was helped. He mentioned a name that seemed familiar." He looked at the Pooka. "Shaglan, was it you that mentioned someone called Mathgen?"

"Mathgen!" the Dagda cried. "It can't be. I saw him die myself!"

"Do you think somehow that evil Druid could be alive and helping the Fomor?" Findgoll asked Manannan anxiously.

"I had heard a tale that Balor had a Druid in the Tower," the tall man answered. "I thought it was one he had captured. But knowing it's Mathgen explains how he learned of the Prophecy, how he found where Lugh was hidden, and why he decided to visit my isle."

"Mathgen," said Findgoll. "That's a name I hoped never to hear again. If it's true that he somehow has survived, then there is a power against us more deadly than Balor himself!"

Images flickered upon the screen in a confused montage: A stricken black ship being whirled away by the winds, a young man rescued by a water-borne chariot, a rejoicing group of people on the shore of a green isle.

"Balor has failed," the hoarse voice forced out.

The images faded and a picture of two people reappeared. Two Fomor officers stood before the creature suspended in its web of life, looking at the wasted mummy's face and the blinded eyes that, somehow, saw so much.

"What must be done?" one of the officers asked. "They will bring the cauldron back to Eire."

"That may not matter now," Mathgen's hideous, echoing whisper replied. "Our delaying them may have already sealed their doom. Bres has begun his march. He should reach Tara long before they can return. With the force he has gathered, he should easily be able to destroy them all. When Lugh and his companions finally reach their 'beautiful ridge,' they will find nothing left of the de Danann race." The lipless mouth stretched to a ghastly smile. "That will be a greater punishment for my old friends than their own deaths."

"And what of our commander?" another of the Fomor wondered. "Can your powers tell us if he has been destroyed?"

In answer, the image projected by the Druid's mind shifted again, this time steadying upon a view of the sea and of a towering wall of fog cutting abruptly across it, shutting all beyond it from sight.

But as the officers watched this scene intently, something appeared. A dark object showed deep within the swirling clouds, growing as it moved toward them until it finally slipped free of the cloaking white. It crawled across the waves with an agonizing slowness, like a badly wounded creature struggling to reach the safety of its den. As it grew larger, it resolved itself into a ship, once sleek and powerful, now battered, mastless, and listing heavily. Still, it was afloat and managing to propel itself haltingly with whatever forces were still functioning within it.

On its sharply canted stern, a giant figure was visible, its body bent to one side like something broken, a massive arm trailing in the sea. The being was motionless, seemingly lifeless. Yet, as the image of it drew clearer, the officers saw the great lid of metal hanging before its single eye shudder. There was a hesitation, as if all energy were being concentrated in this single act, and then it lifted.

Behind the slit that opened, the blaze of an immense and undiminished energy flared angrily.

BOOK IV
THE FOMOR STRIKE

XXVIII

BRES MARCHES

THE FACE THAT rose into view above the hill was more like that of a mole than a man, with tiny ears and mouth and a pointed, wet, quivering snout above which close-set little eyes glinted sharply. The body of this thing was stocky, nearly shoulderless, draped in the ragged Fomor dress, and heavily armed with sword, ax, and iron shield.

It paused on the rim of the hill to gaze carefully across the meadows ahead. Then, satisfied the way was clear, it advanced, making way for others moving up behind.

For an immense swarm of Fomor were marching south through the hills. Their host had turned the fine, peaceful countryside into a nightmare land, peopled with creatures such as those which haunt the most hidden, midnight landscapes of man's mind. Never before had Eire witnessed so vast a gathering of the hideous beings.

At their head, Bres himself rode arrogantly, confident that this army, this tidal wave of brutal force would finally sweep the de Dananns from existence and flush their hated blood from his veins.

One day more would see it done. One day. He smiled as he envisioned his triumphal return to Tara's hall. By tomorrow night Eire would be his once again.

"They were to have returned here days ago!" Bobd Derg pointed out emphatically. "Now, I demand that you let me address the rest of our people! They have a right to know the entire truth!"

High-King Nuada kept up his brisk walk across the fortress yard, forcing the bard to run along beside him. Every day the man had accosted him with this same demand, growing more strident as the days passed and the champions failed to return.

Nuada was tired of the constant argument. Now he tried to ignore Bobd Derg entirely.

But the bard would not be denied. He stepped before his High-King, forcing him to stop. He thrust his lean white face, the cheeks flaring red with his zealous fire, close to Nuada's. The fine, soft, bardic voice was urgent, each word cast separately at Nuada like a hard-thrown spear.

"You cannot pretend I do not exist. You know now that I am right! You know that you have called these people here to their slaughter. You've brought them here to die!"

"*Brought* them here?" Nuada answered, enraged. "Come with me!"

He seized the elbow of the slender bard and, without ceremony, walked him along to the fortress gates. Outside they stopped. Nuada lifted an arm and gestured around him.

"Look at them!" he told the younger man with force.

All about the fortress hill were the gathered de Dananns. Their temporary shelters—tents and crude huts—filled the slopes below the walls. From all over Eire they had come at Lugh's summons. Worn, hungry, battered, most without weapons, they had still come.

"Nearly our whole race is gathered here," Nuada said. "I did not bring them. They were not tricked into coming. They were asked to join the rising and they came by their own choice!"

"By their choice, was it?" Bobd Derg replied sardonically. "And I suppose they would so willingly have come if they had known they would face the combined might of every Fomor warrior in Eire without their promised mystical help!"

"I think they would," Nuada said firmly.

"Then you are living in some dream of your own," the bard retorted. "Look at their condition. They're not mad. They know they are weak, starving, untrained. Few are warriors and most never wished to be. They know that without help they cannot win. Only a promise that their strength would miraculously be restored has convinced them to come."

"You have no faith in your own people's courage, Bobd Derg," the High-King said. "You never believed they would have the courage to rise at all. You were wrong. You are wrong now."

"If what you're saying is true, then there is no reason why they should not know what they will face."

"We made a bond with Lugh," Nuada reminded him

sharply. "We wait until Bres marches against us. If the cauldron has not arrived by then, you are free to reveal the situation to our people. You may ask them then if they choose to give up the fight and abandon Eire. But there is no reason to place this problem before them until we've no other choice."

"You know now, in your heart, that there is no other choice," the bard told him with a savage intensity, his body trembling with an energy that the gaunt frame barely contained. "You know that the cauldron and Lugh and all the rest will not return."

With that, he spun on his heel and stalked away with a quick, nervous stride, moving down into the close-clustered dwellings of the de Danann clans.

Nuada watched him go with deep misgivings. He knew that the troublemaking bard would now go amongst the people and preach his doom to them. He would spread fear, plead for them to abandon Tara, to leave Eire with him and seek the haven of Tir-na-nog once again.

The High-King only wished he felt more confidence than he had expressed. As he looked out on the fields where the de Danann warriors practiced, he had to admit to himself that without the restorative powers of the cauldron, his people would have little chance of withstanding an all-out onslaught of Fomor.

Certainly they had all been rearmed by the skills of Goibnu, Cerdne, and Bridget, along with many other smiths. And those weapons were fine, keen-edged, deadly. But that didn't make the hands that wielded them any less infirm. For the past days these thousands of de Dananns had trained hard, trying desperately to regain some of the warrior skills. The few veterans amongst his household companies had served as teachers for some young men who had never fought, who had been oppressed and afraid all of their lives.

Some semblance of an army had been achieved. Some vague spirit for battle had been rekindled, but like an insect trapped and devoured by a spider, it was only the outer shell. The meat, the blood, the real life, had all been long since sucked away by the Fomor.

He felt a shell himself, shaky and old. He needed a drink to steady him, he thought. But he pushed the thought away with irritation. He couldn't escape that way. He had tried once. Then he had fought his way from drunken despair and retaken his throne as High-King. He had vowed to lead his people to freedom as he should have long before.

He went to work at once, using the activity to keep back the new sense of hopelessness that, like Bobd Derg, had begun to nag at him. He moved amongst the various groups of men, encouraging their work, instructing, demonstrating his own skills to them. He wondered, as he watched the spear throwers at practice, if they were ever going to improve enough to hit a human target in battle.

Toward noon, a movement on the northern hills caught his eye. He stopped in his labors to stare off toward the road that ran from them across the meadows to Tara. A horseman was moving along it at a breakneck pace.

Something in the urgency of the man's ride gave him a foreboding of bad news. Guessing that this rider was heading for the fortress's main gates, he moved toward them to intercept the man.

His guess was right. The rider came through the encampment without slowing his pace, pushing upward toward the gates. As he approached, Nuada recognized him as one of their best scouts. He raised a staying hand and the man saw him, reining in the worn, lathered horse, tumbling from its back to face his king.

The message came from him in broken, breathless sentences. It was what Nuada had been expecting, and fearing, for the last few days.

"My King, Bres is on the march now! There are thousands of Fomor, flooding down through the valleys from the north."

"How long until they reach us?" Nuada asked, keeping all emotion from his voice.

"They are a day behind me, maybe more. By tomorrow they will be here."

"So, Nuada, you can delay no longer," said another voice.

The High-King turned to find Bobd Derg close behind him. The bard had also seen the messenger ride in and had hurried to hear the news.

"Now you have no more excuses not to tell our people the truth," he went on with an air of triumph. "You will see then what they choose to do."

"They will stay and they will fight, no matter what," Nuada told him with barely contained anger.

"Then they will die," the other countered. "You know they will. It will be a slaughter. Our race—all of our people—will be destroyed. And if you do not tell them to escape now, it is you who will be the cause of every death!"

Crowds of de Dananns moved upward from their camps around the hill, pushing through the gateway, filling up the compound within the timber walls. The sounds of their excited talk, their questioning and guessing about the reasons for this call to meet, rose to a constant, uneven hum.

It penetrated to the upper gallery room of the great hall, where Nuada stood alone staring down at one of Gilla's charts spread out on a plank table. He stared down at the points the messenger had indicated as the last position of Bres's army. But it wasn't the markings on the map he saw, it was the hoard of monstrous beings he knew would soon drop down upon them like a war-ax.

In a gesture of anger, he slammed his fist upon the map, as if he could somehow crush those attacking warriors.

"What is it, Nuada?" someone asked.

The High-King looked around as Diancecht, chief physician to the de Dananns, climbed the last stairs to the upper room.

He was a tall man with a dignified bearing. One of the oldest of his people, age had touched him lightly, slightly stooping the shoulders, greying the thick, curling brows and hair, deepening the creases in his lean face.

"What are you doing here?" Nuada asked him irritably. He was in no mood to see anyone just now.

The austere man frowned and answered gruffly: "I only came to see if you were well. You've had very little rest these past days."

Nuada dropped down heavily on his bench, his voice contrite.

"I'm sorry, my old friend. I *am* weary, I suppose. Very weary." He propped his elbows on the tabletop and rested his forehead against his cupped hands. His body sagged.

"Something *is* wrong," Diancecht said, the gruff manner softening at once as he recognized his old comrade's real distress. "What's the matter with you? It's not the drink again, is it?"

"It's not those spirits haunting me," the man replied. "It's the specter of my own past failures. Bodb Derg's talk has shaken me. What if he's right? What if our friends never return? Will I be condemning my people to death if I don't tell them to abandon the fight, to leave Eire?"

"Nonsense," the other said forcefully, moving to the table. "Don't you be letting that enchanting bardic force of his work on you. You know what we have to do. Where's your old will?"

Nuada shook his head. "I don't know. Maybe it was only Lugh and the Dagda pushing me to act. Maybe my own will was lost long ago when I lost my kingship and my hand."

Diancecht leaned his long form across the table and gripped Nuada's hand, pulling it up.

"You see that hand?" he asked hotly. "My work gave it back to you. There's no sign of the joining, no sign it was ever gone. You are a whole man now. A whole man! Both in body and in spirit." He released the hand and looked Nuada fiercely in the eye as he went on. "Listen to me! You don't need Lugh or the Dagda to give you courage. Use your own, man! Have confidence in yourself! Danu does."

Nuada's expression grew puzzled at this remark.

"What do you mean?"

"Why, it's obvious!" the old physician said, beginning to pace restlessly across the gallery. "I've been sure of it since Lugh appeared amongst us to help. If it was Danu who sent him to us, and through him the Lia Fail, then she meant to see us rise against the Fomor and take Eire. And, she meant for you to lead us. Don't you see? Bodb Derg is wrong to think she wants us to fail here and return meekly to her. She knows we have to prove ourselves."

"And if we lose?"

Diancecht stopped pacing and wheeled toward his friend. "Then we die," he said flatly. "And that's a gamble we've faced all of our lives. It's what real living's about. What value would we have for ourselves if we've nothing we're willing to give up our lives for? Danu knew that. She knew we'd never be content until we'd redeemed ourselves."

"But I can't ask the others to sacrifice their lives. I can't make that decision for them."

"You don't have to," the other said. "They'll make it for themselves if you let them. The need for it is part of them. You'll see."

"You are a greater madman than my own father, Diancecht," Bobd Derg said harshly as he entered the upper room.

The two men turned from the window to face him. He stood stiffly, his eyes bright with the fevered energy that fueled his wretched frame.

"I'd hoped that with him gone—along with the rest of your champions—there might be some chance for sanity. I forgot that I'd still have to contend with you, old healer."

"Pray to Danu that you'll not need any healing from me," the tall man answered in chill tones.

Bobd Derg ignored that, looking at the king. "The people are all here now. It's time for us to speak to them. Then this madness will be forever ended."

He strode past them and pushed open the door onto the walkway that linked the upper floor to the outer parapet. He moved out onto it, Nuada close behind, stopping to look down on the crowd jamming the courtyard.

"Children of Danu!" he called, the trained bard's voice ringing out clearly over the crowd, silencing all talk. Hundreds of faces turned upward toward him. "You have been called here to be told the full truth of our situation. Then you may freely decide what you will do."

There were many bewildered glances exchanged at that. What truth was it they were to hear?

"You have all gathered to face a great Fomor army led by Bres," he went on. "We have just learned that this army is now on its way. It is thousands strong and it will arrive at Tara by tomorrow!"

This news raised an uproar amongst the gathered de Dananns.

Bobd Derg raised his arms to silence it.

"I know what grave concerns this raises. Though most of our own people have arrived, we are very weak and very ill prepared. We have neither the warrior's skills nor the strength to fight."

"But, the cauldron!" a man shouted from below. "It was to give us back our strength!"

"The cauldron was to have been here days ago!" the bard replied. "It will not come. You will have no magic to help you in this fight."

"What about Lugh!" called another. "The Prophecy has said he will lead us in destroying the Fomor power!"

"The Prophecy is false!" Bobd Derg shouted. "Lugh Lamfada has likely been destroyed by the Fomor power, along with Morrigan, Findgoll, Angus Og, and my father, the Dagda! They knew that without the cauldron you would have no chance against the Fomor. They took on a dangerous quest to bring it here in time to save you. But they failed! Now you must save yourselves."

"Save ourselves?" shouted the warrior cheiftain called Niet. "You mean, leave Eire? Return to Tir-na-nog?"

"We have no other choice," he said. The full force of his bardic powers were unleashed now, possessing the slender body totally. The voice carried across them, filled with gripping emotions, pleading, cajoling, threatening, all at once. "We were never meant for life here. Our years in Eire must have shown you all that. We are people of peace, lovers of the pleasures of life, at one with those of Tir-na-nog. Why die here needlessly when Danu welcomes us and wants us to return to her?" He looked around at Nuada who watched him stonily. "Even your High-King knows I am right. He knows that the de Dananns have no other choice."

There were murmurings from the gathered people. Bobd Derg had managed to raise doubts and fears in them.

"Nuada, is that true?" someone called up. "Do you think we should leave?"

"Yes!" cried another. "Nuada, please! What shall we do?"

Other voices joined them, pleading for the High-King to speak out.

He looked down at them, torn by his own doubts. He looked around toward Diancecht who watched him solemnly.

"From your heart," the old man said. "Tell them your heart."

Nuada swept his gaze back across the throng whose fate now depended on his words. If he supported Bobd Derg, they would go. If not, they might be destroyed.

His eyes went to the little mound across the yard where sat the small, plain, rounded stone called the Lia Fail—the Stone of Truth. It had proclaimed him king and made the uprising a reality. Now it was revealing another truth to him. He understood suddenly, unquestionably, that Diancecht was right about Danu. She had never meant for them to give up their fight for Eire. She had let them return here willingly, knowing what they must do to be once more their own. The Lia Fail was a sign of that, of her approval for their choice finally to act.

With a renewed sense of assurance, he moved forward to the rail of the walkway to address the crowd.

"My people, listen!" he said in a booming voice, untrained in the bardic arts of moving men, but filled with a kingly force of its own. "I will tell you no lies. There is an army of Fomor coming here, and those who went to fetch the cauldron have not returned.

"It may be that our comrades are dead," he said. "If they are not, they still may not return in time to aid us. Without that aid, we will face an army much stronger than our own. And if we are defeated, Bres will surely see all of us—children, aged, wounded, it won't matter—put to death. He intends to see our race cease to exist."

This raised a new uproar in the gathering. His words were a wave of chill water washing across them. They were even more frightening than those of Bobd Derg, and the bard smiled with satisfaction. It appeared the old king was finally accepting the end of his foolish dream.

Nuada raised his hands for silence, then went on, his voice taking on a new, more vigorous tone.

"But Eire is your land, and I will never tell you to abandon it. That choice must be yours."

Bobd Derg's smile vanished. He now gaped in dismay.

"So, tell me now," the High-King demanded. "Will you leave Eire or will you stay and fight?"

"I say we fight!" cried Febal, lifting his new-made spear above his head.

His cry was quickly taken up by others, running through the crowd, building quickly to a roar of acclamation as weapons were brandished high, creating a sea of glinting weapons within the fortress walls.

"No! No!" Bobd Derg called out desperately. "It means our deaths!"

"Then we will die on our own land!" shouted back a young harper who had gripped his first sword only two days before. Now his thin, pale face was flushed with a battle fire passed to him by warrior ancestors he had never known.

XXIX

LAST CHANCE

THE LITTLE BOAT sat empty on the shore of eastern Eire. Nearby a curious-looking company busied themselves about a massive cart.

"That ought to hold the thing," the Dagda declared with satisfaction, pulling taut a final knot. He stepped back to admire his handiwork.

Atop the cart the huge iron cauldron sat, covered with a heavy lid. Several cables passed over it and down to fastenings along the vehicle sides, securing the precious cargo in place.

"It's going to be a hard thing to move," Aine said, examining the load critically.

"We can move it," Lugh assured her. "Especially with the Pooka's help."

The animal had transformed itself into a brawny oxlike animal, and was allowing Angus to harness it to the cart. Any suspicions the de Dananns still had of it had finally been assuaged by its helpfulness and amiability. Now they talked and joked with it as if it had always been part of their company.

"How long will it be to return to Tara?" the Dagda asked Manannan.

The tall man, still in the clown's ragged dress, was poring over the chart of Eire carefully.

"I'd judge three days by the smoothest route," he said. "We'll not be able to go so directly as when we came."

"Three days," said Lugh, frustrated. "And if we had the Riders to help us, we could be there in less than one."

"We've tried three times now to summon them," Manannan reminded him. "I'm afraid that power of Balor's did them great harm. They may have been destroyed completely this time."

"But it's going to make us very late returning," Lugh said.

"They're likely thinking by now that we won't come. We've got to let them know we're on our way."

"Aye, lad," the Dagda agreed. "Nuada can send some help to meet us. We'll be growing weary of this soon. None of us is the freshest now, and even the Pooka and I can't pull forever. We'll need teams to take the load for us if we're to keep up our speed."

"We may need warriors to help us too," Angus put in. "The Fomor may still be looking to stop us."

They were all aware of that possibility. Though none of the black Tower ships had tried to capture them on the return voyage, more of the Fomor traps might lie ahead.

"We'll ask Morrigan to fly to Tara for us when she returns from scouting, then," Manannan said. "We'll just have to look out for ourselves until she brings some help."

"Now for us," the Dagda said briskly. "Take a hand, everyone. Let's get this bloody great lump moving along." He went to the harness beside the Pooka and strapped himself into it. Findgoll, who argued that he was fully capable of helping, was ordered by the others to ride instead. Lugh, Angus, and Aine took up ropes attached to the cart to aid their larger comrades in the heavy going. There was a rope for Manannan as well, but he didn't take it up at once. He was busy adjusting something about his head.

"There!" he exclaimed at last, looking toward them with a wide and thoroughly inane smile. "What do you think?"

The straggling hair and beard of Gilla Decaire now masked the Sea-God's silver locks and pleasant face. Once again Manannan had become the clown.

"Is that really necessary?" the Dagda asked impatiently.

"I don't mean to be treated like some special being when I'm in Eire," he answered firmly. "I've no power, after all. Less than you, Dagda. This way I'm just a man, and one not to be taken too seriously. If you're my friends, you'll keep my secret as long as I ask. Will you?"

The Dagda shook his head, more certain than ever that the lanky figure was a bit mad. Still, he agreed. So did the others, quite readily. They liked Manannan well enough, but they felt a great deal more comfortable with the clown and were glad to have him back with them.

That decided, they all fell to the ropes. It took a great first effort to budge the heavy cart, but finally the thing began to move and rolled ahead quite smoothly, picking up speed under the powerful urgings of the Dagda and Shaglan. The others were soon able to drop their ropes and trot alongside, ready to help again if a steep spot were reached.

As they moved away from the sea and headed inland, the same concern filled everyone's thoughts. Would they be in time to help?

The fear that they would not kept them moving forward at their best possible speed.

But they had not traveled far from the coast when a familiar black form appeared in the sky ahead. It approached rapidly, and seeing them below, spiraled down to land.

The little company stopped and watched as the great raven settled to the earth before them and shimmered its way into the Morrigan's tall figure.

It was obvious at their first sight of her that something of alarming proportions had happened, for her normally impassive face registered dismay.

"Morrigan, what is it?" Lugh asked. "What's happened?"

"It's Bres," she cawed. "His Fomor are on the march. I made a sweep to the north and saw them."

"How far from Tara?" the Dagda asked.

"A day, perhaps," she told him.

Stunned by this news, Lugh dropped down wearily on the edge of the cart.

"A day," he said, and looked up at the cauldron. "After all this, we're not going to get it back in time?"

"Isn't there any way?" Angus said to Manannan. "If we got help. If Tara sent men—"

"Bres will be upon Tara long before any help from there could reach us," the tall man said. "No, I'm afraid that nothing they can do will get this little pot there any faster."

"And you say it will take us three days to get there on our own," Findgoll said, shaking his head.

"Two, perhaps, at our best speed, moving day and night," Manannan amended. "That's with a wind behind us, of course."

"Too late," said the Dagda, plumping his massive body down next to Lugh's and speaking with despair. "Our people may all be dead by then."

The others sat down in attitudes of defeat. Even the Pooka dropped down on its haunches and wilted in sorrow.

Manannan stood looking about him at this hopeless crew and spoke up cheerfully.

"Oh, come on. There's always something that can be done! We can't all just give up. We're so close! I mean, we got the thing back to Eire. It's just a matter of getting it to Tara now, isn't it?"

"How?" Aine demanded bluntly. "Dear brother, I'm afraid that even you may have run out of luck."

"Oh, are you?" he said, sounding a bit offended by her lack of faith. "Well, my smart young puppy, that we will see." He turned briskly to the young champion. "Lugh, it's time for you to call the Riders of the Sidhe again. With their help we can whisk this little gift of ours to Tara by tonight."

"But you said they were likely destroyed!" Lugh reminded him.

Manannan shrugged. "I was probably wrong. In any case, it's the only possibility we've got now, so get right to it."

"Why don't you have a try?" Lugh asked him, clearly not optimistic about his chances. "You're the Guardian."

"And you are Champion of the Sidhe," the tall man reminded him. "The Riders were put in your care by the Queen of the Four Cities herself, if you'll recall. So if anyone can successfully conjure them up, it's you. And, you might add a special little request for Danu to lend a hand in this. It might help things along."

"He's not likely to get any extra help from Danu this time," Aine added darkly.

"You really are the negative one," her brother told her in a scolding way. "You know, it wouldn't hurt if you put in a word to Danu yourself." He looked around at the others. "And that goes for the rest of you as well. There could be a more persuasive force in numbers. And the added volume just might reach her better too. So gather around here and let's give this young champion of ours some support with our prayers. And, try to be positive about it!"

His bracing, optimistic mood infected them. They shook off the clinging shroud of defeat and moved in around the cart. Lugh stood up beside the cauldron, lifted his eyes to the sky, and began the incantation. Around him, the others made their own private appeals to the mystic Queen. All of them knew that Lugh's success in calling the Riders now might be the only thing saving their people from a massacre.

The young warrior's chant went on, the words lifting into the empty fall sky. Far to the west there came, as if in answer, a low rumble from the thunder of a great storm rising there. But these dark, wind-filled clouds boiling up from the horizon brought no shining horsemen sweeping across Eire with them. Only rain.

It was a fall rain. It had that penetrating chill and snow-sharp scent about it that spoke of coming winter. It had that forlorn quality that suits summer's dying as well. The rain drenched and clung and fell away reluctantly in heavy droplets, weighing down upon everything and giving trees, people, even buildings, the drooping, sorrowful attitude of mourners at a burial.

Its thick cloak increased the blackness of the night. In the enclosure of Tara's high timber walls, scores of torches burned in every sheltered spot in a valiant struggle to provide those busy there with some fitful light.

Everywhere there was a constant bustle as people moved about on their various tasks of preparation. A hospital was being set up under Diancecht's direction inside the large armory building. Chieftains were arriving and entering the main hall to meet the High-King for a final review of battle plans. And parties of warriors worked continuously to move weapons from the smithy to distribute to the companies on the hill outside the walls.

In the large smithy behind the central hall, Cerdne, Goibnu, and Bridget, aided by scores of other craftsmen, worked under shed roofs of thatch through which rain leaked in countless places and made a constant sizzling sound as it dripped upon the red coals of the forges. Skilled artisans in brass and leather and wood helped the smiths to add to a vast supply of weapons. Iron-rimmed shields, keen-edged swords, and elegantly lethal spears were stacked all about them.

Nuada crossed the yard to the smithy, trying with little success to dodge the many puddles in the muddy ground. The workers there glanced up to greet him only briefly, not pausing in their labors.

"You've done well," he told them earnestly. "We'll not lose tomorrow because we're lacking in fine weapons."

"We'll not lose tomorrow at all," said Goibnu, a broad smile glowing whitely for an instant in his smoke-blackened face before he bent back over his hammer.

"Bridget," Nuada called loudly over the clatter of work.

The woman whose oddly divided face had been made all one by the coating of soot looked up at him.

"As soon as you've finished here, Diancecht wants you at the hospital," the king told her. "He'll be in sore need of your healing skills."

Bridget nodded agreement. The mystic healing powers she had gained in Tir-na-nog had saved many a warrior wounded and near death. On the next day, such a talent would be in great demand.

"Excuse me, my King," said a voice beside him.

Nuada turned to see a fresh-faced young warrior smiling up somewhat shyly at him.

"Ruadan!" said Nuada, smiling at the son of Bridget. He noted the weapons adorning the lad, almost too much for his light frame. "Prepared to join the fight, too, are you?"

"Of course!" Ruadan said stoutly. "How could I not join this battle against our greatest enemies?"

Nuada thought to himself how brave it was of such a mere stripling, innocent and untrained in war, to face the savage Fomor. He laid a hand upon Ruadan's shoulder.

"I'm very proud of you," he said with the proper, kingly solemnness.

Ruadan beamed with pleasure at this praise and strode away, holding himself with a warrior's dignity. But Nuada didn't note the troubled frown that creased the face of Bridget as she watched this touching scene.

Nuada left the smithy, returning to the central hall. The chieftains were nearly all gathered there, going over charts spread upon the tables of the High-King's dais. Below it, near the fire, the Druids engaged in their own conference.

On the king's entrance, High-Druid Meglin left the others to approach him. His expression was not a happy one.

"How does it go then, Meglin?" Nuada asked. "Have you and the Druidic circle any bits of sorcery that might help us hold the Fomor at bay tomorrow?"

The man was hesitant. "We may have, High-King. We've worked on some things"—he sighed and shook his head—"but they're not very good. We've had too little time to restore our powers. And, without Findgoll to direct what skills we have . . ."

"I understand," said Nuada. "He'll be sorely missed here, as will the others. Well, do what you can."

The High-King continued on through the hall, toward the gallery steps. There were still some moments before their meeting could begin. He used them to climb to the gallery room and go out, across the bridge to the parapet walk.

He stood looking off toward the east, oblivious to the rain the sharp wind was driving against his back. He strained his eyes into the blackness there, still hoping he would see some sign of help, still praying his champions would miraculously appear through the curtain of rain and night.

He saw only the void of the empty countryside and, beyond the farthest ridge of eastern hills, the flicker of distant lightning.

XXX

ASSAULT ON TARA

BY DAWN, THE rain had ceased, the sky had cleared. A bright sun climbed above the eastern hills and threw a golden, all-revealing light across the plains encircling Tara's hill.

It also lit the Fomor hordes flooding over the northern ridges toward the fortress.

They poured down into the meadows of yellowing fall grass. The horrible seething mass of them was so thick they seemed like swarming maggots on a rotting carcass turned suddenly to the light. From a hilltop Bres watched them move forward with great satisfaction. They were truly a nightmare army, a force of undisciplined, deformed, and brutal creatures. As such he felt revulsion for them. Still, it was those very aspects of their natures that were so valuable to him. They would easily cow the weak and fearful de Dananns they had so long tyrannized. They would be his weapons for the retaking of his Eire.

Now the prize was just ahead of them. He turned his gaze toward it and smiled covetously.

Tara an Rie. The sacred place of High-Kings. Soon that fortress would be his again. It sat there, waiting, a crown to be torn from the brow of the cursed de Dananns.

He rode on, moving down into the van of his force. He meant to lead the final assault personally. He more than half-expected to find no resistance at the fortress. He had no belief in the de Dananns' courage. Quite likely they had fled before him once they realized their "heroes" would perform no more miracles to save them.

In that he was surprised.

As they drew nearer to the hill, he realized that it had been fully fortified. A ditch had been dug around the base of the hill, below the fortress's palisades. Atop a mound of earth piled along the inner edge of this ditch, a second wall had been erected. It was formed of stakes embedded in the earth at intervals, supporting heavy screens of wickerwork. Behind this lower defensive line, he could see the de Dananns swarming as they moved to their positions.

From what he could see of their numbers, they seemed far fewer than his. And glimpses of the de Danann warriors peeping over the wall told him that they were still pitifully weak, quite frail in comparison with his burly animals. He almost laughed aloud at the thought of how absurd their puny resistance would be.

Yet, he did recall that unexpected spirit that had once before brought the starved inhabitants of Tara to rise against him and drive him out, annihilating the Fomor garrison. No, he wouldn't laugh at these people now. As pitiful as they looked, as much as he had already done to strip them of their dignity, possessions, and strength, he would give them no quarter.

They were fools, he thought angrily. Had they run from him, he might yet have shown compassion for them, let them leave Eire alive. Now their stubborn pride had insured that he would see them wiped utterly away. The de Danann spirit would finally be exorcised from him.

He addressed himself to the Fomor officers. He gave his orders only through those of the highest rank.

"Spread your companies out and come against the entire line at once!" he commanded. "Keep the best company in reserve. When a hole has been made, I will lead them through. And let no man harm Nuada Silver-Hand. The pleasure of killing him is reserved for me!"

The orders were passed. The Fomor spread into a thick, ragged line and then surged forward, like a storm-whipped wave rolling toward a beach, to crash upon the de Dananns' fragile-looking wall.

A shower of slender but deadly spears fell upon them as they reached the ditch, decimating their first ranks. Despite Nuada's worry about their throwing skills, the de Dananns had learned something after all. They stole the momentum from the assault, and it was in a trickle, not a flood, that the Fomor came against the barricades.

The wave of Fomor warriors surged about the fortress, trying at point after point to climb the walls or tear them down. But the barricades held, the de Dananns battling courageously to keep the Fomor out.

Bres fumed at the incompetence of this ill-begotten brood of monsters. How did Balor expect him to control Eire with such beings?

He would have to break through the de Dananns himself. For all its courage, the force thwarting him must be nearly exhausted. A wily fighter, a veteran of the war with the Firbolgs, he had analyzed the de Dananns' defenses. He saw a weak spot in the wicker barricades just below the main gates into the fortress. Like a bundle of dried twigs, it was ready to be snapped by one, smart blow. If he could break through here, his forces could swarm in and destroy the whole de Danann line while he himself led a force to seize the fortress. The de Dananns would be trapped with no place to retreat. Their doom would be assured.

He ordered his reserve company against the weak point, riding behind them, ready to charge through the expected breach. The Fomor threw themselves against the wicker walls, hacking into them, trying to rip them down, while the defenders showered them with spears and drove back any enemy who tried to climb across.

"Push through! Push through, you mindless animals," Bres screamed at the warriors. He drew his sword and rode his horse in amongst the attackers, driving them forward like cattle with threats and stinging blows of his sword flat, pushing them against the crumbling barricades.

Finally, the sheer pressure of their numbers seemed to make the wall give way. An entire section splintered apart, opening a wide gap.

Swiftly Bres urged his horse forward, charging through the breach, slashing out at the defenders who scattered before him. His company followed him through, and then other Fomor, forcing the gap wider, spreading out to attack the de Danann warriors on either side.

Suddenly the resistance before Bres ended. He realized that all the defenders had fled, leaving the way ahead clear. The rest of the army of Tara was engaged in defending the remainder of the wall. There was no one to oppose his advance toward the fortress gates. With a sense of triumph already growing in him, he ordered his company to follow and started up the slope, leaving the rest of the Fomor to deal with the de Dananns at the lower barricades. One great desire, one goal drove him now—to reclaim the fortress and his throne.

It took only moments to reach the gates, and he set his men against them at once. He expected to meet some resistance from within, but there was none, and the gates swung inward at the first Fomor push. They were unlocked.

The de Dananns had been more desperate than he'd thought, Bres decided. They had commited every warrior to the fight at the barricades, not sparing any to defend the fortress in case they had to retreat. Now that retreat would be impossible.

Impatient to reassume his sovereignty, he pushed his horse forward through the gates as soon as they had been opened far enough. He rode into the courtyard, still muddy from the night's rain, and searched about him for any sign of challengers. But there were none. The fortress looked totally deserted. Tara was his.

He urged the horse toward the center of the yard. There he pulled up short, staring at a peculiar object directly ahead. A fire had been built before the main entrance to the hall. The ground around it had been trampled to a mire by countless feet. Over this fire a tripod of heavy beams had been erected, and suspended from this on a chain was an enormous black cauldron.

"Welcome, Bres," said a voice from above him.

He looked up toward the walkway linking the hall to the parapet. There stood the little Druid Findgoll, smiling down at him.

"We were certain you couldn't resist the chance to enter Tara first yourself," he went on. "We waited for you."

And, as he spoke, a group appeared from the hall's main doors. Lugh, Aine, Morrigan, the Dagda, Angus Og, and Gilla walked out into the yard, stopping beside the cauldron to face Bres. At the same time a shimmering light streamed from behind the hall, flowing into a ring around the Fomor company. As it closed its circle, it came to a halt, resolving into the separate forms of the shining Riders of the Sidhe, sitting upon their proud steeds as charged with energy and imperious as ever. In one movement, their lances dropped forward to point at the group of warriors, who cowered back into a tight huddle.

Bres, however, seemed very little impressed by this unexpected appearance. He looked over the little band of heroes with contempt.

"So, you did manage to get here after all. Too bad it wasn't enough to save your de Dananns."

"I think you're wrong, Bres," Lugh remarked lightly. "Look again."

Suspicious, the former High-King threw only a quick glance out the gates. But what he saw below the hill captured his gaze at once. The other Fomor who had poured through the breach in the barricades were now stopped, caught in a closing vise of de Dananns led by Nuada himself. And all along the outer wall, the men of Tara had launched a furious counterassault that was driving Bres's army back in panic. He realized with a shock that the weakness of the de Dananns had been feigned. The magic of the cauldron really had restored their strength, and they were now using it to devastate his forces with tremendous zeal.

"Your Fomor friends have set so many little traps for us these last days," Gilla told him gleefully, "we only thought it fair that you be given the fine experience of one yourself!"

Bres jerked back around to face the band. The lot of them were grinning at him with a smugness maddening to him. His face darkened with rage.

"Kill them!" he ordered the Fomor massed behind him.

They, however, had other ideas. They looked fearfully around at the threatening circle of gleaming Riders and toward the rest of their army, now being so efficiently destroyed. They stood unmoving.

"I said kill them!" he cried again, more heatedly.

"If you surrender, you'll not be killed," Lugh promised quietly.

That sounded a much more logical choice to the Fomor. For all of Bres's low opinion of them, they were not wholly fools. They were not eager to die, and they certainly owed nothing to their contemptuous leader. They dropped their weapons.

"You worthless vermin!" he screamed at them. His gaze swung around to the object of his defeat, this boyish champion who had so often thwarted him, who now glowed with his triumph.

Driven nearly insane by his anger, Bres spurred his horse suddenly forward. He charged across the yard, lifting his sword high. His only thought was to destroy his most hated enemy, to strike down Lugh.

His swift attack seemed to raise no alarm amongst the little band. Lugh watched Bres come on without concern, not even drawing his own sword in defense. He had expected some such move from the man. He was prepared.

When he judged the horse was close enough, he simply stepped to one side and said a single word:

"Shaglan!"

From behind him an enormous lionlike beast leaped forward, voicing a tremendous roar.

The effect on the horse was dramatic. Panicked, the animal reared back sharply, neighing shrilly in terror. It rose up onto its hind legs and lost its balance entirely in its effort to turn away, rolling down onto its side.

Taken off guard by this fall, Bres had no chance to jump clear. He was thrown violently from the horse's back, landing heavily, face forward, in the soggy yard. His sword was flung away by the impact, burying its length in the mud. Its finely jeweled hilt, like the man who had held it, was coated with the black ooze.

The great cat hopped lightly to the downed man and lowered its head over him. As Bres struggled to rise, he looked up to find himself staring into a formidable set of fangs.

"Don't kill him, Shaglan," Lugh said.

"Why not?" the Dagda asked in astonishment. "He's a traitor to us. He has the Fomor blood."

"He has de Danann blood too," Lugh reminded him. "He doesn't deserve to die this way."

The big man shrugged. "If that's your wish," he said, not really understanding such compassion.

The Riders had quickly herded the disarmed Fomor back against the inside of the fortress wall, penning them there with a fence of leveled spears. The Dagda stepped forward and hauled Bres up roughly from the mud, smiling at the thick coating of black that reduced the man's form to something barely human.

"Our grand High-King," the champion said scornfully. "You're no different from your pack of filthy beasts now, are you?" He flung the man into the bunched captives. "Here, join your friends. I'm certain they'll be glad to share your company."

His arrogance undiminished by defeat, Bres cast a disdainful look around at the cowed Fomor.

"These witless slugs failed me," he said, sneering, then bent a hate-filled gaze on the Dagda. "But I'll yet see you destroyed!"

"You just give your thanks that you're alive at all now," the champion warned. "And if you move or speak again, I'll kill you myself. That I promise you."

He hefted his great battle-ax meaningfully. Bres continued to glare, but he stayed motionless and silent.

By this time, Findgoll was down from the walkway and had joined his comrades. Together they moved to the main gates of Tara. Their own part in the trap successful, they were ready to help out in the fight below.

But as the little band of heroes came out of the fortress onto the hillside, they realized their help would not be needed. They stood and looked out across the scene of battle and gloried in the spectacle of their people, reveling in their newly reborn vigor, sweeping in pursuit of a routed, shattered Fomor army. The battle-rage fully upon them, they ripped savagely into the rear of the retreating forces. Whether harpers or herdsmen, artists or smiths, they were all warriors now, redeeming their long years of humiliation in Fomor blood.

And it was Nuada himself who was in their forefront. The old High-King, his own vigor and confidence fully restored to him, fought with the skill and power of a young champion. He waded into the midst of Fomor companies, swinging his sword about him with a fury that the bestial warriors could not withstand. He slaughtered without mercy, breaking any resistance, leading his de Dananns forward with such speed that the Fomor finally abandoned any attempt to fight a rearguard action and took up a headlong flight, many even casting away weapons and armor to increase their speed.

"It's few of those poor creatures that will live to reach safety," Gilla remarked.

The strong scent of blood from the battlefield was too great for Morrigan to resist. She transformed herself and flapped into the air. Soon the grim form of the black battle-raven, like some goddess of death herself, swooped low over the field, absorbing the atmosphere of violence, ready to sate her unnatural thirst.

As he realized the remaining Fomor forces were scattering before him, Nuada ordered his own companies to a halt. From the warriors around him a cheer rose, running swiftly along the whole line of men, rising to a roaring crescendo that the watchers on the hill happily joined.

Passing orders to his chieftains to regroup their forces, Nuada quickly climbed onto a horse brought him and galloped back toward the fortress with a troop of mounted warriors, anxious now to see how his champions had fared.

He reined in before them at the gates, a commanding figure on the tall animal, the battle light still shining in his face, the longsword still clutched in his massive hand. He peered through the gates into the fortress yard and beamed with pleasure when he saw how things had gone.

"So, you succeeded in your plan too," he said. "We finally have Bres."

"We should be done with him now," growled the Dagda. "If you'd give me the pleasure—"

"Please, High-King," Lugh said. "Let him live."

"Let him live?" said Nuada in disbelief. "But he is our most dangerous enemy!"

"Not anymore. He's beaten. At least wait until we have some chance to consider fairly his fate."

Nuada shrugged. "All right, young champion, if that's your wish. But you are very forgiving."

"Not really," Lugh answered thoughtfully. "I've just a feeling in me that he should be treated with justice."

Nuada turned to the warriors who had accompanied him.

"See to Bres," he ordered. "Take him to the cell in the armory and watch him well!"

The men dismounted and moved quickly to secure Bres. One of them was the young warrior Ruadan. He moved with apparent eagerness to take hold of this traitor to the de Dananns. But as he helped march the captive away, his eyes met his father's for one, brief moment. And in that moment, a message was exchanged.

With Bres disposed of, Nuada now turned his attention back to his champions.

"There's much yet to be done, my friends. The army must be re-formed. The wounded and dead must be seen to. And then"—he grinned broadly at them—"then we can truly celebrate!"

XXXI

FREEDOM

LIGHTS AND COLORS flickered and flashed across the white expanse of wall. The images flowed together like reflections in a still pool streaked by a sweeping hand. Finally they steadied into recognizable forms.

It was a battlefield depicted there, where thousands of warriors contended in a struggle whose massive carnage stained the grassy meadows red. It was the scene of the battle for Tara.

The wavering glow reflected from this image fell upon the two beings who were the only audience. It played eerily across the grotesque being that hung suspended in its tank of glass, seeming to float like some captive creature of the sea's most sunless depths. It glinted dully from the metal body of the massive, vaguely human form that sat in a giant throne beside the tank, the red slit of its single eye fixed on the rapidly shifting pictures projected upon the wall.

Balor watched, unmoving, as the Fomor army met defeat. He watched as its forces were shattered by the de Dananns, chased back in panic, scattered into the northern hills.

"Bres has failed as you have, Balor," came the horrible whisper of the wasted Druid. "Your Eireland Fomor have been beaten by the de Dananns. Our enemies have their full strength once again."

"It was the power of Manannan that helped them succeed," the giant answered in hard, ringing tones of anger. "And it was Lugh Lamfada, as before. You are right. The Prophecy protects him. He cannot be destroyed."

"Perhaps," the Druid replied thoughtfully. "But this little contest has taught me much about our mutual adversaries. Let the fools have their victory for now. This war is far from over. We'll find a way to see them beaten yet. Somehow, I promise you, I will have my revenge!"

All the great fortress of Tara was filled with a glorious golden light. Within the main hall, scores of torches were set in the thick pillars supporting the high roof. In the stone-lined fire pit, an enormous blaze sent its own glow reflecting in a rich, ruddy gleam from the bronze panels that covered the outer walls, and threw into sharp relief the intricate carvings of serpents, birds, and beasts that intertwined in joyous and sensuous abandon all up and down the red yew pillars. Suspended above this fire was the cauldron, its magic contents undiminished by the multitudes, the simmering broth scenting the air with a marvelous aroma that itself seemed to invigorate.

The vast room was filled to nearly bursting with its crowd of revelers. Chieftains, Druids, warriors, and their families were there, all celebrating with a sense of freedom they'd not known in many years. For today they had truly thrown off the shackles of the Fomor.

Only one figure in the hall seemed not to enter into the spirit of festivity. At the gallery rail of the upper room stood Bobd Derg, gazing down upon the scene below, brooding.

Throughout the hall, winding through the long rows of tables about the fire pit, bards sang their newly composed epics of the victory with great vigor and true, heroic exaggeration,

delighting the rapt listeners who already believed every deed
was true.

Other entertainers circulated too. Harpers and pipers
played their fine, high airs. Jugglers, clowns, and conjurers
whose skills had long gone unused now performed exuber-
antly, unleashing the spirits so many years supressed.

Up on the dais of the High-King, one performer especially
seemed to be enjoying himself. A lanky clown in striped cloak
and great, flopping shoes, he was astonishing the company at
Nuada's table with the juggling of a very peculiar set of objects
that he had pulled one by one from the folds of the voluminous
garment. A full jug of wine, a lighted brand, a keen-edged
dagger, and a very angry kitten were somehow kept up, whirling, with nothing dropped or spilled, while he balanced upon
the tabletop, swaying so precariously that there were gasps of
alarm from his audience at every move.

Amongst the watchers was a strange trio. The Dagda and
Angus, both well along in the drinking, stood with arms linked
about an enormous, shaggy wolfhound who stood upright on
his hind legs between them, opening his mouth often to let
them pour just a bit more ale in. All three were unsteady, but
managing to do their swaying in unison. Morrigan, sitting
furled in her dark cloak nearby, fixed a stern and disapproving
glare on them. Her own thirst had long since been fully assuaged on the battlefield.

The clown's act ended, suddenly and quite dramatically. He
seemed to stumble badly and lose his footing. With a loud
"Whooops!" he crashed heavily onto the tabletop. The kitten
shrieked in fear. But there was no danger. As the clown landed,
he neatly caught all the objects, including the cat, and the
shocked cries of his audience turned to howls of laughter as
they realized this was part of his act. In response he gave them
a broad, foolish grin.

"Gilla, it's truly a marvel you are!" Nuada said heartily,
standing to clap a hand on the clown's shoulder. "But, someday, you'll take a risk too many."

"Not that one!" the Dagda roared. "He'll never find enough
to make him satisfied."

Nuada looked toward the champion and his friends. His
gaze was drawn to the Pooka and he stared at the creature
fixedly.

"Would you mind telling me," he asked it, "are you changing right before me, or has the drink a stronger hold on me than I thought? I was certain you looked a dog before, but now you seem more like a horse to me."

"Ifffff . . ." it began thickly but paused, appearing to have some difficulty with the large horse lips. It tried again. "I've been a great long time without the drinkin'. And it's had its evil way with me a bit, so it has. I'm afraid that what my shape chooses to do now is right out of my control."

"Well, it's good to know that," Nuada said with relief.

Gilla had now pocketed his objects and climbed from the tabletop to sit down by the Druid Findgoll. The High-King lifted his cup of ale high and spoke out loudly to all those at his table.

"I think it's time we gave our praise to our fine company of heroes." He swept the cup around him to include them all. "It was you who gave us our victory."

"It was the warriors of the de Danann who won the victory," the Dagda said. "Nothing we've done would have been of any use without their spirit to fight. They've truly earned the right to call Eire theirs again."

"It's the truth you're speaking," Nuada agreed. "Still, we'd have been surely destroyed without the cauldron's power, and for bringing it, you deserve our thanks." He looked at the Pooka. "And special honors to you, Shaglan. Your courage has proven your honesty and won you a place here." He turned to face the clown. "And you, Gilla," he said with some puzzlement. "Once more you've helped us, and you not even of Eire! What is it that brings you to do it?"

Gilla cast a look around at his companions. Any of them could now reveal the reason to the whole of the de Danann race.

It was the Dagda who finally spoke.

"Why, Nuada, I know the reason!" Gilla held his breath. "The clown's a madman! Everyone knows that!"

The crowd about them laughed. Gilla exhaled with relief and smiled his thanks to the big champion. He got a broad wink in reply.

"It's Lugh Lamfada should be getting the most honors here," young Angus pointed out. "For there'd have been no army hosted and no cauldron, either, without him."

There were cheers of agreement from the company at that. Nuada looked about him for the Champion of the Sidhe without success.

"But, where is Lugh?" he asked. "I've not seen him for some while. And that girl Aine seems to be gone as well."

"Ah well, as to that," said Gilla casually, "I think I saw them leaving the hall a little while ago." He exchanged a knowing look with Findgoll. "Going for a bit of fresh air, I think they were. Don't you?"

The quick-witted little Druid understood at once. Eyes twinkling with merriment, he replied assuredly:

"I do, for certain. I know they said something about being very warm."

Both men were speaking the truth, but the fresh air the young pair was enjoying was not just outside Tara's hall. They were now seated on a hillside far across the meadows from the fortress's hill, while the great horse of the Sidhe stood quietly nearby, glowing softly in the darkness.

Lugh had dismissed the Riders back to whatever otherworldly realm they inhabited. But he had kept the horse. Both feeling a need to be apart from the rest, they had ridden away on it, streaking across the countryside. They had expected the wind of their speed to cool the heat that the ale and the exhilaration of their victory had raised in their bodies. But they had found that the feel of the powerful beast moving rhythmically beneath them and the touch of their two bodies pressed tightly together on its back somehow created an even greater warmth in them.

Now, seated unmoving on the hill, Lugh became aware that there was a touch of fall chill in the air. Though it was no discomfort on his burning skin, he thought that the lightly clad Aine might be uncomfortable.

"Are you cold at all?" he asked. "I could put my cloak about us both for warmth."

"No, I'm not cold at all," she said. Then she smiled. "But you could put your cloak about me anyway."

Such an invitation Lugh was quick to accept, pulling the cloak around her shoulders with one arm, settling the other about her waist to pull her close.

He was very aware of her supple body relaxing against him. He could feel the heat of her bare thigh against his own and the soft swell of her breast against his side.

Across the dark meadows, Tara was clearly visible, marked by the glow of the scores of torches and fires burning in the courtyard where hundreds of de Dananns celebrated. The many lights combined and lifted up from within the circle of the palisades, forming a high golden cone above.

With this first chance for ease and peace in many days, Lugh was able to consider something he'd put aside.

"Aine, do you realize what this victory means? The Prophecy is fulfilled. I'm finally free to seek my own life."

"Are you certain it's finished?" she asked quietly.

"Bres is captured. The Fomor forces in Eire are broken, and without him they'll never be able to organize again."

"There's still the Tower," she reminded him.

He shook his head. "With Balor gone, without their Eireland beasts to fight for them, I don't think those in the Tower are likely to risk themselves just to try mastering us again."

She was silent for a time. When she spoke, it was in a voice that was, for her, strangely hesitant.

"You know, if that's true, then the task of my brother and I is finished too. We could leave Eire. We could go back to Tir-na-nog."

He looked down at her in alarm.

"No!" he said quickly. "You can't do that. Not now. Not when I know—"

She looked up, fixing him with those clear, appraising eyes.

"And just what is it you think you know?"

He met her gaze. There was that indefinable something again, glinting in the lustrous blue depths. Was it an invitation or a challenge he saw there?

"We began something not so long ago," he said boldly. "Would you be willing to continue it or not?"

"Right now we've some peace," she answered gravely. "Right now we're together and alone, and we've no way to know what tomorrow will be bringing us. If such a chance may not come to us again, I don't think we should be letting it go, do you?"

His reply was to draw her tightly against him and drop his mouth to hers. This time she returned his kiss with a passion that more than matched his own.

* * *

On the fortress hill of Tara, the lights of celebration burned on far into the night. Their brightness filled every structure in the great dun, except for one.

In the vast armory room, only a single torch burned. Its wavering red light flicked spots of brightness from the great stacks and rows of arms about it. Its glow fell upon two figures lying still on the earthen floor and showed the spreading dark stains soaking into the hard-beaten clay.

Between the two—dead warriors—a heavy timber door stood open. The faint torchlight was enough to show that the tiny cell beyond the door was empty.

Outside, two figures moved cautiously around the armory building, away from the crowd of revelers before the central hall. They safely crossed an open area to the timber palisade, and crept along it, keeping to its deepest shadows.

Their goal was a small gate used to allow night patrols in and out of Tara. Tonight it was unguarded, its keepers gone to join in the celebrations.

When the pair reached it, one of them quickly unlatched the gate and pushed it open, looking out briefly to be certain the way was clear before turning back to address the other in hushed tones.

"I've arranged everything, Father," said Ruadan. "I've horses waiting in the town below. We'll have no trouble making it away. Everyone is here."

Bres put a firm hand on the boy's shoulder and spoke urgently.

"No, Ruadan. I go alone. You must stay here."

The boy opened his mouth to protest, but Bres stopped him.

"You've got to do it. Don't you see? You're much more valuable to me here. If I can ever raise a new force against them, I'll need your help."

"All right, Father," the other reluctantly agreed. He handed his own sword over. "Here, take this. And go now, quickly, before someone comes."

Bres nodded and slipped out through the gate. Ruadan watched his father until he vanished into the night. Then he carefully latched the gate and turned back toward the lights of the celebration.

For an instant in the revealing glow, his hatred of these victors showed nakedly in his face. Then it was masked with the boyish look of innocent goodwill. He started forward, ready to throw himself with apparent gusto into the merriment.

And outside the walls, Bres made his way down the slope of Tara in the darkness, alone, defeated, and humiliated, but free again! He paused at the hill's base to cast a look back up at the radiant fortress that should have been his. His fist tightened about the hilt of the sword.

ABOUT THE AUTHOR

KENNETH C. FLINT is a graduate of the University of Nebraska with a Masters Degree in English Literature. For several years he taught in the Department of Humanities at the University of Nebraska at Omaha. Presently he is Chairman of English for the Plattsmouth Community Schools (a system in a suburban community of Omaha).

In addition to teaching, he has worked as a freelance writer. He has produced articles and short stories for various markets and has written screenplays for some Omaha-based film companies.

Mr. Flint became interested in Celtic mythology in graduate school, where he saw a great source of material in this long neglected area of western literature. Since then he has spent much time researching in England and Ireland and developing works of fantasy that would interest modern readers.

He is the author of two previous novels, A STORM UPON ULSTER and RIDERS OF THE SIDHE. His next novel, MASTER OF THE SIDHE, will be published by Bantam in 1985.

OUT OF THIS WORLD!

That's the only way to describe Bantam's great series of science fiction classics. These space-age thrillers are filled with terror, fancy and adventure and written by America's most renowned writers of science fiction. Welcome to outer space and have a good trip!

FANTASY AND SCIENCE FICTION FAVORITES

Bantam brings you the recognized classics as well as the current favorites in fantasy and science fiction. Here you will find the most recent titles by the most respected authors in the genre.

☐	24370	RAPHAEL R. A. MacAvoy	$2.75
☐	24103	BORN WITH THE DEAD Robert Silverberg	$2.75
☐	24169	WINTERMIND Parke Godwin, Marvin Kaye	$2.75
☐	23944	THE DEEP John Crowley	$2.95
☐	23853	THE SHATTERED STARS Richard McEnroe	$2.95
☐	23575	DAMIANO R. A. MacAvoy	$2.75
☐	23205	TEA WITH THE BLACK DRAGON R. A. MacAvoy	$2.75
☐	23365	THE SHUTTLE PEOPLE George Bishop	$2.95
☐	24441	THE HAREM OF AMAN AKBAR Elizabeth Scarborough	$2.95
☐	20780	STARWORLD Harry Harrison	$2.50
☐	22939	THE UNICORN CREED Elizabeth Scarborough	$3.50
☐	23120	THE MACHINERIES OF JOY Ray Bradbury	$2.75
☐	22666	THE GREY MANE OF MORNING Joy Chant	$3.50
☐	23063	LORD VALENTINE'S CASTLE Robert Silverberg	$3.50
☐	20870	JEM Frederik Pohl	$2.95
☐	23460	DRAGONSONG Anne McCaffrey	$2.95
☐	23666	EARTHCHILD Sharon Webb	$2.50
☐	24102	DAMIANO'S LUTE R. A. MacAvoy	$2.75
☐	24417	THE GATES OF HEAVEN Paul Preuss	$2.50

Prices and availability subject to change without notice.

Buy them at your local bookstore or use this handy coupon for ordering:

Bantam Books, Inc., Dept. SF2, 414 East Golf Road, Des Plaines, Ill. 60016

Please send me the books I have checked above. I am enclosing $_____ (please add $1.25 to cover postage and handling). Send check or money order —no cash or C.O.D.'s please.

Mr/Mrs/Miss_____

Address_____

City_____ State/Zip_____

SF2—12/84

Please allow four to six weeks for delivery. This offer expires 6/85.